Praise for *Rain Storm*

"[A] superb thriller.... East meets West in Rain, an ultra-cool assassin so perfect for our fictional times."
—*New York Daily News*

"A propulsive thriller plot ... plausible, au courant, and creepy." —*Kirkus Reviews*

"Rain ... owes his literary ancestry ... to the noir private eyes of the 40s—Sam Spade, Philip Marlowe, Lew Archer, and others. The writing here is philosophical, reminiscent of Eric von Lustbader's action novels, but it doesn't interfere with the action sequences.... This is a character-driven action book that will delight any reader." —*The Boulder Daily Camera*

"What truly sets Eisler's series apart is its near total absence of formula and stereotype. Rain is a wholly original, cliché-free character operating in a world created only for him, serving as both his folly and his foil."
—*Publishers Weekly*

"Realistic detail ... separates [Eisler's] international thrillers from the rest of the pack. His goal is to combine the insouciance of Ian Fleming, the realistic detail of Tom Clancy, the ennui of Graham Greene, and the prose power of John le Carré. In *Rain Storm* he takes a major step toward achieving it."
—*The News-Press* (Fort Myers, FL)

"The Rain series keeps on getting better. For espionage fans who favor adventure over ambiguity." —*Booklist*

continued ...

ALSO BY BARRY EISLER

Rain Fall
Hard Rain

RAIN STORM

BARRY EISLER

A SIGNET BOOK

SIGNET
Published by New American Library, a division of
Penguin Group (USA) Inc., 375 Hudson Street,
New York, New York 10014, USA
Penguin Group (Canada), 10 Alcorn Avenue, Toronto,
Ontario M4V 3B2, Canada (a division of Pearson Penguin Canada Inc.)
Penguin Books Ltd., 80 Strand, London WC2R 0RL, England
Penguin Ireland, 25 St. Stephen's Green, Dublin 2,
Ireland (a division of Penguin Books Ltd.)
Penguin Group (Australia), 250 Camberwell Road, Camberwell, Victoria 3124,
Australia (a division of Pearson Australia Group Pty. Ltd.)
Penguin Books India Pvt. Ltd., 11 Community Centre, Panchsheel Park,
New Delhi - 110 017, India
Penguin Group (NZ), cnr Airborne and Rosedale Roads, Albany,
Auckland 1310, New Zealand (a division of Pearson New Zealand Ltd.)
Penguin Books (South Africa) (Pty.) Ltd., 24 Sturdee Avenue,
Rosebank, Johannesburg 2196, South Africa

Penguin Books Ltd., Registered Offices:
80 Strand, London WC2R 0RL, England

Published by Signet, an imprint of New American Library, a division of Penguin
Group (USA) Inc. Previously published in a G. P. Putnam's Sons edition.

First Signet Printing, July 2005
10 9 8 7 6 5 4 3 2 1

PUBLISHER'S NOTE
This is a work of fiction. Names, characters, places, and incidents either are the
product of the author's imagination or are used fictitiously, and any resem-
blance to actual persons, living or dead, business establishments, events, or
locales is entirely coincidental.

The publisher does not have any control over and does not assume any
responsibility for author or third-party Web sites or their content.

If you purchased this book without a cover you should be aware that this book
is stolen property. It was reported as "unsold and destroyed" to the publisher
and neither the author nor the publisher has received any payment for this
"stripped book."

The scanning, uploading, and distribution of this book via the Internet or via any
other means without the permission of the publisher is illegal and punishable by
law. Please purchase only authorized electronic editions, and do not participate
in or encourage electronic piracy of copyrighted materials. Your support of the
author's rights is appreciated.

For Ben and Sarah

If I leave
no trace behind
in this fleeting world
what then could you
reproach?

—DEATH POEM OF UKIFUNE
  IN THE *Genji Monogatari*

PART ONE

We shall not cease from exploration
And the end of all our exploring
Will be to arrive where we started
And know the place for the first time.

T. S. ELIOT, Four Quartets

I

THE AGENCY HAD hired me to "retire" Belghazi, not to protect him. So if this didn't go well, their next candidate for a retirement package would probably be me.

But the way I saw it, saving Belghazi from the guy I now thought of as Karate would be doing Uncle Sam a favor. After all, Karate could fail to make it look natural, or get caught, or do some other sloppy thing, and then there would be misunderstandings, and suspicions, and accusations—exactly the kinds of problems the Agency had hired me to avoid.

Of course, there was also the matter of my getting paid. If Karate got to Belghazi first and I couldn't claim credit, I might be out of a check, and that wouldn't be very fair, would it?

I thought of this guy as Karate because my suspicions about him had first jelled when I saw him doing karate *kata,* or forms, in the gym of the Macau Mandarin Oriental Hotel, where we were both staying and where Belghazi was soon to arrive. Avoiding the facility's tangle of Lifecycles and Cybex machines, he had focused instead on a series of punches, blocks, and kicks to the air that, to the uninitiated, might have looked like some kind of martial dance routine. Actually, his moves were good—

smooth, practiced, and powerful. They would have been impressive in any twenty-year-old, but this guy looked at least twice that.

I do some similar solo exercises myself, from time to time, although nothing so formal and stylized. And when I do work out this way, I don't do it in public. It draws too much attention, especially from someone who knows what to look for. Someone like me.

In my line of work, drawing attention is a serious violation of the laws of common sense, and therefore of survival. Because if someone notices you for one thing, he'll be inclined to look more closely, at which point he might notice something else. A pattern, which would have remained quietly hidden, might then begin to emerge, after which your cloak of anonymity will be methodically pulled apart, probably to be rewoven into something more closely resembling a shroud.

Karate also stood out because he was Caucasian—European was my guess, although I couldn't pinpoint the country. He had close-cropped black hair, pale skin, and, when he wasn't busy with Horse Stance to Spinning Back Kick Number Two in the Mandarin Oriental gym, favored exquisitely thin-soled loafers and sport jackets with hand-rolled lapels. Macau's population of about a half million is ninety-five percent Chinese, with only a small Portuguese contingent remaining to remind anyone who cares that the territory, now a Chinese Special Administrative Region like Hong Kong, was not so long ago a Portuguese colony, and even the millions of annual gambling tourists are almost all from nearby Hong Kong, Taiwan, and mainland China, so non-Asians don't exactly blend.

Which is part of the reason the Agency had been so eager for me to take on the Belghazi assignment to begin with. It wasn't just that Belghazi had become a primary supplier to various Southeast Asian fundamentalist groups whom, post-9/11, Uncle Sam had come to view as a serious threat. Nor was it simply my demonstrated knack for the appearance of "natural causes," which in this case would be necessary because it seemed that Belghazi had protectors among certain "allied" governments whom Uncle Sam preferred not to offend. It was also because the likely venue for the job would require invisibility against an Asian background. And, although my mother had been American, my face is dominated by my father's Japanese features—the consequence of genetic chance, augmented years ago by some judicious plastic surgery, which I had undergone to better blend in in Japan.

So between the conspicuous ethnicity and the *kata* moves, Karate had managed to put himself on my radar screen, and it was then that I began to notice more. For one thing, he had a way of hanging around the hotel: the gym, the café, the terrace, the lobby. Wherever this guy was from, he'd come a long way to reach Macau. His failure to get out and see the sights, therefore, didn't make a lot of sense—unless he was waiting for someone.

Of course, I might have suffered from a similar form of conspicuousness. But I had a companion—a young Japanese woman—which made the "hanging around" behavior a little more explainable. Her name was Keiko, or at least that was how she billed herself with the Japanese escort agency through which I had hired her. She was in her mid-twenties, too young for me to take seriously, but she was pretty and surprisingly bright and I was enjoying her company. More important, her presence made me look less like some kind of intelligence operative or lone-wolf killer assessing the area, and more like a forty- or fifty-something Japanese who had taken his mistress to Macau, maybe for a little gambling, maybe for a lot of time alone at a hotel.

One morning, Keiko and I went down to the hotel's Café Girassol to enjoy the breakfast buffet. As the hostess led us to a table, I scanned the area for signs of danger, as I do by habit whenever entering a room. Hot spots first. Back Corner One: table of four young Caucasians, two male, two female, dressed for a hike. Accents Australian. Threat probability low. Back Corner Two: *Karate*. Hmm. Threat probability medium.

Keep the eyes moving. Complete the sweep. Wall tables: empty. Window seats: elderly Chinese couple. Next table: three girls, fashionable clothes, confident postures, probably Hong Kong Chinese, young professionals on a quick holiday. Next table: pair of Indian men in business attire, sunny Punjabi accents. Nothing that rubbed me the wrong way.

Back to Karate's vicinity with an oblique glance. He had his back to the wall and an unobstructed view of the restaurant's entrance. His seating position was what I would have expected from a pro; his focus on the room offered further evidence. I noticed that he had a newspaper open in front of him, although he wasn't bothering to read it. He would have been better off without the reading material: then he could have scoped the room as though he was bored and had nothing better to do than people-watch.

Or he should have brought a friend, as I had. I could feel him looking at us at one point, and was glad to have Keiko there, smiling into my eyes like a satisfied lover. The smile was convincing, too. She was good at her job.

Who was he waiting for, though? I might have assumed the answer was me—"only the paranoid survive," I think some Silicon Valley type once said—but I was pretty sure I wasn't it. Too many chance sightings followed by . . . nothing. No attempts to follow me, no attempt to recognize my face, no hard-eyed, *that's him* kind of feeling. After over a quarter century in the business and a lot of incidental training before that, I'm sensitive to these things. My gut told me he was after someone else. True, it wasn't impossible that he was only told *where* and *when,* with information on *who* to be provided subsequently, but I deemed that scenario unlikely. Not many operators would agree to take this kind of job without first knowing who they were going up against. It would be hard to know how to price things otherwise.

If the matter had been local—say, a Triad dispute—it was unlikely that a white guy would have been brought in for the job. The Triads, Chinese "secret societies" with deep roots in Macau and the mainland, tend to settle their affairs themselves. Adding up the available data, therefore, and taking myself off the short list of possible targets, I was left with Belghazi as the most likely recipient of Karate's attentions.

But who had hired him? If it had been the Agency, it would have been a violation of one of my three rules: no women or children, no acts against non-principals, no B-teams. Maybe my old friends from the government thought that, because they had managed to track me down in Rio, I was vulnerable, and that they could therefore treat my rules as mere guidelines. If this was indeed their assumption, they were mistaken. I had enforced my rules before, and would do so again.

That afternoon, I made a point of strolling past the gym with Keiko, and, sure enough, there was my friend, earnestly kicking the air at the same time as the day before. Some people just need a routine, and refuse to accept the consequences of predictability. In my experience, these people tend to get culled, often sooner, sometimes later. It's a Darwinian world out there.

Seeing an opportunity, I checked the sign-in sheet. His name was illegible, but he had written his room number clearly enough: 812. Hmmm, a smoking floor. Unhealthy.

I asked Keiko if she wouldn't mind shopping by herself for a little while. She smiled and told me she'd be delighted, which was probably the truth. She might have thought I was going off for a taste of the area's sumptuous buffet of prostitutes. No doubt she assumed I was married—the resulting associated paranoia of which would explain any countersurveillance moves she might have noticed—and I doubted that she would have found the notion of additional philandering excessively shocking.

Watching her walk out the front entrance to catch a cab into town, I felt an odd surge of affection. Most people would think of someone in Keiko's line of work as being anything but innocent, but at that moment, to me, innocence practically defined her. Her job was to offer me pleasure—and she was doing very well at it—and for her, our presence in Macau was no more complicated than that. She was as oblivious to the deadly dance playing out around her as a sheep grazing in a field. I told myself that she would go home with that innocence intact.

I called 812 from the lobby phone. There was no answer. A good sign, although not proof-positive: someone might have been in the room and not answering the phone, or Karate might have written down an incorrect room number, which I certainly would have done. Still, it was worth a look.

I stopped in my room to pick up a few items I would need, then took the elevator to the seventh floor. From there, I took the stairs, the less trafficked route, and therefore the one less likely to present problems like witnesses. On my left wrist, concealed under the baggy sleeve of a fleece pullover, was a device that looked like a large PDA, secured with Velcro. The device, which saw its initial deployment in the second Gulf War, is called SoldierVision. It takes a radar "picture" of a room through walls and feeds the resulting image back to the wrist unit. Not exactly something you might pick up at your local hardware store, and definitely one of the advantages of working with Christians In Action again.

Earlier in my stay I had taken the trouble of securing a master key for just this sort of occasion, although at the time it was Belghazi I had in mind, not Karate. The hotel used punched-hole mechanical key cards, the kind that look like slightly thickened, plain gray credit cards with patterns of two-millimeter holes cut in them. It also used, as part of its campaign to "Protect Our Environment!", a system whereby the key had to be inserted into a wall slot next to the door for the room lights to become operable. When you withdrew the key in preparation for leaving the room, there was about a one-minute delay before the lights would go out. The maids carried master keys, of course, and it had been easy enough to walk past a room that was being cleaned, pull the maid's master from the reader, make an impression in a chunk of modeling clay I'd picked up in a local toy store, and replace the key, all in about six seconds. Using the impression as a template, all I had needed to do was punch the appropriate additional holes in my room key, fill in the inappropriate ones with fast-setting epoxy clay, and presto, I had the same access as the hotel staff.

Karate's room was on the left of the corridor. I used the SoldierVision to confirm that it was empty, then let myself in with my homemade master. I wasn't unduly concerned about disturbing the room's contents in a way that might tell Karate someone had entered in his absence—the daily maid service could account for that.

I walked in and sniffed. Whoever he was, he'd been taking full advantage of his stay on the smoking floor. The room was thick with the lees of strong tobacco—Gauloises or Gitane, something like that—which you can smell outside those Tokyo bistros whose fervently Francophile patrons believe that emissions from a Marlboro or a Mild Seven might ruin the pleasant illusion of an afternoon in a Latin Quarter café.

I pulled on a pair of gloves and did a quick search of the closet and drawers, but found nothing remarkable. The small room safe was closed and locked, probably with his identification and other goodies inside. There was a Dell laptop on the desk, but I didn't have time to wait for its Windows operating system to boot. Besides, if he had enabled the boot log feature, he would see that someone had fired up the laptop in his absence and would get suspicious.

I picked up the room phone and hit the key for room service. Two rings, then a Filipina-accented voice said, "Yes, Mr. Nuchi, how may I help you?"

"Oh, I think I hit the wrong button. Sorry to disturb you."

"Not at all, sir. Have a pleasant day."

I hung up. Mr. Nuchi, then. Who liked French cigarettes.

But no other clues. Nothing even to confirm my suspicion that this guy was a pro, and possibly a rival. Well, there were other ways I might learn more.

I pulled an adhesive-backed transmitter from one of my pockets, peeled off the tape cover, and secured it in a suitably recessed spot along the bottom edge of one of the dressers. The unit was battery-operated and sound-activated. With luck, it would get a good enough feed for me to understand any conversation it picked up. But even short of that, it would help me figure out when Karate was coming and going, and therefore make it easier for me to learn more by following him.

I walked back to the door, used the SoldierVision to confirm that the hallway was clear, and left. The whole thing had taken about four minutes.

BELGHAZI ARRIVED early that evening. I was enjoying a cocktail with Keiko in the lobby, where I had a view of the registration desk, and made him in an instant. He was swarthy, the legacy of an Algerian mother, and his hair, which had been long and unruly in the CIA file photo, was now shaved close to the scalp. I put him at about six feet and a hundred and eighty-five pounds. Dense, muscular build. He was wearing an expensive-looking blue suit, from the cut maybe Brioni or Kiton, and a white shirt open at the collar. In his left hand he gripped the handle of what looked like a computer briefcase, something in black leather, and I caught a flash of gold chain encircling his wrist. But despite the clothes, the accessories, the jewelry, there was no element of fussiness about him. On the contrary: his presence was relaxed, and powerful. He looked like the kind of man who wouldn't have to raise his voice when speaking to his subordinates, who would command the attention of strangers with only a look or a gesture. Someone who wouldn't need to threaten violence to get what he wanted, if only because the hint of it would always be there, in the set of his posture, the look in his eyes, the tone of his voice.

Even if I hadn't had access to the file photo, the long-distance feel I had developed for this guy from his bio would have been enough for me to make him. Belghazi, first name Achille, had been born of a French army officer stationed in Algeria during France's "pacification" efforts there, and of a young Algerian woman whom the officer brought back to Paris but did not take as his wife. Illegitimate status hadn't seemed to slow Belghazi down, though, and he had excelled in school, both academically and athletically, making a name for himself afterward as a photojournalist. His fluent Arabic had made him a natural for covering conflicts in the Arab world: the Palestinian refugee camps, the Mujahideen in Afghanistan, the first Gulf War. Playing on his contacts among the combatants, and on those he developed at the same time among foreign military and intelligence services, Belghazi had become a conduit for small arms deliveries to various Middle Eastern hot spots. His operation had grown organically as his supply-side and customer-side contacts broadened and deepened. His latest efforts were concentrated in Southeast Asia, where various emerging fundamentalist and separatist groups within the region's sizeable Muslim populations provided a growing customer base. He was known to have a taste for the finer things, too, along with a serious gambling habit.

He was with two large men, also in suits and similarly swarthy, whom I made as bodyguards. One of them started a visual security sweep, but Belghazi didn't rely on him. Instead, he did his own evaluation of the room and its occupants. I watched in my peripheral vision and, when I saw that he was finished and had turned his attention to the front desk, I looked over again.

A striking blonde had just come through the front doors. She was wearing a black pant suit and pumps. Practical, but classy. What you'd see on a traveler carrying a first-class ticket. She was tall, too, maybe five-nine, five-ten, with long legs that looked good even in pants, and a ripe, voluptuous body. A porter followed her in, gripping a pair of large Vuitton bags. He paused near her and leaned forward to ask something. She raised a hand to indicate that he should wait, then started her own visual sweep of the room. I hadn't expected that, and quickly returned my attention to Keiko until the blonde's gaze had passed over us. When I glanced over again, she was standing beside Belghazi, her arm linked through his.

Something about her presence was as relaxed and, in its way, as commanding as his. Everything about her seemed natural: her hair, her face, the curves beneath her clothes.

A minute later she, the porter, and one of the bodyguards headed toward the elevators. Belghazi and the other bodyguard remained at the front desk, discussing something with the receptionist.

The front door opened again. I glanced up and saw Karate.

Christ, I thought. *The gang's all here.* I wondered half-consciously whether he'd been tipped off somehow.

Karate walked slowly through the lobby. I saw his gaze move to Belghazi, saw his eyes harden in a way that would mean nothing to most people but that meant a great deal to me. From this gaze I understood that Karate wasn't looking at a man. No. What I saw instead was a hunter acquiring a target.

And, I knew, but for my long-practiced self-control, had anyone been watching me as I confirmed my suspicions about why Karate was here, they would have seen an identical involuntary atavism ripple across my own features.

A few minutes passed. Belghazi and his man finished at the front desk and made their way to the elevator. I gave them four minutes, then told Keiko I needed to use the restroom and would be right back.

I went to a house phone and asked the operator to connect me to the Oriental Suite. There were only two suites in the hotel—the Oriental and the Macau—and, judging from his file, I had a feeling Belghazi would be occupying one of them.

No answer at the Oriental. I tried again, this time asking for the Macau.

"Hello," a man's voice answered.

"Hello, this is the front desk," I said, doing a passable imitation of a local Chinese accent. "Is there anything we can do to make Mr. Belghazi's stay with us more comfortable?"

"No, we're fine," the voice said.

"Very good," I said. "Please enjoy your stay."

THAT NIGHT, while Keiko was out, I sat in the hotel room and used an earpiece to listen in on Karate. He was in his room, from the sound of it watching CNN International Edition. Go to sleep, or go out: I would take my cue from him. I was already dressed in a pair of charcoal worsted pants, navy pullover, and comfortable, rubber-soled walking shoes in case we wound up with the second option, a night on the town.

I looked out at the massive cranes and earth moving equipment that Macau was using to build yet more bridges to China's Guangdong province, the low mountains of which crouched a few kilometers distant. The machines rose from the harbor like mythological creatures provoked from the seabed, hulking, misshapen, slouching toward land but held fast by the muck below.

The cranes reminded me of Japan, where I'd lived most of my adult life and where reclaiming land from the sea for the construction of redundant bridges and unneeded office parks is a national sport. But where the ubiquitous construction in Japan always felt familiar, almost comforting in its obviousness, here the excess was mysterious, even vaguely menacing. Who made the decisions? Who rigged the environmental impact statements to ensure that the projects were approved? Who profited from the kickbacks? I didn't know. In many ways, Macau was a mystery.

I had spent the previous three weeks here, moving from hotel to hotel, keeping a low profile, getting a solid feel for the place. Before accepting the Belghazi assignment, I hadn't known much more about the place than what I picked up from reading the *Far Eastern Economic Review*: Portugal's return of the territory to China in 1999 had been amicable, as these things go, and the territory's five percent ethnic Portuguese population was unusually well integrated, speaking Cantonese and mixing with the locals in a way that might make most British-derived Hong Kongers blush; its service economy was staffed largely by Filipinos and Thais; for a territory that until recently had been the ball in a five-hundred-year game of Great Power Ping-Pong, it had an unusually firm sense of its own identity.

At the end of my three-week sojourn, I knew much more: how to dress, walk, and carry myself to look like one of the millions of visitors from, say, Hong Kong; the layout and rhythms of the stores and streets; the codes and mores of the casinos. All of which would confer an important advantage in the job at hand.

I heard the phone ring in Karate's room. The television went quiet.

"Allo," I heard him say. A pause, then, *"Bien."*

French, then, as I had suspected from the nicotine permeating his room. And with a cultured Parisian accent. My French was mostly left over from high school, and the receiver reception was muffled and obscured by periodic static. This was going to be tough.

"Oui, il est arrivé ce soir."

That I understood. Yes, he arrived tonight.

Another pause. Then, *"Pas ce soir."* Not tonight.

Pause. Then, *"Oui, la réunion est ce soir. Ensuite cela."* Yes, the meeting is tonight. Then after that.

Pause. A thicket of words I couldn't pick apart, followed by, *"Tout va bien."* Everything is fine. Another impenetrable thicket. Then, *"Je vous ferai savoir quand ce sera fait."* I'll let you know when it's done.

Click. Back to CNN.

A half hour later, the TV went off again. I heard his door open and close. He was going out.

I grabbed a dark windbreaker and took the stairs to the ground floor. A professional could be expected to use the rear entrance, which would represent the less trafficked, less predictable alternative, and I ducked out through the back doors on the assumption that this was the route Karate would be using. There were three exits back here—one from the hotel, one from the beauty parlor, one from the restaurant—but all of them fed into the same courtyard, which in turn fed onto a single walkway, meaning a single choke point.

There was an open-air parking garage next to the hotel. I walked into it and hugged the wall, obscured by bushes lining the wall's exterior.

He appeared a minute after I'd gotten in position.

The streetlights illuminated him and cast shadows into the garage where I stood silently by. I watched him stroll past me down the tree-lined walkway in the direction of the Avenida da Amizade, named, like most of Macau's thoroughfares, by the Portuguese centuries earlier. The soft drape of his navy sport jacket was too stylish for his surroundings—dress in Macau, I had learned, was almost slacker casual—but I supposed that as a white island in an Asian sea he was going to stand out regardless.

Past the parking garage he turned right into an alley. I glanced back at the hotel exit—all quiet. So far he seemed to be alone, with no countersurveillance to his rear. I moved out to follow him. He reached the Avenida da Amizade and waited for a break in the traffic before crossing. I hung back in the shadows and waited.

On the other side of the street he turned left, looking back over his shoulder, as any pedestrian would, to check for oncoming traffic before crossing. I permitted myself the trace of a smile. His "traffic check" was an unobtrusive bit of countersurveillance. It was nicely done, casual, and I saw from the quality of the move that I was probably going to have a hard time following him solo.

He moved down the wide boulevard in the direction of the Hotel Lisboa, the territory's biggest casino and best-known trolling ground for prostitutes, and after a moment I crossed the street and trailed after him. The streetlights around us were widely spaced, with ample pools of darkness between them for concealment, and Karate couldn't have spotted me even had he looked backward to do so.

A few hundred meters farther on, he cut down the

steps of an underground passageway. The passageway was H-shaped, its lengths running parallel to the Amizade and its middle running perpendicular beneath it. I moved just a little more quickly to close the gap, and arrived at the entrance in time to see him disappearing into the middle of the tunnel and under the street.

Now I faced a dilemma. If I followed him in and he glanced back, he would make me. If I stayed put and he emerged on the opposite side of the street and hurried on to develop distance, I could easily lose him.

I thought for a moment. Until now, his countersur-veillance had been subtle, disguised as ordinary pedestrian behavior. But he was abandoning subtlety now: after all, a pedestrian out for a stroll doesn't typ-ically cross a street one way and then, a short stretch later, cross back. He knew what he was doing. The question was, which way would he play it? Double back, to catch a follower? Or hurry out the other side, to lose him?

If I had been working with a team, or even just a teammate, there wouldn't have been a problem. We would have just tag-teamed him in, knowing that if one of us got spotted, the other would fall into place after. But this time I didn't have that luxury. All I had was in-stinct and experience, and these were telling me that the tunnel move was a feint, an attempt to draw a follower into the tunnel, weed him out of the crowd, then turn around and catch him. So I moved past the passageway on the right, hiding in the shadows of one of the av-enue's stunted palm trees, hoping I was right.

Fifteen seconds went by. Thirty.

If I had been wrong, this was my last chance to try to cross the street. If I waited until he had emerged, he would see me coming.

Just another second, just another second, c'mon, asshole, where are you...

Boom, there he was, moving up the vertical side of the H, still on my side of the street. I let out a long, quiet breath.

He strolled another hundred meters along the Avenida da Amizade, then cut right. I did the same, in time to see him turn left, down a scooter-choked alley walled in by office buildings to either side. I fell in behind him, window unit air conditioners buzzing like insects in the dark around us.

Three minutes later we arrived at the Lisboa. I followed him in, wondering whether he was hoping to use its many entrances and exits as part of a preplanned surveillance detection route. If so, he'd made a mistake. The Lisboa was too crowded at night; a pursuer could stay close in here without your ever knowing it. Even if he'd had a team positioned for countersurveillance, the nighttime crowds would present insurmountable opportunities for concealment. Maybe he'd designed this route during the day, when the hotel was less crowded? That would have been a mistake, too. Times of day, days of the week, changes of season, changes of temperature—all can make for an environment dramatically different from the one you originally reconnoitered.

I moved in closer and stayed with him, knowing that if he snaked off into the crowded, multilevel hive of the casino I might easily lose him. But he avoided the gaming area, strolling instead in a slow, clockwise loop around the ground floor's shopping arcade, where clusters of prostitutes from nearby Guangdong province circled like hungry fish in a spherical aquarium. We moved with them, past gamblers flush with fresh winnings, whom the girls eyed with bold invitation, eager to retrieve a few floating scraps from the casino food chain; past middle-aged men from Hong Kong and Taiwan with sagging bodies and febrile eyes, their postures rigid, caught in some grim purgatory between sexual urgency and commercial calculation; past security guards, inured to the charms of the girls' bare legs and bold décolletage and interested only in keeping them moving, circling, forever swimming through the murk of the endless Lisboa night.

Karate left the building through a secondary exit. I still wasn't sure what he had hoped to accomplish by going inside. The shopping arcade, like the hotel itself, was too crowded for meaningful surveillance detection. Maybe he had planned this part of the route poorly, as I had initially speculated. Or maybe he had simply been window-shopping in anticipation of indulging himself later that night. Not impossible: even professionals occasionally slip, or pause to fulfill some human need.

His subsequent behavior supported the "indulgence" hypothesis: after the Lisboa, I didn't spot him doing anything further to check his back. He must have satisfied himself with the provocative tunnel stunt. It wasn't an ineffective move, actually, and probably would have been enough to flush someone else. Hell, it would have flushed me, if my instincts had been a little less sharp or if I hadn't done my three weeks of homework.

He continued northwest on the Avenida Henrique. The street was straight, dark, and heavily trafficked, and I was able to follow him from far back. My eyes roved constantly, searching the hot spots, the places I would have set up countersurveillance or an ambush. Nothing set off my radar.

At Senado Square, the area's main pedestrian shopping commons, he turned right. The square would be crowded, even at this evening hour, and I increased my pace to ensure that I wouldn't lose him. There he was, moving up the undulating lines of black and white tile, to the left of the illuminated vertical jets of the square's central fountain, along the low, pastel-colored porticos of the Portuguese-style storefronts, incongruous amid the surrounding Asian sounds and scents. I followed from about ten meters back. Hong Kong pop blared urgently from a storefront. The smells of roasted pork and sticky rice wafted on the air. Thick groups of shoppers drifted back and forth around us, chatting, laughing, enjoying the comfortable closeness of the arcade and the carefree camaraderie of the evening.

We moved off Senado and onto quieter streets. Karate browsed among the street stalls—fruit, lingerie, traditional Thai costumes at three for a Hong Kong dollar—but bought nothing. He seemed to be heading in the direction of St. Paul's, the site of a once-splendid Portuguese church, over the centuries gutted again and again by fire, and standing now only as a sad façade, a haunted relic, illuminated at night like a bleached skeleton propped at the apex of a long series of steep stairs, where it broods in ruined majesty over the city that has grown like weeds around it.

Gradually our surroundings became more residential. We passed wide, open doorways. These I checked automatically, but they offered no danger, only miscellaneous domestic scenes: four elderly women absorbed in a game of mahjong; a group of boys surrounding a television; a family at the supper table. We passed an old shrine, its red paint peeling in the tropical moisture. Incense from the brazier within pervaded my senses with the recollected emotions of childhood.

Karate reached the corner of the street and turned

right. In this warren of dim alcoves and alleyways, I could easily lose him if he developed distance, and I increased my pace to stay with him. I turned the same corner he had gone past a moment earlier—and nearly ran right into him.

He'd turned the corner and stopped—a classic countersurveillance move, and hard to beat if you're working solo. No wonder he'd been taking it easy: the tunnel stunt had been a false finish to the run, and I'd fallen for it. *Shit.*

I felt an adrenaline dump. Audio faded out. Movement slowed down.

Our eyes locked, and for a suspended second we stood totally still. I saw his brow begin to furrow. *I've seen this guy,* I knew he was thinking. *At the hotel.*

His weight shifted back into a defensive stance. His left hand pulled forward the left lapel of his jacket. His right reached toward the gap.

Toward a weapon, no doubt. *Shit.*

I stepped in close and grabbed his right lower sleeve with my left hand, pulling it away from his body to prevent him from deploying whatever he had in his jacket. With my right I took hold of his left lapel and thrust it up under his chin. His reaction was good: he stepped back with his left leg to regain his balance and open up distance, from which he might be able to employ something from his karate arsenal. But I wasn't going to give him that chance. I caught his right heel with my right foot and used my fist in his throat to shove him back in *kouchigari,* a basic judo throw. His balance ruined and his foot trapped, he went straight back, his left arm pinwheeling uselessly. I maintained my tight hold on his right arm and twisted counterclockwise as we fell, keeping my right elbow positioned squarely over his diaphragm, nailing it hard as we hit the pavement.

I scrambled to his right side, raised my right hand high, and shot a hammer-fist toward his nose. His reflexes were good, though, despite the shock of hitting the ground. He turned his head and deflected the blow with his left hand.

Still, he was out of his element on the ground, and quickly made a mistake. Rather than dealing with the immediate threat—my dominant position and freedom to attack—he went for his weapon again. I swam my right arm inside his right and jerked it back into a chicken wing. He sensed an opening and tried to sit up, but I felt that coming. Using the chicken wing to arrest his forward momentum, I swept my left arm around his head counterclockwise, from front to back, locked my hands behind his near shoulder blade, and leaned back, the back of my arm pressing down against his face. The move bent his neck back to the limit of its natural range of motion and took his shoulder half out of its socket, but I went no further. I only wanted to make him comply, not kill him. At least not yet.

"Who are you working for?" I said.

In response, he only struggled. I put some additional pressure on his neck, but quickly relaxed it, lest he conclude that I was trying to finish him, in which case I couldn't reasonably expect him to cooperate.

He got the message and the struggling stopped. Not likely that he practiced any *kata* that involved being held on the ground in a neck crank. *"Je ne comprends pas,"* I heard him say, his body tense in my grip.

Bullshit you don't comprehend, pal, I thought. *I just heard you watching CN fucking N.*

"Pour . . . Pour qui travaillez-vous?" I tried asking.

"Je ne comprends pas," he said again.

All right, the hell with it. I squeezed again, harder than before, holding the pressure a second longer this time before backing off.

"Last time," I said in English. "Tell me who you work for or you're done."

"All . . . all right," I heard him say, his voice muffled by my arm across his face. I leaned forward slightly to hear better.

As I did so, he arched into me and jerked sharply upward with his right arm, trying to get clear of the chicken wing, to reach whatever he had in his jacket. I shifted to the left and yanked the arm back hard. But his move had only been a feint, and as I shifted I saw, too late, that his true intention had been to reach for his belt with his other hand. Before I could stop him, in one smooth motion he had popped a button on the leather and yanked free the buckle, which was attached to a double-edged steel blade.

Fuck. Without thinking I arched savagely back, pressing my left forearm hard across the back of his neck and squeezing with the strength of both arms. There was a split instant of raw corporeal resistance, and then his neck snapped and his body spasmed in my arms. The knife clattered to the ground.

I laid him out on the pavement and quickly patted him down. My hands were shaking from the effects of adrenaline. I was suddenly aware of my heart, pounding crazily inside me. Damn, that had been a nice move. He'd nearly gotten away with it.

He was traveling light: no wallet, no ID. Just his hotel key in a pants pocket and there, in a shoulder holster, what he'd been reaching for when he saw me. A Heckler & Koch Mark 23. Attached to it, a Knights Armament suppressor, one of the two models H&K approves for the Mark 23.

A belt knife and a silenced H&K. I doubted that he just waltzed them through airport security on his way to Macau, although I supposed it was possible the security guards were too preoccupied with nail clippers and cuticle scissors to notice. Still, my guess was that the mysterious Mr. Nuchi had local contacts, and that the weapons had been waiting for him or were otherwise procured after he had arrived. I filed the thought away for later consideration.

There was nothing else that could tell me more about who he was or who had sent him. Or who he had been on his way to meet.

I stood and glanced around me. Left, right. Nothing. The street was graveyard still.

I moved off into the shadows, my head reflexively sweeping right and left as I walked, searching for danger. I left the weapons, having little use for them in the current operation and not wishing to contaminate myself with anything connected to what the police might find at the crime scene. After a while, my pulse began to slow.

Who the hell was he? Who had he been on his way to meet? I hated the feeling of knowing so little about him. A name—Nuchi—which might have been an alias. And a probable nationality. But no more.

But I supposed that, overall, it wasn't a bad outcome. I was nearly certain that, regardless of who had sent him, Karate had been here to take out Belghazi. That was no longer a possibility.

And things certainly could have turned out worse. If he'd had that H&K out when I'd first turned the corner, instead of reaching for it afterward, it might have been me lying back there in the dark.

I stayed on the narrow streets, the dark alleys. My

pulse slowed more. My hands settled. The buildings to either side seemed to grow taller, and the weak light dimmer, until I felt as though I was zigzagging along the channel of a steep ravine, a dark urban gorge cut through the faded concrete façades by a long-vanished river. The rusted fire escapes were escarpments of rock, the hanging laundry tangled vines, a lone sodium-arc roof light a yellowed, gibbous moon.

I made my way back to the hotel. By the time I reached the rear entrance, my heart rate was normal again. I started thinking ahead, thinking about Belghazi.

Right, Belghazi. The main event. No more sideshows. I'd get close, do it right, and get out. After that, a big payday. Big enough so that afterward I would get clear of this shit forever.

Or at least for a reasonably long while.

2

THE NEXT MORNING, Keiko and I enjoyed another leisurely breakfast in the hotel's Café Girassol, then whiled away an hour browsing the hotel shops, all of which offered splendid views of the lobby. But Belghazi never showed.

Around noon, I went to an Internet café to check the electronic bulletin board that I was using to communicate with Tomohisa Kanezaki, my contact inside the CIA. Before going further, I downloaded a copy of security software and installed it, as I always do, to confirm that the terminal I was using was free of "snoopware"—software, some commercial, some hacker-devised, that monitors keystrokes, transmits screen images, and that can otherwise compromise a computer's security. Hackers love to remotely place the software on public terminals, like the ones you see in airports, libraries, copy shops, and, of course, Internet cafés, from which they then harvest passwords, credit card numbers, bank accounts, hell, entire online identities.

This one was clean. I checked the bulletin board. There was a message waiting: "Call me."

That was all. I logged out and left.

Outside, I turned on the encrypted cell phone the

Agency had provided me, punched in the number I had memorized, and started walking to make it harder for anyone to triangulate.

I heard a single ring on the other end, then Kanezaki's voice. *"Moshi moshi,"* he said.

Kanezaki is an American *sansei,* or third-generation Japanese, and he likes to show off his language skills. I rarely indulge him. "Hey," I said.

"Hey," he said, conceding. "I've been trying to call you."

I smiled. Kanezaki was part of the CIA, which in my book rendered him automatically untrustworthy. Of course, he probably had the same misgivings about me. But in Tokyo I had declined a contract that his boss wanted to take out on him, and in fact had warned him about it. You'd have to be a world-class ingrate not to appreciate a favor like that, and I knew Kanezaki felt he owed me. He'd feel that way not just because of what I had done, but also because he was much more American than Japanese, and Americans, whose self-image is so tied up with "fairness," wind up making themselves suckers for the concept. His sentiment would take us only so far, of course—in my experience, one of the guiding principles of human relations seems to be "what have you done for me lately"—but it was something, a small antidote against the potential poison of his professional affiliations.

"Unless I'm talking on it," I said, "I leave this thing turned off."

"Saving the battery?"

"Guarding my privacy."

"You're the poster boy for paranoia," he said, and I could see him shaking his head on the other end. I smiled again. In some ways I liked the kid in spite of his choice of employer. I'd been impressed by the countermeasures he'd taken against his boss after my warning, and some part of me enjoyed being able to watch his development from naïve idealist to increasingly seasoned player.

"Our friend just got in," he said.

"I know. I saw him last night."

"Good. You know, we're tracking him. If you'd leave the cell phone on, we might be able to contact you with some timely information."

Although I didn't know for sure, I suspected the Agency had been keeping tabs on Belghazi through a compromised cell or satellite phone. I wasn't going to make the same mistake.

"Sure," I said, my tone neutral to the point of sarcasm.

There was a pause. "You're not going to leave it on," he said, his tone half-resigned, half-bemused.

I laughed.

"We'd have a better chance of success if we could work together," he said, earnest as ever.

I laughed again.

"All right, do it your way," he said. "I know you will anyway."

"Anything else?"

"Yeah. It would really be nice if you could account for some of those disbursements."

"C'mon, we've been over this. I need the cash to get into the high rollers' rooms. I saw a guy from China drop a million U.S. at one of the baccarat tables the other night. That's where our friend plays. I need to get near him, and they don't allow spectators. Or low rollers."

He was probably just giving me a hard time to try to make me feel like I'd won something. I knew this whole program was as off the books as anything the Agency had ever run. The last thing Kanezaki or his superiors would want would be a paper trail for the General Accounting Office to follow.

"What if you actually win something?" he said.

"I'll be sure to report it as taxable income."

He laughed at that, and I said, "We're done?"

"Sure. Oh, just one more thing. A little something. Last night someone got killed in your neighborhood."

"Yeah?"

"Yeah. Broken neck."

"Ouch."

"You would know."

I knew what he was thinking. Kanezaki had once watched me take someone out with a neck crank.

"Actually, I wouldn't know," I said. "But I can imagine."

I heard a snort. "Just remember," he said, "even if we're not there in the room with you, we're still watching."

"I've always suspected that you guys self-select for voyeurs."

"Very funny."

"Who's being funny?"

There was a pause. "Look, it might be that I owe you. But not everyone here feels that way. And you're not just dealing with me. Okay? You need to watch yourself."

I smiled. "It's always good to have a friend."

"Shit," I heard him mutter.

"If I need anything, I'll contact you," I told him.

"Okay." A pause, then, "Good luck."

I pressed the "end" key, purged the call log, and turned the unit off.

He hadn't seemed particularly perturbed about the late Karate. Possibly indicating that the CIA wasn't affiliated with him. Or maybe there was an affiliation, and Kanezaki-san was simply out of the loop.

I kept walking. Macau breathed around me, deeply, in and out, like a winded animal.

IN THE EVENING, Keiko and I decided to enjoy a little gambling at the Lisboa. I couldn't continually set up for Belghazi in the hotel lobby without drawing attention to myself. And trying to wire his room the way I had Karate's would have been too risky—if his bodyguards swept for bugs and found something, they might harden their defenses. So I decided my best shot at intercepting him would be not to follow, but to anticipate him.

This can be easier than it might sound. All you have to do is put yourself in the other party's shoes: if I were him, what would I do? How would I look at the world, how would I feel, how would I behave? Just good, sound, Dale Carnegie stuff. Appreciating the other guy's viewpoint, that kind of thing. I'm-okay-you're-okay. I'm-okay-you're-going-to-die.

Performing this exercise with someone as security-conscious as Belghazi, though, is tough, because the security-conscious tend to eschew patterns in favor of randomness. Random times; random routes; when possible, random destinations. They deliberately avoid getting hooked on anything—lunch at a certain restaurant, haircuts at a certain barber, bets on the horses at a certain track—that the opposition can dial into.

But Belghazi's security consciousness wasn't perfect. His behavior suffered from what software types call a "security flaw"—in this case, his compulsion to gamble.

That compulsion was probably part of what had enabled the Agency, and, perhaps, Karate, to track him to Macau to begin with. It was the same compulsion I was now working with to get inside his head. Because, if you're addicted to high-stakes baccarat and you're in

Macau for a few days, there's really nowhere but the Lisboa. Everything else feels small-time.

Belghazi would know better, of course. And maybe he'd heed that knowledge and put his chips down someplace less exciting, less glamorous, less predictable. But I didn't think he would. If he had that kind of self-control, he wouldn't be playing the tables in the first place. No, he'd gamble, all right, and rationalize by telling himself that there was nothing to worry about, that no one knew he was in Macau anyway, that besides, he always traveled with the bodyguards, just in case.

Keiko and I enjoyed a dinner of Macanese cuisine—an exotic mix of Portuguese, Indian, Malay, and Chinese influences—at the O Porto Interior, a charming but somewhat out-of-the-way restaurant. The location gave me ample opportunity to check our backs on the way to our meal, and also afterward, when we got in a cab and headed to the Lisboa.

I had spent time in all of Macau's casinos, of course, while reconnoitering the territory, but that had been only part of my preparation for the Belghazi operation. I needed to be comfortable not just with gambling in Macau, but with gambling generally, and I wanted more exposure to the tics and rites of the subculture so that I could better absorb them, reflect them back, achieve the proper level of invisibility as a result. Macau was a start, but I knew that the persona I was inhabiting—moneyed Japanese gaming enthusiast—would lack crucial verisimilitude if the persona in question had never set eyes on Las Vegas.

So I had spent a week there, staying at the Four Seasons on the south end of the strip because it seemed to be the only good hotel that could be accessed without first fording a casino floor, and I knew I would need refuge from the smoke and the noise and the frenzy. I played baccarat at the upscale Bellagio; roulette at the off-strip Rio; craps at the fading Riviera, whose attempts to match the gayness and glitter around her felt forced, artificial, like makeup layered on by a woman who recognizes that she was never beautiful to begin with and has now, in addition, grown colorless and old.

When I couldn't stand it anymore, I would wander off into the desert west of the strip and walk. The noise faded quickly. The lights took longer to escape, and even after miles they still obscured the stars in the desert sky. But eventually it would all come to seem sufficiently inconsequential in the distance, and I would stop and look back on what I had left behind. Standing silently on those indigenous reefs of sand, breathing the still, desiccated air, I decided that the improbable town I now beheld was a sad and lonely place, the shows and the restaurants and the neon all just a gaudy bandage wrapped around some irrefutable psychic wound, the city itself a bizarre and passing spectacle in the eyes of the reptiles that watched as I did unblinking from afar, who must have understood in their primitive consciousness and from this distant vantage that soon enough it would all be scrub and sand again, as it had always been before.

The reprieve was inevitably brief. I would return to the strip and all would be excess: Hummers purchased on tax breaks for use on flat asphalt, without even a pothole to challenge them; quarter-mile-long buffets vacuumed down by impossibly corpulent diners; pensioners drugged by a lifetime of television and enticed to this place by a craving for more spectacle, more and ever more.

I had thought that 9/11 might have changed some of

this, might have been the occasion for reflection, for focus. But if the trauma of attack had produced any such effect, the benefits had been short-lived. Instead, during my mercifully brief time stateside, I saw that nothing had really changed. Sacrifice was the duty only of the few, who were of course hypocritically lauded by the many, the latter barely pausing in their infantile partying to wish the soldiers good luck at war.

But none of it mattered to me. I had seen it all before, when I had first returned from Vietnam. I'd done my bit of soldiering. It was someone else's problem now.

Keiko and I got out of the cab in front of the Lisboa, and I felt my alertness bump up a notch. I don't like casinos, in Macau, Las Vegas, or anywhere else. The entrances and exits tend to be too tightly controlled, for one thing. The camera and surveillance networks are the best in the world, for another. Every move you make in a gaming hall is recorded by hundreds of video units and stored on tape for a minimum of two weeks. If there's a problem—a guy who's winning too much, a table that's losing too much—management can review the action and figure out how they were being scammed, then take steps to eliminate the cause.

But it's not just the operational difficulties. It's the atmosphere, the scene. For me, gambling when there's no hope of affecting the odds always carries a whiff of desperation and depression. The industry recognizes the problem, and tries to compensate with an overlay of glitz. I suppose it works, up to a point, the way a deodorizer can mask an underlying smell.

We went in through a set of glass doors and rode a short escalator up to the main gaming hall. There it was, triple-distilled, a circular room of perhaps a thousand square meters, jammed tight with thick crowds shifting and sliding like platelets in a congealing bloodstream; high ceilings almost hidden above clouds of spot-lit, exhaled tobacco smoke; a cacophony of intermingled shouts of delight and cries of despair.

Keiko wanted to play the slot machines, which was fine, freeing me as it did to roam the baccarat rooms in search of Belghazi. I gave her a roll of Hong Kong dollars and told her I'd be back in a few hours. More likely, if things went according to plan, I would go straight to the hotel. In which case, when we hooked up again, I'd tell her that I'd looked for her but couldn't find her, and had assumed that she'd gone back ahead of me.

I set out for the stairs that would take me out of the low-stakes pit and up to the high rollers' rooms above. I passed rows of pensioners, each mechanically communing with a slot machine, and I thought of pigeons taught to peck a lever in exchange for a random reward. Next, several interchangeable roulette tables, the troupe hovering around them younger than the slot players they would eventually become, their jaws set, eyes shining in cheap ecstasy, lips moving in silent entreaty to the selfsame gods that even at the utterance of these foolish prayers continued to torment their worshipers with Olympian caprice.

I bought chips with four hundred thousand Hong Kong dollars—about sixty thousand U.S. I'd already squeezed Kanezaki for that much and more in "expenses"—the disbursements of which he had complained earlier. Then I wandered from room to room, never actually going inside, until I found what I was looking for.

Outside the Lisboa's most exclusive VIP room, on the fifth floor, the highest in the casino, were the two bodyguards, flanking the entrance. Belghazi must have felt sufficiently safe inside not to bother himself arguing about the "no spectators" rule. And sure, the guards could effectively monitor the entrance this way, and deal appropriately with anyone they deemed suspicious.

Unfortunately for them, I'm not a suspicious-looking guy. And their presence told me exactly where to go.

I walked right past them and into the room. Only one of the three baccarat tables was in play. The rest were empty, save for their dealers, of course, who stood with postures as crisp as the starched collars of their white shirts, ready for the players who would surely drift in as the evening deepened into night; and for a few attractive Asian women whom I made as shills, there to attract passing high rollers with their bright smiles and plunging necklines.

I glanced over at the active table. There they were, Belghazi and the blonde, both dressed tastefully and a bit more stylishly than the other players: Belghazi in a white shirt, open at the neck, and navy blazer; the blonde in a white silk blouse and black bolero. Most of the fourteen player slots were taken, but Belghazi and his girlfriend had empty seats to either side of them. They were the only foreigners in the room, and had probably taken the isolated seats so as not to offend anyone who might consider a foreigner's presence unlucky. I didn't have such qualms. Quite the contrary tonight, in fact.

I'd been in this room before, and had seen bets of as high as one hundred thousand U.S. for a single hand. Some of the patrons here, I knew, might gamble all night, and on into the next night. A few of Belghazi's cohorts, their eyes glassy, their complexions pasty beneath the chandelier lighting, looked as though they might have done just that.

The dealer turned over the player's hand and cried

out, "Natural eight!" An excited murmur picked up around the table: eight was a "natural," and could be beaten only by a nine. The round would be decided based on the cards already on the table—nothing new could be dealt. With almost painful deliberation, the dealer next turned over the bank's cards, calling out, "Natural nine!" as he did so. There was an outburst of cheers and curses, the former by those who had bet on the bank's hand that round, the latter by those who had bet on the player's. As the dealer passed the cards across the table to the other two dealers, who began paying off the winning bets, many of the players dipped their heads and began marking up the pads the casino had provided, attempting to discern some pattern in the randomness, a lucky streak they might lunge at and manage to grab.

I walked over and took the seat to Belghazi's right, so that he would naturally look away from me to talk to the blonde or to follow the action of the player in Seat 1, who was designated to act as the bank. I noticed the computer briefcase, nestled against his leg where he would feel it if it were somehow to move.

He turned to me. "I've seen you, haven't I," he said in French-accented English, his dark eyes narrowing a fraction. The effect was half attempt at recollection, half accusation. The blonde glanced over and then away.

This was a slight breach of high roller etiquette, which is generally predicated on respect for the other players' anonymity. "Maybe at the tables downstairs," I answered, concealing my surprise. "I have to build up the bankroll a bit before a trip to the VIP rooms."

He shook his head twice, slowly, and smiled, still looking into my eyes. "Not downstairs. At the Oriental. With a pretty Asian woman. She's not with you tonight?"

"You're staying at the Oriental?" I asked, sidestepping his inquiry as would any self-respecting philanderer who'd just been questioned about his mistress by a stranger.

"It's a good hotel," he replied, doing a little sidestepping of his own.

I was impressed. I had been taking care not to stand out or to otherwise become memorable, and he had spotted me anyway. He was well-attuned to his environment, to the patterns that might at some point make the difference between winning and losing. Or living and dying.

The dealer advised us that it was time to place our bets. "Yes," I said, putting down the minimum of about U.S. ten thousand on the bank, "but this is the place for baccarat." Belghazi nodded and put down fifty thousand on player, then turned to the banker to watch the hand get dealt. I saw from this movement that he wasn't truly concerned about me. If he had been, he wouldn't have turned his back. No, he had only been reflexively probing, firing into the tree line, checking to see whether he'd hit anything and whether anyone fired back.

The banker handed the first card to the dealer. As he did so, I leaned forward and crossed my hands, my right fingers settling across the Traser P5900 I was wearing on my left wrist. On the underside of the watch was a thumbnail-sized squib containing a little cocktail, one unlikely to be served by the casino's bar girls. The concoction in question consisted primarily of staphylococcus aureus—a rapid-onset food poisoning pathogen—and chloral hydrate, a compound that causes nausea, disorientation, and unconsciousness within one to four hours. The first would get Belghazi back to the hotel in a hurry. The second would ensure that he slept soundly, if not ter-

ribly comfortably, when he got there. I eased the squib
free and held it at the junction of my right middle and
forefinger. I'd wait for the right moment—one of Belghazi's head-turns, or a big win or loss for one of the players, or some other distraction—and then make my move.

I realized there was an important side benefit to my
plan: the symptoms of staph infection are so acute, and
set in so quickly, that there was a good chance Belghazi
would return to the hotel room without, or at least
ahead of, the blonde. And, even if she came back with or
only shortly behind him, he might very well send her
away for a while, so he could endure the effects of his
rebelling stomach in privacy.

I won the first round. So far so good: I didn't know
how long this would take, and, even with baccarat's favorable odds and leisurely pace of play, Kanezaki's
money wouldn't hold out forever.

A pretty attendant came by. Belghazi ordered a tonic
water. At fifty thousand a hand, I supposed he wanted
to exercise a little alcohol discipline. I followed suit.

The blonde leaned toward Belghazi and said, *"Je vais
essayer les tables de dés. Je serai de retour bientôt."* I'm
going to try the craps tables. I'll be back in a little while.
She got up and left.

Perfect. I stole a glance, just a quick one, the kind Belghazi would find neither surprising nor disrespectful.
She was wearing a black skirt to match the bolero. Her
legs were stunning, and she walked with the unpreten-
tious confidence of someone who long ago came to understand that she is beautiful and today finds the fact
neither remarkable nor worthy of flaunting.

Belghazi doubled his bet on the next round. I stayed
with the minimum. This time we both won.

The attendant came by with the drinks, carrying them

perched on a silver tray. She placed Belghazi's on the table next to him, then leaned forward and moved to do the same with mine. He was watching the banker, who was getting ready to deal. *Now.*

I half rose from my seat, reaching for my drink with both hands as though concerned that I not spill it during the transfer. As my right hand passed over Belghazi's glass, I paused for an instant and squeezed, and the seal at the squib's bottom, thinner than the surrounding plastic, parted silently and released the contents within. I used my torso to obscure the move from above, where the overhead cameras might otherwise have recorded it. *Done.* I eased back into my seat, tonic water in hand.

Belghazi ignored his drink during the next round, and during the one after. The ice in his glass was melting, and I began to grow concerned that one of the attendants would come and replace it. I had another squib, of course, but didn't want to have to repeat the risky maneuver of getting it into his glass.

As it turned out, there was no need. At the end of the fifth hand, he picked up his glass and drank. One swallow. A pause, then another. He put the glass down.

That was enough. It was time for me to go. I played one more hand, then collected my chips. "Good luck," I said to him, moving to stand.

"So soon?" he asked.

I'd been there less than an hour—a twinkling, by the standards of the room's diehards. He was still probing, I saw. He had a cop's instinct for irregularities. I nodded and smiled. "I've learned to quit while I'm ahead," I told him, holding up my chips.

He smiled back, his gaze cool as always. "Yes, that's usually wise," he said.

On my way out of the casino I stopped to use one of the restrooms. A full bladder would be a nuisance later this evening, and I also wanted to thoroughly wash my hands. Staph is nasty stuff, and I had no wish to consume some of it inadvertently.

I took a cab to the Oriental and went straight to my room. Keiko was out, presumably still gambling with the money I'd given her. I grabbed what I needed from the safe, placed it in a small backpack I'd brought along for just this occasion, and went straight to Belghazi's suite. He would start feeling sick shortly and could be expected to return soon after that, and I needed to let myself in ahead of him. If he got in first, he might engage the dead bolt—low tech, but inaccessible from the exterior—and I would lose this opportunity.

I used the SoldierVision before going in. The blonde had said she was going to play craps, but people change their minds. The room was empty. I let myself in with my homemade master key. It would have been nice if I could have just stood in the closet or lain down under the bed, but those would be among the first places the bodyguards would check if they performed even a cursory sweep. Instead, I moved quickly to the larger of the suite's two bathrooms. I saw two sets of toiletries arranged across the expansive marble countertop around the sink—Belghazi's, presumably, and the blonde's.

There was a vertical slab of marble joined to the front edge of the countertop, extending about a quarter of the distance to the floor. I took a SureFire E1e mini-light from the backpack—three inches, two ounces, fifteen bright white lumens—squatted, and looked under the slab. Hot and cold water pipes ran down from the sink handles above and disappeared into the wall. I saw the curved bottom of the ceramic sink, and an attached drainage pipe snaking down, then up, then, with the other pipes, into the wall behind.

I smiled. If Belghazi had taken a more modest room, I wouldn't have been able to get away with this, and would have had to come up with something less optimal. As it was, the countertop was sufficiently grand to leave a sizeable gap between the back of the vertical marble façade and the underside of the sink basin behind it. It would be a bit of a squeeze, but there was just enough room in there for a man of my size.

I reached into the backpack and took out a specially designed nylon sling, which, unfurled, looked something like an uncomfortably thin black hammock with four aluminum cams on its ends. I squatted down again, held the SureFire in my mouth, and looked for places to secure the cams. I could have replaced the cams with suction cups or with several other means of attachment, but there was no need: the marble countertop must have weighed at least a couple hundred pounds, and it was buttressed by a series of wooden supports, each of which provided a convenient gap for a cam. I attached the cams, tightened the horizontal straps of the sling, then hauled myself and the backpack up into it. I lay on my side, curled around the curve of the sink, the backpack tucked under my upper arm. It was uncomfortable, but not intolerable. I'd certainly put up with worse, and didn't expect to have to wait long in any event.

I knew that the bodyguards, if they were any good, were likely to inspect the suite before Belghazi entered. But I also knew that, in his current condition, Belghazi would want to be alone and would therefore probably order them out—if he allowed them in at all—before they had done a thorough sweep. Still, ever the good

Boy Scout, I was equipped with a CIA-designed, .22-caliber single shot pistol, artfully concealed inside the body of an elegant Montblanc Meisterstück pen, which I now removed from the backpack. If pressed, I would use the disposable pen to drop whoever was closest to me and, in the ensuing melee, improvise with whoever might be left. Of course, if it came to this, I wouldn't be paid, so the gun was only for an emergency.

I didn't have to wait long. Twenty minutes after I had gotten in position, I heard the door to the suite open. A light came on in the outer room. Then the sound of feet, rapidly approaching. The door to the toilet stall slammed against the wall, followed immediately by the sounds of violent retching.

Another set of footsteps. A male voice: *"Monsieur Belghazi . . ."*

The bodyguard, I assumed. There was more retching, then Belghazi's voice, low and ragged: *"Yallah!"* I didn't know the word, but understood what he was saying. Get out. Now.

I heard the bodyguard walk off, then the sound of the exterior door opening and closing. Belghazi continued to groan and retch. In his haste he hadn't bothered to turn on the bathroom light, but there was some illumination from the suite beyond and I could make out shadows under the sink where I was suspended.

I heard a metallic thump on the marble floor and wondered what had caused it. Then I realized: his belt buckle. Staph causes diarrhea, and he was struggling to keep up with the onset of symptoms. The sounds and smells that followed confirmed my diagnosis.

After about ten minutes I heard him stumble out of the room. The bedroom light went off. A safe assumption that he had collapsed into bed.

I raised my arm slightly and looked at the illuminated dial of the Traser. I would give him another half hour—long enough to ensure that the chloral hydrate had been largely processed through his system and therefore maximally difficult to detect, but not so long that he might start to wake up. The staph would turn up in a pathologist's exam, of course, but staph occurs naturally, if unfortunately, in food, so its presence postmortem wouldn't be a problem. With luck, in the absence of any other likely explanation, the staph might be blamed for the heart attack Belghazi was about to suffer.

In fact, the heart trouble would be the result of an injection of potassium chloride. I would try for the axillary vein under the armpit, or perhaps the ophthalmic vein in the eye, both hard-to-detect entry points, especially with the 25-gauge needle I would use to go in. An injection of potassium chloride is a painless way to go, recommended, at least implicitly, by suicidal cardiologists the world over. The potassium chloride depolarizes cell membranes throughout the heart, producing a complete cardiac arrest, immediate unconsciousness, and rapid death. Postmortem, other cells in the body naturally begin to break down, releasing potassium into the bloodstream, and thereby rendering undetectable the presence of the very agent that got the ball rolling to begin with.

Twenty minutes passed, with no sound other than Belghazi's occasional insensible groans. I rolled out of the harness and lowered myself silently to the floor. Just a few more minutes, and I would begin preparing the injection. I had a small bottle of chloroform that I would use if he started to stir during the procedure.

I heard a card key sliding into the suite's door lock. I froze and listened.

A moment passed. I heard the door open. It clicked closed. The light went on in the bedroom.

I reached into the backpack and withdrew the Montblanc. I heard the sound of footsteps in the room. Belghazi, softly groaning. Then a woman's voice: *"Achille, tu vas bien?"* Achille are you all right? To which Belghazi, clearly out of it, continued only to groan in reply.

The blonde, I thought. I slipped the pen into my left hand and used my right to ease out my key chain, and the shortened dental mirror I keep on it. I padded silently to the edge of the door and angled the mirror so that I could see the suite's bedroom reflected in it.

It was her, as I had expected. She must have had her own key.

I grimaced. Bad timing. Another ten minutes and this would have all been over.

I watched her shake Belghazi once, then harder. "Achille?" she said again. This time there wasn't even a groan in response.

I saw her take a deep breath, hold it for a beat, then gradually push it out, her chin moving in, her shoulders dropping as she did so. Then she strode quickly and quietly over to a wall switch and cut the lights. The room was now lit only by the ambient glow of buildings and streetlights without. I watched her glance at the room's gauze curtains, which were closed.

She moved to a desk across from the bed. I glanced over and saw Belghazi's computer case, the one I had seen him with in the lobby and then again in the casino. Interesting.

She unzipped the case and took out a thin laptop, which she opened. Then she walked over to the bed, gingerly took one of the pillows from next to Belghazi's head, came back to the desk, and held the pillow over the laptop's keyboard. It took me a second to figure out what she was doing: muffling any chimes or other music heralding that the operating system was stirring to life. A nice move, which showed some forethought, and maybe some practice. She wouldn't have known where Belghazi had left the volume of the machine when he had last used it; if it had been turned up, the computer's musical boot tones might have disturbed his slumber.

After a few minutes, the trademark Windows logo appeared on the screen, the accompanying notes barely audible under the cushion of fluffy down pressed southward from above. The woman paused for a moment, then removed the pillow and returned it to its original place on the bed. I noted that she hadn't tossed it on the floor, or otherwise thrown it randomly aside. She was keeping the room as she found it, which is to say the way Belghazi had left it, down to the details. Another sign that she had good instincts, or that she was trained. Or both.

The woman walked back to the desk and pulled a cell phone from her purse. She spent a moment configuring it in some fashion, then pointed it at the laptop. She started working the phone's keypad.

Several minutes went by. She would input some sequence on the phone's keypad, look at the laptop for a few seconds, and repeat. Occasionally she would glance at Belghazi. I could see the laptop screen while she was doing this and it hadn't changed. My guess was that the computer was password-protected, that her "cell phone" was more than it seemed, and that she was using the device to interrogate the laptop by infrared or by Bluetooth, most likely trying to generate a password or otherwise get inside.

Five minutes went by, then another five. We were get-

ting to the point where Belghazi might have metabo-
lized enough of the drug to regain consciousness. Another five minutes, ten at the most, and I would have to
abort.

But how? I wasn't worried about getting out. Belghazi wouldn't be in any kind of condition to stop me,
even if he were fully awake when I made my departure,
and I didn't expect that the woman would pose a significant obstacle. But if Belghazi saw me, especially after
making my acquaintance at the Lisboa earlier that
evening, or if the woman reported that there had been
an intruder, I would be facing an even tougher security
environment. I'd have a hell of a time getting a second
chance.

I heard Belghazi groan. The woman froze and
glanced at him, but he stirred no further. Still, she must
have decided he might be waking up, because a second
later she dropped the cell phone back in her purse, set
the purse on the floor, and logged off the laptop, using
the pillow as she had before to eliminate any farewell
melody. When the screen had gone dark, she closed the
lid and placed it back in its case, returned the pillow to
the bed, and began to undress.

Shit.

The situation was deteriorating. I couldn't count on
her to get to sleep quickly enough, or to stay asleep
deeply enough, to enable me to slip out unnoticed. Hell,
from what I'd seen so far, she looked like she might
sleep as lightly as I do. Also, from the care she had dis-
played so far, I knew she would have engaged the suite's
interior dead bolt, that most likely she would have done
so deliberately, as part of a mental checklist, and that
she would therefore remember doing it. If she found it
disengaged in the morning, she would be more likely to

conclude that someone had been in the room than she would be to doubt her recollection.

Kill them both? Impossible to do "naturally," under the circumstances. Kanezaki had stressed that payment was conditioned on no evidence of foul play, so I wouldn't use overt violence unless I had to. Besides, what I do, I don't do to women or children. There had been one recent exception, but that had been personal. I had no such extenuating issues at work with Belghazi's companion. On the contrary, I found myself liking this woman. It wasn't just her looks. It was her moves, her self-possession, her air of command. And the instincts and brains I thought I had just silently witnessed.

There was one possibility. It was risky, but certainly no worse than the other alternatives among my currently meager range of options.

I waited until the woman had fully disrobed, the moment when she would feel maximally helpless and discomfited. She was just moving toward the bed, presumably to get into it, when I strode into the bedroom.

She startled when she saw me, but overall kept her composure. "What the hell are you doing here?" she asked in a low voice, in some sort of European-accented English. She stressed the "you" in the question, and sounded more accusatory than afraid.

"You know me?" I whispered back, thinking, *What the hell?*

"From the casino. And I've seen you in the hotel. Now what are you doing here?"

Christ, she was as observant as he was. "Any luck with Belghazi's computer?" I asked, trying to regain the initiative. My gaze was focused on her torso, the area I always watch, after confirming that the hands are empty, because aggressive movement tends to originate in the midsection. In this instance, though, the view was distracting. She looked even better naked than she had in the black couture I had seen her in earlier.

She kept her cool. "I don't know what you're talking about."

I flashed the SoldierVision, still secured to my wrist, and bluffed. "Really? I've got it all right here on low-light video."

She glanced at the device, then back to me. "On a SoldierVision? I didn't know they recorded video."

Damn, she knew her hardware. Whoever she was, she was good, and I needed to stop underestimating her. "This one does," I said, improvising. "So why don't we make a deal? I don't know who you're working for, and I don't care. As far as I'm concerned, this never happened. You didn't see me, and I didn't see you. How does that sound?"

She was silent for a long moment, seemingly oblivious to her nakedness. Then she asked, "Who are you with?"

I smiled. "Don't ask, don't tell."

She was silent again. My gaze dropped for a moment. Her body was beautiful: simultaneously muscular and curvaceous, like a figure skater's or that of an unusually tall gymnast, with delicate, pale skin that seemed to glow faintly in the light diffused through the curtains.

I looked up again. She was watching my eyes. "You're probably bluffing about that video," she said, her voice even, "but I can't take the chance. I can't let you leave with it."

I was impressed by her aplomb. I nodded my head in Belghazi's direction. "He's going to come out of it any minute now. If he wakes up and I'm here, it'll be bad for both of us."

She rolled her eyes as though exasperated and said, "I'm going to get dressed."

I almost bought it. It seemed natural enough—she was naked in front of a stranger, she wanted to put clothes on. But her nakedness hadn't seemed to bother her a moment earlier. And exasperation wasn't an expression she wore very convincingly.

"Don't," I said sharply. The pen was in my pocket now, and I wouldn't be able to deploy it in time. Even if I could have, pointing a Montblanc at someone tends to be less attention-getting than, say, employing a Glock 10-millimeter for the same purpose. I wouldn't have been able to use the pen to control her, only to shoot her, and I didn't want to do that.

She ignored me. I saw that she was going for her purse, not her clothes.

She must have had a weapon there. I closed the distance in two long steps and kicked the purse aside. As I did so, she straightened and I saw her left elbow whipping around toward my right temple. By reflex I moved in closer to get inside the blow and started to get my hands up. Her elbow missed the mark. But she instantly snapped her hips the other way and caught me with the other elbow, from the opposite side. *Boom.* I saw stars. Before she could chain together another combination, I dropped down, wrapped my left arm around her closest ankle, and drove my shoulder into her shin. She went down hard on her back.

To keep her from landing an axe kick with her free leg or otherwise attacking with her feet, I got a hand on her thigh and shoved away from her. I stood and backed up, watching her carefully.

"Are you crazy?" I said, my voice low. "What's he going to think if you wake him up?" That was the point, though, wasn't it. If she'd wanted, or been willing, to wake him, she already would have done so. She didn't want him to know about me, maybe because of the "video," maybe for other reasons, as well. Trying to take me out had been a calculated risk. Then there would only be one side of the story afterward.

There was a dull throbbing in my head where she'd connected. I moved over to the purse and picked it up to make sure she couldn't try to get to it again. I didn't know what was inside: lipstick Mace, edged credit cards, a pen-gun like mine, maybe.

Belghazi groaned again. I'd need at least a few minutes to prepare him for the injection, even assuming I could do it without interference from my new sparring partner, and it looked like I'd run out of time.

"It would have been nice if we could have met under different circumstances," I said, rubbing my sore left temple, taking a step toward the door.

"How are you going to get past the bodyguard?" I heard her say.

That off-balanced me. I had expected them to depart after they saw Belghazi to his room.

I aimed the SoldierVision at the wall and checked the monitor. Sure enough, there was a human image just on the other side of the door. *Oh, shit.*

"Give me the video," she said, "and I'll send the guard away. You can go."

I shook my head slowly, trying to figure out a way to improvise out of this.

Belghazi groaned again. She glanced at him, then back to me. "Look," she whispered sharply, "I don't know who you are, but you're obviously no friend of his. You've figured out that I'm not his friend, either. Maybe we can help each other."

"Maybe," I said, looking at her.

"But show me some good faith. Give me the video."

I shook my head again. "You know I can't. You wouldn't, in my place."

Her eyes narrowed a fraction. "I don't think there even is a video. So when he wakes up, it's going to be your word against mine. And I promise, he'll be inclined to believe me, not you."

I shrugged. "What if I told him to check the boot log on his computer? I'm sure Belghazi has it enabled. Or to take a good look at your 'cell phone'?"

She didn't have an answer to that one.

"But I agree that we can help each other," I said. "And here's how we can do it. I'm going to hide again. You get the bodyguard in here, tell him Belghazi seems really sick, he's been throwing up and is barely conscious, and you need to get him to a hospital. You and the bodyguard walk him out of here. No one's going to search the room after he's been in it, and as soon as you're gone, I'll be gone, too. You can have the video after that."

She was silent for a long moment. If I were caught here now and Belghazi got ahold of the "video," or if I blabbed about his boot log or her cell phone, her cover, whatever it was, would be blown for certain. If I were to leave with the "video," she'd be taking a risk, but she might be okay. She understood these odds, and she knew that I understood them, too.

"How do I contact you?" I asked, closing the deal.

She pursed her lips, then said, "You can look for me in the casino after eight tomorrow night."

"The Lisboa?"

"No, here, the Oriental."

"What do I call you?"

She looked at me, her eyes coolly angry. "Delilah," she said.

Belghazi groaned again. I nodded once and moved quickly back to the bathroom. I took out the Meisterstück, then hauled myself back into the sling under the sink.

A moment later, I heard the door to the suite open, followed by a muffled conversation in French. Delilah's voice and a man's. I heard them come into the suite, where they started trying to rouse Belghazi. I could pick out a few words in French: "sick," "hospital," "doctor." Then Belghazi's voice, low and groggy: *"Non, non. Je vais bien."* No, no, I'm fine. Delilah's voice, closer now, urging him to see a doctor. More demurrals, also closer.

Shit, he had gotten up and they were coming my way. I willed myself to relax and breathed silently through my nose.

"Je vais bien," I heard him say again from just outside the bathroom. His voice sounded steadier now. *"Attendez une minute."* I heard his feet lightly slapping the marble floor, coming closer. Then the sound of a faucet turning, of water coursing through the pipes around me. I turned my head and looked down. A pair of feet and lower legs stood before the sink. If I'd wanted to, I could have reached down and touched them. I noted two bare lines running the length of his shinbones, where the hair had been worn away, along with a slight rippling effect in the surface of the bone itself—both signature deformations of Thai boxers and other practitioners of hardcore kicking arts. The bones enlarge in response to the trauma of repeated blows, eventually developing into a nerveless and brutally hard striking surface. Belghazi's file had said something about Savate—a French style of kickboxing. It looked like that information had been correct.

I heard him splashing water on his face, groaning *"merde"* as he did so. Then the rhythmic sounds of a hasty scrub with a toothbrush—an ordinary enough urge after vomiting.

The sounds of the toothbrush stopped. The water was turned on again. Then something clattered to the floor, practically underneath me.

I turned my head and saw it: he had dropped the toothbrush. *Fuck.*

My heart rate, which had been reasonably calm under the circumstances, kicked into overdrive. Adrenaline surged from my midsection into my neck and limbs. I tightened my grip on the Meisterstück. I breathed shallowly, silently. My body was perfectly still.

Belghazi knelt and reached for the toothbrush. I saw the top of a close-cropped scalp; the bridge of a nose, bent from some long-ago break; the upper plane of a pair of prominent cheekbones; his shoulders and back, thickly muscled, covered with dark hair.

All he had to do was glance up, and he would see me.

But he didn't. His fingers closed around the toothbrush and he straightened. A moment later the water stopped running, and he padded out of the bathroom.

I heard voices again from the bedroom, but could only make out a bit of what they were saying. It seemed that Belghazi was adamant about not seeing a doctor. Christ, I was going to have to spend the night slung up under the sink like a rock climber sleeping alongside a mountain.

I heard Delilah's voice. Something about *"médecine."* The door to the suite opened and closed.

Two minutes passed. Silence from the suite. Then the sounds of footsteps, rapidly approaching. Someone burst into the bathroom and blew past me into the toilet stall. The stall door slammed, followed immediately by the sounds of Belghazi retching.

I heard Delilah's lighter footsteps. She headed straight for the sink and squatted down so she could see me. She must have given it some thought and realized that this would be the only decent place to hide. Again I was impressed.

"I've sent the guard to get some medicine," she whispered. "This will be your only chance."

Without a word I rolled out of the harness and dropped silently to the floor on one hand and the balls of my feet. I started to reach up to undo the equipment, but Delilah stopped me with a hand on my shoulder. "Leave the rig," she said. "There's no time. I'll take care of it later."

From behind the stall door, Belghazi exclaimed, *"Merde!"* and retched again. I nodded at Delilah and headed for the exit. She followed me closely. I paused before the door and used the SoldierVision to confirm that the hallway was clear before leaving.

I moved into the empty corridor. She shut the door behind me without another word.

3

I'D BEEN LIVING in Brazil for almost a year when they finally got to me. It had rained that day, the sky full of oppressive, low-lying clouds that clung to Rio's dramatic cliffs like smoke from some faraway calamity.

After leaving Tatsu in Tokyo, I had finished preparing Yamada-san, the ice-cold alter ego I had created as an escape hatch for the day my enemies might succeed in tracking me to Japan, as indeed they had, for his departure to São Paulo. São Paulo is home to some six hundred thousand of Brazil's approximately one million ethnic Japanese, the largest such community outside Japan, and the kind of place in which a recent arrival like Yamada-san might easily lose himself.

Yamada found a suitable apartment in Aclimação, a residential neighborhood near Liberdade, São Paulo's Japanese district, from which he made the necessary arrangements to establish his new business of shipping high-quality, low-cost Brazilian judo and jujitsu uniforms to Japan—a business which, if conditions were favorable, he might one day expand to include additional exportable items. Many of his neighbors were of Korean and Chinese extraction, which suited Yamada because such Asian faces made it easier for him to blend. A more heavily Japanese setting, such as that of Liberdade itself, would have conferred the same advantages, but could have been problematic, as well, because Japanese neighbors would have been more inclined to probe the specifics of his background, and to discuss it among themselves afterward. To the extent that he did need to share some of his past with his Japanese neighbors, Yamada would explain that he was from Tokyo, a simple *sarariiman,* or salary man, who had suffered the double indignity of being laid off by one of Japan's electronics giants and then being abandoned by his wife of twenty years, for whom he could no longer provide as she expected. It was a sad, although not uncommon story in those difficult economic times, and Yamada's neighbors, with typical Japanese restraint, would nod sympathetically at the telling of his lament and press for no further details.

Yamada obsessed over the study of Portuguese—tapes, tutors, television, music, films, even a series of professional women, because, Yamada knew, there is no more natural or productive route to the acquisition of a language than the sharing of a pillow. Every few weeks, he would leave town to travel, to acquaint himself firsthand with his adopted land: the vast *cerrado,* the central plains, with its handful of frontier towns and vanishing Indian tribes, and its bizarre, planned city, Brasília, stuck on the land as though by extraterrestrials in imitation of an earthen metropolis; the prehistoric enormity of Amazonas, where the scale of everything—the trees, the water lilies, and, of course, the river itself—first diminishes and then extinguishes the traveler's sense of his own human significance; the baroque art and architecture of Minas Gerais, left behind like a conflicted apology by the miners who centuries earlier had raped the region's land for its diamonds and gold.

Yamada avoided Bahia and in particular its capital, Salvador. Rain knew a woman there, a beautiful half-Brazilian, half-Japanese named Naomi, with whom Rain had enjoyed an affair in Tokyo and to whom he had made a promise when she was forced to flee to Brazil. Yamada wanted to go to her there, but at the same time hesitated to do so, finding himself unsure, at some level, of whether he was attempting to forestall the inevitable or simply hoping to relish the anticipation of its arrival. Occasionally Yamada was troubled by such thoughts, but his new surroundings, exotic after so many years in familiar Japan, his travels, and his constant study of the language, were all strongly diverting.

Yamada's linguistic progress was excellent, as one might expect of a man who already spoke both English and Japanese as a native, and after six months he judged himself ready to relocate to Rio; more specifically, to Barra da Tijuca, known throughout Rio simply as Barra, a middle- and upper-middle-class enclave extending for some nineteen kilometers along Rio's southern coast. He chose a suitable apartment at the corner of the Avenida Belisário Leite de Andrade Neto and the Avenida General Guedes da Fontoura. It was a good building, with entrances on each of the streets it faced, and nothing but other residences all around, therefore offering, had Yamada been inclined to reflect on such matters, multiple points of egress and no convenient areas from which some third party might set up surveillance or an ambush.

In Barra the Yamada identity finally began to feel truly comfortable. Partly it was that I'd lived as Yamada for so long at that point; partly it was that the São Paulo stopover had been only one step removed from Japan, and therefore from those enemies who were trying to find me there; partly it was the inherent difficulty of feeling uncomfortable for long in Rio, its rhythms, indeed its life, defined as they are by the culture of its beaches.

In my new environs I became a Japanese *nisei,* one of the tens of thousands of Brazil's second-generation ethnic Japanese, who had decided to retire to Rio from São Paulo. My Portuguese was good enough to support the story; the accent was off, of course, but this was explainable by virtue of having grown up in a Japanese household and having spent much of my childhood in Japan.

I was intrigued at how distant a notion Japan seemed to present to my *nisei* cousins. It seemed that, when they looked in the mirror, they saw only a Brazilian. If they thought about it at all, I imagined, Japan must have felt like a coincidence, a faraway culture and place not much more important than the other such places one reads about in books or sees on television, something that meant a great deal to their parents or grandparents but that wasn't particularly relevant to them. I found myself somewhat envious of the notion of forgetting where you had come from and caring only about who you are, and liked Brazil for offering a culture that would foster such a possibility.

And Barra offered this culture triple-distilled. My *nisei* story was thin, I knew, but it didn't really matter. Barra, the fastest growing part of the city, its skyline increasingly crowded with new high-rises, its neighborhoods ceaselessly changing with departures and arrivals, is much more focused on the future than it is with anyone's particular past. It's the kind of place where, a month after you've been there, you're considered an old-timer, and I had no trouble fitting in.

Rio, home to a sports- and fitness-mad population, has numerous health food outlets, and it was easy for me to indulge my taste for protein shakes and *acai* fruit smoothies. These, along with antioxidants, fish oil, and other dietary supplements, enhanced my recovery times and enabled me to adhere to a regimen of five hundred daily Hindu squats, three hundred inclined sit-ups, three hundred Hindu push-ups, and other esoteric body weight calisthenics that maintained my strength and flexibility.

I varied my mornings and evenings training at Gracie Barra, jujitsu's modern Mecca, where the fecund Gracie family had taken the teachings of a visiting Japanese diplomat and adapted them into a system of ground fighting so sophisticated that the art is now more firmly established in Brazil than it ever was in Japan. I trained frequently and hard, having missed the opportunity to do so during the year I had spent underground in Osaka and in São Paulo thereafter. The academy's young black belts were impressed with my skills, but in truth their ground game was stronger than mine—although certainly less ruthless, if applied in the real world—and I relished the opportunity to once again polish and expand my personal arsenal.

In the afternoons I would ride an old ten-speed out to one of the city's more isolated beaches—sometimes Grumari, sometimes even less accessible slivers of sand, which I reached on foot, where only the most determined surfers, and perhaps some nude sunbathers, might venture. After a month my skin had become dark, like that of a true *carioca,* or Rio native, and my hair, brown like my mother's now that I no longer dyed it black to make myself look more Japanese, grew streaked like a surfer's.

Sometimes I would swim out to one of the nearby islands. I would sit on those deserted outcroppings of gray and green and consider the rhythm of waves against rock, the occasional sighing of the wind, and my mind would wander. I would think of Midori, the jazz pianist I had accidentally met and then deliberately spared after killing her father, a man whose posthumous wishes I had tried to carry out later, an effort that had perhaps earned ambivalence, but that could never lead to forgiveness, from the daughter. I would remember how on that last night she had leaned in from astride me and whispered *I hate you* even as she came, the newly acquired certainty of what I had done to her father damning the passion she otherwise couldn't prevent, and I would wonder foolishly if she might ever play in one of Rio's jazz clubs. And I would look back on my new city and see it as an island, not unlike the one from which I viewed it: a beautiful place, to be sure, but still one of exile, sometimes of regret, ultimately of loneliness.

I kept the apartment in São Paulo. I took care to travel there from time to time to maintain appearances, and managed Yamada's new export operation remotely, mostly by e-mail. Some simple commercial software turned the lights on and off at random intervals during preset hours so that it looked as though someone was living there, and so that the electric bills would be consistent with full-time residency. A faucet opened to a continual slow drip accomplished the same end with regard to water bills. In addition, I stayed from time to time in various short-term hotel/apartments elsewhere in Rio, adding a certain shell game dynamic to the other challenges a pursuer might face in attempting to locate me.

But all this security cost money, and, although I had saved a good deal over the years, my means were not unlimited, and what I did have was kept in a variety of anonymous offshore accounts that effectively paid no interest. Dividend-paying stocks and IRAs and 401(k)s weren't part of the plan. I told myself that after a couple of years, or a few, when the trail someone might try to follow had grown cold, and their potential motivations sufficiently remote, I might be able to scale back on some of the precautions that posed such a burden to my finances.

Time passed. And, much as I enjoyed it, Rio came to feel like a way station, not a destination; a breather, not the end of the march. There was an aimlessness to my days there, an aimlessness that my focus on jujitsu alleviated but didn't dispel. From time to time I would remember Tatsu telling me *you can't retire,* spoken with equal parts confidence and sadness, and those words, which I had first taken to be a threat and then understood to be merely a prediction, came in my memory to bear the weight of something else, something more akin to prophecy.

I grew restless, and my restlessness proved fertile ground for memories of Naomi. The way she had whispered *come inside* in my ear on that first long night together. The way she would slip into Portuguese when we made love. The way she had offered to try to help Harry, who had been not just an asset of mine, but a rare friend, an offer that had been as sincere as it was ultimately useless. And the way I had promised her the last time I saw her that I would find her in Brazil, that I wouldn't leave her waiting and wondering what had ever happened to me.

The way you did Midori.

I've paid for that one, thank you.

It had been good with Naomi, that was the thing.

Warm and sweet and emotionally uncomplicated. It wasn't what I had with Midori, or almost had, but I was never going to have that again and preferred to spend as little time as possible flagellating myself over it. Going to her would be selfish, I knew, because in Tokyo our involvement had almost gotten her killed, and, despite the change of venue and all my new precautions, it was far from impossible that something like that could happen again. But I found myself thinking of her all the time, wondering if somehow it could work. Japan was far away. I was Yamada now, wasn't I? And Naomi was whoever she was in Brazil. We could start over, start afresh.

I should have known better. But we all have stupid moments, rationalization, even blindness, born of weakness and human need.

Naomi's Japanese mother had died many years earlier, but she had told me her father's name, David Leonardo Nascimento, and had let me know that I could find him in Salvador. Nascimento is a common name in Brazil, but there was no Leonardo, David, in the Salvador white pages, to which I had access via a Rio public library. An Internet search proved more productive: David Leonardo Nascimento, it seemed, was the president of a Salvador-based company with real estate, construction, and manufacturing interests.

I could have simply called and asked how I might get in touch with Naomi, but I didn't want too long a gap between the time when I contacted her and the time when we might actually meet. I told myself that this preference was logical, the outgrowth of my usual security concerns, but I knew at some level that it was driven also by personal factors. I didn't want to have to catch up over the phone, to answer questions about where I

was and what I was doing, to explain my long delay in
tracking her down. Better to get it all out of the way in
person.

Salvador was a two-hour flight from Rio, and in making my way through this new city I was struck, as always
when traversing colossal Brazil, by the contrasts among
the land's regions. Salvador, nearer the equator, was
hotter than Rio, the air somehow richer, moister. In Rio,
the ubiquitous granite cliffs seem to offer glimpses of the
land's strong skeleton; in Salvador, everywhere there
was red earth, more akin to a soft covering of skin. And
the people were darker-hued: a reflection of the area's
African heritage, which revealed itself also in the
baroque carving of the town's colonial churches; in the
blood-pounding beat of its *candomblé* music; in the flowing, dancing moves of its *capoeiristas,* with their hypno-
tizing mixture of dance, fighting, and gymnastics, all set
to the tune of the stringed *berimbau* and the mesmeriz-
ing beat of the *conga*.

Nascimento was well buffered by secretaries, and
there was a fair amount of back and forth before I was
able to actually get ahold of him. When I did, he told
me that Naomi had left word with him about a friend
from Japan, someone named John, but that this had
been some time ago. I acknowledged the delay and
waited, and after a moment he told me that his daughter was living in Rio, working at a bar called Scenarium,
on the Rua do Lavradio. He gave me a phone number.
I thanked him and went straight to the airport, smiling
at the irony. All these months of avoiding Salvador,
only to learn that Naomi and I were living practically as
neighbors.

That evening, after taking steps to ensure that I
wasn't being followed, I caught a cab to Lapa, the neigh-

borhood around Scenarium, among the oldest in the city. I got out a few blocks away, per my usual practice, and waited until the cab had departed before moving in the direction of the bar.

I made my way along antique streets composed of rows of cobblestones convulsed over the centuries into valleys and hillocks by the ceaseless stirrings of the earth below. A few widely spaced streetlights offered weak respite against the surrounding gloom, and passing figures appeared indistinct, insubstantial, like phantoms from the area's colonial past, shifting in confusion among the faded façades and broken balconies, lost souls trying to locate once-thriving addresses that existed now only as monuments to dilapidation and disuse. Here and there were signs of new life—a repaired balustrade, a reglazed set of windows—and somehow these small portents made the shattered relics on which they blossomed a strangely vibrant foreground to the modern high-rises towering beyond: tenacious, more resolute, the ravaged sockets of their empty doors and windows seeming almost to smile at the prospect of the eventual passing of their newer, taller peers, who would age without inspiring any of the devotion that promised to restore these ancients to the vigor of their youth.

I turned onto the Rua do Lavradio and saw Scenarium. The bar occupied all three floors of two adjacent buildings, the façades of each suffering, like so many of their brethren in the area, from considerable age and neglect. The light and music emanating from the interior were startlingly vibrant and alive by contrast. A long queue of cars waited in the street in front, as though in awe or homage. I stood before the large, open entranceway for a moment, surprised to note that my heart was beating rapidly, remembering the concentrated time I had spent with Naomi in Tokyo, and how long it had been since I had promised I would be in touch.

I walked in and glanced around. Hot spots first, by instinct and long habit: seats facing the entrance, partially concealed corners, ambush positions. I detected no problems.

I moved inside. The interior was vast, and decorated like a Hollywood prop warehouse. Everywhere there were antiques and curios: iron cash registers, a red British telephone booth, a cluster of parasols, busts and statues, shelves of colored bottles and jugs. Even the tables and chairs looked vintage. Had it been less capacious, it would have felt cluttered.

The ceilings were high and of bare wood, the walls stone and alabaster. In the center of the room, about ten meters in, the ceiling disappeared and the room was open to the second and third floors above. Below this space, a three-man band was performing *"De Mais Ninguém,"* "No One's But Mine," Marisa Monte's modern classic of *choro,* a style that might loosely be thought of as Brazilian jazz, given that both *choro* and jazz are based on improvisation and the mixture of African and European musical elements. But *choro,* though less widely known, is in fact older than jazz, and has a distinct and sometimes melancholy sound of its own. The crowd, clustered around warrens of wooden tables and five across at couches along the walls, was singing along passionately.

I made my way to a staircase in back, which I took to the second floor. This, too, was crowded with diners, and no less replete with ancient odds and ends, but was somewhat less boisterous than the area below.

The third floor was quieter still. For a few moments, I

leaned against the railing surrounding the open center of the floor, gazing down at the band, at the patrons at the tables before the stage, and at the waiters crossing between, and felt an odd sadness descend, both remote and heavy, as though I was watching this lively scene not so much from on high but rather from an impossibly detached and alienated distance.

A waiter came by and asked in Portuguese if he could bring me anything.

"I'm looking for Naomi," I told him.

"She's downstairs, in the office," he said. "Who shall I tell her is looking for her?"

I paused, then said, "Her friend from Japan."

He nodded and moved off.

I walked over to the end of the room and out onto one of the balconies overlooking the Rua do Lavradio. I leaned against the railing, pitted and worn as driftwood, and felt the old surreal calm steal over me, the kind I always feel just before the final moments of a job, like a sniper relaxing into his shot. There was nothing I could do now. It would turn out the way it would turn out.

A few minutes passed. I heard the floorboards behind me creaking with someone's rapid approach. I turned and saw Naomi, her hair longer than it had been in Tokyo, her caramel skin darker, and when she saw that it was me her face lit up in an enormous smile and she made a sound of almost childlike delight, and then she was in my arms, pulling me close and squeezing hard.

She smelled the way I remembered, sweet, and somehow also wild, her own scent, which I will always associate with heat and wet and tropical ardor. Her body felt good, too, petite but ripe in all the right places, and her shape, suddenly in my arms, along with her scent, flooded my mind with a jumble of conflicted memories.

She pulled back after a long moment and glanced down at what she had already felt was there, then punched me in the shoulder, hard. Her face was mock-angry, but I saw some real distress in her eyes, as well.

"Do you know how many times I promised myself I wouldn't do that?" she asked in her Portuguese-accented English.

"How many?"

"A lot. Most recently as I was coming up the stairs over there."

"I'm glad you didn't listen."

"Why didn't you call me? Why did you wait so long? I thought that maybe you weren't interested. Or that, after everything that had happened, something bad had happened to you."

"You were wrong about the first one, but were almost on the mark with the second."

"What happened?"

Her green eyes were so earnest. It made me smile. "I had to settle some things in Tokyo," I said. "It took a while."

"You came all the way from Tokyo?"

"I've been moving around a lot."

"Are we going to keep secrets after everything that happened between us?"

"Especially after that," I said, telling her the truth. But she looked hurt, so I added, "Let's just spend a little time together first, okay? It's been a while."

There was a pause. She nodded and said, "You want a drink?"

I nodded back. "Love one."

"A single malt?" she asked, remembering.

I smiled. "How about a *caipirinha,* instead?" The *caipirinha* is Brazil's national cocktail. It's made with *cachaça*—a Brazilian liquor made from distilled sugar-cane juice—along with lime, sugar, and ice, and I'd grown fond of the drink during my time in the country.

"You know a lot about Brazil," she said, looking at me.

I realized it might have been safer to go with the single malt, which she had been expecting. *"Go ni itte wa, go ni shitagae,"* I said with a shrug, switching to Japanese. When in Rome, do as the Romans do.

She smiled. "It's a good choice," she said. "We make a great *caipirinha.*"

I raised my eyebrows. "'We'?"

Her smile widened. "I'm one of the owners."

"I'm impressed," I said, looking around and then back to her. "How did that happen?"

She smiled and said, "First, the *caipirinha.*"

We sat near the windows, open to the air outside, in the semidark of the third floor. A waiter brought us a pitcher of *caipirinha* and two glasses, and, as Naomi had promised, the drink was expertly made: astringent but sweet, cold and strong, redolent of the tropics. Unlike whiskey, with its decades of associations, the taste of *caipirinha* holds no memories for me.

I asked her how she wound up coming to own a place like Scenarium, and she explained that it was part serendipity, part her father's connections. The government was investing in restoring the Lapa district—which explained some of the renovations I had noticed—and was offering tax breaks to new businesses in the area. She had some money saved, and some entertainment business expertise, from her time in Tokyo, so her father had put her in touch with a group that was hoping to open a bar/restaurant.

"What about you?" she asked me. "What have you been doing?"

I took a sip of *caipirinha*. "Figuring some things out. Trying to get a new business going."

"Something safer than the last one?"

She didn't know the specifics. Just that whatever I did had a tendency to put me in touch with some shady characters and that it had nearly gotten both of us killed in Tokyo. "If I'm lucky," I told her.

"It looks like you're staying in shape," she observed.

I smiled. "Pilates."

"And you're tan. You get that dark in Tokyo?"

She was zeroing in. I should have expected that.

Maybe you did. Maybe you wanted that.

But I wasn't ready to tell her. "You know how it is, with all that fluorescent lighting," I said.

She didn't laugh. "I'm getting the feeling that you've been in Rio for a while."

I didn't say anything.

"Why did you wait so long?" she went on after a moment. "To look me up. I'm not mad. And only a little hurt. I just want to know why."

I drank some more and considered. "I can be a danger to the people I get close to," I said after a moment. "Maybe you noticed that, in Tokyo."

"That was a long time ago. In another place."

I nodded, thinking of Holtzer, the late CIA Chief of Tokyo Station, and how he'd reappeared in my life in Tokyo like a resurgent disease, very nearly managing to have me killed in the process. Of how the Agency had patiently watched Midori, hoping she would lead them to me. "It's never that long ago," I said.

We were quiet for a while. Finally she asked, "How long will you be in Rio?"

I looked around. "I don't want to complicate your life," I said.

"You came all the way out here to tell me that? You should have just sent me a damn postcard."

I had tried to resist her charms in Tokyo because I knew it would all end badly. None of that had changed.

Yet here I was.

"I'd like to stick around for a while," I told her. "If that's okay with you."

She offered me a small smile. "We'll see," she said.

We made love that night, and again and again on the nights that came after. She had a small high-rise apartment near the Lagoa Rodrigo de Freitas, just slightly removed from the crowded beaches and trendy boutiques of Ipanema. From one of her windows there was a view of nearby Corcovado, or Hunchback Mountain, topped by the massive, illuminated statue of *Christo Redentor,* Christ the Redeemer, his head bowed, his arms outstretched in benediction to the city below him, and on some nights I would gaze out upon this edifice while Naomi slept. I would stare at the statue's distant shape, perhaps daring it to do something—strike me down if it wanted, or show some other sign of sentience—and, after an uneventful interregnum, I would turn away, never with satisfaction. The statue seemed to mock me with its muteness and its immobility, as though offering the promise, if of anything, not of redemption, but rather of a reckoning, and at a time of its choosing, not of mine.

One rainy morning, about a month after I'd gone to see Naomi at Scenarium and started spending time with her, I left her apartment for a workout at Gracie Barra. It was a Friday, and training would be in shorts and tee-shirts, without the heavy cotton *judogi.* I took the stairs to the third floor, kicked off my sandals, and stepped onto the mat.

On the far side of the room a heavily muscled Caucasian man was hanging from the bar in front of the cartoon Tasmanian Devil that serves as the academy's logo and mascot. He was barefoot and bare-chested, wearing only a pair of navy shorts, and his torso gleamed under a coating of oily sweat. He saw me come in and dropped to the floor, the move smooth and silent despite his bulk.

The sandy-colored hair was longer now, longer even than the ponytail he had once sported, and he wore a goatee that had originally been a full beard, but I recognized him immediately. I knew him only as Dox, his nom de guerre. He was an ex-marine, one of their elite snipers, and, like me, had been recruited by the Reagan-era CIA to equip and train the Afghan Mujahideen, who were then battling the invading Soviet army. We had each spent two years with what Uncle Sam at the time affectionately referred to as the *Muj,* more recently regarded with less warmth as the Taliban and al-Qaeda, and I hadn't seen him, or missed him, since then.

He walked over, a grin spreading as he approached. "Wanna roll around a little?" he asked in the hayseed twang I remembered.

I noted that he had no place to conceal a weapon or transmitter. I wondered whether the attire had been chosen deliberately, to reassure me. Dox liked to play the hick, and a lot of people bought the act, but I knew he could be subtle when he wanted to be.

This was obviously not a social call, but I wasn't concerned for my immediate safety. If Dox had any ill intent, the third floor of Gracie Barra would be a poor place to carry it out. He was an obvious foreigner, would have checked in at the front desk, and would be dealing with dozens of witnesses.

"Let me warm up first," I said, without returning his grin.

"Shit, man, I'm already warmed up. Pretty soon I'm going to be warming down. Been here almost an hour, waiting for someone new to train with." He jumped up and down a few times on his toes and flexed his considerable arms back and forth.

I looked around. Although morning classes at Barra tend to be more sparsely attended than the evening equivalent, there were about twenty people practicing on the mat, some within earshot. I decided to hold off on the questions I wanted to put to him.

"Why don't you go with one of these guys?" I asked, looking over at some of the other men who were training.

He shook his head. "I already went with a few of them." He smiled, then added, "Don't think they liked me. Think they find me . . . unorthodox."

"Unorthodox" was in fact the origin of the nom de guerre. He had been one of the younger guys in our happy few, having left his beloved Corps under cloudy circumstances not long before. There was a rumor that he had roughed up a superior officer, although Dox himself never spoke of it. Whatever it had been, it did seem to impel the young man—who, unlike most of his peers in Afghanistan, had been just a little too young for service in Vietnam—to try to prove himself. He liked to accompany the *Muj* on ambushes despite his "train only" mandate, and was well respected because of it. He made his own way, developing a reputation for unusual, even bizarre tactics, usually involving improvised explosive devices that left the Soviets firing at an enemy that had long since faded back into unreachable mountain caves. Nor did he confine himself to training new snipers—he went out and did some hunting himself.

His physical conditioning methods, I remembered, were also unconventional: he lifted weights with fuel drums, and would sometimes stand on his head, his hands laced behind his neck, for a half hour or more. A lot of people had underestimated him because of his unusual habits, his good ol' boy routine. I wasn't going to make that mistake.

"I'll let you know when I'm ready," I told him, rotating my head, loosening my neck.

He gave me the grin again. "I'll be right here."

He walked over to the wall and popped up into a headstand. Christ, he was still doing that shit.

I stretched and worked through a series of Hindu squats, neck bridges, and other calisthenics until I felt sufficiently limbered. Then I stood and signaled to Dox, who had been watching from his headstand. He dropped his legs to the floor, came to his feet, and strolled over.

"You're good, man, I can see it. Rolling through on those neck bridges smooth. You're staying in shape."

Although he'd been damn effective in the field, in other contexts Dox had always talked too much for my taste. He still had the habit, it seemed. "You want to start standing, or on the ground?" I asked.

"Whatever you want, man," he said. "It's your place."

If he'd intended the comment to rattle me, he'd failed. But I did feel some irritation, mild for the moment. I thought I might not be able to respond as quickly as decorum ordinarily demanded when he tapped out from a submission hold.

I nodded and started circling. He got the idea and followed suit.

We closed and I took the back of his neck in my right hand, my elbow down, pressed in against his clavicle and chest, controlling his forward movement. He grabbed a similar hold with his right and yanked my head toward his, the movement fast enough to almost be a head butt. I looked down in time to take the impact on the top of my skull, where it didn't do anything more than hurt. My irritation edged up a notch. But before I had a chance to react further, he started muscling me with the neck hold, jerking me left, right, forward and back. He was using his hand and elbow confidently, which showed some training, and he was strong as hell.

Time to change tactics. I snapped his neck toward me, and then, as he pulled back, used the hold to launch myself into the air under him. I wrapped my legs around his waist and dragged him down to the mat. I had expected him to try to retreat from my "guard," as the position is known in jujitsu, but instead he went the opposite way, grabbing and twisting my head in both pawlike hands and attacking the underside of my jaw with the top of his head. It felt like someone was trying to run a pile driver up through my skull. To relieve the pressure, I unlocked my ankles from around his back, brought my knees to his chest, and started pushing him away.

Once again, his reaction showed training: he wrapped his right arm around my left ankle from the inside out and dropped back to the mat, trying for what I recognized as a sambo foot lock. Sambo is a variety of Russian wrestling. It's distinguished by, among other things, its emphasis on foot, knee, and ankle locks, some of which can be applied so swiftly and can cause such extensive damage that they've been outlawed from various grappling competitions.

I shot my right foot into his neck and jerked the other leg back, just barely getting it clear from between his biceps and ribs. He tried to scramble away, and as we scuffled I managed to throw my right leg over his left and across his body and to catch his left toes under my right armpit. Before he could kick free, I over-hooked his heel with the inside of my right wrist; clasped my hands together and clamped my elbows to my sides; and arched back and twisted to my left in my own little demonstration of sambo prowess, a classic heel hook.

Despite the technique's name, the attack is to the knee joint, not the heel. The heel serves only as the lever, and I had a nice grip on Dox's. He tried to kick with his right leg, but from this position the kicks were feeble. I twisted a fraction more and he gave up that strategy.

"Tap, tap," he said. "You got me."

"Who sent you here?"

"Hey, I said 'tap!' Come on, now!"

I twisted another fraction and he yelped. "Who sent you?" I asked again.

"You know who sent me," he said, grimacing. "Same outfit as last time."

"Yeah? How did they know where to look?"

"I don't know!"

He tried to push my leg off. I squeezed my knees tighter and twisted his heel another millimeter.

"Fuck!" he said, loud enough for other people to hear. "C'mon, man, I seriously don't know!"

His breathing was getting more labored, as much from pain as from exertion. I looked in his eyes.

"Hey, Dox," I said, my voice calm, almost a whisper. "I'm going to count to three. If you haven't told me what I want to know by then, I'm going to twist as hard as I can. Ready? One. Two. Thr—"

"The girl! The girl! They paid her, or something. I don't know the details."

I almost twisted anyway.

"What girl?"

"You know. The Brazilian chick. Naomi something."

I was less surprised than I would have imagined. I'd have to think about that, later.

"Who's your handler?"

"Jesus Christ, man, I'll tell you what you want to know. You don't have to . . . fuck! Kanezaki! Ethnic Japanese guy, about thirty, wire-rimmed glasses, says he knows you."

Kanezaki. I should have known. I'd let him live when I'd first found him trying to tail me. I wondered briefly whether that had been a mistake.

I noticed that several people were watching us, including Carlinhos, the founder of the academy and its chief instructor. No one was moving to interfere, recognizing, as Brazilians do, that this problem was *homem homem*—man to man—and not yet their concern. Still, I didn't want to draw any more attention to myself. I released his leg and disengaged.

The tension ran out of his body and he slumped onto his back, cradling his injured knee. "Oh, man, I can't believe you did that," he said. "That was totally unnecessary, man."

I didn't respond.

"What if I really hadn't known, huh? What then?"

I shrugged. "Surgery to reconstruct the anterior and posterior cruciate ligaments and menisci, then maybe a six- to twelve-month rehabilitation. Lots of painkillers that wouldn't work nearly as well as you'd want."

"Shit," he grunted. A minute or so passed. Then he sat up and looked at me. He flexed his leg and flashed his indefatigable grin.

"I almost had you, man. And you know it."

"Sure," I said, looking at him. "Almost." I stood. "Where did you learn the sambo?"

The grin widened. "Since the dreaded Iron Curtain got lifted, I've been working some with the Ruskies."

"They let you in, after some of the shit you pulled on them in 'Stan?"

He shrugged. "It's a whole new world, partner, with whole new enemies. I'm helping them with their Chechen problem now, so we're like old buddies."

I nodded. "Let's go somewhere where we can talk."

We grabbed our bags and left without changing. I still had the bug and transmitter detector Harry had once made for me. It lay quietly in my bag, powered up from its daily charging, and I knew neither Dox nor his belongings was wired. But that didn't mean he was alone.

I took him along a circuitous series of quiet neighborhood streets. Twice we got in and out of taxis. I stayed with generic countersurveillance techniques, not wanting to take specific advantage of the area's features lest he conclude by my intimate knowledge of the local terrain that I must be a resident. He knew what I was doing and didn't protest.

By the time we had reached the beach at São Conrado, I knew we were clean. The rain had stopped and we strolled down to the edge of the water. The tide was receding, giving up wet sand like a defeated army abandoning terrain it could no longer control.

A minute passed. Neither of us spoke.

A ball from a nearby game of beach soccer rolled our way. Dox picked it up and threw it back at the brown-skinned kid who was chasing after it. The kid waved his thanks and went back to the game. I watched him for a moment, wondering what it would be like to grow up like that, in a city by the sea with nothing worse to do than play soccer on the sand.

"We done with the spy stuff?" Dox asked me.

I nodded, and after a moment he went on.

"Nice setup you got going here," he said. "Good weather, the ocean . . . And man, the women! I've been falling in love maybe three times a day. First morning, I got to my hotel, girl at the reception desk, man, they practically had to resuscitate me she was so fine."

"You could be a travel writer," I told him.

"Hey, I'd take it. It's tough for guys like us, you know? You get a certain résumé, you only get hired for certain jobs."

"You seem to be doing all right," I observed.

He kicked some sand and looked out at the ocean. "Sure is nice here, though. You been here long?"

The hayseed accent was getting thicker. I wasn't going to fall for it, but no sense calling him on it, either. Better to have him assume that I was underestimating him the way he was used to being underestimated.

"Couple months," I told him. "I move around a lot. So people like you can't find me."

He frowned. "C'mon, what else was I going to do? The lucky ones find a gig bodyguarding rich assholes, doing threat assessments, living the good life in the guest quarters of a house in Brentwood, hardening the soft targets who should have gotten culled early on to improve the gene pool like nature intended. The really lucky ones teach Hollywood types how to act like soldiers, or they get to blow shit up for the cameras. The unlucky ones? Mall security guards and rent-a-cops. I didn't get a shot at the first, and fuck the second. So here I am."

"Why not go with Blackwater, one of those outfits?"

He shrugged. "I tried it. But I discovered that the corporate world just didn't offer me appropriate financial opportunities. And you know what they say about opportunity, buddy. It only knocks once."

We were silent again for a moment. I asked, "Why'd they send you?"

He reached down and rubbed his knee. "You know why. We know each other, they figure you trust me." He smiled. "Don't you?"

"Sure," I told him. "Completely."

"Well, that's it," he went on, pretending he was too slow to understand sarcasm. "Plus, I figure they want you to hear from me that what they've got in mind is real, get you interested that way. I'm like a customer reference, you know what I mean?"

"Sure," I said again.

"Okay, so here's the score. I've been doing some work for Uncle Sam, deniable shit, off the books. High risk, high 'they'll fuck you in the end' potential, but lucrative."

"Yeah?"

"Yeah. They thought you might be interested. But contacting you wasn't my idea, by the way. I didn't even know you were still around, man. A lot of people we knew in 'Stan, they're not breathing so much these days."

"Whose idea, then?"

"Look, there's a program. Something new, something big. They're hiring people like me and you, paying good money, is what I'm saying."

"Dox, do you know what a 'pronoun' is?"

He frowned. Then his face brightened. "Ah, I know what you mean. I keep saying 'they' and shit like that. Not telling you who really."

I looked at him and waited.

He smiled and shook his head. "C'mon, man, you know who 'they' is. Christians In Action." He shivered in mock excitement. "The Company."

"Right."

"They've got some sort of new mandate. You should hear it from them."

"I'd like to hear it from you first."

"Hey, I don't have all the details. And I can't give you the specifics about what I've been up to. I'll just tell you that they're paying me a lot of money to make certain people who are causing problems stop causing problems. They want to make the same offer to you."

"Through your handler?"

He nodded. "I've got a number for you to call."

I wrote the number down in code, then left him there and made my way back to Naomi's apartment. The move was predictable, and I took extensive precautions. The caution was mostly reflex, though. If they'd wanted to kill me, they wouldn't have sent someone I knew to contact me first. They would have known that doing so would only tune up my alertness, possibly even convince me to run.

No, I had a feeling Dox's story was straight. But no sense being sloppy, regardless.

I thought on the way to Naomi's about what Dox had told me. The Agency must have connected the bodies outside Naomi's Tokyo apartment with the contemporaneous death of Yukiko, the ice bitch who had set up and then disposed of Harry after the *yakuza* had used him to find me. They knew, despite the absence of real proof, that I'd been involved in all those killings. They knew that Naomi and Yukiko had both been dancers at the same Nogizaka club. It wouldn't be too great a leap to deduce, from the pieces they had, a connection between Naomi and me.

I used the intercom at the front entrance. Naomi was surprised that I was back, but she buzzed me in. I took the stairs. She was waiting, holding the door open for me.

I went in. The room smelled of brewing coffee. Her hair hung wet against the shoulders of a white terry-cloth robe—she had just gotten up and out of the shower, it seemed.

"Someone was following me this morning," I told her.

"Following you?" she asked.

"Yeah. Not in a good way."

"A mugger?"

"Not a mugger. A pro. Someone who knew just where to go."

She looked at me, her expression more frightened than confused.

"Tell me what's going on, Naomi."

There was a long pause, then she said, "I didn't tell them anything."

"Tell who?"

"I don't know exactly. They call every month or so. It started when I came back to Brazil from Tokyo. Someone came to Scenarium and started asking me about you."

"Describe him."

"He called himself Kanematsu. American, but ethnic Japanese. He had slicked hair and wire-rimmed glasses. Thirtyish, I think, but younger-looking. He told me he was with the U.S. government and that he was a friend of yours but wouldn't say more than that."

Kanezaki again, operating under a pseudonym. "What did you tell him?" I asked.

She looked at me, her expression an odd mixture of vulnerability and defiance. "I told him I knew you, yes, but that I didn't know where you were or how to find you."

If that was true, it was also smart. If she'd denied even knowing me they would have known she was lying. They would have assumed the rest was a lie, too, and might have started to pressure her.

"And after that?"

She shrugged. "I get a call once a month or so. Always from the same guy. And I always tell him the same thing."

I nodded, considering. "What did they offer you?" I asked.

She looked down, then back at me. "Twenty-five thousand U.S."

"Just for putting them in touch with me?"

She nodded.

"Well, it's good to be appreciated," I said. "Did the guy you met leave you any way of contacting him?"

She got up and walked into her bedroom. I heard a drawer open, then close. She came back and wordlessly handed me a card. It included an e-mail address and a phone number. The latter had a Tokyo prefix. It was the same number I had just gotten from Dox.

"Twenty-five thousand is a lot of money," I said, flipping the card around in my fingers.

She stared at me.

"You were never tempted to take it?" I asked.

Her eyes narrowed. "No."

"Not even with everything you've invested in the restaurant? That kind of cash would be a big help."

"You think I'm going to give you up?" she asked, her voice rising. "For money?"

I shrugged. "You never told me about any of this. Until I pressed you."

"I was afraid to tell you."

"And you kept the card. A keepsake? Souvenir?"

There was a pause. She said, "Fuck you, then."

I told myself I should have seen this coming.

I told myself it was all right, that I wasn't disappointed, that it was better this way.

I wondered in a detached way whether it was all part of some cosmic punishment for Crazy Jake, the blood brother I had killed in Vietnam. Or perhaps for the other things I've done. To be periodically tantalized by the hope of something real, something good, always knowing at the same time that it was all going to turn to dust.

Maybe she didn't tell them anything. Maybe they nailed you some other way.

Then why didn't she say anything to you? And why did she keep that card?

I had convinced myself that, in Rio, I had become safe enough to see her. I realized now that I'd been wrong. The disease I carried was still communicable.

And still potentially fatal. Because, even if I could trust her to stay quiet, the Agency was watching her. She had become a focal point, a nexus, just like Harry had been. And Harry had wound up dead. I didn't want that to happen to her.

Well, now for the hard part. *You don't have to like it,* a boot camp instructor had once told me. *You just have to do it.*

I looked at her for a long moment. Her eyes were

angry, but I saw hope in them, too. Hope that I would put my arms around her and pull her close, apologize, say I'd just been startled, that I'd been out of line.

I got up and looked into those beautiful green eyes, now widening with surprise, with hurt. I wondered if she could see the sadness in mine.

"Goodbye, Naomi," I said.

I left. I told myself again that I wasn't disappointed, that I wasn't even terribly surprised. I learned a long time ago not to trust, that faith is to life what sticking your chin out is to boxing. I told myself it was good to get some further confirmation of the essential accuracy of my worldview.

I took extra precautions to ensure I wasn't being followed. Then I went to a quiet beach near Grumari and sat alone and looked out at the water.

Don't blame Naomi, I thought. *Anyone would have given you up.*

Not Midori, was the reply. And then I thought, *No, you're just trying to turn her into something too good to be true, something impossible.*

But maybe she really was that good, and now I was just trying to dampen it, debase it, cheapen the consequence of what I'd lost.

I guess you can never really know, I thought. *But then how do you decide?*

Doesn't matter how it gets decided. Just that you do the deciding.

I shook my head in wonder. Midori was still throwing me off, all these months later and half a world away. Making me doubt myself, my judgments.

What does that tell you?

That one I didn't answer. I already knew.

I sat and thought for a long time. About my life in Rio. About how Naomi had come into it, and how she was then suddenly gone. About what I ought to do now.

A breeze kicked up along the sand. I felt empty. The breeze might have been blowing straight through me.

I supposed I could just leave it all behind me. Bolt for the exit again, go somewhere new, invent another Yamada.

I shook my head, knowing I wasn't ready for that, not so soon after the last time. The thought of doing it all again felt like nothing but dread.

Which made the conclusion that followed suspect, a possible rationalization. The conclusion went like this: *It would be better to know what they want, anyway. To take the initiative, rather than passively waiting for whatever they have in mind.*

All right then. I left the beach, and called Kanezaki from a pay phone. There was a decent chance they would track the call to Rio, but they obviously already knew I was here.

The phone rang twice. "Yeah," I heard him say. He sounded groggy.

It was early afternoon in Rio, and Tokyo was twelve hours ahead. "Hope I didn't wake you," I said.

"Don't worry about it," he said, recognizing my voice. "I had to get up to answer the phone, anyway."

I was surprised to hear myself chuckle. "Tell me what you want."

"Can we meet?"

"I'm in Rio for a few more days," I told him. "After that I won't be reachable."

"All right, I'll meet you in Rio."

"Glad I was able to provide you with the excuse."

There was a pause. "Where and when?"

"Have you got a GSM phone, something you use when you travel?" Unlike Japanese cell phones, a GSM unit would work in Brazil and most of the rest of the world.

"I do."

"All right. Give me the number."

He did. I wrote it down, then said, "I'll call you on this number the day after tomorrow, when you're in town."

"All right."

I hung up.

Two days later, I called him. He was staying at the Arpoador Inn on the Rua Francisco Otaviano in Ipanema, an inexpensive hotel located right on Ipanema's famous beach.

"How are we going to do this?" he asked.

"Have a cab take you to *Cristo Redentor,* Christ the Redeemer," I told him. "From there, head southwest on foot along the road through the Parque Nacional da Tijuca, the national park. I'll find you in there. Start out from the statue in one hour."

"All right."

An hour later I had made myself comfortable on a trail overlooking the road through the national park, about a kilometer from the statue. Kanezaki appeared on time. I watched him pass my position, waited to ensure that he was alone, then cut down to the road and caught up with him from behind.

"Kanezaki," I said.

He spun, startled to hear my voice so close. "Shit," he said, perhaps a little embarrassed.

I smiled. He looked a little older than he had the last

time I had seen him, leaner, more seasoned. The wire-rimmed glasses no longer made him look bookish. Instead, they gave his face . . . focus, somehow. Precision.

The bug detector was silent. I patted him down, took his cell phone for safekeeping, and nodded my head toward the trail from which I had just descended. "This way," I said.

I led him back to a secondary road in the park, where we walked until we found a cab. A few deft countersurveillance maneuvers later, we were comfortably ensconced in the Confeitaria Colombo, a coffee shop founded in 1894 that, but for the tropical atmosphere and the surrounding sounds of animated Portuguese, can convey the illusion of an afternoon in Vienna. I used English to order a basic espresso, not wanting Kanezaki to see any more of my familiarity with the local terrain, and he followed suit.

"We want your help again," he told me, as soon as the espressos had arrived and the waitress had moved off. Right to the point. Like Tatsu. I knew there was a relationship there, each believing the other to be a source, with Tatsu's view being the more accurate. I wondered if Kanezaki was emulating the older, more experienced man.

"Like you wanted it last time?" I asked, my eyebrows arched slightly in mild disdain.

He shrugged. "You know I was in the dark about all that as much as you were. This time it's straightforward. And sanctioned."

"Sanctioned by whom?"

He looked at me. "By the proper authorities."

"All right," I said, taking a sip from the porcelain demitasse. "Tell me."

He leaned forward and put his elbows on the table.

"After Nine-Eleven, Congress took the shackles off the Agency. There's a new spirit in the place. We're pushing the envelope again, going after the bad guys—"

"The few, the proud . . ." I interjected.

He frowned. "Look, we're really making a difference now—"

"Be All You Can Be . . ." I started to sing.

His jaw clenched. "Do you just enjoy pissing me off?" he asked.

"A little bit, yes."

"It's petty."

I took another sip of espresso. "What's your point?"

"I wish you'd just listen."

"So far I've listened to five clichés, including something about shackled envelopes. I'm waiting for you to actually say something."

He flushed, but then nodded and even managed a chuckle. I smiled at his composure. He had matured since I had last seen him.

"Okay," he said. "Remember that Predator drone that took out Abu Ali and five other Qaeda members with a Hellfire missile in Yemen in November 2002? That was one of ours."

"That's what was in the papers," I said.

"Well, what's not in the papers is the full extent of this kind of clandestine activity. The Agency has won a tug-of-war with the Pentagon over who's responsible for these things. The Pentagon tried, but they can't move fast enough to act on the intelligence we produce. So we've been tasked with the action ourselves. And we're doing it."

I waited for him to go on.

"So now we have a new mandate: no more Nine-Elevens. No more sneak attacks. We've been charged with doing whatever it takes—and I mean whatever—to disrupt the international terrorist infrastructure: the financiers, the arms brokers, the go-betweens."

I nodded. "You want me for the 'whatever' part."

"Of course," he said, almost impatiently, and this time I was sure he'd gotten the habit from Tatsu, who had a way of uttering those two syllables as though barely managing to avoid instead saying, *Are you always this obtuse?*

He took a sip from his cup. "Look, some of the individuals in question enjoy a lot of political protection. Some of them, in fact, are technically U.S. citizens."

"'Technically'?"

He shrugged. "They could be classified as enemy combatants."

I closed my eyes and shook my head.

"What?" he asked.

I smiled. "Just thinking about the way the end justifies the means."

"Sometimes it does."

"Their end, or only yours?"

"Let's save the philosophical discussion," he said. "The point is, even post-Nine-Eleven, even in the current, security-minded climate, it wouldn't do to just take some of these people out. Certainly not with a Hellfire missile. Better if their demise were to look . . . you know, natural."

"Assuming that I were interested, and I'm not, what would be in it for me?"

"You're not interested? You're going to a lot of trouble to meet me, for someone who's not interested."

A year ago my protestation would have flustered him. Now he was counterpunching. Good for him.

"It's no trouble. I was here because of a woman.

When I found out she was working for you, I had to break things off. So here I am, killing a few days before heading home."

If he was surprised to learn that I knew about his connection with Naomi, he didn't show it. He looked at me and said, "Some people think Rio is your home."

I returned his stare, and something in my eyes made him drop his gaze. "If you want to play fishing games with me, Kanezaki," I said, "you're just wasting time. But if I think your I-took-a-course-at-Langley-on-verbal-manipulation-techniques bullshit contains an element of threat, I'll take you out before you even have a chance to beg me not to."

I felt fear flow off him in a cold ripple. I knew what he had just seen in his mind's eye: the way I had broken his bodyguard's neck, an act that would have looked as casual to Kanezaki as unzipping to take a leak. Which is exactly the way I had wanted him to see it. And remember it.

"The money could set you up well," he said, after a moment.

"I'm already set," I answered, which was a lie, unfortunately.

We were both quiet for a moment. Then he said, "Look, I'm not doing any verbal manipulation here. Or at least no more than you'd expect. And I'm definitely not threatening you. I'm just telling you that we could really use your help to accomplish something important, and that you could make a lot of money in the process."

I suppressed a grin. It was nicely done.

"Tell me who and how much," I said. "And we'll see if there's anything worth discussing after that."

The target was Belghazi, of course. The first of many,

Kanezaki told me, if I was interested. Two hundred thousand U.S. a pop, delivered any way I wanted, fifty thousand upfront, the rest upon successful completion. On expenses I'd be out of pocket, which minimized paperwork—and paper trails—for the bean-counting set, a rule we wound up having to change somewhat given the sums I needed to operate in the VIP rooms of the Lisboa. The only catch was that it absolutely had to look natural.

It was about what I would have guessed. Enough to create the incentive, but not so much that I wouldn't be tempted to do it again later. Not a bad deal for them, really—about the cost of a Hellfire or two, and a lot less than a cruise missile. And more deniable than either.

"I'll think about it," I told him. "And while I'm thinking, pay Naomi what you owe her."

"She didn't hold up her end," he said, shaking his head, not bothering to deny the connection. "So she's out of luck."

"What was 'her end'?"

"She was supposed to contact us if you contacted her."

I looked at him. "If she didn't contact you, how . . ."

"Voice analysis. Like a lie detector. We used it every time I called her. Every time I asked whether you'd shown up, she said no. On the last time, the machine detected significant stress patterns."

"So you knew she was lying."

"Yeah. We sent people to watch her. You know the rest."

I looked away and considered. So she had been telling me the truth—she really hadn't given me up. Damn.

Or maybe she had, and Kanezaki was just protecting her. There was no way to know, and I supposed there never would be.

"Pay her anyway," I said.

He started to protest, but I cut him off. "She still led you to me, even if it was inadvertent. Pay her the fucking finder's fee."

"I'll see what I can do," he said, after a moment.

I wondered briefly whether this was bullshit, too, designed to make me feel that I'd won something. Again, no way to know.

"I'll contact you," I said. "If you've paid her, we'll talk more. If you haven't, we won't."

He nodded.

I thought about adding something about leaving her alone, some threat. But all an admonition would accomplish would be to reveal, more than I already had, that I cared, thereby making Naomi more interesting to them. Better to say nothing, and simply steer clear of her thereafter.

Maybe you could have trusted her after all. The thought was tantalizing.

And sad.

It didn't matter. Even if there had been some possibility of trust, my reflexive assumptions, my accusations, had extinguished it.

I thought of an apology. But there are things that just aren't subject to an "I'm sorry" or a "please forgive me" or a "really, I should have known better."

Let it go, I thought. The twenty-five grand would have to do.

"Now tell me about Dox," I said.

He shrugged. "I needed someone you knew, so you

could see that the program, and the benefits of the program, were real. If it weren't for that, then, other than your history, you would never have known about him."

"Are there others?"

He looked at me over the top of his glasses. The look said, *You know better than to ask something like that.*

I looked back.

After a moment, he shrugged again and said, "I'll just say that men like you and Dox are rare. And even he can't operate in some of the places you can. Asia, for example. Also he tends to be a little less subtle in his methods, meaning not well suited for certain jobs. Okay?"

We left it at that. He gave me the URL for a secure bulletin board. I called him a few days later on his Japanese cell phone. He was back in Tokyo. He told me Naomi had gotten the money.

I used a pay phone to call her at Scenarium. The club was noisy in the background. She said, "I didn't want the fucking money. I could have had it, but I didn't want it."

"Naomi . . ." I started to say. I didn't know what I was going to add. But it didn't really matter. She had already hung up.

I looked at the phone for a long time, as though the device had somehow betrayed me. Then I put it back in its cradle. Wiped it down automatically. Walked away.

I went to an Internet café and composed a message. The message was brief. The salient part was the number of an offshore account, to which they could transfer the fifty thousand down payment.

I heard laughter and looked up. Some kids at the terminal next to me, playing an online game.

I wondered for a moment how I had gotten here.

And I wondered if maybe this is what Tatsu had

meant when he said I could never retire. That I would inevitably ruin every other possibility.

We shall not cease from exploration, some poet wrote. *And the end of all our exploring will be to arrive where we started, and know the place for the first time.*

How incredibly fucking depressing.

4

AFTER LEAVING BELGHAZI'S suite, I took a long, solitary walk along the waterfront. I wanted to think about what had just happened, about what I wanted to happen next.

Delilah. Who was she? How would her presence affect my operation? The same questions, of course, that she would be asking about me.

I knew from her deportment that she was trained. Therefore likely to be working with an organization, rather than on some sort of private mission. And that, despite public appearances, she was no friend of Belghazi's. She was with him because she wanted something from him, something he kept, or that she thought he kept, on his laptop, but that she hadn't yet managed to get.

I considered. By conspiring to get me out of the suite, she had sided, at least temporarily, with me. We shared a secret. That secret might become the basis for cooperation, if our interests were sufficiently aligned.

But she also had reason to view me as a threat. There was some hard evidence of her operation against Belghazi, in the form of her dual-purpose cell phone and the boot log on Belghazi's computer, which the wrong people could find if they knew where to look. If someone like me were to steer them to it, for example.

I realized that my knowledge of that potentially damning evidence gave Delilah a reason to want me out of the way. "Out of the way" might take a variety of different forms, of course, but none of them would be particularly attractive from my standpoint.

Still, it wouldn't make sense for her to do anything too aggressive without first trying to learn more. If she had struck me as stupid or inexperienced, I might have concluded otherwise. But she'd obviously been around for a while, and she was smart. I thought I could reasonably expect her to play things accordingly.

I smiled. *You mean, to play it the way you would.* Yes, that was probably true.

Again, she would be coming to similar conclusions, *mutatis mutandis,* as the lawyers like to say, about me.

So the risk of a meeting seemed manageable. Moreover, avoiding her, and losing an opportunity to acquire additional information, would make proceeding against Belghazi more difficult, possibly more dangerous. Not an easy call, but in the end I decided to go see her at the Mandarin casino.

I used the cell phone to call Kanezaki. It was late, but he answered after only one ring.

"It's me," I said.

"Is it a coincidence, or do you just enjoy calling me in the middle of the night?"

"This time it's both."

"What do you need?"

"Information," I said. "Anything you have on a woman I ran into, although I don't have much for you to go on. She uses the name Delilah, probably among others. I think she's European, but I'm not sure what nationality. She's tall, blond, striking looks."

"You need this information operationally, or are you trying to get a date?"

Maybe he thought that busting my chops would foster "camaraderie." Or that it would otherwise put us on a more equal footing. Either way I didn't care for it.

"Also, she's shacking up with our friend," I said.

"That's not much to go on."

"Is there an echo on this line?" I asked, my voice an octave lower. It seemed he'd recently learned the value of playing up the difficulty of accomplishing whatever he was tasked with, the better to play the hero when he subsequently pulled it off. He was overusing the technique the way a child overuses a new word.

There was a pause that I found satisfying, then he said, "I'm just saying that it might be hard to find anything useful with the particulars you've given me."

"I'm not interested in your assessment of how difficult it might be. What I need is the information. Can you get it or not?"

There was another pause, and I imagined him reddening on the other end of the line. Good. Kanezaki seemed to be getting the idea that I worked for him. Although I supposed this sort of misapprehension was probably common enough among the world's newly minted Secret Agents, I didn't like being the subject of it. It might be beneficial for him occasionally to be reminded that I work for myself. That he was a stagehand, not one of the actors.

I heard a voice in the background, muffled but audible. "That's John, isn't it," the voice said. "Let me talk to him!"

Christ, I knew that twang. It was Dox.

There was an exchange that I couldn't make out, followed by a hiss of static and a clatter. Then Dox was on the phone, his voice booming and full of amusement.

"Hey, buddy, sounds like you're having yourself a good time there! Are we talking blonde, or brunette? Or Asian? I love those Asian ladies."

He must have snatched the phone over Kanezaki's protests. Secret Agents get no respect.

"What are you doing out there?" I asked, smiling despite myself.

"Oh you know, just a meeting with my handler. Going over this and that. What about you? Guess you decided to take advantage of Uncle Sam's magnanimity. Good for you, and tough luck for the bad guys."

"You mind putting him back on the phone?"

"All right, all right, no need to act short with me. Just wanted to say hello, and welcome aboard."

"That was good of you."

There was a pause, then Kanezaki's voice came back on. "Hey."

"Sounds like you've got a little date of your own out there," I said, unable to resist.

"I wouldn't call it that." He sounded glum.

I chuckled. "Not unless you've done hard time with a cellmate named Bubba."

He laughed at that, which was good. I needed him to understand who was in charge, but didn't want to beat him down too hard. His goodwill, his naïve sense of fairness, was a potential asset, and not something to toss away needlessly.

"I'll check the bulletin board," I told him. "If you find anything about the woman, just put it up there."

"Okay."

I paused, then added, "Thanks."

"Don't mention it," he said, and I thought he might be smiling.

AT ABOUT six o'clock the following evening, I dropped by the Mandarin casino. Delilah had said eight, but I like to show up for meetings early. It helps prevent surprises.

I used the street entrance, preferring to avoid the hotel for the moment. Keiko was out, but I wanted to minimize the chances of my running into her while she was coming or going. I walked up the escalator, nodded agreeably to the guards, and went inside.

The room was large, and largely empty. The pace would pick up later in the evening. For now, the action comprised just a few lonely souls. They seemed lost in the expanse of the room, their play joyless, desultory, as though they'd been looking for a livelier party and found themselves stuck with this one instead.

I spotted Delilah instantly. She was one of a handful of people quietly attending the room's lone baccarat table, and the only non-Asian in sight. She was dressed plainly, in black pants and a black, shoulderless top. Her hair was pulled back and I saw no signs of makeup or jewelry. If she'd been trying to downplay her looks, though, she hadn't been notably successful.

I checked the usual hot spots and saw nothing that set off any alarms. So far, my assessment that she wouldn't yet do anything precipitous seemed correct. But it was too soon to really know. After all, the casino, with its cameras, guards, and other forms of security, would have made a poor place for an ambush. An attack, if one were to come, would happen later.

I bought a handful of chips, then took a seat next to her.

"Early for baccarat," I said, meaning it's early for our appointment, but trying to be oblique in case anyone nearby spoke English.

"For both of us, it seems," she replied, putting her chips down on player and looking up at me sidelong.

I smiled, then placed a bet on the bank. "I hate to get a late start. You get there, the place is already filled up, the odds aren't as good."

She returned the smile, and I got my first good look at her eyes. They were deep blue, almost cobalt, and they seemed not only to regard, but somehow to assess, with intelligence and even some humor.

"Yes, early is better," she said. "It's a good thing not everyone realizes it. Otherwise you could never beat the crowds."

I noted that her English, though accented, was idiomatic. She would have learned it young enough to pick up the idiom, but not quite young enough to eradicate the accent.

The banker dealt the cards. I said, "Looks like we're the only ones who recognize the advantages of a timely arrival."

She followed my gaze, then looked back at me. "Let's hope so."

The dealer turned over the cards. Delilah won, I lost. She collected her chips without looking at me, but made no attempt to hide her smile.

I wanted to get her someplace where we could talk. The casino was a good starting point because it offered us a relatively safe, neutral venue. Also, it provided automatic cover for action: if anyone, Belghazi, for example, saw us here, our presence together would look like a coincidence, each of us presumably having arrived separately for a few rounds of cards or the dice. A corner table in a bar, or a park bench in the shadows, or a walk along the harbor, would offer none of these advantages. But we weren't going to get anywhere at the baccarat table. Besides, I was losing money.

"I was thinking about going somewhere for a drink," I said. "Care to join me?"

She looked at me for a moment, then said, "Sure."

We left through the street exit. As soon as we were out of earshot of the casino's few patrons, she said, "Not the hotel bar. I'm too well known here. We'll get a taxi in front of the hotel and go somewhere else. There's not much chance that any of my acquaintances will show up right now, but just in case, we ran into each other in the Mandarin casino. It was dead. I mentioned that I was going to try the Lisboa. You asked if I wouldn't mind you catching a cab over with me. Okay?"

I was impressed, although unsurprised. She was obviously in the habit of thinking operationally, and was as matter-of-fact about it as she was effective. I'd already concluded that she was trained. To that assessment I now added a probable minimum of several years of field experience.

"Okay," I said.

I took us to the Oparium Café, a place I'd found near the new Macau Cultural Center along the Avenida Baia Nova while waiting for Belghazi and getting to know the city. The ground floor featured an oppressively loud band playing some sort of acid-funk and a bunch of deafened teenagers gyrating to the beat. Not the kind of place you'd find someone unfamiliar with the area, especially someone whose tastes ran to things like the Macau Suite at the Mandarin Oriental.

We went upstairs, where it was darker and quieter, and sat at a corner table in a pair of oversized beanbag chairs. The other seating consisted mostly of couches, some of them occupied by couples, a few of them locked in intimate embraces that the shadows only partially obscured. A pretty Portuguese waitress brought us menus. They were written in Chinese and Portuguese. Delilah smiled and said, "I'll have what you're having."

In the dim light her eyes looked more gray than blue. I liked the way the lighting softened her features, the way it rendered her eyes, even her smile, alluringly ambiguous.

I glanced at the menu and saw that they didn't serve any single malts worth drinking. Instead I ordered us a couple of *caipirinhas,* which I knew from recent experience would be delicious in the tropical heat.

The waitress departed. We were quiet for a moment. Then Delilah leaned toward me and, looking into my eyes, asked, "Well? You have something you want to give me?"

I looked at her. Why was it that her question seemed suffused with double entendre? She was attractive, of course, more than attractive, but that wasn't all of it. She had a way of looking at me with a sort of confident sexual appreciation, that was it. As though she was seeing me just the way I might hope a desirable woman would see me.

And she made it seem so natural, so real. I would have to be careful.

"Like what?" I asked, curious to see her reaction if I hit a few back at her.

"Do I need to be more explicit?" she asked, maybe suggestive again.

I wondered what response she was expecting. I knew that my information about her cell phone and the computer boot log would make her view me as a potential threat. And she would probably expect me to try to exploit the video, to hang its existence over her head as a way of protecting myself. I decided to surprise her.

"The thing about the video was a bluff," I told her. "I think you know that. I was afraid that, without it, you might take a chance on waking Belghazi."

She paused, then said, "You're not concerned that, without it, I might take other chances now?"

I shrugged. "Sure I am."

"Then why are you telling me?"

I looked at her. "I'm not a threat to you."

She raised an eyebrow. "This is like, what, a dog showing its belly?"

I smiled. "Well, I've already seen yours."

She smiled back. "Yes, you have."

The smile lingered, along with her eyes, and I felt something stirring down south. But I thought, *Don't be stupid. This is how she plays it, how she gets people to drop their guard.*

"Well, you don't have a video for me," she said, after a moment. She was still looking into my eyes. "So what do we do next?"

The stirring worsened. I decided I'd have been better off if I could have just removed the damned thing and left it in a drawer for the evening.

But I saw a less extreme means of defending myself.

I thought for a moment about the scores of other men she would have played before me, about how, in her eyes, I was just a new fool, another mark to be led by his dick and manipulated. The thought irritated me, which was what I needed. It short-circuited my unavoidable mechanical reaction and gave me back some of the air I wanted to project.

"Hey, Delilah," I said softly, letting her see a little coldness in my eyes, "let's cut the shit. I'm not here to flirt with you. We might be able to help each other, I don't know. But not if you keep trying to play me like I'm some testosterone-addled fourteen-year-old and you're my date at the prom. Okay?"

She smiled and cocked her head, and of course her poise only added to her appeal. "Why would I be trying to play you?" she asked.

I wanted to snap her out of this mode, move her outside her comfort zone. So far, I hadn't managed.

"Because you're good at it," I said, still looking at her, "and people like to do what they're good at. Hell, if they gave out Academy Awards for what you do, I think you'd get Best Actress."

Her eyes narrowed a fraction, but other than that she kept her cool. Still, I thought I might be heading in the right direction.

"You seem to have a rather low opinion of yourself," she said.

I smiled, because I'd been half expecting something like that. Most men won't do anything that could lessen their perceived chances of taking a gorgeous woman to bed. They're horrified even at the thought that something might accidentally dim the temporary glow of an attractive woman's sexual adulation, lest all those longing looks be exposed as farce, deflating the always fragile façade of the needy male ego. Delilah knew the dynamic. She had just explicitly acknowledged, even invoked it.

"Actually, I have a rather high opinion of myself," I said. "But I've seen you working Belghazi, and he's smarter than most. I know what you can do, and I want you to stop doing it with me. Assuming you can stop, of course. Or have you been running this game for so long that you can't help yourself?"

For the first time I saw her lose a little poise. Her head retracted a fraction in a movement that was not quite a flinch, and her eyes dilated in a way that told me she'd just received a little helping of adrenaline.

"What do you want, then?" she asked, after a moment. Her expression was neutral, but her eyes were angry, her posture more rigid than it had been a moment earlier. The combination made her look quietly dangerous. I realized this was my first peek at the person behind the artifice, my first chance to see something other than what she wanted me to see.

The crazy thing was, it made her look better than ever. It was like seeing a woman's real beauty after she's removed the makeup that only served to obscure it, a glimpse of a geisha the more stunning shorn of her ritual white camouflage.

"The same thing you do," I told her. "I want to make sure we don't trip all over each other trying to do our jobs and both get killed in the process."

"And what are our jobs?"

I smiled. "This is going to be tricky, isn't it," I said.

"Very," she said. Her expression had transitioned from I'm-pissed-and-trying-not-to-show-it to something reserved and unreadable. I knew what I'd said had rattled her, although I wasn't sure precisely what nerve I'd managed to touch, and I admired her swift recovery.

"Why don't we start with what we know," I said. "You want something from Belghazi's computer."

She raised her eyebrows but said nothing. That hint of incongruous good humor was back in her eyes.

"But you haven't managed to get it yet," I went on. "Belghazi keeps the computer with him all the time. When you finally got a crack at it, you couldn't get past the password protection."

"We should talk about the other things we know," she said.

"Yes?"

"Like what you want with Belghazi."

I shrugged. "I've got other business with Belghazi. What's on his computer doesn't interest me."

"Yes, you seemed uninterested in his computer. More interested in him."

I said nothing. There was no advantage in confirming any of her insights.

"And he was right there. Unconscious. Helpless. I asked myself, 'Why did this man leave without finishing what he came for?'"

"You don't know what I came for," I said, but of course she did.

"You'd knocked me down, and I obviously didn't have a weapon," she said, looking at me. "I couldn't have done anything to prevent you. And you knew it. But you didn't follow through."

I shrugged, still looking for a way to throw her off. "Maybe I didn't want to harm a naked woman," I said.

She shook her head. "I've known some hard men, men who can act without compunction. I recognize the type."

"I wasn't expecting you. You startled me."

She smiled, and I knew I wasn't changing her diagnosis. "Maybe. Or maybe your 'business' with Belghazi has to be carried out in a . . . circumspect way. So that no one would know that any business was done. And you couldn't pull that off with someone else in the room."

I hadn't expected her to follow this line of reasoning. I'm usually good at putting myself in the other person's shoes, anticipating his next move. But she had out-played me on this one. Time to try to regain some initiative, give myself a second to think.

"It's funny, I'm asking myself some of the same things about you," I said. "For example, 'Why hasn't she or her people just taken the computer and run?'"

She smiled just a little, maybe conceding the point.

"Let me guess," I went on. "If Belghazi realized that the information on the computer had been compromised, he would implement countermeasures. No, let me amend that. Because if Belghazi were the only one you were worried about, you'd just put him to sleep yourself and take the briefcase at your leisure. So he's not the only one who might take countermeasures if it's discovered that the computer has been compromised. There are others, people or organizations who would be affected by the information you're trying to acquire. And when you acquire it, it's critical that they not know. Is that about it? Maybe I'm not the only one whose moves might have to be 'circumspect.'"

She cocked her head slightly as though I'd finally started to say something interesting. "Yes," she said. "Yes, stealing is easy. Stealing without the victim knowing he's been robbed, this takes some doing."

The waitress brought our *caipirinhas* in frosted glasses and moved away. Delilah tipped hers back and took a long sip. "Like you," she went on. "Killing is easy. Killing and making it look like something else? That would require some . . . artistry."

She used "this" and "that" slightly mechanically, as I would expect from someone who had acquired English later in life. "Stealing" was "this." "Killing" was "that." The first was hers, the other, mine. I didn't think these verbal cues were deliberate. I took them as small, additional signs that my conclusions about what she was after were correct.

We were silent for several moments, each digesting what the other had said, reassessing the situation.

She said, "It seems that we're in mirror-image positions. Maybe we can help each other."

"I'm not sure I follow you," I told her, although I thought I did.

She shrugged. "Your presence makes it difficult for me to do my job. My presence makes it hard for you to do yours. Mirror images."

"Your mirrors might be a little distorted," I said, taking a swallow of the *caipirinha*. "If something happens to you, Belghazi would be alarmed. Or his demise might not look 'circumspect.' But if something happens to me . . ."

Her smile broadened in a way that reminded me of Tatsu, the way he would be pleased when I made a connection he was expecting would be beyond me, and I knew that she was well aware of this flaw in her "mirror image" theory.

"Yes," she said, "that's true. My people made the same point when we discussed the situation. Some of them wanted to send a team in to remove you."

"Did you tell them they'd have to get in line?"

She laughed. "I told them I thought that kind of hostile action would be a mistake. I saw the way you assessed the room when you came into the casino. I see the way you subtly check your back all the time. Even this table, you chose it because it was in the corner. So you could sit with your back to the wall."

"And you, too."

"You knew I wouldn't let you put my back to the stairs, especially after you chose the place. This was a compromise."

"That's true."

"Anyway, you've got that weight about you, the feel of experience and competence, even though I think you're adept at concealing it. I told my people that removing you wouldn't be easy and would probably involve a mess. The kind of mess that could alert Belghazi that something was wrong. He has very keen instincts, as I think you know. I doubt that anyone has gotten as close to him as you did."

"Only you."

She smiled, and I saw the bedroom eyes again. "I have resources that you don't." She took a sip of *caipirinha.* "So I think my description of our positions as 'mirror image' is apt."

"All right. What do you propose?"

She shrugged. "I told my people that moving against you would be a poor option, although we couldn't rule it out if you insisted on behaving unreasonably. If you gave us no choice."

I looked at her, letting her see some coldness again. "I doubt that your people were able to get you any background on me," I told her, "but if they had, they would have told you that I react poorly to threats. Even irrationally."

"I'm not threatening you."

"Convince me of that."

"Look, you know what we want from Belghazi. And we know what you want. Stand down for a few days. Let me get what I need. When I have it, I can get you access."

"I already have access."

She shook her head. "That was one in a million. You or someone else must have put something in what he was eating or drinking. If that happens to him again, he's going to know something is wrong. He'll react accordingly, stiffen his defenses. And he moves around a lot. You tracked him here, all right, but are you sure you could track his next move?"

She sipped again. "But if you work with me, you have someone on the inside. Once we have what we need, we don't care what happens to him."

I thought for a moment. There was something obvious here, something she was avoiding. I decided to test it.

"I've got a better idea," I said. "Help me get close, and I'll do what I'm here to do. You can take his computer when I'm done."

She shook her head. "That won't work."

"Why not?"

She shook her head again. "It just won't. I can't tell you why. We have to do it my way. Give me a little time, and then I'll help you."

It was what I thought. The information on Belghazi's computer would lose its value if Belghazi died before Delilah accessed it.

I looked at her and said, "Even if I needed your help, and I don't, why would I trust you? Once you've gotten what you wanted from the computer, you'd just walk away."

She shrugged. "But that's your worst case, isn't it? You wait a few days and then I'm out of your way. Your best case, though, is that I stick around to help you. And I'll tell you why you can believe me. Because it would be very much to our advantage if, after we acquire what we need from his computer, Belghazi were to expire naturally. As opposed to . . . violently."

"You'd have to be pretty confident that I could make that happen."

She shrugged again. "Your behavior in his suite tells me that you intend for it to happen that way. And if you are who we think you are, we're also confident that you have the capability."

I raised my eyebrows.

"You were right, I had my people run a background check on you," she went on. "I didn't have too much for them to go on: Asian male, about fifty, American-accented English, adept at close-quarters combat, good with surreptitious entry, very cool under pressure."

"Sounds like something you came across in the personals," I said.

She ignored me. "And probably intending to put Belghazi to sleep in a way that would look natural."

"Any response?" I asked, my tone mild.

"We had nothing specific in our files," she said, "but we did come up with some interesting information from open sources, primarily *Forbes* magazine. A series of articles written by a reporter named Franklin Bulfinch, who died not so long ago in Tokyo. His articles suggested that there is an assassin at work in Japan, an assassin expert at making murder look like anything but." She paused, looking at me. "I think we may be dealing with this man."

Whoever they were, they were good, no doubt about it. I liked the way they used open sources. Your typical intelligence service suffers from the belief that if it's not stamped Top Secret and not nestled between the service's own mauve-hued folders, it's not worth considering. But I've been privy to some of the secret stuff, as well as to the work of the Bulfinches of the world. I know the spooks would learn more reading *Forbes* and *The Economist* than the magazines would learn from perusing "intelligence assessments."

"How long are we talking about?" I asked.

"Not long. Two days, maybe three."

"How do you know that?"

"I can't tell you that. But we know." She took a sip of *caipirinha.* "Just trust me."

I laughed.

She retracted her head in mock indignation. "But I trusted you. I got you out of his suite, didn't I?"

"When you thought I had a videotape. That's not trust, it's duress."

She smiled, her eyes alight with humor. "You need me to get to him, and you can't get to him while I'm in the way. This means you'll have to trust me. Why use an ugly word like 'duress'?"

I laughed again. What she said was true. I didn't have a lot of attractive alternatives. I would have to try "trusting" her.

Because direct means of contact would be unacceptably dangerous, we agreed that, if I needed to see her, I would place a small, colored sticker just under the buttons in the Oriental's four elevators. I had seen the stickers in a local stationery store. The elevator placement would enable me to leave the mark in private, would give Delilah the opportunity to check for it several times a day without going out of her way or otherwise behaving unusually, and would be so small and discreetly placed that anyone who didn't know what to look for could be expected to take no notice. She would do the same if she needed to see me. The meeting place would be the Mandarin Oriental casino; the time, evening, when Belghazi liked to gamble at the Lisboa.

"I don't see how Belghazi would hear that we left the casino together tonight," she said. "But just in case, we'll use the original story, that I told you I was going to the Lisboa and you asked if we could share a taxi. There are taxis lined up in front of the Oriental all evening, so even if he were inclined to do so, he would never be able to check the story."

"There are cameras all over the Lisboa casino," I said,

wanting to see how many moves ahead she was thinking. "There won't be a record of your having gone in
tonight."

"I know. But he has no access to those security tapes.
Even if he did, I would tell him that I wanted to get rid
of you because you seemed a little too interested, so I
went shopping in the hotel arcade, instead. There are no
cameras there."

"What about me?" I asked, already knowing the answer but enjoying her thoroughness.

She shrugged. "You're Asian, much harder to pick out
of the crowd, so it would be harder to be certain that
you weren't there tonight. And even if they could be
certain, how would I know why you had decided not to
go in? Maybe you hadn't wanted to go to the Lisboa
tonight at all, you were only trying to pick me up.
Maybe you were discouraged when I brushed you off,
and left."

I took a long swallow from my glass. "Which would
also explain our failure to acknowledge each other if we
happen to pass each other in, say, the Mandarin lobby.
Ordinarily people who've shared some time at the baccarat table and a cab afterward wouldn't act like
strangers afterward."

She smiled, apparently pleased that I was keeping up
with her. "Maybe you were unhappy about the results of
our meeting and are in a bit of a sulk?"

"Maybe. But you can't count on any of this. Even
when there's a reasonable explanation for something,
people can overlook it and go straight to assuming the
worst."

"Of course. But again, the overwhelming odds are
that no one noticed us and no one cares. The rest is just
backup."

I nodded, impressed. I knew her explanations would go even deeper, positioning her for increasingly remote possibilities. Belghazi learns she was seen in this bar with me; she tells him she was bored because he was gone so much. When I invited her, she came along, then thought better of it. She had lied to him because she didn't want him to be jealous or to think poorly of her. Confessing to some lesser offense to obscure the commission of the actual crime.

Yeah, she was good. The best I'd come across in a long time.

"I'll leave first," she said, getting up. She didn't need to explain. We didn't want to be seen together. She started to open her purse.

"Just go," I told her. "I'll take care of it."

She cocked an eyebrow. "Our first date?" She said it only with that attractively wry humor, not playing the coquette.

I smiled at her. "Maybe you better pay up after all. I don't want you getting the wrong idea."

She looked at me for a moment, as though considering whether to say something. But in the end she only smiled, then turned and left. I imagined her checking the street through the windows downstairs before moving through the door.

I finished my *caipirinha*. The couples on the couches continued in their embraces, their soft laughter just reaching me above the music from the ground floor.

I paid the bill and left. I wondered if Keiko would be waiting for me back at the room.

Strangely enough, I hoped the answer was no.

5

KEIKO AND I spent the next two days doing the things tourists do. We visited Coloane Village and Taipu. We went to the top of the Macau Tower. We toured Portuguese churches and national museums. We gambled in the Floating Casino. Keiko seemed to enjoy herself, although she was a pro and I couldn't really know. For me, it all felt like waiting.

I found myself wishing I didn't need the cover Keiko provided. She was a sweet girl, but much as I enjoyed her body I had tired of her company. More important, I didn't like that Belghazi and Delilah both knew that I was staying at the Mandarin. The risk was manageable, of course: Belghazi had no way of knowing that I presented a threat, and Delilah had reason to refrain from moving against me, at least for the time being. The risk was also necessary: if Belghazi somehow learned that I had checked out of the hotel but saw me again in Macau, it would look strange to him, suspicious. I knew he was attuned to such discrepancies. So I had to stay put, and simply stay extra alert to my surroundings.

Twice we took the TurboJet ferry to Hong Kong. I gave Keiko money to indulge herself in the island's many boutiques, a small salve for what I recognized as my recent remoteness. While she shopped, I wandered, observing, imitating, practicing the Hong Kong persona that helped me blend here and in Macau: the walk, the posture, the clothes, the expression. I bought a pair of nonprescription eyeglasses, a wireless, sleek-looking design that you see everywhere in Hong Kong and only rarely in Japan. I picked up one of the utilitarian briefcases that so many Hong Kong men seem to carry at all times, part of the local culture, I think, being comprised of a constant readiness to do business. I bought clothes in local stores. I was confident that, as long as I didn't open my mouth, no one would make me as anything but part of the indigenous population.

At the outset of the second of these Hong Kong excursions, I noticed an Arab standing in the lobby of the Macau Mandarin Oriental as we moved through it. He was new, not one of Belghazi's bodyguards. I noted his presence and position, but of course gave no sign that he had even registered in my consciousness. He, however, was not similarly discreet. In the instant in which my gaze moved over his face, I saw that he was looking at me intently, almost in concentration. The way a guy might look, in a more innocent setting, at someone he thought but wasn't entirely sure was a celebrity, so as not to appear foolish asking the wrong person for an autograph. In my world, this look is more commonly seen on the face of the "pedestrian" who peers through the windshield of a car driving through a known checkpoint, his brow furrowed, his eyes hard, his head now nodding slightly in unconscious reflection of the pleasure of recognition, who then radios his compatriots fifty meters beyond that it's time to move in for the kidnapping, or to open up with their AKs, or to detonate the bomb they've placed along the road.

General security for Belghazi, maybe. Watching hotel comings and goings, looking for something out of place, someone suspicious.

But my gut wouldn't buy that. And I don't trust anything more than I trust that feeling in my gut.

Delilah, I thought. I felt hot anger surging up from my stomach. I don't get suckered often, but she had suckered me. Lulled me into thinking that our interests could be aligned.

But they *were* aligned, that was the thing. What she had told me made sense. Moving against me, rather than trusting me to wait as I had told her I would, was unnecessarily risky. And even if she had decided to take the risk, she would know not to be so obvious. A non-Asian, standing in the lobby of the hotel, getting all squinty-eyed and flushed with excitement at my appearance? Not on her team. She was good, and she knew I was good. She wouldn't have used such a soft target approach.

But I might have been missing something. I couldn't be sure.

Drop it. Work the problem at hand.

Okay. Keiko and I kept moving, smiling and talking, just a couple of happy tourists, wandering around in a daze. I might have turned around and taken us out through the back entrance. But that would have interfered with the spotter's sense that I was clueless, and that sense might offer some small advantage later. Besides, I didn't think they'd move against me in a public place, if a move was what this was about. Macau is a peninsula, after all, and they'd want a venue that would enable them to slip away. So I stayed with the front entrance, where we caught a taxi for the brief ride to the Macau Ferry Terminal.

We arrived and got out of the cab. I didn't see anything in front of the building that set off my radar. The lobby of the first floor, likewise. But the place to pick someone up here would be the second floor, where passengers boarded. If you wanted to know whether someone was traveling to Hong Kong, the departure lounge would be the only real choke point in the complex.

And that's exactly where I saw the second guy, another Arab, this one a bearded giant with a linebacker's physique. He was wearing an expensive-looking jacket and shades and standing off to the side of one of the ATMs in the lobby, the machine offering both cover for action and a clear view of the departure area. Again, I offered no sign that I had noticed anything out of the ordinary.

The Arabs stuck out sufficiently to make me wonder for a moment whether they might have been deliberate distractions—decoys to mask the other, in this case Asian, players. Possible, I decided, but not likely. No one else was setting off my radar. And flying all these guys in from wherever would have been an expensive and time-consuming way to gain the marginal advantage of distraction they might offer. No, I sensed instead that the momentary problem I faced was probably no deeper than what was immediately apparent. Sure, these guys knew they stuck out. They just didn't give me enough credit to understand that I would find their sticking out highly relevant, and to act appropriately. They didn't grasp the critical fact of how I would interpret their relative conspicuousness. Shame on them.

The ferry ride to Hong Kong lasted an hour. There were no Middle Eastern types on board, or anyone else who rubbed me the wrong way.

We presented our passports to the customs authorities at the Shun Tak terminal in Hong Kong, then moved into the main lobby outside the arrivals gate.

I spotted the third one immediately. Another Arab, long hair, mustache, navy suit, white shirt open at the collar, stylish-looking pair of shades. Unlike the majority of the people waiting here to greet passengers from Macau, who were standing right in front of the arrivals exit, he was leaning casually against the railing at the back of the open-air center of the lobby. Apparently, my new friend was afraid to get too close, afraid he'd get spotted. In trying to find a less conspicuous position, though, he'd only made himself stand out more.

We took the down escalator at the front of the lobby. On the floor below, we had to walk around to the opposite side, then turn one hundred eighty degrees to catch the next escalator down. As we made the turn, I saw our pursuer, who I now thought of as Sunglasses, riding the escalator we had just used.

I paused to take a look in the window of a cigar store before catching the second escalator down. I moved so that Keiko was facing me, her back to the window.

"Keiko," I said in Japanese, "do me a favor. Take a look behind us. Just glance around, okay? Don't let your eyes linger on any one person. Tell me what you see."

She looked past me and shrugged. "I don't know, lots of people. What am I supposed to be looking for?"

"Do you see a foreigner? Arabic-looking guy? Don't stare, just take a quick peek, then look at other people, look at the stores. You're just bored waiting for me to finish window-shopping and you're looking around, okay?"

"What's going on?" she asked, and I heard some concern in her voice.

I shook my head and smiled. "Nothing to worry about." I stepped into her field of vision to make her stop scoping the lobby, then placed my hand on her lower back and started moving her along with the pressure of my palm. "Okay, don't look back. Just tell me what you saw."

"There was an Arab man in a suit."

"What was he doing?"

"Talking on a cell phone. I think he was watching us, but he looked away when he saw me looking around. Do you know him?"

"Sort of. It's a little hard to explain."

What did Ian Fleming say? Once is happenstance, twice is coincidence, three times is enemy action. And I don't believe in waiting for even that much evidence. It was past time to act.

We caught a cab on the ground floor. I held the door as Keiko got in. Out of my peripheral vision I saw our friend loitering in front of a 7-Eleven a few meters from the taxi stand. I knew that, as soon as I was in and the door had closed behind me, he would be getting a cab of his own.

I used my dental mirror as we pulled away and saw that I had been right. Keiko watched me but didn't say anything. I wondered what she was thinking. The driver didn't seem to notice. He was absorbed in the variety show he had on the radio, the announcer's voice frantic with artificial hilarity.

I had the driver take us to the Citibank next to the Central MTR subway station. One of my alter egos keeps a savings account with Citi. I carry his ATM card whenever I go out.

We went inside the bank, and Keiko waited while I withdrew fifty thousand Hong Kong dollars—about seven thousand U.S. The amount was over the ATM limit and I had to take care of it at the teller window.

The clerk put the money in an envelope. I thanked him and walked over to Keiko.

"How about some shopping?" I asked her, showing her the bulging envelope. We were surrounded by Hermès, Prada, Tiffany, Vuitton, and others that I knew she craved. "I'd like to buy you some new things, if you want."

She smiled and her eyes lit up. *"Hontou?"* she said. Really? Probably she was glad that whatever that weirdness with the Arab guy was seemed to be over.

I walked us to the Marks & Spencer up the street, a destination that interested me less because of the store's wares than because of its design. The front was all plate glass, and offered a clear view of the street outside. Keiko and I browsed among the silk and cashmere, and I watched Sunglasses and two recently arrived companions setting up outside, two in front of the HSBC bank, the other in front of a Folli Follie jewelry store.

The way they were assembling, I was getting the feeling that they were no longer just in "following" mode. If they had been, they wouldn't have positioned themselves so closely together—a configuration that tends to be counterproductive for surveillance, but has certain advantages for a hit. They were getting ready, ready to move, and they wanted their forces in place, concentrated, good to go when the moment was right.

All right, time for me to head out. Alone.

I walked over to Keiko and took her gently by the arm.

"Keiko, listen to me carefully. Something bad is going on. I'll tell you what you need to know to get out of it."

She shook her head slightly as if to clear it. "I'm sorry?"

"There are some men following me. The Arab with the cell phone is one of them. They intend to do me harm. If you're with me, they'll harm you, too."

She gave me a hesitant smile, as though hoping I was going to smile back and tell her the whole thing was a joke. "I'm sorry," she said, "I don't . . . I don't understand." The smile widened for a second, then faltered.

"I know you don't, and I don't have time to explain. Here, take this." I handed her the envelope. "There's enough in there to get you back to Japan, and then some. You've got your passport. Get to the airport and go."

"Are you . . . is it that you're not happy with me?" she asked, still thinking like a professional. But of her profession, not of mine.

"I've been very happy with you. Look at me. What I'm telling you is the truth. You need to get away from here now if you don't want to get hurt. It's me they're after. They don't care about you." Before she could ask any more questions, I added, "Here's what you need to do. Stay put for ten minutes. I'm going to leave and those men will follow me. After ten minutes, you leave, too. Go into one of the women's stores nearby. Tell them you're being hassled by a guy and want to lose him. He's following you, waiting for you outside. They'll let you out the back, which the men won't be expecting. If it doesn't work at the first one, try another."

"I don't—"

"Just listen. Use cabs. Go into stores that men don't visit—lingerie, things like that. That'll make it harder to follow you because I don't think these guys work with women. Go in the front and out the back. Take a lot of elevators. It's hard to stay with someone in an elevator without getting spotted. Stay in public places."

She shook her head. "Why would . . . I don't—"

"I don't think anyone will follow you. You don't matter to them. But I want to make sure, all right? I don't want to take chances. When you know you're alone, get to the airport and leave Hong Kong on the first flight you can get. Then go to Japan. Go home. You'll be safe there."

She shook her head again. "I have . . . I have things at the hotel. I can't just go."

"If you go back to the hotel, they'll pick you up again and follow you in the hope that you'll lead them to me."

"But—"

"Your things aren't worth dying over, Keiko. Are they?"

Her eyes widened.

"Are they?" I asked, again.

She shook her head. In agreement or disbelief, I couldn't tell.

I wanted to go, but she needed to hear one more thing. "Keiko," I said, looking at her closely, "in a few minutes, certainly in an hour, this conversation will start to seem unreal. You'll convince yourself that I was making this all up, trying to get rid of you, something like that. You'll be tempted to go back to the Mandarin to try to find me. I won't be there. I can't go back any more than you can. You seem like a smart girl and you've got a lot of good things ahead of you. Don't be stupid today. This isn't a game."

I turned and left. I'd done all I could do. She would either act tactically or she wouldn't.

I headed for the MTR subway's Central Station. I didn't know if they were armed, and the way they were configured around me I couldn't be confident of dropping all three and getting away clean. Also, there were a number of uniformed policemen in the area. The police presence would likely inhibit my friends for the moment, as it was inhibiting me. I decided to take them sightseeing someplace, somewhere casual where we could all let our hair down.

This would be tricky. From the way they had been following us, my gut told me they were waiting for the right venue to act. Someplace unusually empty, or someplace extremely crowded. Someplace that would give them a chance to act and then get away without being stopped, or even remembered by witnesses. Until they found that place, I could expect them to continue to refrain. If they thought they were losing me, though, or if they sensed that I was playing with them in some way, they might decide the hell with it and do something precipitous.

I hoped I was right about them. It was hard to be sure. I was used to dealing with western intelligence services and *yakuza,* not potential fanatics spawned by the culture that had once invented arithmetic but whose most notable recent contribution to world civilization was the suicide bomber.

I took the escalator down to the MTR station, maintaining a brisk pace to make it harder for them to overtake me in case I had been wrong about where they might make their move. The station was filled with surveillance cameras, and for once I actually welcomed their presence. Unless Larry, Moe, and Achmed wanted whatever they had in mind to be captured on video, they would have to wait a little longer. And a little longer was all I needed.

That is, if they even noticed the cameras, of course. Assuming your enemy is intelligent can be as dangerous as assuming he's stupid.

A Tsuen Wan–bound train pulled in and I got on it. My friends entered the same car on the other end. I'd been right, at least so far. They were hanging back, not yet wanting to get too close, not yet realizing that I'd already spotted them.

I decided to take them to Sham Shui Po, a colorful

community in West Kowloon, one of the many areas I had spent some time getting to know while setting up for Belghazi, contingency planning for circumstances like the one at hand. On a more auspicious occasion, we might have been hoping to take in the two-thousand-year-old Lei Cheng Uk Han Tomb or the century-old Tin Hau Temple. Or bargain hunting on Cheung Sha Wan Road, the area's "Fashion Street," where garment manufacturers sell directly to the public. Or hunting for secondhand electronic goods and pirated CDs and DVDs in the area's outdoor flea markets. But today I wanted to offer them something a little more special.

I stepped off the train at Sham Shui Po station, moved through the turnstiles, and took the C1 exit to the street. The teeming scene in front of the station made familiar Tokyo look deserted by comparison. The street stretching out before me between rows of crumbling low-rises and slumped office buildings looked like a river of people gushing through a ravine. Cars jerked through congested intersections, pedestrians flowing around them like T-cells attacking a virus. Laundry and air-conditioning units hung from soot-colored windows, high-tension wires sagged across overhead. Signs in Chinese characters leered from buildings like lichens clinging to trees, their paint gone to rust, colors faded to gray. Here was an emaciated, shirtless man, asleep or unconscious in a lawn chair; there was a plumper specimen, leaning against a lamppost, clipping his fingernails with supreme nonchalance. An indistinct cacophony blanketed the area like fog: people shouting into cell phones, street stall hawkers exhorting potential customers, cars and horns and jackhammers. A couple of pigeons soared from one rooftop to another, flapping their wings in seeming amusement at the seething mass below.

My friends would be trying to take all this in, process it, decide what it meant for them and for their chances of getting away with what they were here to do. It would take them a few minutes to work all that out. They didn't know that a few minutes was all they had left.

I browsed the open-air stalls and popped in and out of a few electronics stores, checking unobtrusively as I did so to ensure that my friends weren't getting too close, that they hadn't yet made up their minds. To them, it would look like I had left Keiko shopping for clothes while I indulged a taste for computer gadgets and pirated software. And I did make a couple of purchases as I browsed. A pair of athletic socks—thick, knee-length, light gray. A plain navy baseball cap. And a dozen Duracell look-alike D-cell batteries. All for about twenty Hong Kong dollars. I smiled at the bargains to be had in Sham Shui Po.

While we walked, I shoved the baseball cap in a back pocket. Then, working in front of my waist and mostly by feel to ensure that my pursuers wouldn't see, I pushed my left hand into one of the socks and pulled the other sock over it, doubling them up. I slipped eight of the batteries inside, discarding the rest in a trashcan, and tied off the sock just above the batteries to make sure they would stay clumped together. I wrapped the open end of the sock around my right hand twice like a bandage, using three fingers to secure it and holding the weighted end between my thumb and forefinger. As I turned a corner, I released the weighted end. It dropped about twenty centimeters, stopping with a heavy bounce as the batteries reached the limit of the material's extension. I looped the material around my right hand until the weighted end nestled into my palm, then hooked my thumbs into my front pockets as I walked, concealing the improvised flail from the men behind me.

I took them in a counterclockwise arc that ended at a three-story food market half a kilometer from the station entrance. I went inside, checking as I did so to make sure that they were still an appropriate distance behind me. I had no trouble picking them out of the crowd. They were the only non-Asians around.

Which was a problem for them, but not an insurmountable one. The market was so massively crowded and clamorous that, if they could get close, they could put a knife in a kidney or a silenced bullet through my spine without anyone noticing when it happened or remembering it afterward. If I were in their shoes, this was the place I'd make my move.

I moved up one of the alleys of food stalls toward the escalators I knew were at the other end. Meat hung from hooks around me, the air sharp with the smell of fresh blood. Butchered eels writhed on bamboo serving plates, their severed halves twitching independently. Mouths on disembodied fish heads slowly opened and closed, the gills behind them rippling, trying still to draw breath. Hawkers gestured and shouted and coaxed. Masses of shrimp and crabs and frogs twitched in wire baskets. A severed goat's head twirled from a hook, its teeth clenched in final rictus, its dead eyes staring past the tumult at some bleak and final horizon.

I broke free of the thick crowd just before I reached the escalator. I took it two steps at a time, dodging past the stationary riders, knowing the men behind me would read my sudden acceleration as a sign that I'd made them and was trying to escape. As soon as they cleared the crowds as I had, they would pursue. And if they caught me, they wouldn't take another chance. They would act.

At the top of the escalator, I looked back. There they

were, at the bottom, trying to squeeze past the people in their way. Perfect.

There was a double set of green doors just ahead and on the left. They were propped open; beyond them was a loading area in front of a freight elevator. At the top of the escalator I shot ahead, out of the field of vision of the men behind me, and ducked left into the loading area. I moved left again and hugged the wall, wedged partly behind one of the open doors, looking out through the gap at the hinged end. From here I would see them as they moved past. I tested the door and found it satisfyingly mobile and heavy. If they saw me and tried to move inside, I'd slam the door into them and attack with the flail as best I could. But it would be better if they went past me entirely.

They did. I watched them moving through the gap in the door. When the last had gone by, I took three deep breaths, giving them another couple of seconds.

I moved out. Adrenaline flowed through my gut and limbs. There they were, stopped where the corridor ended in a "T," looking left and right, trying to make out which way I had gone among the thick crowds of shoppers to both sides. They were clustered up tight, the guy in the middle slightly ahead of the other two. Probably they thought proximity would afford them safety in numbers. In fact, they were turning themselves into a single target.

When I was six meters away, the one in the center and slightly ahead of the other two started to turn. Maybe to consult; maybe, if he had any sense, to check his back. I increased my pace, hurrying now, needing to close the distance before he turned and saw that his understanding of who was hunting and who was hunted had become suddenly and fatally inaccurate.

When I was four meters out, the lead guy completed his turn. He started to say something to one of his comrades. Then his eyes shifted to me. His head froze. His eyes widened. His mouth started to open.

Three meters. I felt a fresh adrenaline dump in my torso, my limbs.

His partners must have seen his face. Their shoulders tensed, their heads began to turn.

Two meters. The guy to my right was closest. He was turning to his left, toward whatever had made his partner start to bug out. I saw the left side of his face as he came around, slowly, everything moving slowly through my adrenalized vision.

One meter. I stepped in with my left foot, bringing my left arm up across my body, partly as defense, partly as counterbalance. I let my right hand drift back, the flail uncoiling on the way, then whipped my arm around, the palm side of my fist up, my elbow leading the way, my hips pivoting in as though I was doing a one-armed warm-up with a baseball bat. The weighted end sailed around and cracked into the back of his skull with a beautiful bass note thud. For a split instant, his body completely relaxed but he stayed upright—he was out on his feet. Then he started to slide down to the ground.

The flail swung past him, my body coiling counterclockwise with the continued momentum of the blow, the flail wrapping itself halfway around my thigh. The guy to my left had now completed his turn. I saw him look at me, the universal expression for "oh shit" moving across his face, his right hand going for the inside of his jacket. Too late. I snapped my hips to the right and backhanded the flail around. He saw it coming, but was too focused on deploying his weapon and couldn't concentrate on getting out of the way. It caught him in the side of the neck—not as solid a shot as his buddy had received but good enough for my purposes. I saw his eyes lose focus and knew I'd have at least a couple seconds before he was back in the game.

The third guy was smarter, and had more time and space to react. While I was dealing with the other two, he had stepped back and gotten himself out of swinging range. He was groping inside his jacket now, his eyes wide, his movements frantic. The flail was passing between us, back to my right side. I saw him pulling something out of the jacket with his right hand. I let the flail's momentum bring it around and under, releasing my grip at the last instant and sending the whole thing sailing toward him like a softball pitch aimed at the batter. He saw it coming and jerked partly out of the way, but it caught him in the shoulder. He stumbled and managed to get out a silenced pistol, a big one, trying at the same time to regain his balance. But his motor skills were suffering from a large and probably unfamiliar dose of adrenaline, and the long silencer made for an equally long draw. He bobbled the gun, and in that second I was on him.

I caught the gun in my left hand and used my right foot to blast his legs out from under him in *deashi-barai,* a side foot sweep that I had performed tens of thousands of times in my quarter century at the Kodokan. I went down with him, keeping my weight over his chest, increasing the impact as he slammed into the floor. I felt the gun go off as we hit the ground, heard the *pffft* of the silenced report and a crack as the round tore into the wall behind me. Keeping control of the gun, making sure it was pointed anywhere but at me, I rose up to create an inch of space between our bodies, spun my left leg over and past his head, and dropped back in *juji-gatame,* a cross-body armlock. I took the gun from him and broke his elbow with a single sharp jerk.

The second guy had now recovered enough to get a gun out. But, like his partner, he was adrenalized and having trouble with fine motor movements. His hand was shaking and he hesitated, perhaps realizing that if he pulled the trigger he might hit his partner, over whose torso my legs were crossed and whose ruined right arm was pulled tight across my chest.

I straightened my right arm and focused on the front sight, placing it on the second guy's torso, center mass. The gun was a Glock 21 in .45 caliber. Healthy stopping power. I willed myself to slow it down, make it count.

The guy under me jerked and my aim wavered. *Fuck.* I squeezed my legs in tighter and leaned back closer to the floor, trying to offer the second guy a reduced profile. I knew from experience that bullets tend to skim close to the ground rather than bounce off it. The guy under me would function as a human sandbag for any shots that hit the deck short of our position.

The second guy moved the gun, trying to track me, the movements overlarge and shaking. Then, maybe because he saw the cool bead I was drawing on him, his nerve broke. He started shooting in a spray-and-pray pattern, his eyes closed, his body hunching forward involuntarily. *Pffft. Pffft. Pffft.* Small clouds of dust kicked up along the concrete around me, puffing out lazily in my adrenalized slow-motion vision. I heard the sounds of ricochets. Someone screamed.

Slow. Aim. Breathe. . . .

I double-tapped the trigger. The first round caught him in the shoulder and spun him around. The second missed, going off into the wall near the ceiling. I compensated and fired again. This time I nailed him in the back near the spine and dropped him to the floor.

I lurched to my feet and moved toward him. Around us, people were running from the scene, pushing up against the mass of other shoppers. The immediate area was suddenly empty.

I walked up to the one I had just dropped. He was on his stomach, writhing, groaning something unintelligible. I shot him in the back of the head.

The first one I'd hit with the flail was flat on his back, his legs splayed back under him, seemingly unconscious. I shot him in the forehead.

I turned to the last one. He was on his ass, scrambling away from me on his feet and good arm. His face was green with pain and terror. I shot him in the chest and he collapsed to the ground, his legs still kicking. I took three long steps forward and shot him again, in the forehead. His head rocketed back and he was still.

I looked around. Pandemonium now. Screams and shouting and panic.

I needed to get the hell out. But I also needed information. Under other circumstances, I would have tried to keep one of them alive for questioning, but in a public place like this that course was impossible.

I scooped up the flail and shoved it into one of the outer pockets of the navy blazer I was wearing. I was glad I'd thought to tie the thing off—if I hadn't, the batteries might have rolled all over the place after I'd thrown it, with my fingerprints on them.

I walked over to the last guy I'd shot and opened his jacket. Cashmere. The label under the breast pocket proclaimed Brioni. This guy was wearing three or four thousand bucks on his back. The shirt, admittedly not shown to its best advantage soaked in blood, looked similarly fine. His neck was adorned with a nice gold chain. His pockets, though, were empty. Nothing but a wad of Hong Kong dollars and a packet of fucking breath mints. Smart, not carrying ID. If they get pinched, they dummy up, call the embassy, maybe, get bailed out. But which embassy? Whose?

I went to the next guy, knowing this was taking too long, hating the risk. Another Brioni jacket, along with a gold Jaeger-LeCoultre watch. But that was all.

The third guy had a cell phone clipped to his belt. Yeah, that was him, the one Keiko and I had passed at Shun Tak terminal. Sunglasses. I pulled the phone free and opened his jacket. More Brioni. More empty pockets, save for the shades from which he had derived his short-lived nickname. The pants pockets were empty, too.

I looked up, then behind me. The corridors were packed with fleeing people. A stampede panic tends to feed on itself long after the originating cause is gone. Probably most of these people didn't even know what they were running from, hadn't seen or heard anything. My escape routes weren't going to open up anytime soon.

Elevator, I thought. I ducked into the loading area and pressed the down button with a knuckle. I stood there for an agonizingly long time, feeling exposed, until the damn thing finally arrived. The doors opened. I stepped inside, hit the ground floor and "close" buttons. The doors slid shut and the elevator lurched downward.

I pulled the baseball cap out of my pocket and jammed it down onto my head. I pocketed the cell phone, slid the gun into my waistband, and shrugged off the blazer, exposing the white shirt underneath. In the immediate aftermath, witnesses would remember only gross details—color of the clothes, presence of a necktie, that sort of thing. The new hat and disappeared jacket would be enough to get me out of here. I pulled out the shirttails and let them fall over the gun.

The elevator doors opened. It was calmer down here, but there was an unusual agitation in the crowd and it was clear that something had happened. I moved down one of the corridors, easing past shoppers who were looking behind me, searching to see what was going on back there. My pace was deliberate but not attention-getting. I kept my face down and didn't meet anyone's eyes.

By the time I had reached the entrance where we had first come in, the collective rhythm of the people around me was normal, just food shoppers absorbed in the serious business of picking out the freshest fish or the most delectable cut of meat. I moved past them and into the street.

I folded the jacket and slipped the gun inside it, wiping it down as I walked, making sure I covered all the surfaces. I did it by feel. Barrel. Trigger guard. Trigger. Butt.

Fingerprints were only part of the problem, of course. When you're stressed, you sweat. Sweat contains DNA. Likewise for microscopic dead skin cells, which, like sweat, can adhere to metal. If you're unlucky enough to get picked up as a suspect, it's inconvenient to have to explain why your DNA is all over the murder weapon. The dead men's clothes, which I had touched while searching them, were less of a problem. They wouldn't take prints, and I probably hadn't handled them sufficiently to leave a material amount of sweat or skin cells behind.

I turned into an alley choked with overflowing plastic garbage containers. An aluminum leader ran down the side of one of the alley walls and into an open drain beneath. I moved the leader out of the way and dropped the gun into the drain, seeing a satisfying splash as I did so. I checked behind me—all clear. I committed the batteries to the same final resting place, wiping each with the socks as I did so, then moved the leader back into position and walked on. Unlikely that the gun or batteries would ever be discovered where I had left them. Even if they were found, the water would probably wash away any trace DNA. And even if DNA were present, they'd need me in custody as a suspect to get a match. A good, layered defense.

There was still a potential problem with witnesses, of course. I didn't stick out here the way the Arabs had, but I didn't exactly fit in, either. It's hard to explain the clues, but they would be enough for the Sham Shui Po locals to spot, and perhaps to remember. My clothes were wrong, for one thing. I had been dressed for a day of lunch and shopping in Central, not for the hivelike back alleys of my current environs. The locals here were dressed more casually. And what they were wearing fit differently, usually not that well. Like the area itself, the colors on their clothes were slightly dulled. These people weren't getting their delicates dry cleaned, starched, and returned on hangers. They weren't laundering their things in Tide with Bleach and Extra Stain Removing Agents and Advanced Whiteners, or drying them on the gentle cycle in microprocessor-controlled driers. They hung their things on lines, where they would evaporate into the polluted air around. These and other differences would tell. Whether witnesses would be able to articulate them, I couldn't say. So I needed to take every possible measure to ensure that it wouldn't matter if they could.

I turned a corner, balled up the jacket, and stuffed it deep into a ripe pile of refuse in a metal container. I unbuttoned the shirt I was wearing and gave it a similar burial. I was now wearing only pants and a tee-shirt, and looked a little more at home.

I made a few aggressive moves to ensure that I wasn't being followed, then took the MTR to Mong Kok, where I found a drugstore. I bought soap, rubbing alcohol, hair gel, and a comb. Next stop, a public restroom, reeking of what might have been decades-old urine, where I shit-canned the baseball cap and changed my appearance a little more by slicking my hair. I used the alcohol and soap to remove any traces of gunpowder residue that could show up on my hands under UV light. By the time I walked out of the lavatory, I was starting to feel like I had things reasonably well covered.

I bought a cheap shirt from a street vendor, then found a coffee shop where I could spend a few minutes collecting myself. I ordered a tapioca tea and took a seat at an empty table.

My first reaction, as always, was a giddy elation. I might have died, but didn't, I was still here. Even if you've been through numerous deadly encounters, in the aftermath you want to laugh out loud, or jump around, shout, do *something* to proclaim your aliveness. With an effort, I maintained a placid exterior and waited for these familiar urges to pass. When they had, I reviewed the steps I had just taken to erase the con-nection between myself and the dead Arabs, and found them satisfactory. And then I began to think ahead.

Three down. That was good. Whoever was coming after me, I had just significantly degraded their forces, degraded their ability and perhaps also their will to fight. The paymasters must not have had ready access to local resources. If they had, they wouldn't have sent a bunch of obvious out-of-towners. Now, when word got back that the last three guys who signed up for this particular mission had all wound up extremely dead as a result, they might have a harder time recruiting new volunteers.

My satisfaction wasn't solely professional, of course. The fuckers had been trying to kill me.

I took out the cell phone. Christ, I'd forgotten to turn it off while I moved. Shame on me. Getting sloppy. All right, let's see if I'd just created a problem for myself.

The unit was an Ericsson, the T230. It had a SIM card, meaning it was a GSM model, usable pretty much everywhere but Japan and Korea, which employ a unique cell phone standard. I examined it for transmitters and didn't find any. I thought for a minute. Did the T230 incorporate emergency services location technology? I tend to read almost compulsively to stay on top of such developments, but even so things slip through the cracks. No, the T230 wasn't that new a model. I was okay on that score, too.

Still, I knew that some intelligence services had refined their cell phone tracking capabilities to the point where they could place a live cell phone to within about twenty feet of its actual location. Any worries on that score? Probably not. Whoever was coming after me had limited local resources. I doubted they would have the contacts or expertise that tracking the phone would require.

Under the circumstances, I decided it would be worth hanging onto the unit, and leaving it powered on. It could be interesting to see who might call in.

I checked the stored numbers. The interface was in Arabic, but the functions were standardized and I was able to navigate it without a problem.

The call log was full—he hadn't thought, or hadn't had time, to purge it. I didn't see any numbers I recognized. But the guy I'd taken it from had been talking to someone when I spotted him at Shun Tak station. Unless he'd made or received ten calls in the interim, there would be a record inside the phone of the numbers he'd dialed and of those that had dialed him. I had a feeling that some of those numbers would be important.

I drank my tea and left. I took out Kanezaki's cell phone and called him from it, moving on foot as the call went through.

"*Moshi moshi,*" I heard him say.

"It's me."

"What's going on?"

"I'm concerned about something."

"What?"

"Three guys just tried to kill me in Hong Kong."

"What?"

"Three guys just tried to kill me in Hong Kong."

"I heard you. Are you serious?"

I didn't detect anything in his voice, but it was hard to tell over the phone. And he was smoother now than when I'd first met him.

"You think I make this shit up to amuse you?" I said.

There was a pause, then he asked, "Are you all right?"

"I'm fine. Just concerned."

"Are you in danger now?"

"Not from the three who were after me."

"You mean—"

"They're harmless now."

Another pause. He said, "You're concerned about how they found you."

"Good for you."

"It wasn't me."

I already half-believed that, I supposed. Otherwise, I wouldn't have warned him by calling. Or I would have conceived of the call simply as a way to lull him, to set him up. I couldn't imagine why he would have turned on me, but you never have the full picture on things like that. Circumstances change. People develop reasons where they had none before.

"Who else knew I was in Macau?" I asked. "They tracked me from there. One of them was waiting to pick me up when I arrived at Shun Tak in Hong Kong."

"I don't . . . Look, I have absolutely no reason to try to fuck you. No reason. I don't know who they were or how they got to you. But I can try to find out."

"Convince me," I said.

"Give me what you've got. Let me see what I can do."

I decided to give him a chance. I didn't see any downside. I also didn't see a good alternative.

"They look Arab to me," I said. "Maybe Saudi. They dress like they've got money. One of them was carrying a cell phone with an Arabic interface, and was using it to make or receive calls while they were following me. I'll put all the numbers from the phone's log on the bulletin board. You can run those down. They had at least one partner on Macau, probably more, and probably all of them transited Hong Kong recently. They were sloppy, they might all have arrived at the same time, maybe even on the same plane."

"That's a lot. I can work with that. You think there's a connection with our friend?"

Belghazi. There were only a few Arabs in my life, and they were all recent arrivals. Although my thinking might not go down well with the antiprofiling crowd in the U.S., it was hard not to suspect that they were all connected.

But I didn't see anything to be gained from speculating aloud. "You tell me," I said.

"I'll try."

"You need to convince me," I said again.

We'd known each other long enough for him to understand my meaning. "How do I contact you?" he asked.

"I'll check the bulletin board."

"It would be more efficient if you would just leave the cell phone on."

"I'll check the bulletin board."

He sighed. "Okay. And you can always call me at this number. Give me twelve hours. Anything else?"

"The blonde?" I asked.

"Nothing. Still working on it."

I hung up.

I found an Internet café, where I uploaded the information to the bulletin board. Then I sat for a minute, thinking.

The three guys who had come after me here in Hong Kong were obviously in touch with someone in Macau. In fact, I was pretty damn sure that the one with the cell phone, Sunglasses, had called his Macau contact to confirm that I had arrived. The guy in Macau would now be waiting for news of the operation. The bodies of his buddies had only been cooling for about an hour now. Chances were good that he wouldn't have heard yet of their tragic demise. He certainly wouldn't be expecting, and he wouldn't be prepared, to see me in Macau without first getting a heads-up from Hong Kong. And, even if he had somehow heard about the way things had turned out here, the last thing he would expect me to do would be to head straight back to the place where the ambush had obviously initiated: the Macau Mandarin Oriental.

In either case, I realized I had an opportunity to surprise someone. Which is always a nice thing to be able to do.

I headed back to Shun Tak to catch the next ferry to Macau. I tried not to think too much about what I was about to do. Charging an ambush is counterinstinctive: when your lizard brain identifies the direction the threat is coming from, it wants you to run away.

But your lizard brain doesn't always know best. It tends to focus on short-term considerations, and doesn't always adequately account for the value of unpredictability, of deception, of surprise. Of taking a short-term risk for a longer-term gain.

The hour-long ferry ride felt long. Maintaining a razor-edge readiness is exhausting, and, once the mad minute is over, the body badly wants to rest and recuperate. I tried to clear my mind, to take myself down a few levels—enough to recover, but not so much that I would be less than ready for whatever I might encounter on Macau.

With about twenty minutes to go, the cell phone rang. I looked down at it and saw that the incoming number was the same as the one last dialed. Almost certainly the Macau contact, then, checking in, wanting to know what had happened. I ignored the call.

We arrived at the Macau Ferry Terminal and I walked out into the arrivals lobby. The lobby was too crowded for me to know whether I had a welcoming committee. That was okay, though. One of the advantages of Macau is that you can access the city from the first floor of the ferry terminal—either by foot on the sidewalks, or by taxi—or you can go to the second floor and use the extensive series of causeways. If you're waiting for someone at the ferry terminal, therefore, you have to be just outside the arrivals area, ready to move out or up, depending on the route taken by your quarry. So even though I couldn't spot a pursuer yet, it would be easy for me to flush him if he was there.

I took the escalator to the second floor, where I paused in front of one of the ATMs as though withdrawing some cash—a common enough maneuver for visitors heading for the casinos. I glanced back at the escalator I had just used, and saw an Arab coming up it. The big bastard, the bearded giant I'd noticed that morning. The shades and expensive jacket looked familiar at this point. Christ, they might as well have worn uniforms. Hi, my name's Abdul, I'll be your assassin today.

They must have gotten nervous when the Hong Kong team had failed to check in, and put this guy back in position to be on the safe side. That, or he'd been waiting here all day. It didn't matter. He'd seen me. His next move would be to telephone his Macau partners, if he hadn't already. Which would be the end of the surprise I wanted to share with them all. I would have to improvise.

If he was surprised to see me, and I imagined he was, he didn't show it. He looked around, his demeanor casual, a simple tourist just arrived in Macau and taking in the wonders of the ferry terminal.

Why didn't they call me first? I knew he'd be wondering. *They were supposed to call me when he was on his way back, just as I called them to alert them that he was coming.*

Because dead people don't use phones, pal. You'll see in a minute.

I walked out onto the open-air plaza in front of the entrance to the second floor and walked a few meters toward the causeway. Then I stopped and looked behind me.

He had just come through the doors on the right side

of the plaza and was starting to raise his cell phone to his face when I turned back. When he saw me, he lowered the cell phone and stopped as though suddenly interested in the nonexistent view.

I nodded my head at him and gave a small wave of acknowledgment, the gesture communicating, *Oh there you are, good.* I started walking over.

His head turtled in a fraction and his body tensed in the internationally approved reaction to being spotted on surveillance. It's hard to describe, but it looks a little like what a gowned patient does when the doctor picks up a long instrument and advises, *This might be a little uncomfortable.* He looked around, then back to me, doing a decent imitation of someone wondering, *Huh? Was that me you were waving to? Do we know each other?*

I walked straight up to him and said in a low voice, "Good, you're here. They told me you'd be waiting on the first floor, by arrivals, but I didn't see you."

He shook his head. His lips twitched, but no sound came out.

"There's been a mistake," I said. "I'm not the guy you want."

His lips twitched some more.

Shit, I thought, *he doesn't understand you. Hadn't counted on that.*

"You speak English, right?" I said. "They told me we could use English."

"Yes, yes," he stammered. "I speak English."

I glanced quickly left and right as though suddenly nervous, then back at him, my eyes narrowed in sudden concern. "You're the right guy, right? They told me someone would be waiting for me."

"Yes, yes," he said again. "I am the right guy."

So many "yeses" in a row. We'd established the proper momentum.

A group of three Hong Kong Chinese emerged from the terminal. I watched them walk past us as though I was concerned that they might hear us, then said, "Let's talk over there." I gestured to the external wall of the terminal, where we could stand without being seen from inside the building. I walked the few steps over and waited. A moment later, he followed.

Damn, if I could maneuver him just a little more, get him to a slightly quieter place, I might even manage to interrogate him. That would be ideal, but also far riskier than the relatively straightforward approach I had in mind. I considered for a moment, then decided it wouldn't be worth it.

"From the look on your face," I said, "I'm getting the feeling that you haven't heard."

"Heard what? I'm sorry, I'm not understanding you."

The Hong Kong group was now out of earshot and still walking away. The plaza was momentarily empty.

"Yes, I can see that," I said. "All right, let's just go back to the hotel. We'll straighten everything out there."

That sounded harmless enough. His compatriots would be positioned at the hotel. They could explain to him what the hell was going on. Besides, he was half a head taller than me, and probably outweighed me by forty or fifty pounds. What did he have to worry about?

He nodded.

"Okay, let's go," I said. I moved as though to walk off toward the causeway, then turned back to him. "Good God, is that bird shit on your shoulder?" I asked, staring as though in disbelief.

"Hmm?" he said, his gaze automatically going to the spot I had indicated.

That's the trouble with wearing four-thousand-dollar cashmere jackets. You panic at the littlest things.

As he turned his face back toward me, I shot my left hand behind his neck and snapped his head forward and down. At the same instant, I swept my right arm past his neck and around it, encircling it clockwise, bringing my right forearm under his chin and catching it with my left hand. The back of his head was now pinned against my chest. I tried to arch back, but the bastard was so big and strong that I couldn't get the leverage I needed.

I felt his hands on my waist, groping, trying frantically to push me away. All the muscles of his neck had popped into sharp and cablelike relief. We struggled like that for a long couple of seconds. Twice I tried to shoot in with my hips, but that was exactly the movement he was in mortal fear of at the moment and I couldn't get past his massive arms.

Okay, change of plans. I took a long step back, jerking him forward and down. He lost tactile contact with my hips and flailed with his arms, trying desperately to reacquire me. Too late. I dropped to my back under him and arched into a throw. There was a moment of structural resistance, and it seemed that the musculature of his neck bulged out even larger. Then I felt his neck snap and his body was sailing over me, suddenly limp and lifeless.

I twisted to my right and he hit the concrete past me and to the side with a thud that felt like a small earthquake. I let go and scrambled to my feet. He was on his back, his head canted crazily to one side, his tongue protruding, the limbs twitching from some last, random surge of electrical signals to the muscles.

This time I didn't bother checking the pockets. I had a feeling I wouldn't find anything more useful than what I had already, and didn't want to take a chance on being seen with or even near the corpse.

I moved off, across the plaza and down the causeway, my heart slamming bass notes through my torso and down to my hands and feet. I breathed deeply through my nose, trying not to let my internal agitation break through to the surface, where it might be noticed and draw attention.

Someone was leaning over the railing up ahead, smoking a cigarette. As I got closer I saw who it was: the spotter from the Mandarin Oriental lobby, the one who'd gone all squinty-eyed on me that morning. He was looking past me, maybe trying to figure out what had happened to his buddy, who should have been trailing in my wake. As I got closer he turned his head back to center, just a guy hanging out on the causeway, enjoying a cigarette, taking in the scenery, watching the traffic cruising up and down the four-lane street beneath him. Thinking his biggest problem right then was finding a way to avoid having me spot him for what he was.

Thinking wrong.

I kept my head down as I approached him, acting distracted, oblivious to his existence. I'd been moving quickly and did nothing now to alter my pace. My heart was still hammering and I felt a fresh adrenaline dump moving in like rolling thunder.

When I was about a meter away from him and beyond the range of his peripheral vision, I took a deep step in, dropped into a squat just behind him, and wrapped my arms tourniquet-tight around his legs just above the knees. I felt his body go rigid, heard him suck in a breath. In my adrenalized, slow-motion vision, I logged every detail: the height of the guardrail; rust marks on the metal; chewing gum ground black into the

cement tiles from which his feet were about to fatally
separate.

I exploded up and out and launched him into the air
over the railing. His arms flailed and he shrieked as he
went airborne, a high, atavistic sound of sheer animal
panic, and I felt a spasm of terror rip through his body
as I let him go. The cigarette tumbled out of his mouth.
His limbs swam crazily, uselessly, against the air around
him. Then he was gone, below my field of vision. The
shriek continued, cut off a second later by the sound of
a resounding, dull thud twenty feet below. Tires
screeched. Another thud. Crunching sounds. More
screeching tires. Then silence.

I continued on my way to the New Yaohan department store. As the causeway curved right, the accident
scene became visible. Traffic was stopped, and a number
of people were clustered around something on the
ground. Really, they ought to make those guardrails
higher. It's dangerous.

Two people, Chinese civilians, were heading toward
me. Shit. I averted my eyes and changed my posture,
dropping my shoulders, adopting a more rolling gait,
giving them a persona to remember, a persona that
wasn't mine. I felt them looking at me closely as I
passed. They might have seen what had happened; if
they had, they would be in mild denial about it and trying to come up with some other explanation for the evidence of their senses, what the psychologists call
"cognitive dissonance" and "reality testing."

I briefly considered heading straight back to the terminal and returning to Hong Kong. Two bodies, two potential witnesses . . . the police might not be happy. But
I decided to take the chance. The bodies were of foreigners, and so unlikely to produce undue domestic

alarm. And Macau was no stranger to gangland killings, killings that the authorities had worked hard to down-play lest they inhibit the lucrative gambling tourism trade. If they could quickly rule these deaths "accidental" or otherwise act to minimize fallout, I expected they would.

I kept walking. From here I could take a variety of routes, and if anyone else was following me they'd have to be set up close by. I saw no one. I'd still watch my back, make the appropriate evasive moves to be certain, but, for a few precious minutes, I was reasonably sure that I wasn't being followed. If there was anyone left that I might ambush, they would likely be at the hotel.

Keeping my head down and my pace brisk but not attention-getting, I cut through the New Yaohan, moved down the causeway to the street, and walked the ten minutes to the Mandarin Oriental. As I reached the back entrance, the cell phone buzzed. I looked at the display, and saw one of the numbers I had seen in the phone's call log. Shit, five down, but someone was still left, checking in, wanting an update, or instructions, or just the sound of a familiar voice in an unfamiliar country.

I went inside. If they had someone else in position it would be here, the other place where they could reasonably expect to pick me up. Maybe another Arab, sitting in the spacious lobby, calling from a cell phone, waiting for a friend to show up.

I used the back entrance, checking the hot spots along the way. So far, so good.

I walked in through the café entrance. Because I hadn't seen anyone in back, I knew they weren't covering the entrances. That meant the next choke point would be the elevators. And there was only one spot where you could wait without drawing attention and watch the elevators: at the end of the café closest to the lobby. As I moved inside, that was the first spot I checked.

Delilah was sitting there, wearing a black skirt and a cream-colored silk blouse, a pot of tea and an open book on the table in front of her.

Son of a bitch, I thought. *I was right.* My first reaction, when spotting the Arab surveillance in the lobby earlier that day, had been to suspect her. I had tried to talk myself out of that. Now I realized I should have just accepted it. You don't give people the benefit of the doubt. Not in this line of work.

She glanced over and saw me coming before I'd reached her.

"I've been waiting for you all day, damn it," she said.

That brought me up short. "I'll bet you have," I said, looking around.

"Yes, I have. To tell you not to go to your room. There's someone in there."

I looked at her closely. "Yeah?"

She looked back. "You don't believe me?"

I was suddenly unsure again. Which was frustrating. Ordinarily, I know exactly what to do, and I do it.

"Maybe I do," I said. "Let me see your cell phone."

Her eyes narrowed a fraction. Then she shrugged. She reached into her purse and pulled out a Nokia 8910, the sleek titanium model.

I popped open the sliding keypad and the screen lit up. The service provider was Orange, a French company, and the interface was in French. I checked the call log. No entries—she'd purged it. No surprise there. She was smart. I turned the unit off, then back on. As it powered back up, the phone number appeared on the screen. I didn't recognize it. It wasn't one of the ones I'd seen on the unit I'd taken from the guy at Sham Shui Po.

The exercise proved nothing, though. She might have had another phone with her. I could ask for her purse, rifle through it. But then, when I didn't find anything, I'd wonder if she hadn't just left the other phone in her room, or hidden it somewhere, or whatever. I knew she was in the habit of thinking several moves ahead.

I handed the unit back to her. "Who's in my room?"

"I'm not sure. My guess is it has something to do with your reasons for being in Macau."

"If you're not sure—"

"I overheard him in the lobby of the hotel this morning. He was speaking in Arabic, so he assumed no one around could understand him."

I raised my eyebrows. "You speak Arabic?"

By way of answering, she said something suitably incomprehensible. It sounded Arabic to me.

"All right," I said. "Tell me what you overheard."

"He said he would wait in your room in case you returned unexpectedly from Hong Kong. He didn't use names, but I don't know who else they could be talking about."

I considered. It's not all that hard to get into a hotel room if you have some imagination and know what you're doing. I would have known he was in there before I entered, of course. That morning, while Keiko waited for me in the lobby, I'd taped a hair across the bottom of the doorjamb, as I do whenever possible before leaving a place where I'm staying. I'd hung the Do Not Disturb sign on the door to make sure the maids didn't spoil the setup. If the hair was broken when I returned, I'd know that someone had been in the room, and might still be there.

"Why are you warning me, then?" I asked.

She looked away for a long moment, then back at me.

"I think your cover is blown," she said. "Forget about this job. Leave Macau."

A contrivance? A way to get me out of her hair? Maybe. But if she really did have a confederate in there, warning me could easily get him killed, which your standard confederate ordinarily won't appreciate. And if the room was empty, I'd be sure to find out when I checked it, and I'd know the whole thing had been a ruse.

"It would serve your interests if I walked away from this," I said. "So you'll have to forgive me if I doubt your motives."

"I don't care what you think about my motives. I could have let you go into your room. Then you wouldn't walk away, you'd be carried out. My interests would be served in either case. So do what you want. I have to go."

She stood up and started walking toward the elevators.

"Wait a second," I said, moving with her.

She ignored me, then stopped in front of the elevators. "I don't want to be seen with you," she said. "Just go."

"Look," I started to say. I heard the ping of an arriving elevator and we both glanced over. The doors opened.

Another Arab started to come out. He saw us. He looked at my face, then to Delilah. He froze. His mouth dropped open.

He'd clearly recognized me. He'd also clearly seen that I'd been chatting with Delilah. The way he'd looked from me to her—he was connecting us.

He started to step back into the elevator. His hand reached out for the buttons.

It happened fast. I didn't think about it, didn't think about the risk. I leaped into the elevator and body-checked him into the wall. His head slammed against the wood paneling and bounced off. He got his arms up on the rebound and grabbed at me. I returned the favor, catching his shoulders with an inside grip and shooting a knee into his balls. He doubled over with a loud grunt. I stepped behind him and slipped my left arm around his neck in *hadaka-jime,* the inside of my elbow pressing up against his trachea, my biceps digging into his carotid. I put the same side hand over my right biceps and brought my right hand to the back of his head. I squeezed hard. He struggled wildly for less than three seconds, then went limp, the blood supply to his brain interrupted.

Delilah had stepped into the elevator with us. The doors were closing—she must have pressed the button. "Five," I said. "Hit five."

She did as I asked. But had she moved inside to help this guy, then hesitated when she saw that it was impossible? I wasn't sure.

As soon as the doors closed, I released the choke and hoisted his limp body onto my shoulder. If we were seen now and we played it right, someone might think I was just carrying a friend who'd passed out from too much drinking. Not an ideal scenario, but less problematic than being seen dragging the guy by his ankles with his face blue and contorted.

"That's him," she said. "The one I overhead in the lobby."

I nodded. Maybe it was true. Maybe he'd gotten antsy when no one was checking in or returning his calls, and had decided to move on.

Second floor. Third. Fourth. No stops along the way.

The doors opened on five and we filed out and started walking down the hallway. Still all clear.

I felt the guy's limbs begin to move in what I recognized as a series of myotonic twitches. It happens sometimes when someone emerges from an unconsciousness induced by blood flow interruption. I'd seen it many times training judo at the Kodokan and recognized the signs. He was waking up. *Shit.*

I leaned forward and dumped him on the ground. His arms and legs were jerking now, his eyes starting to blink.

I stood behind him and sat him up. Then I leaned over his left side until we were almost chest to chest, wrapped my right arm around his neck from front to back, grabbed my right wrist with the other hand, and arched up and back. His arms flew up, then spasmed and flopped to his sides as the cervical vertebrae separated and his neck broke.

I took hold of one of his jacket lapels and stepped in front of him. Lifting and hauling back on the lapel, I went to my knees, snaked my head under his armpit, then stood, shrugging him up by degrees until I had him up in a fireman's carry. I reached into my pants pocket and pulled out my room key. "Here," I said, flipping it to Delilah. "Five-oh-four. Open the door."

She caught it smoothly and headed off down the hallway.

I stayed with her. I wanted to see whether that hair had been disturbed. I stopped her outside the door and squinted down to see.

The hair was broken. Which didn't prove anything more than her cleared cell phone had; it simply failed to prove that she had been lying about someone being in my room.

My next thought, of course, was *bomb.* The guy goes in, plants it, gets out. No timer, because they didn't know when I was coming back. It would be rigged, to the door, a drawer, something like that. Backup in case the ambush in Hong Kong failed.

Delilah must have been thinking the same thing. That, or she was doing a good job acting. She was running her fingers lightly along the doorjamb, tracking closely with her eyes. I didn't think a device, if there was one, would be triggered to the door. First, you'd need sophistication to pull it off: mercury switches, vibration switches, a way of arming the device electronically afterward for safety. Simpler means would require time spent outside the door, where the technician could be seen. In all events, working with the door would likely mean less time and less privacy than would be offered by the many other possibilities inside.

Still, it paid to check. Triggering a device to the door would ordinarily leave some evidence in the jamb, where the bomb maker would have placed something that would close a circuit when the door was opened.

Delilah stopped, apparently satisfied, and put the key in the lock. She pushed open the door wide enough to move inside—no wider than someone who had, say, taped a mercury switch vertically to the floor behind the door would have opened it to leave. She paused for a moment, then opened it wider. We went in, looking for trip wires along the way.

The door closed behind us. I set the body down next to it and we each quickly examined the room. Mercury switches, pressure release switches, photocell switches . . . there are a lot of ways to rig a room. The main thing is to look for anything unusual, anything out of place. We checked the desk chair, the edges of every drawer, the closet doors, the minibar cabinet, the underside of the bed, the drapes, the television. Neither of us spoke. The sweep took about ten minutes.

I stopped a moment before she did. She was bending forward, her back to me, running her fingers along the edge of the bedstand drawer. The black skirt was pulled taut across her ass, the exposed back of her legs deliciously white by contrast.

She stood up and looked at me. Her brow was covered with a light sheen of perspiration. The silk of her blouse shimmered and clung in all the right places.

"That was too close," she said, shaking her head. "This has to stop."

I nodded, looking at her. I couldn't tell if the thumping in my chest was from the exertion of killing, hoisting, and carrying Elevator Boy, or from something else. My awareness of her shape, of her skin, made me think maybe it was option #2. Horniness is a common reaction of the postcombat psyche, Eros reasserting over Thanatos. If I didn't change my lifestyle soon, I might not live long. But I'd never have to worry about Viagra, either.

"No one saw us," I said, pulling myself back from the direction my body and the reptile portions of my brain wanted to go in, focusing on the situation. "And there are no cameras in the elevators or hallways."

"I know that," she said.

"All right. Tell me what you know about this."

"Nothing more than what I just told you." She inclined her head toward the figure slumped on the floor by the door. "Saudi. I could tell by his accent."

"You speak Arabic well enough to recognize regional accents?"

She shook her head at the question. "We can talk about that another time. The only thing we need to talk about now is getting you off Macau. I've had enough of you fucking up my operation."

I felt some blood drain from my face. "I'm fucking up *your* operation?" I said, my voice low. "I could as easily—"

"I was almost just seen with you," she said, her hands on her hips, her eyes hot and angry, "by someone who until I can be convinced otherwise I will assume is working for Belghazi. Do you understand what will happen to me if he comes to suspect me?"

"Look, I didn't ask you to—"

"Yes, you're right, I should have just let you walk into that man's ambush. I should have, too. You would be gone, and that's what I need."

"Why, then?" I said, thinking that maybe I'd have more luck finishing my sentences if I kept them short.

She looked at me, saying nothing.

"Why did you warn me?"

Her nostrils flared and her face flushed. "It's none of your business why I do or don't do something. I made a mistake, all right? I should have just stood aside! If I could do it over and do it differently, I would!"

She stopped herself, probably realizing that she had been raising her voice. "I want you to leave Macau," she said, more quietly.

I wondered for a moment whether her outburst had been born of frustration. Frustration that whatever she had just set up to get rid of me had failed to get the job done.

"I know how you feel," I said. "Because I want the same thing from you."

She shook her head once, quickly, and grimaced, as though what I had said was ridiculous. "We both understand the situation. We've already discussed it. Even if our positions were symmetrical before, they're not any longer. He's on to you. Even if I were to leave, and I won't, you can't finish what you came here to do."

"I don't know that."

"My God, what more proof do you need?"

I stopped for a moment and thought. She was probably right, of course. But I still hadn't heard back from Kanezaki. I might learn more from him. And maybe from her, too, if I could find a way to get her to tell me.

She wanted me to be gone. Wanted it so much that whatever had happened in the elevator might have been a bungled attempt to make it happen. Regardless, a minute ago the issue had caused her to lose some of her considerable cool.

Which created a bargaining chip. I decided to play it.

"Meet me later," I said. "I'm going to check on a few things in the meantime, and then we'll fill each other in. If I'm convinced at that point that I've got no chance of finishing this properly, I'll walk away."

"I'm not meeting you again. It's too dangerous."

"Not if we do it right."

There was a pause, then she said, "Tell me what you have in mind."

"Where's Belghazi right now?"

"He's off Macau."

"Where?"

"He has meetings in the region. I'm not supposed to know where."

Not being supposed to know and not knowing were quite different things. She was afraid that, if she told me, I might try to go after him. Not an unreasonable concern.

"When will he be back?" I asked.

"He wasn't sure. A day, maybe two."

"All right. Take a trip to Hong Kong. Tonight. There are lots of Caucasians there and it's much bigger than this place. You'll have an easier time blending in. If he asks, you tell him Macau started to feel small, you got bored, you wanted to do some shopping, take in the sights."

There was a long pause. Then she said, "Where do I find you?"

"I haven't decided that yet. Give me your cell phone number and I'll call you from a pay phone. Ten o'clock tonight. I'll tell you where then."

She looked at me for a moment, then nodded. I grabbed a pencil and a piece of paper from next to the telephone and wrote down the number she gave me, in code, as always, so that she wouldn't be compromised if I were ever found with the paper.

She walked to the door. I watched her glance down at the body as she stepped over it. She checked through the peephole, opened the door a crack, looked through it, and moved out into the corridor. The door closed quietly behind her.

I had to be careful now. I knew there were only two possible reasons that she'd agreed to meet me. One, because she was afraid that, if she didn't, I might go after Belghazi again and screw things up for her. In this sense, I was coercing her, and I was aware that coercion is an inherently dangerous way to gain someone's cooperation.

Two, she wanted another shot at using a little coercion herself.

I realized that she hadn't even asked what I was going to do about the dead guy. I decided to take that as a compliment: she knew I would handle it and hadn't felt the need to inquire.

In the end, it took me the rest of the afternoon to make Elevator Boy disappear as he needed to. I could have simply left him in the room, but doing so would have undone all my efforts to disconnect myself from the other dead Arabs. Hmm, the police would be saying, three dead Saudis in Hong Kong, another two near the Macau Ferry Terminal, and now this one, in a hotel room? Dumping him in one of the Oriental's stairwells would have been a marginal improvement, but it would still mean the police would focus on the hotel where I had been staying. I didn't want that kind of attention. Sure, I'd checked in under an appropriate alias and could have just evaporated, counting on the alias to break the connection between the perpetrator and the crimes, but I decided that the risk of bringing that much heat down on the alias was greater than the risk of cleaning up the mess and avoiding the heat entirely.

Of course, the "cleaning up the mess" option involved a bit more than just tidying up after a dinner party. I had to shop for proper luggage, in this case a Tumi fifty-six-inch wardrobe, billed as "The Goliath of Garment Bags"; sheet plastic to prevent contamination of the interior of the bag during transportation; and plenty of towels to absorb any leakage. As for the packing itself, suffice to say that Elevator Boy, although not a particularly large man, wasn't just a couple of suit jackets, either, and I had to make a few unpleasant adjustments to get the desired fit. The Goliath worked as advertised, though, and I was able to wheel it and its unusually heavy load out of the hotel, eschewing offers of assistance from two bellhops along the way. Under the causeway a kilometer or so from the hotel, I ducked behind a pillar and unloaded the Goliath's contents, then continued on my way, wheeling the bag along behind me with considerably less effort than before. I left it far from the body and the hotel, at the other end of the causeway, where I knew someone would quickly and happily "steal" it, marveling at his good luck in acquiring such expensive, high-quality luggage, and saying nothing to anyone about where it had come from.

Back at the room, I took an extremely long, extremely hot shower. I changed, packed my things, and headed down to the lobby. At the hotel checkout counter, I told them that my plans had changed suddenly, that I needed to check out earlier than planned. They told me they would still have to charge me for that evening. I told them I of course understood their policy.

I took a cab to the ferry terminal. I saw no police barricades, technicians sniffing for evidence, or other evidence of official interest in what had happened here earlier. On the contrary, in fact: it seemed that things had been quickly cleaned up and returned to normal. I had been right about law enforcement priorities on Macau.

I went to the TurboJet counter to buy a ticket. The ticket clerk informed me that only first-class seats were available on the next departing ferry. I told her first class would be wonderful.

Once aboard, I settled into my first-class seat and watched the lights of Macau fade into the distance. I felt myself beginning to relax.

Yeah, there were problems. There had been a breach in the security I depend on to do my work and get away alive afterward. And, although the evidence was so far circumstantial, it looked like Belghazi was on to me, which would make it a hell of a lot harder to get close to him and finish what I had started.

The thing in the elevator had been a close call, too. But it had turned out all right. Maybe that was an omen. Nothing like a little luck to give you that wonderful sense of well-being. That, and having killed and survived someone trying to do the same to you.

I smiled. Maybe I would write a self-help book. Live off the proceeds.

I would worry about the problems later. There was nothing I could do about them on the ferry. My relaxation deepened, and I actually indulged a light snooze on the ride over. I woke up refreshed. The Hong Kong skyline was already looming before me, its proud towers eclipsing the silhouetted hills behind them, dense crystals of light that seemed to have erupted out of the earth to embrace the sky and dominate the harbor.

The City of Life, the local tourist board liked to call it. It seemed a fair description to me. At least for the moment.

PART TWO

This world—
to what may I liken it?
To autumn fields
lit dimly in the dusk
by lightning flashes.

MINAMOTO-NO-SHITAGO,
nobleman, scholar, poet

6

I CALLED THE Hong Kong Peninsula from a pay phone and reserved a Deluxe Harbour View room. I like the Peninsula because it occupies an entire city block in Kowloon's Tsim Sha Tsui district, has five separate entrances, multiple elevators, and more internal staircases than you can count. Not an easy place to set up an ambush.

Also, it's one of the best hotels in Hong Kong. And hey, it had been a rough day. A little luxury along with the usual dose of security didn't seem objectionable.

I could imagine what Harry would have said: *You trying to impress her?*

Nah. It's just about the security, I would have told him.

He would have known not to believe that. It made me miss him, and for a moment I felt bleak.

I made my circuitous way to the hotel and checked in. I paid for the room with a credit card under the name of Toshio Okabe, a sufficiently backstopped identity I use from time to time for just such transactions. A porter escorted me to room 2311. The room was on the south side of the new tower and, as promised, had a stunning view of Hong Kong across the harbor.

I shaved in the shower, then soaked for twenty minutes in the oversized tub. I'd been forced to stay mostly at more anonymous, downmarket properties to protect myself since leaving Tokyo two years earlier, and damn if a Deluxe Harbour View room at the Peninsula didn't feel good.

I changed into a pair of charcoal gabardine trousers, a fine cotton mock turtleneck of the same color, and a pair of dark brown suede split-toe lace-ups and matching belt. Then I spent a half hour refamiliarizing myself with the hotel layout—the placement of the internal staircases and which ones could be accessed without a staff key; the positions of the numerous security cameras; the movements of security personnel. When I had decided on how I would arrange to meet Delilah while continuing to ensure my own safety, I went out.

I stopped at an Internet café. There was a message waiting from Kanezaki on the bulletin board. Six guys matching the descriptions of the ones I'd taken out had left from Riyadh for Hong Kong two days earlier. Plus, the Saudi embassy in Hong Kong was involved in the investigation of the recent deaths in Hong Kong and Macau. And Delilah had mentioned that the guy she had overheard had a Saudi accent. Apparently, she'd been telling the truth, at least about that. It looked like my erstwhile friends had indeed been Saudi. A connection with half-Algerian, Arabic-speaking Belghazi seemed likely under the circumstances. What I didn't know was why. Or how.

The last part of the message said, "Checking on the phone numbers and on the woman. Nothing yet. Will be in touch."

I typed, "Follow up on the Saudi connection to our friend. Monitor Riyadh to Hong Kong air traffic for movement of similar teams." Not likely that they could have put together another unit so quickly, but it couldn't hurt to be watching for one.

I uploaded the message, purged the browser, and left.

I thought about Delilah. European, I'd been thinking, although I hadn't been able to place the slight accent. I'd been half-assuming, pending further information, that she was French. Partly it was her appearance, her dress, her manner. Partly it was her involvement with Belghazi, who, when he wasn't moving around, was said to be based in Paris. Even her Arabic could fit the theory: France has a substantial Algerian population, and there is a long and violent history between the two countries. The French intelligence services, domestic and foreign, would have well-funded programs in Arabic. Delilah might have been one of their graduates.

But there was another possibility, of course, one I was beginning to think was increasingly likely. I decided to look for a way to test it.

I bought a prepaid cell phone from a wireless store, to be used later. I dropped it in a pocket, then used a pay phone to call Delilah.

"The Peninsula," I told her. "Room five-forty-four." I wasn't ready to tell her the correct room number, or even the correct floor. Not with all the reasons she had for wanting to see me off. We would do this sensibly.

"Thirty minutes," she said, and hung up.

There was a liquor store near the phone. On impulse, I went inside. I found a bottle of thirty-year-old Laphroaig for twenty-five hundred Hong Kong dollars— about three hundred U.S. Extortionate. But what the hell. I stopped at an HMV music store and picked up a few CDs. Lynne Arriale, *Live at Montreux*. Eva Cassidy, *Live at Blues Alley*. Bill Evans Trio, *Sunday at the Village Vanguard*. All the next best thing to being there.

I went back to my room at the Peninsula and took two crystal tumblers and a bucket of ice from over the minibar. I set them down on the coffee table with the Laphroaig, along with a bottle of mineral water. I popped the CDs into the room's multidisk player and chose "random" and "repeat." A moment later, the music started coming through a pair of speakers to either side of the television. I paused for a minute, and listened to Eva Cassidy doing "Autumn Leaves," the lyrics and the melody the more poignant by virtue of the singer's untimely death. The song's melancholy notes seemed to clarify, and somehow to frame, my feelings about Delilah—part pleasant anticipation at seeing her again, part deadly concern at her possible role in what had recently come at me in Hong Kong and Macau.

I used the room's speakerphone to call the prepaid cell phone I had just bought, picked up the call, and left, closing the door behind me. I plugged a wire-line earpiece into the cell phone and listened. The music was soft but audible. As long as I could hear it in the background, I would know the connection was good.

I took the stairs down to the fifth floor. Room 544 was at the end of a hallway, with the entrance to an internal staircase opposite and about three meters ahead of it. I waited inside the doors that led to the staircase, where I could see the room through a glass panel. If anyone had managed to listen in on my call to Delilah, which was unlikely, or if she had decided to inform her people of my whereabouts, which I deemed less unlikely, I would see them coming from here. If they tried to use the staircase, as I had, I would hear them. And, if for some reason that I had completely missed, someone tried to get into my room while I was out, I would know it through the cell phone. Layers. Always layers.

Delilah arrived fifteen minutes later. As she passed my position, I checked the direction she had come from to ensure that she was alone. When I saw that she was, I opened the door and said, "Delilah. Over here."

She turned and looked at me. She didn't seem particularly surprised, and I wasn't surprised at that. She was familiar with my habits and wouldn't have expected me to just be waiting at the appointed place at the appointed time.

I held the door open as she walked past me. Harry's detector was in my pocket, sleeping peacefully, the batteries fully juiced from an earlier daily charging. She wasn't wired.

I led her along various stairways and internal corridors back to the room, listening in on the earpiece while we moved. All I heard from my room were the quiet notes of Lynne Arriale. Neither of us spoke along the way. We encountered no surprises.

I unlocked the door to the room and we went inside. "Sorry about the procedures," I said, removing the earpiece. I turned off the cell phone and left it by the door.

The apology was perfunctory. So was the shrug she offered in response. I bolted the door behind us.

Feeling secure for the moment, I took in a few more details. She was wearing a midnight blue dress, something with texture, maybe raw silk. It was cut just above the knee, with three-quarter-length sleeves, an off-the-shoulder neckline, and a deep V cut in the back and front. Her shoes were patent leather stilettos with sharp toes. There was a handbag to match the shoes, and a gold Cartier watch with a gold link band encircling her left wrist. It was a man's watch, large and heavy on her wrist, and its incongruous heft served to accentuate her femininity. Her hair was swept back and away from her face in a way that accentuated her profile. Overall the look was controlled and sleek, sophisticated and sexy. None of it, especially the shoes, would be ideal for escape and evasion, if it came to that, so I realized she must have chosen it all for some other operational imperative. There are all sorts of weapons in the world, and I reminded myself that when this woman was dressed for work she was anything but unarmed.

She reached into her purse and took out her cell phone to show me that it was turned off and unconnected to anyone who might be listening in. Then she opened the purse so I could see there was nothing else inside that might have been problematic. I nodded to show that I was satisfied.

She raised her arms away from her sides and looked at me. She smiled in that sly, subversive way she had—teasing, but also amused, and inviting the recipient of the smile to join in the amusement. "You're not going to search me?"

I didn't think it would be necessary. And it certainly wouldn't be wise. If I put my hands on her body, my previous reaction, when I had watched her leaning over the bedstand in my room at the hotel in Macau, would have seemed shy and retiring by comparison. She knew that, and she was showing me that she knew.

"Why would I want to do that?" I said, aware that my heart had started a little giddyup just at the prospect. "We trust each other, right?"

She lowered her arms, letting the smile linger for a moment, maybe acknowledging that I'd handled her suggestion about as well as anyone could under the circumstances.

"Shall I take off my shoes?"

"Why?" I asked, thinking of that idiot shoe bomber who had tried to bring down a flight from Paris.

She shrugged. "Isn't that the custom in Japan?"

Cute. A way to confirm a biographical detail, to increase or decrease the probability that the guy her people had read about in *Forbes* had been me. She'd have to do better than that.

"I think they do it in houses, not so much in hotels," I said. "Either way is fine."

She bent forward, raised her right leg behind her, and reached around to a strap at the back of her ankle. She didn't need to touch the wall or otherwise support herself to perform this maneuver. Her balance was good. But I had already seen that, in Belghazi's suite when she had nearly put me down with that elbow shot.

She repeated the procedure for the other shoe. In the half-light where we stood by the door I caught a tantalizing glimpse of skin and curves as the front of her dress slipped momentarily away from her body. The view wasn't accidental, I knew, but it was undeniably good.

I took off my shoes, as well, and followed her into the room. I'd left the lights on low so that their reflection against the floor-to-ceiling window glass wouldn't obscure the view of the harbor and the lights of the Hong Kong skyline beyond it, but still I saw her logging the room details before appreciating the panorama outside. I couldn't help smiling at that. A civilian would never have paused before taking in that spectacular scenery.

She glanced over at the coffee table. "Laphroaig?" she asked.

"The thirty-year-old," I said, nodding. "You know it?"

She nodded back. "My favorite. I like it even better than the forty. That sherry finish—divine."

Not bad, I thought. I wondered what else she would know. She was obviously adept when it came to languages, clothes, spycraft. And now whiskey. Food? Wine? Poetry? Tantric sexual techniques? I tried not to speculate too much on that last one.

"Can I get you a glass?"

"I'd love one. Just a drop of water."

I poured us each a healthy measure in the crystal tumblers, adding a drop of water to hers as she had requested. I handed her her glass, raised mine, and said, *"L'Chaim,"* smiling into her eyes as I did so.

She paused, looking at me. "I'm sorry?"

I smiled innocently. "'To life,' right? Isn't that the custom in Israel?"

For one second I thought she looked angry, and then she smiled. *"Kanpai,"* she said, and we both laughed.

It was a good recovery. But that pause, and the momentary reaction that had followed, seemed telling.

We sat by the coffee table. Delilah took the couch with her back to the wall, her right side to the window. I took the stuffed chair next to the couch. My back was to the wall next to the window, so I didn't have the view. But I preferred to look at her, anyway.

We sipped for a moment in silence. She was right—the thirty-year-old, finished in sherry casks, mingles ocean tang and sherry sweetness like no other whiskey, offering a nose and taste unparalleled even among Laphroaig's other outstanding bottlings.

After a minute or two she asked, "How much do you know about me?"

"Not a lot. Mostly speculation. Probably about what you know about me."

"You think I'm Israeli?"

"Aren't you?"

She smiled. The smile said: *Come on, you can do better than that.*

I shrugged. "Yeah, you're right. Beautiful woman, speaks Arabic, knows how to handle herself and then some, trying to set up a guy who supports various Islamic fundamentalist groups . . . I don't know what I could have been thinking."

"Is that really all you're going on?"

"What else would there be?"

She took a sip of the Laphroaig and paused as though considering. Then she said, "No one works completely alone. Even if it's just the people who are paying you, there's always someone you can go to for information. If you share your theories about who I am with whomever you work for, it could make things dangerous for me."

I hadn't even considered that. I tend to focus only on whether a given action might create danger for me. Selfish, I suppose. But I'm alive because of it.

"We're both professionals," she went on. "We do what we have to. If you need information, you'll seek it out. But what you learn might buy you little. It could cost me a great deal."

"Why don't you just level with me, then," I said. "Tell me what I need to know."

"What more do you need?" she asked, looking at me. "We've already learned too much by accident. We understand each other's objectives, and we understand the situation we're in. The more you push, the more you compromise my ability to carry out my mission. And the more dangerous you make it for me personally. The people I work with recognize all this. At some point, they may decide to overrule me when I tell them not to try to remove you."

I put down my glass and stood up. "Delilah," I said, my voice dropping an octave the way it does when I feel I'm seconds away from having to take decisive action, "we're here to try to find a way to coexist. Don't make me decide that you're a threat."

"Or what?" she said, looking up at me.

I didn't answer. She put her glass down, too, then stood and faced me. "Will you break my neck? Most men couldn't—I'm not so delicate, you know—but I know you could."

She took a step closer. I felt an adrenaline surge and couldn't put it in the right context. A second ago I'd reacted to her the way I reflexively do when something suddenly reveals itself as dangerous, but now . . . I wasn't sure. My respiration wanted to speed up and I controlled it, not wanting her to see.

"Maybe I am a threat to you," she said, her voice even. "Not because I want to be, but because of the situation. So? You're a professional. Do what you have to do. Eliminate the threat."

She took a step closer, close enough for me to smell her, to feel something coming off her body, heat or some electrical thing. I felt another adrenaline rush spreading through my chest and gut.

"No?" she asked, looking into my eyes. "Why? You know how. Here." She reached down for my hands and brought them up to her neck. Her skin was warm and smooth. I could feel her pulse against my fingers. It was beating surprisingly hard. I could hear her breath moving in and out through her nose.

I hadn't meant to bluff, but somehow I had. And now she was calling. *Fuck.*

But she wasn't completely sure of herself. There was that rapid pulse, and the sound of her breathing.

And of mine, I realized. I looked for some way to regain the initiative, regain control of the situation. But looking into those blue eyes, seeing her face framed by my hands encircling her neck, her expression simultaneously fearful and defiant, I was having trouble.

She lowered her arms to her sides now and tilted her chin slightly upward, the posture maximally submissive, and yet, somehow, also mocking, insolent. I looked down at the shadowed hollows of her clavicles, one side, then the other, and was almost defeated by the thought of how easy it would be to sweep my hands down over her shoulders, catching the material of the dress on the way, bringing the garment and the lingerie beneath down to her wrists and belly in one smooth motion, exposing her breasts, her skin, her body.

It was there if I wanted it. I knew that, and I knew this was by design, our moves to be choreographed on her terms, where she would offer what I wanted like a kind homeowner offering milk to a starving kitten, maybe petting the little stray on the head while it greedily lapped at the leavings.

I was suddenly angry. The feline imagery helped. I removed my hands from her neck and took a careful step away from her. My mouth had gone dry. I picked up my Laphroaig. Took a swallow. Sat back down, as casually as I could.

"I was right about you," I said, leaving her standing there. "You really can't help yourself. This is all you've got."

Her eyes narrowed a fraction, and I knew I was right. I'd competed against guys like this in judo. They had one money move, a technique that always worked for them, but if you could get past that one, if you could survive it, they were off their game and couldn't recover.

"What's it like?" I went on, feeling more in control now. "Can you even talk to a man without trying to give him a hard-on? What are you going to do a few years from now, when your pheromones start to dry up? Because there's nothing more to you. Maybe there was, a long time ago, but there's nothing left now."

Her eyes narrowed more and her ears seemed almost to flatten in an oddly feral attitude of anger. *Good,* I thought. *I needed that.*

"Are you going to sit down?" I asked, gesturing to the couch. "I'm not going to fuck you. And I'm not going to kill you. Not here, not now. It took all afternoon to get rid of that guy from the elevator, and I'm not going through that again tonight."

She smiled in a way that made me wonder if she had just imagined herself killing me, and dipped her head toward me as if to say, *All right. Touché.*

She moved back to the couch and finished what was in her glass. I picked up the bottle to pour her another. She raised the glass as I did so and I noticed that both our hands were shaking. I knew she saw it, too.

"Why don't we call that one a draw," I offered.

She smiled and took a swallow of what I'd poured her. "I think you're being generous," she said.

"I'm being honest."

She smiled again, a little more brightly this time. "You're good, you know. Exceptional."

"Yeah, so are you."

She took another swallow and looked at me. "It would have been interesting to see what would have happened if we'd met under other circumstances."

"You want it to be more interesting than it already is?" I asked. We both laughed, and the tension broke.

Then we were silent for a moment, maybe collecting

ourselves, adjusting to the new dynamic. I decided to try to keep things comfortable for a while, thinking it would be useful to make her feel good after that harsh exchange. I was aware that I also just *wanted* the exchange to be comfortable, that I didn't want to spar with her and certainly didn't want to fight, and I wondered for a moment where my decision was really coming from.

"You know, you almost dropped me in Belghazi's suite," I said.

She shrugged. "I had surprise on my side. I don't think you were expecting much from a naked woman."

"Maybe not. But you used what you had at your disposal, and you used it well. Who trained you?"

The question was straightforward, and I knew she wouldn't take it as another attempt to glean something revealing.

She looked at me for a long moment, then said, "It's Krav Maga."

Krav Maga is the self-defense system developed by the Israeli Defense Forces. These days it's taught all over the world, so experience in the system certainly doesn't mean the practitioner is Israeli. But Delilah already knew that I suspected her nationality and her affiliations. In this context, her acknowledgment served also as a tacit admission.

I wondered how best to pursue the slight opening she seemed to have deliberately created. I said, "I like Krav Maga. It's practical."

"It's all in how it's taught," she said, nodding. "And how you train. Most martial arts are taught as religions. They're about faith, not facts."

I smiled. "People need to believe something, even if they have to invent it."

She nodded again. "Even if it's wrong. But we don't have that luxury. We need something that works."

We. She was getting ready to tell me something.

But don't push it. Let her get to it the way she wants to.

"How'd they train you?" I asked.

"You know how. A lot of scenario-based conditioning. A lot of contact. My nose was broken during training, can you see it? I had it fixed, but you can still see the scars if you look closely."

I looked, and saw a hairline mark at the bridge, the remnants of a bad break repaired by a good plastic surgeon. It wouldn't have meant anything if you hadn't known to look for it.

"Sounds pretty rough," I said.

"It was. They took it further for me than for most because my missions are special. I'm alone in the field for a long time, usually without access to a weapon, or at least not to a traditional weapon."

We were silent again. She took a sip of the Laphroaig and asked, "And you?"

"Mostly judo," I said. "The Kodokan." If she'd trained in Krav Maga, she would know both.

She looked at me. "I thought neck cranks were illegal in judo."

"They are," I said, seeing that I'd been right about her knowledge. "I learn the special stuff elsewhere. Books and videos. I used to practice it with a couple partners who shared some of my interests."

"What else?" she asked. "The way I saw you move, you don't learn that doing judo as a sport. Even with the extra books and videos."

"No. You don't. It helps to have spent a decade or so in combat. You develop a certain attitude."

Silence again. Then she said, "So you are who I think you are."

I shrugged. "I think you know part of it, yes."

"Well, you know part about me, too."

There it is, then. "You're Israeli," I said. "Mossad."

She looked away and cocked her head slightly as though considering what I had said, meditating on it. Then she said, "What difference does it make who I am, who I'm with? From your perspective, none."

She wasn't going to tell me, I'd been wrong about that. Or maybe she already had told me, in her own oblique way, and I'd missed it. I wasn't sure.

She took a sip of the Laphroaig and went on. "But from my perspective, your affiliations matter a great deal. The information we were able to put together on you suggested that you work for the Japanese Liberal Democratic Party. But I don't see what interest the LDP could have in Belghazi. So I assume that, at least this time, you're being paid by the Americans. And that concerns me."

"Why?"

She waved her hands outward, palms to the ceiling, as if to say, *Isn't it obvious?* "They're big and factional-ized," she said, "so they're not discreet. You have to be careful with them. You never know quite who you're dealing with."

"How do you mean?"

Now she put her hands on her hips, leaned back on the couch, and dropped her shoulders. The gesture read, *Is he just playing dumb, or is this the genuine article?* She started talking a moment later, so I figured she had de-cided it was #2. It shouldn't have bothered me—on the contrary, in fact—but it did, a little. I assuaged my pride by reminding myself that it's generally good to be underestimated.

"Did they explain to you why they want Belghazi removed?" she asked.

"They did."

"Did you believe them?"

I shrugged. "I was barely listening."

She laughed. "They must have told you about his arms networks, though, terrorists, fundamentalist group connections, blah, blah, blah."

The disparaging idiom, rendered in her accented English, surprised me, and I laughed. "What, were they making it up?" I asked.

She shook her head. "No. It's all true. And I'm sure that some parts of the U.S. government are upset over it, and might even be trying to do something about it. Some parts."

"Meaning?"

She smiled and said, "You know, you haven't even told me your name."

I looked at her and said, "Call me John."

"John, then," she said, as though testing the sound of it. "You were saying, 'Some parts.'"

She shrugged. "Let's just say that America is a very big place. It has a lot of competing interests. Not all of them might think Belghazi is such a bad guy."

"Meaning?" I said again.

"Have you thought about why they want you to be 'circumspect' about the way you go about this particular assignment?"

"I have a general idea."

"Well, consider this." She leaned forward and brought her hands up, her fingers slightly splayed and her palms forward, as though framing a photograph. "Whatever faction hired you, they're being oblique. They need deniability. Who do they need deniability from? And have you considered the position this puts you in?"

The relatively marked body language was new. I was seeing a different part of her personality, maybe a part that she ordinarily kept hidden. *Interesting.*

I thought for a moment. "The same position I'm always in, I would say."

"Qualitatively, maybe," she said, waving a hand, palm down, perhaps unconsciously erasing my point. "Quantitatively, the situation might be worse. Who do you think sent the man in the elevator?"

I paused, thinking, *I half thought it was you.* Instead I said, "I don't know."

The wave stopped and she stabbed the air with her index finger. "Correct. Any number of players could now be trying to counter you. Anyone who stands to benefit from what Belghazi does."

Or who wants to keep him alive long enough to get access to his computer, I thought. I wondered if she was telling me all this to throw me off her scent. Or maybe she was trying to emphasize the hopelessness of my situation, to encourage me to quit. Maybe.

"I've always known that being in this business was a poor way to win a popularity contest," I said.

She laughed. I picked up the bottle and refreshed first her glass, then mine.

I liked her laugh. It was an odd collection of incongruities: husky, but also sweet; womanly, in the sophistication that informed it, but somehow also girlish in its delighted timbre; spiced with a hint of irony, but one that seemed grounded more in a sense of the absurd than in sarcasm or cruelty. I smiled, feeling good, and realized I was getting a little buzzed from the whiskey.

She leaned back and took a sip, pausing with the glass under her nose. I liked that, liked that she appreciated the aroma. I did the same.

"The one thing you do know," she said, "is that someone is on to you. Do you understand what that means for me? Someone could make the connection. And I don't operate the way you do. I don't have the luxury of being able to hide. To do what I need to do, I need to be close, and stay close."

So now an appeal to sentiment. A two-pronged approach: logic, to the effect that the situation had changed and I could no longer accomplish my mission; emotion, to the effect that, if I continued to try, she would pay the price.

"I understand what you're saying," I told her. "But I also understand where you're coming from. The second is what gives me pause about the first."

It made me feel a little sad to say it. Things had been so relaxed for a while. Christ, the whiskey was getting to me. I'm not usually sentimental.

"That's fair," she said, nodding. "Nonetheless, what I've told you is accurate. Do a little digging—leaving me out of it, if you can, please—and you'll see."

I nodded. "The digging is already happening. Discreetly, you're not part of it." Not entirely true, but how my inquiry to Kanezaki might affect her was something I would think about later.

I took a sip of the Laphroaig. "Anyway, I need to figure out where this leak is coming from, so I can close it."

"You think the problem is on your side?"

I shrugged. "Wouldn't be the first time. I learned a long time ago that democracies are dangerous to work with. They're hindered by all those annoying checks and balances, all that meddlesome public opinion, so they have built-in incentives to find ways of doing things off the books. Sometimes it gets a little hard to follow who you're dealing with."

She smiled. "Want Castro whacked? Hire the Mafia."

I smiled back. "Sure. Or, if Congress won't cough up the appropriations, fund the Contras through the Sultan of Brunei."

"Or bankroll almost anything by getting the Saudis to pay for it."

"Yeah, don't worry, I see your point."

She moved her hands up and down like a pedestrian trying to slow down an oncoming car, the gesture both impatient and suppliant. "Sorry to belabor it. But you have to understand, Nine-Eleven put America into a bad state of schizophrenia. The country committed itself to a 'war on terrorism,' but still pays billions of oil dollars to the Saudis, knowing that those dollars fund all the groups with whom America purports to be at war. Fifteen of the nineteen Nine-Eleven hijackers were Saudi, but no one wants to talk about that. Can you imagine the reaction if the hijackers had been Iranian, or North Korean? I think if America were a person, a psychiatrist would classify her as being in profound psychological denial. I don't know how you can trust an employer like that."

"Do you trust yours?" I asked.

She looked down. Her hands descended gently to her lap. After a moment, she said, "It's complicated."

"That's not exactly a ringing endorsement."

She sighed. "I trust their intentions. Some of the . . . the policies are stupid and outmoded. But I don't have to agree with every decision to know I'm doing the right thing."

From her body language and her voice, I knew that

my question had troubled her. But not for the reasons she had just articulated. There was something else.

"Do they trust you?" I asked.

She smiled and started to say something, then stopped. She looked down again. "That's also . . . complicated," she said.

"How?"

She looked left and right, as though searching for an answer. "They trained me and vetted me," she said after a moment. "And I'm good at what I do. I'm resourceful and I have a track record to go on."

She took a sip of the Laphroaig and I waited for her to go on.

"But, let's face it, what I do, I sleep with the enemy. Literally. It's hard for people to get past that. They wonder what it makes me feel, whether it might . . . infect me, or something."

"How does it make you feel?" I asked, unable not to.

She looked away. "I don't want to talk about it."

I nodded and we were silent for a moment. Then I said, "You're taking a lot of risks with this operation. Maybe more even than usual. Some people might argue that, with me in the picture, with the guy at the hotel, things have gotten unacceptably hot for you, that you should get out. But you haven't."

She smiled, but the smile didn't take.

"Are you trying to prove something?" I asked. "Trying to earn someone's respect by putting your life on the line here?"

"What would you know about that?" she asked. Her tone was a little sharp, and I suspected I was on to something.

I smiled gently. "I fought with the U.S. in Vietnam.

Against 'gooks' and 'zipperheads' and 'slopes.' Look at my face, Delilah."

She did.

"You see my point?" I said. "It took me years to realize why I was willing to do some of the things I did there."

She nodded, then drained what was left in her glass. "I see. Yes, you would understand, then."

"Are they worth it, though? They send you out on these missions, at huge risk to you, you bring back the goods, and still they don't trust you. Why bother?"

"Why bother?" she asked, tilting her head to the side as though trying to see something she had missed in me before. "Have you ever seen an infant with its legs torn off by a bomb? Seen its mother holding it, insane with grief and horror?"

A rhetorical question, for most people. Not for me.

"Yes," I said, my voice quiet. "I have."

She paused, looking at me, then said, "Well, the work I do prevents some of these nightmares. When I do my job well, when we disrupt the flow of funds and matériel to the monsters who strap on vests filled with explosives and rat poison and nails, a baby that would have died lives, or a family that would have grieved forever doesn't have to, or minds that would have been destroyed by trauma remain intact."

She paused again, then added, "I should quit? Because my superiors who ought to know better don't trust me? Yes, then I can explain to the bereft and the amputees and the permanently traumatized that I could have done something to save them, but didn't, because I wasn't treated sufficiently respectfully at the office."

She looked at me, her cheeks flushed, her shoulders rising and falling with her breathing.

I looked back, feeling an odd combination of admiration, attraction, and shame. I took a big swallow of the Laphroaig, finishing it. I refreshed her glass, then mine.

"You're lucky," I said, after a moment.

She blinked. "What?"

I closed my eyes and rubbed my temples for a moment. "To believe in something the way you do . . ." I opened my eyes. "Christ, I can't imagine it."

There was a long pause. Then she said, "It doesn't feel lucky."

"No, I'm sure it doesn't. I used the wrong word. I should have said 'fortunate.' It's not the same thing."

I rubbed my temples again. "I'm sorry I said what I said. That you shouldn't bother. Over the years, I've developed the habit of . . . preempting betrayal. Of thinking that the possibility of betrayal, and defending against it, is paramount. And maybe that's true for me. But it shouldn't be true for everyone. It shouldn't be true for someone like you."

For a few moments, neither of us spoke. Then she asked, "What are you thinking?"

I waited a second, then said, "That I like the way you use your hands when you talk." Telling her part of it.

She glanced down at her hands for a second, as though checking to see whether they were doing something right then, and laughed quietly. "I don't usually do that. You pissed me off."

"You weren't only doing it when you were pissed."

"Oh. Well, I do it when I forget myself."

"When does that happen?"

"Rarely."

"You should do it more often."

"It's dangerous."

"Why?"

"You know why. You have to protect yourself."

Her expression was so neutral that I knew she had to be consciously controlling it. She took a sip of the Laphroaig and asked, "And you? What do you do?"

"I don't get close."

"I told you, I don't have that luxury."

I looked at her and said, "I've never thought of it as a luxury."

She looked back. The look was noticeably long. Definitely frank. Possibly inviting.

I got up and sat down next to her on the couch. One of her eyebrows rose a notch and she said, "I thought you just said you don't get close." But she was smiling a little, those warm notes of irony and humor in her eyes.

"That's the problem with making your own rules," I said. "There's no one around to straighten you out when you break them."

"I thought you said you weren't going to fuck me."

"I'm not."

I looked at her for another moment, then leaned slowly forward. She watched me, her eyes focusing on mine, then dropping momentarily to my lips, and moving back to my eyes again.

I paused. Our faces were a few centimeters apart. There was the hint of rare perfume, maybe something she had bottled uniquely for her in expensive cut glass at an exclusive shop in Paris or Milan. The scent was there but you couldn't quite get ahold of it, like the remnant of a dream upon waking, or an afterimage fading from the retina after an intense flash of light, or the memory of a face you knew and loved a lifetime earlier. Something just real enough to bring you in, to make you want to pull it closer, to get it back before it flickers away again and is irretrievably lost.

I inclined my head further and kissed her. She accepted the kiss but didn't exactly embrace it, and after a moment I drew back slightly and looked at her.

"Some people might call what you're doing 'mixed signals,'" she said. She was smiling a little, but her tone was serious enough.

"I have a conflicted nature. All the military shrinks said so."

"A few minutes ago you were slapping me down, remember?"

I shook my head. "That wasn't you. It was your alter ego. I'm not interested in her."

"How do you know you'll be interested in what's behind her?"

"I like what I've seen so far."

She looked at me. "Maybe you were right. Maybe I can only be an actress. A poseur."

"That would be sad if it were true."

"You're the one who said it."

"I was trying to get under your skin."

"You did."

"Show me I was wrong."

"I don't know that you were."

I looked at her legs and breasts with mock lasciviousness, then said, "All right, I'll take the alter ego."

She laughed, then stopped and looked at me, another long one. She leaned forward and we kissed again.

The kiss was better this time. There was an uncertainty about it, the tentativeness of a cease-fire, the sense of something moving slowly but with a lot of momentum behind it.

She opened her mouth wider and our tongues met. Again the feeling was tentative: an exploration, not a hasty charge; a testing of the waters, not a heedless plunge.

A minute passed, maybe two, and the kiss grew less cautious, more passionate; less deliberate, more a thing unto itself. It waxed and waned as though in obedience to some force that was slipping from our control. I took in all the different aspects of her mouth, each shifting through my consciousness like images illuminated by a strobe light: her tongue; her lips; her teeth; her tongue again; the delicious feel of the whole, this new threshold to so much of whoever she was.

She took my lower lip between her teeth and lips and held it there for a moment, then released it and gradually eased away. We looked at each other. She smiled.

"I like the way you taste," she said.

"Yeah, I was thinking the same thing. Must be the Laphroaig."

She made a sound of agreement that was something like a purr. "That's part of it. The other part is you."

I smiled at her. "The exotic taste of the Orient?"

She laughed. "Just you."

We made love on the bed. There was some jocular debate in the midst of the proceedings about who should be on top, debate that we resolved by recourse to each of the alternatives in question, along with several others. Her body was as luscious and beautiful as that glimpse in Belghazi's suite had promised, and she moved with an unaffected experience and enthusiasm that made me think of the confidence I had first seen in the lobby of the Mandarin Oriental.

We used a condom, something I assumed was one of several practical items she would typically keep in her purse. It was smart. In my unfortunately infrequent encounters with real passion, I'm rarely as careful as I ought to be. The rationalization goes something like: *With all the bullets and mortar rounds I've survived, I must be immune to sexually transmitted diseases*. Stupid, I know. More likely, fate will indulge its taste for irony by killing me with AIDS or some other unpleasant alternative.

We lay on our sides afterward, facing each other, heads propped languorously on folded pillows. She reached over and traced my lips with a fingertip.

"You're smiling," she said.

I raised an eyebrow. "What did you think, I was going to frown?"

She laughed. Her words, her attitude, it all felt authentic enough. But she was a pro. If she was letting her hair down, I had to assume it was tactical, a means to an end. And I still couldn't be sure about her motives, about what she might have tried back at the Mandarin Oriental. A shame, to have that knowledge lying on the bed coldly between us, but there it was.

I asked her, "How did you get involved in your work?"

She shrugged. "Sometimes I ask myself the same thing."

"Tell me."

"I answered an ad in the newspaper, same as you."

I waited. There was no sense saying more. If she didn't want to talk about it, she wouldn't.

We were quiet again. Then she said, "I was a skinny kid, but when I was fourteen, my body started to develop. Boys, men, started looking at me. I didn't know why they were looking, exactly, but I liked it. I liked that I had something they wanted. I could tell it gave me a kind of power."

"You must have driven them crazy," I said, remembering what it was like to be that age, testosterone-poisoned and single-minded as a heat-seeking missile.

She nodded. "But I wasn't interested in boys my age. I don't know why; they just seemed so young. My fantasies were always about older men."

She pulled herself a little higher on the pillow. "When I was sixteen, a friend of my father's from the army moved to our city because of a job opportunity. He stayed with us for a couple months while he looked for an apartment and got settled. His name . . . I'll call him Dov. He was forty, a war hero, dark and handsome and with the softest, most beautiful eyes. Every time I looked at him I would get a strange feeling inside and have to look away. He was always proper with me, but sometimes I would catch him looking at me the way men did, although it seemed that he was trying not to.

"When I realized he was looking at me that way, it was . . . exciting. Here was this *man*, this war hero, handsome and intelligent and so much older and more sophisticated than I was, and still I had this power over him. I started . . . experimenting with the power. Testing it, in a way, to try to figure out what it was. I would laugh at something he said and hold his eyes a moment too long. Or brush against him when I walked past. I didn't intend for it to lead anywhere; I didn't even know that it could lead somewhere with a man like Dov, or where that place might be.

"One day, when he was home and my parents were out, I put on what I thought of as my sexiest outfit—a white bikini top and matching sarong. I knocked on his door. My heart was beating hard, the way it always did when I was near him or even thought of him. I heard him say, 'Come in,' so I did. He was sitting at the small desk in his room, and when he saw me he stood up, then flushed and looked away. My heart started beating harder. I told him I was going to walk down to the

beach—we lived near the ocean—and asked him if he
wanted to go for a swim. He didn't say anything—he
just looked at me for a second, then away again. I realized I could hear his breathing. I was so young at the
time, I didn't even know what that might mean, but it
excited me. And I felt awkward because he hadn't answered me. I didn't know what to say, so I fanned my
face a little and said, 'It's so hot in here!' which it suddenly was. He still didn't say anything, he just looked at
me with the oddest expression—smiling, but almost a
little sick, too, as though he was in pain and trying to be
brave about it—and I saw that his hands were trem-
bling. It made me nervous that he wasn't answering me,
so, just trying to think of something to say, I said, 'It's
okay if you don't want to swim,' and I realized my voice
was as shaky as his hands.

"His lips moved, but no words came out. Then he
reached out and touched one of my cheeks with the
back of his fingers. I was surprised and took a quick step
away. He pulled his hand back and told me quickly he
was sorry. I didn't know what he meant by that or why I
had stepped back; all I knew right then was that I
wanted him to touch me, wanted it more than anything,
and without another thought I took his hands in mine
and said, 'No, no, it's okay!' Then he looked at me with
his beautiful, dark eyes, took my face in his hands, and
kissed me. It was my first real kiss and I felt like I would
faint from the pleasure of it. I could hear myself moaning into his mouth and he was moaning, too. And you
know what? When he put his hands on my body, just my
hips and my breasts, I came. That was another first for
me—I didn't even know what was happening, I couldn't
breathe, there was this explosion of pleasure and then I
was sagging against him and crying. He held me and

stroked my hair and told me over and over that he was sorry, and I couldn't speak so I just kept shaking my head and crying because it was so wonderful, he was so wonderful."

I smiled, wanting to believe that the story was true, that she was showing me something more of the person behind what she had called the "poseur." Maybe she was. Even if it was a pseudonym, Dov was an Israeli name. From what I could tell of the timelines, Israel's Six Day War might have been the conflict in which he had distinguished himself. Her city by the sea? Tel Aviv? Eilat?

Or maybe it was a story she had told so many times and for so many reasons that she'd come to believe it herself. Maybe it was part of a campaign to get me to develop an attachment, to warp my objectivity, cloud my judgment.

But I could remind myself of all those unwelcome possibilities later. I didn't see the point of dwelling on them now.

"Did he make love to you?" I asked.

"No. Not that time. Although he could have. He could have done anything with me."

"What happened after?"

She smiled. "We promised each other that it would never happen again, that it was wrong because he was so much older and if my parents found out it would be a disaster. But we couldn't stay away from each other. My brother was in the army then, and he was killed that year. I don't think I could have gotten through that without Dov. He understood war and had lived through a lot of loss. He was the only one who could comfort me."

"That must have been hell for your parents."

"They were devastated. A lot of people didn't think

we should even have been fighting where we were, so their feeling was, 'our beautiful son died for what?' It wasn't like losing someone in the other wars, which everyone knew had been forced on us. It was more like . . . more like just a waste. You know what I mean?"

She could only have been talking about Lebanon. If she was making all this up, it was an impressive piece of fabrication.

I looked away, thinking about my first trip stateside from Vietnam, when the best you could expect from your average fellow American when he learned you'd been in the war was polite embarrassment and a desire to change the subject. Often you could expect much worse.

I said, "One of the cruelest things a society can do is send its young men off to war with a license to kill, then tell them when they get home that the license wasn't valid. America did the same thing in Vietnam."

She looked at me and nodded. We were quiet for a moment. I asked, "How did things turn out with Dov?"

She smiled. "He moved away. I went to college. He has a wife and two sons now."

"You still see each other?"

She shrugged. "Not very often. There's his family, and my work. But sometimes."

"Your parents never found out?"

She shook her head. "No. And he never told his wife. He's a good man, but you know? We can't help ourselves. There's something there that's just too strong."

I nodded and said, "Most people only dream of a connection like that."

She raised her eyebrows. "What about you?"

I looked away for a moment, thinking of Midori. "Maybe once."

"What happened?"

Nothing really, I could have said. *Just, she figured out I killed her father.*

"She was a civilian," I said, finessing the point. "She was smart enough to understand what I do, and smart enough to know that our worlds had to stay separate."

"You never thought about trying to get out of this world?"

"All the time."

"It's hard, isn't it."

There's no home for us, John. Not after what we've done. As spoken by that philosopher, my blood brother Crazy Jake.

I nodded and said, as though to his ghost, "There are things you do that you can't wash off afterward."

"What was it between you?"

"I screwed up. I hurt her."

"Not that. The good part."

"I don't know," I said, imagining her face for a moment, the way she would look at me. "There was this . . . frankness about her. In everything she did. I could always tell how I made her feel. She was experienced and sophisticated, even renowned, in her field, but somehow when I was with her I always felt I was with the person she was before all that. The real her, the core that no one else could see. I made her happy, you know? In a way that made no sense and caught me completely off guard when it started to happen. I don't think I've ever had anything like that before. I can't imagine I will again. Making her happy"—I paused, thinking it would sound corny, then said it anyway—"was the thing that made me happy."

"You're not happy now?"

"This very moment? I feel pretty good."

She smiled. "Generally."

I shrugged. "I'm not depressed."

"That's a pretty minimalist way of defining happiness."

"I take pleasure in things. A good single malt, good jazz, the feeling when the judo is really flowing. A hot soak afterward. The change of seasons. The way coffee smells when it's roasted the way it ought to be."

"All things, though."

I was quiet for a moment, thinking. "Yeah, mostly. I suppose that's true."

"Someone once said to me, 'If you live only for yourself, dying is an especially scary proposition.'"

I looked at her, but didn't say anything. Maybe the comment hit home.

"You don't trust," she said.

"No." I paused, then asked, "Do you?"

"Not easily. But I believe in some things. I couldn't live without that."

We were quiet for a while, thinking our separate thoughts. I said, "You can't do this forever. What's next?"

She laughed. "You mean when my 'pheromones dry up'? I don't know. What about you?"

I shrugged. "I'm not sure. Maybe retire someplace. Someplace sunny, maybe by the ocean, like where you grew up. A place with no memories."

"That sounds nice."

"Yeah. Don't know when I'll get there, though."

"Well, in your line of work, you've got a longer shelf life than I do, I suppose."

I laughed. "What about a family? You're still young."

"I don't know. I don't think I could give up Dov, so I'd need a pretty understanding husband."

"Don't tell him."

"I'd have to not tell him about what I've been doing

for the last dozen years, too. You know, if a man learns that you can be an actress in bed, he'll always wonder afterward whether you're acting with him. Men tend to be insecure about those things."

I realized that the comment might have been directed at me. Maybe a probe, to see if I would admit to something along those lines. Better to sidestep. I said, "It must be hard being so close with someone like Belghazi, knowing what he does."

She nodded. "You have to be able to compartmentalize. But it's not so bad with him. He's not one of the killers. He's much higher up the food chain than that. Besides, he's intelligent and not unkind. Attractive. Remember, I like men. It's part of what makes me good at what I do."

"But after you've gotten what you want from him . . ."

Her expression occluded slightly. "Someone else will take care of that. Maybe you, if we can manage this relationship properly."

"How will you feel then?"

"The way I always do. But you don't shrink from doing what's right just because it's not comfortable."

I looked at her, impressed. Most people don't realize it, but ninety percent of morality is based on comfort. Incinerate hundreds of people from thirty thousand feet up and you'll sleep like a baby afterward. Kill one person with a bayonet and your dreams will never be sweet again.

Which is more comfortable?

Which is worse?

Maybe it doesn't matter. In the end, you get over everything. We're such resilient creatures.

It was strange, lying in bed with her. The room felt like a haven. I realized my ease of mind was borne both of the precautions I had taken and of my confidence that she wouldn't have allowed herself to be followed. But also, perhaps, of some part of me that wanted to feel this way, for its own reasons, independent of the evidence of the outside world. Not a good sign, I knew. And possibly an indication that I was growing less well adapted to the game, and less able to survive in it.

Delilah got up and took a shower. She brought her purse in the bathroom with her, knowing I would have gone through it if she hadn't. Not that I would have found anything useful. She was too careful for that.

I lay on the bed and listened to the water running. I knew there was at least a theoretical possibility that she would use her cell phone while she was in there, alerting her people to my whereabouts. My gut told me the possibility was remote, but my gut might have been feeling the effects of whiskey and lovemaking. The fact was, she would still be concerned about the danger I posed to her operation. I had to stay sensible.

When she came out she was already dressed. She looked relaxed and refreshed. I had pulled on one of the Peninsula's plush bathrobes and was sitting on the bed, as though ready to turn in for the night.

She sat down next to me and said, "What do we do now?"

I put my hand on her thigh. "Well, I'm ready for round two, if you are."

She laughed. "About the situation."

"Oh, yeah. Can you send text messages with your phone?"

"Of course."

I gave her the URL of one of my encrypted bulletin boards. "The password is 'Peninsula,'" I told her. "The name of this hotel. Tell me when you've gotten what you need from Belghazi and where I can find him then."

"You'll do that?"

I shrugged. "I'm still waiting to hear from my contacts, who should be able to shed some light on who came after me and why. And how. For the moment, I don't have access to Belghazi, anyway. Standing down seems sensible."

"It is. Whoever was coming at you in Macau won't have unlimited resources. It will take them time to get new forces in position."

"I know," I said.

"But you need to be careful. I know you know this, I know you're a professional. But Belghazi is a dangerous man. Remember when I told you that I've known men who could act without compunction? Never more so than with him."

"What do you mean?"

"In Monte Carlo, I saw him kill a man. With his feet and bare hands."

"Yeah, he's got a Savate background, I know."

She shook her head. "More than a background. He has a silver glove in Savate and was a ring champion in Boxe-Francaise. He works out on sides of beef. With his kicks he can break individual ribs."

"He ought to market it. 'Belghazi's meat tenderizer.'"

She didn't laugh. "And he carries a straight razor."

"Good for him," I said.

She looked at me. "I wouldn't take it lightly."

"You know what they teach salesmen?" I asked, looking at her. "Don't sell past the close. I already told you I would stand down, for now. You don't need to keep trying to persuade me."

She smiled, and for an instant I thought the smile looked strangely sad. "Ah, I see," she said.

We were quiet for a moment. Then she said, "Tell me,

do you think I went to bed with you ... tactically? To manipulate you?"

I looked at her. "Did you?"

She dropped her eyes. "That's something you have to decide for yourself."

There was a kiss, oddly tentative after our recent bout of passion, and then she was gone. I waited fifteen seconds, then slipped off the bathrobe and pulled on my clothes. The rest of my things were still in my bag. I waited a minute, looking through the peephole and using the SoldierVision to confirm that the corridor outside the door was empty. It was. I moved out into it, taking various staircases and internal corridors until I reached the ground floor. I used one of the rear exits, which put me on Hankow Road, cut across Nathan, and took the elevator down to the MTR. I made some aggressive moves to ensure that I wasn't being followed. I wasn't. I was all alone.

7

I SLEPT AT the Ritz Carlton, across the harbor. It was a shame to have to leave the Peninsula, but Delilah knew I was there, and might share that knowledge. Better to sever the potential connection.

I woke up the next morning feeling refreshed. I thought about Delilah. She badly wanted those two days of grace, the day or two during which Belghazi had "meetings in the region." I assumed that whatever he was doing on this trip was what Delilah and her people had been waiting for. They must have been expecting that something from the trip would wind up on his computer, something important, and that's when they would act.

But why had she tried to access it that night in his suite, then? Opportunistic, maybe. A warm-up. Yeah, could be that. But no way to be sure. At least not yet.

And all my conjecture assumed that she was telling me the truth, of course. I couldn't really know. I needed more information, something I could use to triangulate. I hoped I'd get it from Kanezaki.

I showered and shaved and enjoyed a last soak in the room's fine tub before going down to the front desk to check out. The pretty receptionist looked at me for a moment, then politely excused herself. Before I had a chance to consider what this could be about, she had returned with the manager, a thin specimen with a pencil mustache.

"Ah, Mr. Watanabe," he said, using the alias I had checked in under, "we believe a man might be looking for you. A police matter, it seems. He says it is important that you contact him. He left this phone number." He handed me a piece of paper.

I nodded, doing nothing to betray my consternation, and took the paper. "I don't understand. Why didn't you call me about this?"

"I'm very sorry, sir. But the man didn't even know your name. He left a photograph at the front desk. It was only just now, when the receptionist saw you, that she realized you might be the gentleman in question."

"Is that all? Was there anything else? Did the man leave a name?"

He shook his head. "I'm sorry."

"May I see the photo?"

"Of course." He reached down and produced what I recognized as an excellent forgery—a digitized image of my likeness. The face in the photo wasn't a dead ringer, but it was more than close enough.

I thanked them, paid the bill, and left, checking the lobby more carefully than I had when I had entered it. Nothing seemed out of order.

I did a series of thorough surveillance detection moves, wondering how the hell someone could have tracked me, and who it could have been. Having someone stay on you when you think you've gotten clean feels highly unpleasant.

When I was confident I was alone, I found a pay phone. I punched in the number the hotel had given me.

The phone on the other end rang twice. Then a voice

boomed out, *"Moshi moshi,"* Japanese for hello, in a thick Southern twang.

"Jesus Christ," I said. Dox.

"Well, some people think so, but no, it's just me," he said, with annoying good cheer. "Did I get the Japanese right?"

"Yeah, it was perfect."

"I think you're just saying that. But thank you anyway."

"What do you want?"

"Ain't you going to ask how I found you?"

"Not until I put you in another leglock."

He laughed. "I told you, you don't need to do that. I'll tell you what you want to know. In person."

I paused, then said, "All right."

"Where are you now? Still at the hotel?"

That's when it hit me. I knew how he'd done it.

"Yeah," I said, testing my theory.

"Well, okay, good. I'll come to you. Tell me, though, I don't know Hong Kong so well, what's the best way to get there again?"

I smiled. "Taxi."

"Sure, that makes sense. But give me some directions. I like to know where I'm going."

Yeah, that was it. I'd been right. "Just tell the driver the name of the hotel," I said. "I'm sure he'll be able to find it."

There was a pause, during which I imagined him looking decidedly nonplussed. "Damn, what was the name of the place again?" he asked, trying valiantly.

I laughed and said nothing. After a moment, he said, "All right, all right, you got me. I'll meet you anywhere you want."

"Why would I want to meet you at all?"

"All right, I was out of line. Just wanted to see if I could sneak one past you, but you're too slick. But you'll still want to hear what I've got to tell you. Believe me on that."

I thought for a moment. Of course I wanted to meet him. I needed to know what all this was about. But I would have to take precautions. Precautions that could prove fatal to Dox if things didn't go the way I wanted them to.

"Where are you now?" I asked.

"In a coffee shop in Central, ogling a table of Chinese girls. I think they like me."

"They must not know about your sheep proclivities," I said.

He laughed. "Shoot, partner, not unless you told them."

"Stay put for a while. I'll call you back."

"Where are you going?"

"I'll call you back," I said again, and hung up.

If this had been Tokyo, I could have told him immediately where we should meet and how. I had studied the city for the twenty-five years I'd lived there, and knew dozens of venues that would have worked. But Hong Kong was less familiar to me. I needed to map things out.

I walked to the causeway, then headed west, toward Sheung Wan, looking for the right locale. It was Sunday, and the area was animated with the chatter of thousands of the island's Filipina maids, who were out enjoying a weekly day of relief from their labors. They sat on flattened cardboard in the shade of the long causeway ceiling and picnicked on *pancit palabok* and *sotanghon* and *kilawing tanguige* and other comfort food and felt, for a few brief moments, that they were home again. I liked how physical they were: the way they braided each other's hair, and held hands, and sat so close together, like children finding solace, a talisman against something fearful, in simple human contact. Despite their transplanted lives and the loss of what they left behind, there was something childlike about them, and I thought that it was probably this seeming innocence, joined incongruously to an adult sexuality, that drove so many western men mad for Southeast Asian women. Such charms are not lost on me, either, but at that moment, desire wasn't really what I felt for them. What I felt, dull and somehow surprising, was more akin to envy.

I continued down the causeway, then moved south into the Western District, named entirely for its position relative to Central and without reference to culture or atmosphere. In fact, characterized as it is by the craggy faces of ancient herbalists concocting snake musk and powdered lizards and other such antique pharmacopoeia; the aroma of incense from its temples and of cooking from snake restaurants and dim-sum bakeries; the cries of its fishmongers and street cleaners and merchants, Western feels significantly more "eastern" than the rest of Hong Kong.

I stopped in one of the innumerable bric-a-brac shops on Cat Street and bought several secondhand items, all of which were intended to distract the shopkeeper and would soon be discarded, save one: a gutting knife with a four-inch blade and a horn handle. The knife was nestled in a leather sheath and the blade was satisfactorily sharp.

In my wallet was an old credit card, around which I keep wrapped several feet of duct tape. Thousand and one uses, they say, one of which, it seemed, was securing a gutting knife to the underside of a causeway banister. If I saw anyone following us or detected any other signs of duplicity, I would lead Dox past the banister, retrieve the knife, and finish him with it.

I would have preferred to keep the blade on my person, but Dox wasn't stupid, despite the appearance he cultivated, and I knew he'd be looking for signs of a weapon. Adequate concealment on my body was possible, of course, but would make for an unacceptably time-consuming deployment. Better to have the element of surprise. Likewise, it would have been sensible to wear some extra clothing, with a running suit or something similar between the outer and inner layers, which I could quickly peel off afterward if things got messy. But I knew this was also something Dox would spot. There was a compromise, though. I purchased a dark nylon jacket and a carton of baby wipes, which I stashed under a trashcan in a public restroom not far from where I had placed the knife. If I had to deal with Dox and got bloody in the process, I could duck into the restroom and quickly make myself presentable again.

I continued east on the causeway, then into the International Financial Center, which houses a large shopping mall. I wandered around until I had found a suitable setup: a third-floor vantage point overlooking a second-floor bookseller called Dymock's. From the third floor I could monitor not only the entrance to the bookstore, but the nearby second-floor entrance to the mall and the approaches to my position, as well. If I saw something I didn't like, I could disappear in any one of a number of directions.

I called Dox from a pay phone.

"Moshi moshi," he said, in his thick drawl.

I wondered briefly whether I was giving Dox too

much credit in thinking that his hayseed thing was only an act.

"Still ogling those girls?" I asked.

"Them and some new ones," he said, his voice booming with good cheer. "There's enough of me for all of 'em."

"Meet me in the Dymock's bookstore in the IFC shopping mall."

"The what? I don't . . ."

"Save the hillbilly stuff for someone who cares," I interrupted. "The International Financial Center shopping mall. Second floor. At Hong Kong station on the MTR. It should take you less than fifteen minutes to get there. Longer than that and I'm gone."

"All right, all right, no need to get unpleasant about it, I'm on my way."

"I'll be watching along the way, Dox. If you're not alone, I'm going to take it personally."

"I know, I know."

He did know, too. We'd worked together. He'd seen what I could do.

I hung up, went back to my position, and waited.

I didn't know the details, of course, but then I didn't really need to. Dox knew I was in Hong Kong because that's where I'd placed the call to Kanezaki. Somehow he'd created that photograph of me. He'd known me before and had seen me recently; maybe he had worked with a technician the way a witness works with a police sketch artist. Or maybe they had a military-era photo and had digitized it to account for the effects of plastic surgery and the intervening decades. Regardless, Dox would have taken the photo around to hotels on Hong Kong and Kowloon. He knew me, so he would start with the best and work his way down. That's why he knew I was at a hotel, but didn't know which one.

I realized he'd probably been to the Peninsula, too, but I had left there in too much of a hurry to bother with a formal checkout. Maybe he would have flashed some sort of government ID, U.S. Customs requesting a favor, something like that. Or maybe he even had local liaison. Sure, the Ritz manager had said something about this being a "police matter." Maybe the Agency had asked the local gendarmerie for assistance. Great.

I shook my head a little sadly. Staying at high-end hotels when I'm moving around is one of the few luxuries I have. Now I saw that the habit had become a liability. I would have to jettison it.

I tried not to take it personally. Dox, Kanezaki, they had their reasons. They were just doing their jobs.

Well, if it got to be too much, I would just do mine. No hard feelings, guys. You know how it is.

Ten minutes later I watched him enter the shopping mall through the second-floor entrance to my right. For the moment, he seemed to be alone. If he was with anyone, they were hanging back beyond the entrance.

As he went to turn into the bookstore I called to him. "Dox. Up here."

He looked up and smiled. "Hey there."

"Use the escalator to your right," I told him. "Hurry."

He did. While he moved, I waited to see whether anyone came in the entrance behind him, trying to keep up. No one did.

When he reached the top of the escalator, I started moving. "Turn left," I said. "Just head through the mall. I'll be right behind you. I'll tell you what to do next."

"Don't you get tired of this stuff?" he asked, giving me a hangdog look.

I watched the escalator behind him. "Go," I said. "Now."

He did. I watched the escalator and the entrance for a moment longer. All clear. Then I caught up to him and fell in just behind and to the right of him. Harry's detector stayed quiet.

We came to a maintenance corridor. "Here," I said. "Turn right."

He did. We walked a few meters in. "Stop," I said. "Face the wall."

He gave me a long-suffering sigh, but did as I asked. I patted him down. No weapons. I took his cell phone, turned it off, and pocketed it.

"Will you give that back when school's over?" he asked.

"Sure," I said. "If you're good. Now head out."

I looked back the way we had come from. Nothing set off my radar. So far, so good.

I took him through a provocative series of maneuvers that would have forced a pursuit team into the open. If I'd seen anything, I would have taken him past the knife and ended the bullshit then and there. But he was alone.

I took him to a hole-in-the-wall restaurant deep in Pok Fu Lam, far enough from the island's tourist areas to draw only the most intrepid sightseers. The area was arguably a slum, but I liked it. In some ways, I found its crumbling four-story buildings, their paint faded and peeling from decades of subtropical moisture, their ornate balconies and carved balustrades by contrast strangely proud, even defiant, to be more pleasing than the trademark wealth and power of the districts east. Dox, enormous, bearded, and, most of all, Caucasian, looked decidedly out of place among the other diners, but he didn't seem to mind. The menu was entirely in

Chinese, but I knew the characters and was able to point to what I wanted.

"What is this?" Dox asked, after the soup had arrived and we had begun to eat. "It's tasty."

"Good for you, too," I said. "A Chinese Olympic running coach used to feed it to his star athletes."

"Yeah? What's in it?"

"The usual stuff. Spring water. Mountain vegetables. Turtle blood and caterpillar fungus."

He paused, the spoon halfway to his lips. "You serious?"

"Well, that's what it said on the menu."

He nodded as though considering. "Those Chinese runners are quick. If it's good enough for them, I guess I can have some, too." He slurped the rest down with a smile.

I wasn't surprised. I'd seen Dox dine on equally unusual fare in the field in Afghanistan. Always with relish.

When we were done with the soup, I asked him to tell me what was going on.

"Well now," he said, leaning back in his chair. "You wouldn't believe the things they've trained me on. Forging ID, hacking computer networks, locks and picks, flaps and seals . . . And not just the training, they give me the toys! I've got a twenty-five-thousand-dollar color laser copier, special paper, inks, hologram kits, magnetic stripe encoders, shoot, buddy, I can whip up fake ID that'd make your hair stand up! You want something, you just let me know."

"You didn't come here just to make a sales pitch for fake ID, did you?" I asked.

He seemed to brighten at that, and I wondered if Dox had come to the conclusion that my occasional barbed remarks were actually terms of endearment. That would be perverse.

"I had a weird meeting with a guy the other day," he said, grinning. "Came all the way to see me in Bangkok, where I was relaxing and revivifying at the time. Told me his name was Johnson. But his real name is Crawley. Charles Crawley. The Third. Imagine, a family that would want to perpetuate a silly name like that when they could have named him something imaginative like Dox."

"How'd you get his real name?"

The grin widened. "Shit, I could smell lies all over that boy. So I pretended to get a call on my cell phone while we were talking. I used the phone to take his picture."

He must have had one of the units with a built-in digital camera. In these matters it used to be that you only had to worry about the odd amateur who happened to be carrying a camcorder, like Zapruder or that guy who caught the police working over Rodney King. Now it was anyone with a damn cell phone.

I pulled out the unit I had confiscated from him. "This phone?" I asked.

He nodded. "Go ahead, take a look."

I hit the "on" button and waited for a moment while the phone powered up. Yeah, it was an Ericsson P900, new and slick, with a built-in camera and a lot more. I handed it to Dox. He worked the buttons for a moment, then gave it back to me. I saw a surprisingly sharp image of a fine-boned, thirty-something-year-old Caucasian with curly wheat-blond hair, blue eyes, a thin nose, and thinner lips. The picture had been taken from an odd, and apparently surreptitious, angle.

"Weaselly-looking little fuck, ain't he. I got a few more if you want to take a look. Just press that advance key there."

I did as he indicated and scrolled through, getting a

better sense of what Crawley looked like. Photos aren't always good likenesses. If you see more than one, you increase your chances of being able to recognize the subject in person. Which I was beginning to think I might want to do.

When I was done, I turned the phone off and handed it back to Dox. He was still smiling. "If you want, I can forward the photos directly to your cell phone," he said. "Or to an e-mail account. Hell, if you feel like having fun, we can post old Crawley's face on any bulletin board you'd like! Dumbass didn't even know what I was doing. Shame on him for failing to keep up with the ever-advancing march of technology."

"Who is he?" I asked.

"Well, his résumé says he's with the Consular Affairs section of the State Department."

I couldn't help smiling. "Looks like Consular Affairs has a pretty wide-ranging brief these days."

He smiled back. "They certainly do."

"How'd you find this out?" I asked.

"Come on, buddy, I can't tell you all my sources and methods! You know magicians don't like to show how they do their tricks."

I looked at him and said nothing.

"All right, all right, just having a little fun with you. No need to get so serious on me with those scary eyes and all. I ran the photos through a new Agency database. The database compiles images from electronic media—online versions of newspapers and magazines, video, whatever. You feed in your photo, the system goes out and tries to find a match using something called XML—entensible markup language, something like that. It's like Google, but with pictures instead of words. I think they stole it from some start-up company."

"It worked?" I said, thinking, *Christ, what are they going to come up with next?*

"Well, sure, it worked. Gave me a couple thousand false positives, though. The Agency has a little way to go before Google has any reason to panic, I'll tell you that. But you know me, I like to party, but I can be patient, too. I went through all the hits until I came across the unforgettable face of Mr. Crawley." He reached into his pocket and took out a piece of paper, unfolded it, and handed it to me. "See there? That's him, standing next to the Ambassador to Jordan at a press conference the Ambassador was giving in Amman. Doesn't he look important?"

"Very. What did he want?"

He leaned forward. "Well, here's where it gets interesting. He told me he represented very, very, senior interests in the U.S. government. But that, for national security reasons, these interests had to maintain good old 'plausible deniability' about certain courses of action and couldn't meet with me personally as a result, much as they of course would otherwise like to. Yeah, 'certain courses of action,' I think that was how he put it. I think he liked hearing himself talk. Anyway, he told me that there was this former undercover operative who'd gone rogue and killed a bunch of friendlies in Hong Kong and Macau, and who needed to be 'removed,' is what he said. I said, 'Removed?' Having fun with the guy now, you understand. And he nods and says, with his voice serious, the way I guess he imagines Really Important Government representatives should talk about these things, 'We want his actions terminated.' Lord help me, I couldn't stop myself, I said to him, with my eyes all wide now, 'With Extreme Prejudice?' And he just nods once, like he was afraid if his head had gone up and down more than that it could get him into trouble."

"And then?"

"Oh, after that, the usual praise for my past service to my country and appeals to my patriotism. You know the drill. Then he tells me he's got twenty-five thousand dollars for me right now, and another seventy-five thousand upon completion, if I take on this little service that Uncle Sam wants of me."

"And you said?"

"I told him it would of course be an honor to serve my country on this most auspicious occasion. He gives me a key to a coin locker, shakes my hand, thanks me— again!—for my 'patriotism,' and walks away. I go to the locker, and who does it turn out this 'rogue operator' is? Well, none other than my friend from the good old days in 'Stan, the intelligent and charming Mr. John Rain."

I nodded, considering, then said, "Why are you telling me all this? Didn't you say, 'opportunity only knocks once'? Why not do the job, take the money?"

He smiled at me. The smile said, *I knew you were going to say that.* I supposed it made him feel good to prove that, at least on certain occasions, he was capable of thinking ahead of me.

"I'll tell you, buddy, there are some things a marine won't do, not even to an army type like you. I figure we veterans have to stand up for each other, since no one else seems to want to. Besides, I didn't much care for the way old Crawley treated me. Shoot, that boy made me out for nothing but a dumb cracker, didn't he. Just like you do, if you don't mind my not mincing my words."

I looked at him. "I don't think you're half as dumb as you act, Dox. And you might not even be as dumb as that."

He laughed. "I always knew you loved me."

"What about the money?"

"Shit, I'd rather take twenty-five thousand for nothing than a hundred thousand for doing something that didn't sit right with me, wouldn't you?"

"Maybe. But won't Crawley want the money back?"

"Well, he might, and I might like to give it to him. Trouble is, I can't remember where I put it. Think maybe I invested it with a securities trader or some other unscrupulous type. It might already be gone."

I smiled. "Crawley might be angry about that."

"I expect he will be. He might even try to hire another 'patriot' to 'remove' me for taking advantage of him. But that would cost him another hundred grand. No, I think I know Mr. Crawley's type. I think he'll decide it's best to just swallow the insult and live to fight another day. That is, if he lives another day. I know the news I'm giving you might make you righteous angry. It would me."

He picked up his soup bowl, raised it to his mouth, and drained it. "Aaaaah," he said, setting the bowl down on the table and leaning back in his chair. "Nothing like caterpillar fungus. You know, there's one more thing. You may not have noticed it at the time, but you were always decent to me in 'Stan. I was the only one there who hadn't served in Vietnam, and the other guys were a little cliquish, I always thought. Made me feel like I wasn't welcome. You weren't like that. Not that you ever acted like we were long-lost brothers, but you didn't seem to have a problem with me, either."

I shrugged. "You were good in the field."

He nodded and started to say something, then looked down and swallowed. What I'd said had been as dry to me as it was true, and I wasn't expecting any particular response in reaction. So it took me a second to realize that Dox was struggling with his emotions.

After a moment he looked at me, his eyes determined, almost fierce. "And that's all that should count," he said.

I thought of the rumors I'd heard in Afghanistan about how he'd had to leave the Corps after getting physical with an officer. "Somebody once tell you otherwise?" I asked.

He drummed his fingers on the table, looking into the dregs of his caterpillar soup. Then he said, "I'm a damn good sniper, man. Damn good. I'd never been in combat before 'Stan, but I knew what I could do. Top of my class at Sniper School at Quantico. But there was one instructor who had it in for me. Because, even though my skills were top-quality—spotting and target detection, stalking and movement, marksmanship—I didn't always act like what a sniper is supposed to act like."

I couldn't help a gentle smile. "You're a little more reserved than most snipers," I said.

He smiled back. "Yeah, snipers tend to be a soft-spoken breed, it's true. They start out that way, and their work reinforces the tendency. But I'm not like that, and never was. When I'm in the zone, I'm as stealthy and deadly as anyone. But when I'm not in the zone, I need to cut loose sometimes. That's just who I am."

I nodded, surprised at the sympathy I felt. "And not everyone liked that."

He shrugged. "You know, regular military types aren't comfortable with snipers. They think we're cold-blooded killers, assassins, whatever. Sure, it's okay to return fire in a mad minute firefight, or mortar someone from a mile away, but moving through the woods like a ghost? Picking up your quarry's sign like he's just a deer or something? Stalking him, or waiting in a hide, then blowing his brains out with Zen-like calm? You should hear the way the regulars will beg for your help when they've got a problem that only a sniper can solve, though. Then you're everybody's daddy. Of course, that's only until the problem's solved. Anyway, what snipers do, it all makes the hypocrites uncomfortable."

I nodded. "I know."

He nodded back. "I know you do. Truth is, partner, in a lot of ways, you act more like a sniper than I do. I don't know what kind of marksman you are, but you've got that habit of stillness about you. And you know what it's like to hunt humans. You don't have a problem with it."

There was a short stretch of silence, during which I considered his words. It wasn't the first time I'd been the recipient of that particular "praise," but I wanted to hear Dox's story, not tell him mine.

After a moment, he said, "Anyway, yeah, the regular marines thought I was one of the sociopaths, and the snipers thought I was a freak. The fact that my scores were higher than theirs just pissed them off. Especially a certain officer. Now, all snipers get subjected to stress during training. When you're trying to shoot, the instructors will be screaming at you, or playing loud music they know you hate, or otherwise trying to fuck with you. That's all good, it produces dead shots and you better be able to deal with stress if you want your skills to work in the real world. But this guy kept doing more and more, 'cause none of the shit he was coming up with was throwing me off. Finally he started 'accidentally' jarring my rifle while he was screaming at me, and even though I could give a shit about the screaming, of course his bumping into my rifle was enough to throw off my shot. Well, the first time I didn't say anything. The second time I stood up and got in his face. Which is what that fuck was hoping for. He wrote in my fitness report that I had 'anger management' issues and in his opinion was 'temperamentally unsuited' to be a sniper. When I found out about that, I busted him up good."

I nodded, thinking of how the young eager beaver CIA officer Holtzer had been in Vietnam had run a similar game with me, and how he had elicited a similarly stupid, albeit satisfying, reaction. Holtzer had gone on to become the CIA's Station Chief in Tokyo, and had carried a grudge all the way to the grave I finally sent him to.

"They court-martial you?" I asked.

He shook his head. "No, enough people knew this guy was an asshole so that someone pulled some strings and saved me from all that. But the fitness report was permanent, and my career wasn't going anywhere after all that. At least not until the Russians decided to try and swallow Afghanistan. Then Uncle Sam needed tainted people like me, and all was forgiven."

"It always seemed like you had something to prove over there," I said.

He smiled. "Well yeah, I did. You know, I had a lot of personal kills in 'Stan—three of them at over a thousand yards. Not bad for someone 'temperamentally unsuited,' I'd say. Carlos Hathcock would have been proud."

Carlos Hathcock was the most successful sniper ever, with ninety-three confirmed kills in Vietnam, one of them a twenty-five-hundred-yard shot with a .50-caliber rifle, and maybe three times that many unconfirmed.

"You know, I met Hathcock once," I said, thinking of what Dox had just said about my sniper's stillness. "In Vietnam. Before anyone knew who he was."

"No! You met the man?"

I nodded.

"Well, what did he say to you?"

I shrugged. "Not much. He was sitting by himself at a

table in a bar in Saigon. The only empty seat was at the table, so I took it. We just introduced ourselves, really, that was all. I had a beer and left. I don't think we exchanged more than a couple dozen words."

"No? He didn't say anything to you?"

I was quiet for a moment, remembering. "When I left, he told me I should be a sniper."

"Damn, man, he saw your soul. That's like being blessed by the Pope."

I didn't say anything. My army fitness reports; the darkly humorous observations of my blood brother, Crazy Jake; that parting comment from Hathcock; now Dox's thoughts, too. I wished I could just accept their collective judgment, accept what I am. Accept it, hell. I wished I could fucking embrace it. Other people seemed able to.

We were quiet for a few moments. I asked, "Why do you suppose Crawley has gotten it into his head to try and take me out?"

"That I don't know. All I could get out of Mr. Crawley was that bullshit about how you'd gone rogue and the details could only be distributed on a 'need to know' basis."

"And you don't need to know."

He sighed in mock dejection. "Even though I am a 'patriot' and all. Kind of hurts my feelings, when I think about it. Well, there is that twenty-five grand to perk me back up if I get overly blue."

"How did Crawley know how to contact you? Or even who you are?"

He nodded as though considering. "Well, I'm reasonably confident that our Mr. Crawley is in fact in the service of our current employer, in some capacity or other. If that's the case, he might have access to my particulars."

"You think Kanezaki is involved?" I asked.

He shrugged. "Can't help thinking that, can you? He sure is in the middle of a lot of the shit, for a young guy."

"He's a quick study."

"Yeah, I've got the same feeling. But I'll tell you, I don't think he's behind this. It's my sentimental side showing, I know, but I think that boy's got an okay heart."

"How long will he be able to keep it that way, working with who he works with?"

"Well, that's a question now, I'll admit it."

We were quiet for a few moments. "I can reach you at the number I've got?" I asked.

"Anytime you want," he said. "What are you going to do?"

"Make a few calls," I told him. "Figure out what makes sense."

He flashed me the grin. "You always were the cautious type."

"It's part of the reason I've lasted so long."

"I know that. Hell, I meant it as a compliment."

I stood and put some bills on the table. Then I held out my hand. "You're a good man, Dox."

He stood and smiled back, a lower wattage but more genuine version of the grin. We shook. "Watch your back now, you hear?" he said.

I nodded and left.

After making sure I was clean, I took the Peak Tramway to Victoria Peak, then walked Lugard Road through its forests of bamboo and fern. I found a quiet place and sat, listening to the cicadas.

The first thing I thought, as always, was *set up.*

Someone, maybe Crawley, maybe someone he works with, is after you. They get Dox to lay out a line of bullshit, knowing that I'll come after Crawley as a result. Straight into an ambush.

No. Too uncertain. No one could count on Dox to be convincing, not to that degree.

Then they gave Dox the job for real. Plan A was he takes the job and kills me. Plan B is he spills everything to me, in which case I go after Crawley. Back to an ambush.

No. Too uncertain. When would I come at Crawley? Where? How? Besides, Crawley would have to be awfully comfortable with risk to invite retaliation from me.

Dox, or someone else, has his own reasons for wanting Crawley taken out, and he's trying to goad you into doing it.

That one was worth chewing over, but in the end I judged it unlikely. Dox was a pretty direct guy in his way. If he wanted Crawley to go to sleep, he'd sing the lullaby himself. I would keep the possibility in mind, but it seemed in this case that the most likely explanation was also the simplest: Dox was telling me the truth.

Now what to do about it. The most direct approach would be to brace Crawley. Ask him a few questions. Use my charm.

But not yet. First, I needed to see how all of this tied in with Belghazi. A half-Arab target, an Arab assassination team, a CIA officer trying to take out a contract on me? Even for a guy like me, who's made a few enemies along the way, it was hard to think that the timing was all just a coincidence. I wanted more information before acting, and I thought Kanezaki might be able to provide some of that.

8

I CALLED TATSU from a pay phone.

"*Nanda?*" I heard him say, in typically curt greeting.
What is it?

"*Hisashiburi,*" I said, letting him hear my voice. It's
been a long time.

There was a pause. He said in Japanese, "I've been
thinking of you."

Coming from Tatsu this was practically sentimental.
"You're not getting mushy on me, are you?" I asked.

He laughed. "My daughters say I am."

"Well, they would know."

"I'm afraid they would. And you? Are you well?"

"Well enough. I need a favor."

"Yes?"

"I'll send you a message," I said, referring to our electronic bulletin board.

There was a pause, then he said, "Will I be seeing you?"

"I hope so."

Another pause. "*Jaa,*" he said. Well, then.

"Take care, old friend."

"*Otagai ni na,*" he said. And you.

I uploaded the message at an Internet café. Then I
made my way to Hong Kong International Airport. I

caught a flight to Seoul, and from there to Narita International in Tokyo. And so, that very evening, I was mildly surprised at being back in Japan.

From Narita, I took a Narita Express train to Tokyo station, where I emerged to find my former city hunched up against characteristically rainy and cold late autumn weather. I stood under the portico roof at the station's Marunouchi entrance and took in the scene. Waves of black umbrellas bobbed before me. Wet leaves were plastered to the pavement, ground in by the tires of oblivious cars and the soles of insensate pedestrians, by the weight of the entire, indifferent metropolis.

I watched for a long time. Then I turned and disappeared back into the station, borne down by a feeling of invisibility that was nothing like the one I had assiduously cultivated while living here.

I bought a cheap umbrella for an extortionate thousand yen and caught a Yamanote line train to Nishi-Nippori, where I checked into an undistinguished business hotel, one of dozens in this part of *shitamachi*, the scarred yet stalwart low city of old Edo. With the lights off, I could have been anywhere. And yet I was keenly aware that I was in Japan, I was in Tokyo.

I slept poorly, awaking to another gray and rainy day. I made my way to Sengoku, where I had lived for so many years before getting burned by Holtzer and having to leave for more anonymous climes.

Outside Sengoku station, I discovered that the features of an area I had remembered with some fondness had been erased. In their place had grown a McDonald's on one corner, a Denny's on the other. There was a chain drugstore; a chain convenience store; and other chains, all intended, no doubt, to offer increased choice and variety. A more pleasant, more efficient shopping experience. The city's implacable engines of progress grinding on, I supposed, the homogenous expression of some increasingly senescent collective unconscious.

I reminded myself that all I owned of Sengoku were memories. The neighborhood itself was someone else's to ruin.

I opened my umbrella, crossed the street, and walked until I passed my old apartment. And here, away from the station's newly gaudy façade, I was surprised to find that all was almost exactly as I remembered: the gardens with their carefully tended plantings, the stone walls draped in patterns of gentle moss, the buildings of ancient wood and tile roofs, standing with dignity and determination beside their younger brick and metal cousins. Children's bicycles were still clustered around doorways; umbrellas dripped as they always had from stands before small stores. The periphery had changed, I saw, but the core remained resolutely the same.

I laughed. What I had just seen at the station had been disappointing, but had also allowed me some compensatory sense of superiority. What I found afterward came as a relief, but carried with it a profound feeling of insignificance. Because I understood now that in Sengoku, life had just . . . gone on. The neighborhood was as untroubled by my loss as it had been unaware of my presence. When I had lived here, I realized, I had dared to think that perhaps I had belonged, that in some way my living here mattered. Now I could see that these thoughts had been, in their way, narcissistic. Certainly they had been mistaken.

I thought of Midori, of what she had once told me of *mono no aware,* what she had called the "sadness of being human," and wished for a naked second that I could talk to her.

I took a final look around, trying to recollect the life I once had here. There was a feeling that lingered, certainly, something insubstantial that expressed its longing for corporeity in the form of a series of long sighs, but nothing I could really grasp. The interior of the town was just the same, yes, and yet, imbued with the unfair weight of my memories, it was now all hauntingly changed. I didn't belong here anymore, and I felt like an apparition, something unnatural that was right to have left and foolish to have returned.

I walked back to the station and called Kanezaki from a pay phone.

"I was just going to upload something for you," he said.

"Good. Where are you now?"

"Tokyo."

"Where in Tokyo?"

There was a pause. He said, "Are you here?"

"Yes. Where are you now?"

"The embassy."

"Good. Be outside Sengoku station in thirty minutes. Take the Mita line from Uchisaiwaicho."

"I know how to get there."

I smiled. "Walk up the west side of Hakusan-dori, toward Sugamo. When you get to Sugamo station, turn around and walk back. Repeat as necessary."

"All right."

"Come alone. Don't break the rules." There was no need to mention penalties.

I waited on Hakusan-dori northeast of Sengoku station, the umbrella held low to obscure my features, ready to bolt into the hive of alleys and streets behind me if something went wrong and Kanezaki violated the procedure I had established.

Twenty-five minutes later, he emerged onto the sidewalk and began walking toward me. He seemed to be alone. When he had pulled even with me, I called out to him. He looked over. I motioned that he should cross the street, and watched that no one performed the identical move behind him.

For the next half hour, I kept us moving on foot, by subway, and by taxi. Harry's bug detector was silent. I ended the run at a place called Ben's Café in Takadanobaba, in the relatively quiet northeast of the city.

We walked past the ivy-covered trellis and modest signage outside. Kanezaki took a deep breath as we walked through the door.

"Damn, it smells good in here," he said.

I nodded. I find few smells as welcoming as the accumulated aroma of years of reverential coffee preparation.

"You know, if anyone ever catches on to your coffee shop and café habit," he said, as we settled down at one of the small wooden tables, "they could probably track you."

"Probably. Assuming they had the manpower to cover the thousand or so that I like in Tokyo."

Actually, Ben's had been one of my favorites, and I was glad to be back. The place has the feel of a college town coffeehouse, which in some ways it is, given the proximity of Waseda University and some smaller schools in the area. It's got that laid-back air, the murmur of laughter and conversation always accompanying the house music at just the right, relaxing pitch; the eclectic regulars, in this case Japanese and foreign, neighborhood residents as well as sojourners from more distant corners of the city; the overflowing community bulletin board advertising support groups and theater and poetry readings. Cozy but not cramped; cool but not self-important; welcoming but not overly familiar, Ben's would surely qualify as a Living Metropolitan Haven, if the government ever decided to grant such designations to Tokyo's periodic sensory overload shelters.

We each ordered the house blend, a mixture of Brazilian and Guatemalan beans, roasted fresh that morning. We didn't spend any more time on pleasantries.

"What have you got for me?" I asked him.

"This time, a lot."

"Good."

"To start with, the woman. Check this out. Twice before, a player we would describe as part of the terrorist infrastructure—finance and logistics, not a foot soldier— has been spotted with a striking blonde. Each time, within two months of the spotting, the guy in question is found shot to death."

I looked at him. "Why didn't you tell me this the first time?"

"This information isn't indexed. I can't just search the files for 'hot blonde and dead terrorist infrastructure,' okay? I came across these commonalities the old-fashioned way, by reading a lot of thick files. Which takes time."

That was fair. "All right."

"We don't have anything else on this woman. No name, nothing. No one has ever made the connection before, and I probably wouldn't have, either, if you hadn't gotten me looking in the right direction."

My face betrayed nothing, but I thought, *This is what Delilah was afraid of.*

"And?" I asked.

He shrugged. "Well, I don't think this woman's

presence in the lives of two, and now maybe three, soon-to-be-departed infrastructure types is a coincidence. My guess is, she's working for someone, setting these guys up."

"One of Charlie's Angels?"

He chuckled. "More like the Angel of Death."

"Seems a little thin."

He looked at me, and I realized I might have protested just a bit too much. "Maybe," he said. "But both of the guys she was seen with were killed while traveling, not at choke points like their homes or in the company of known associates. One while passing through Vienna, the other vacationing in Belize. Meaning someone was tracking them, tracking their movements. Tracking closely."

I shrugged. "Could be the woman, but there are other ways to triangulate on a moving target. You didn't need to sleep with Belghazi to tell me where I could find him."

Reasonable enough, but I could feel that he sensed I was arguing with him, and was suspicious about why. I needed to rein that shit in.

Kanezaki picked up his coffee and looked at it for a moment, then said, "There's more. Both bad guys died of a single twenty-two-caliber gunshot to the eye. Even from close up, and the victims were hit close up, that's a hell of a shot. Whoever pulled the trigger is confident enough to use something with low penetration power because he knows he can place one shot where it needs to go to get the job done."

He. Interesting.

"The woman's not the shooter?" I asked.

"I don't think so. I think she's the spotter. She's like a very specialized mole. She gets vetted by the target, passes the test, gets inside. The target is still taking other precautions, of course, and thinks he's safe. But there's a flaw in his security, and he's sleeping with it. Then, when the woman judges that the moment is right, she makes a phone call. That night, the guy she's with runs into a bullet. She's not there when it happens, and she vanishes afterward. No one knows she was involved."

He took a sip of coffee. "You know, I once read an article about unexplained car accidents. It seems a significant percentage of automotive fatalities gets filed under 'unknown causes.' Broad daylight, bright sunshine, a guy flips his car and dies. A lot of times when this happens, it turns out the windows were rolled down. So one theory is, the guy is driving along, listening to the radio, enjoying the beautiful day, and a bee flies into the car. The guy freaks, tries slapping at the bee, gets distracted, boom. The bee flies away. 'Unknown causes.' I think that's what we're dealing with here."

"Who's she working for, then?"

"Don't know. A lot of possibilities, because these guys have lots of enemies. Could be a business competitor, someone moving in on the weapons contracts or the cash transactions to get better access to the skim. Could be the French—they've got their fingers in everything and you never really know what the hell they're doing or why. But my guess is, it's an Israeli operation."

I nodded, both impressed by and not particularly liking his insights. It was one thing for me to have an idea of who Delilah was, who she was with. I could use the information any way I liked, I could control the situation. It was another thing to have the CIA taking an interest. "Why?" I asked.

He shrugged. "Because the Israelis have the most constant and immediate motive to disrupt the infrastructure and they're always trying to do so, any way they can. Because Israeli assassination teams like to work with twenty-twos—they're small and concealable and relatively quiet. The teams that killed the Septemberists who did Munich were using twenty-twos. And because the shooter is so good. And likewise for the woman. The guys she's setting up and knocking down aren't lightweights, so if she's doing what I think she's doing, she must be damn good at it. Mossad quality."

"You think she's Mossad?"

He nodded. "I think she's part of the Collections branch. Collections does the target assessment and evaluation, after a committee has decided on the hit. Specialists, called Kidon, or Bayonets, part of the special Metsada unit, are the actual triggermen. So the division of labor here, it has an Israeli feel to me. Have you seen her again?"

"No," I said, reflexively.

He paused for a moment, then said, "I was almost hoping you had. It's not impossible that she could have been behind whoever attacked you in Hong Kong."

Oddly enough, the notion seemed less likely when proposed by Kanezaki than it did when I was grappling with it myself.

"They were Arabs," I said.

"Mossad uses Arab factions all the time. False flag ops. But anyway, I don't know for sure that she's Israeli. I told you, she could also be working for a faction. Or she could be a freelancer." He smiled. "You know those freelancers, they'll work for anyone."

"Even the CIA," I said, not returning the smile.

"That's true. But she's not one of ours. I would know about it."

"I wouldn't overestimate how much you know about

what your organization is up to. Your motto could be, 'Don't worry, our right hand doesn't have a clue about the left.'"

He chuckled. "That can be true at times."

We were quiet for a moment.

I didn't want him to think I was protecting Delilah. Didn't want him to think there was anything personal motivating me. In my experience, giving the CIA emotional information is like handing a hot poker to a sadist. Better to have him think my attempts to downplay the woman's significance were motivated by something else.

"Anyway, I don't think the woman is as important as I first did," I said. "I only saw her the once. She's probably not the one in your files. I'm sure I can handle Belghazi just fine."

He raised an eyebrow. "You worried that, if we think someone else is going to take out Belghazi, we'll take you off the case?"

I could have smiled. He was good—a lot better than when I'd first gotten to know him—but he had just gone for the head fake I'd offered.

I frowned, overplaying it just slightly to convince him his suspicions were right, to make the impression stick. Pretending to ignore his question out of annoyance, I said, "I want to hear what you know about the team that just came after me."

He was quiet for a long moment. Then he said, "All right, I'll level with you. I think there's a leak on our side. But I don't want to say more until I've had a chance to run it down."

I was getting that feeling from him, that feeling of *this guy is an agent, I can run him just like they taught me down at the Farm, string him along, take him where I want him to go.*

I looked at him for a long moment, letting him feel the coldness in my eyes. "'I'll level with you,'" I repeated, saying it slowly. "You know, I've never liked that phrase. To me it always sounds like, 'Up until now I've been full of shit.'"

"No, it sounds like, 'Up until now, I've been judiciously holding something back.'"

"If you think I can appreciate the difference, you must assume I'm capable of CIA-class subtlety," I said, still looking at him.

His color deepened. He was remembering his security escort, the one whose neck I had broken.

"Look," he said, raising his hands, palms forward, "I've seen you act precipitously before, okay? You can be very direct, and I admire you for it, it's why you're so good at what you do. But if I tell you something half-baked that turns out to be wrong and you go off and act on it, there are going to be very serious repercussions. For everyone involved."

I said nothing. My expression didn't change.

"Besides," he went on, and his urge to keep talking satisfied me that his discomfort was increasing, "it's not like you've been totally aboveboard with me either, okay? You expect me to believe you haven't seen the woman again? I don't buy it. Whoever she is, the one in the file or someone else, she didn't travel all the way to Macau with Belghazi for a single cameo appearance. Trust works two ways, okay?"

Maybe I'd been wrong a moment earlier, thinking he was still a bit unseasoned. He was sharp, and getting sharper all the time. Shame on me for underestimating him.

But I'd give him a pat on the back later. For now, I needed to keep up the pressure.

"Did you have a fucking death squad come after you in the last week, Kanezaki?" I asked, my eyes still cold and direct. When he didn't answer, I said, "No, I didn't think so. Well, I did. In connection with a job for which you retained me. So let's just cut the 'love is a two-way street' bullshit right now or I'm going to conclude that you've been dissembling."

There was a long pause. Then he said, "All right. Belghazi is part of a list. A hit list. Of course, it's not called a 'hit list.' Even post-Nine-Eleven, no one would use a description like that."

I raised my eyebrows, thinking that maybe the geniuses who had once named an e-mail sniffing program 'Carnivore' had finally taken a class on marketing.

He took a sip of coffee. "The list is officially called the 'International Terrorist Threat Matrix,' or ITTM, for short. Unofficially, it's just called 'the list.' It was created and is continually updated by the Agency, in our capacity as central clearinghouse for all intelligence produced by the intelligence community. Its purpose is to identify the key players in the international terrorist infrastructure. Like the FBI's Most Wanted List, but broader. You know, a 'Who's Who.'"

"Are you still 'leveling' with me?" I asked.

He put his coffee down and looked left and right, as though searching for words. "See, that's what I'm talking about, the tendency to be precipitous," he said. "Will you just let me finish? Because I'm trying to tell you what you need to know."

It was a fair rebuke. I said nothing, and, after a moment, he went on. "The list existed before Nine-Eleven," he said, "but it's been substantially revised and expanded since then. And, since then, it has also doubled as a hit list—a nice, deniable hit list, because it's really just a wiring diagram and has been around in one form or another for a long time. So no one had to worry about giving the order to draw up a brand-new list that might make for riveting testimony in front of a hypocritical Congressional committee sometime down the road."

"A hit list that isn't a hit list."

"Exactly." He took a deep breath. "Now, a few days ago, I received a visit from a guy who works in another division of the Agency."

"Crawley?" I asked, watching him.

His eyes widened and he flinched just slightly—not enough to make me think he was deliberately creating the response for my benefit. And he flushed, an even more involuntary reaction. A full two seconds went by. Then he said, "Look, it doesn't matter who it was. Let's leave names out of it, all right?"

"Sure," I said, indulging him for the moment. His response had already been as eloquent as I could have hoped for.

"Now, this person . . . he wanted to see the list. Which is strange."

"Strange, how?" I asked.

"Well, first of all, no one wants to see the list. Key people know it exists, of course, but they don't want to know more than that. They want to be in a position to deny knowledge if it comes to that. You know, 'oh the ITTM? Yes, I seem to remember once hearing something about a Who's Who or something. . . .' That kind of thing."

He picked up his coffee and took another sip. "Now, of course, this guy's request was outside official channels. Just a phone call to arrange a meeting, then a personal visit at the embassy in Tokyo. No paper trail. Which tells me he was being careful."

"Why?"

He shrugged. "At first I thought the list. He wanted to be able to deny the meeting if he needed to, or, barring that, to be able to characterize it according to his 'best recollections.' Which, if you've noticed when it comes to official questioning, are never particularly good."

"Why do you say, 'at first'?"

"He asked a lot of general questions, but I could see that most of them were designed to hide his real interest."

"Which was?"

"First, is Belghazi on the list. Second, did we send someone to Macau to take Belghazi out."

I thought for a moment. "Why didn't you mention this to me earlier? You said the visit happened several days ago."

"I didn't think this was something that might affect you. I thought it was just the usual bureaucratic turf fighting. This guy is part of a division that could make a claim to being responsible for Belghazi, so I figured they were ticked that another division might be operating against him. Worst case, maybe they complain to the Deputy Director, 'Hey, Kanezaki's playing with our marbles,' that kind of thing. I didn't expect something like what seems to have happened, okay?"

"What division are we talking about?"

He paused, then said, "NE. Near East Division. The Middle East."

"What did you tell him in response to his questions?"

"That my understanding was that access to the list is granted by the Counter Terrorism Center, and that he should check with them. As to whether we were operating against Belghazi or anyone else, in Macau or anywhere else, that information was also need-to-know through the CTC."

"His reaction?"

He shrugged. "You know, he huffed and he puffed, but what could he do?"

"What did he do?"

"My guess is he went to the CTC."

"Would they have given him what he wanted?"

"Maybe. He's a pretty heavy hitter. If he complained about being out of the loop on Belghazi, they might have given him information to appease him, massage his ego."

"Why didn't he go to the CTC first, then?"

"I think two reasons. First, because he wanted to deal with the most junior person he thought would be able to produce what he needed. Maximum intimidation, maximum low profile, maximum deniability."

"Second?"

"Second, because I'm responsible for coordinating certain aspects of the list for Asia. Hong Kong and Macau are part of my purview. And, like I said, he seemed to have Macau on the brain."

"Meaning?"

"Meaning something happened in Macau recently that got his attention. Maybe something like, a French national who turns out to be a known independent contractor is found dead there with a broken neck. Which he asked about, specifically."

"Yeah, you mentioned something about that. The guy was a contractor?"

"I just said so," he said, looking at me.

He was catching on to the way I was leading him by feeding back pieces of what he'd just said. Good for him.

I smiled. "What did our friend want to know about the contractor?"

"Was he on our payroll."

"Was he?"

"No."

I looked at him. No way to tell whether he was lying. For now.

"Who was the contractor working for, if he wasn't working for you?"

"I don't know."

"Who do you think?"

He shrugged. "Why would you care? My guesses, about the woman, for example, are usually way off base."

I laughed. "That's true," I said. "But I find them amusing anyway."

He smiled, apparently having figured out that it was smart not to let me get a rise out of him. "I really don't know," he said. "And there are a lot of other things I don't know, either. I'm already speculating to fill in the gaps. I think what happened was, Belghazi's people learned about the dead French guy and got spooked. 'Who was he? Could he have been after Belghazi? Who hired him?' Belghazi is a professional paranoid. You know the type. I'm sure he would have investigated."

"You're saying there's a connection between Belghazi and the Agency guy who visited you recently?"

He was quiet for a moment, then said, "Let me tell you about those phone numbers you gave me."

"All right."

"First, the cell phone you picked up operates on a plan from Saudi Telecom, although the subscriber is an obvious corporate front that hasn't led us anywhere yet. Second, whoever was using the phone placed repeated calls to a certain Khalid bin Mahfouz, who's a general with Saudi intelligence. Mahfouz liaises with key members of some of the groups the Saudis fund—Hamas, Islamic Jihad, Hezbollah. Mahfouz controls the funding to these groups, so if he asks them for a favor—say, muscle for an unrelated job in an unrelated place, he gets what he asks for."

"Is Mahfouz on the list?"

"I'm sorry, other than what I've of necessity told you, you don't need to know who is on or not on the list."

"Then tell me how this leads to Belghazi."

"Belghazi makes sure Mahfouz gets a cut of all Belghazi's weapons deals. So if Belghazi has a problem, he calls Mahfouz. Belghazi spreads around a lot of patronage. He can ask for a lot of favors."

"All very interesting," I said, "but so far the connections you're offering me seem a little thin."

"I know they're thin. I don't have all the answers, but I'm trying, all right? And I'm telling you things that I probably shouldn't, partly because I owe it to you after what just happened in Hong Kong and Macau, partly because I'm concerned that, if you're not satisfied that I'm leveling with you, you're going to do something unwarranted, possibly involving me."

"All right, keep going, then."

He exhaled forcefully, his cheeks puffing out slightly as he did so. "Do you know that, in mid 2002, word leaked to the press that the semiofficial Defense Policy Board, which recommends policy to the Pentagon, had written a report concluding that, quote, 'The Saudis are active at every level of the terror chain, from planners to financiers, from cadre to foot soldier, from ideologist to cheerleader'? The Secretary of the State was mobilized within hours to quash the report and distance it from the purported actual views of the Bush administration. Then, last summer, Bush ordered twenty-eight pages of a Congressional report on Nine-Eleven redacted, ostensibly to protect national security, in fact because the redacted portions provided details on Saudi financing of terrorist groups."

"A conspiracy?" I asked.

He shrugged. "More like a conspiracy of silence. Everyone in Washington knows what's going on, but bringing it up goes over about as well as a discussion of incest in the family. But the lack of discussion doesn't make it all any less pervasive."

He took a sip of coffee. "So here's what I know. Fact one, someone in NE Division is very concerned that Belghazi might be on the list, and that we might have sent someone after him in Macau. Fact two, shortly after the NE Division guy visits me, six Saudis show up in Macau and Hong Kong to try and take you out. Fact three, the six Saudis are connectable to Belghazi through Mahfouz. Fact four, there are elements of the U.S. government that are intent on protecting the Saudis."

We were quiet for a moment. "Then the speculation," I said, "is that Crawley—sorry, the guy from NE—finds out about me and warns Belghazi, who contacts Mahfouz for help, who sends in the Saudi team?"

"Yes."

I considered. If the facts were true, the speculation was reasonable. But I wasn't entirely comfortable with the way Kanezaki had presented it all to me. He'd given me a few juicy tidbits, then paused to allow me to reach my own conclusions. And I could too easily imagine him taking diligent notes in a "How to Run Your Assets" course at Langley: *Let the subject reach his own conclusions . . . the conclusions we reach ourselves are always more convincing than the ones someone else proposes. . . .*

"How did Belghazi get on the list?" I asked. "Given

that various important personages at the Agency seem less than thrilled to find him there."

He shrugged. "Like you said, sometimes the right hand doesn't know what the left is doing. And, like I said, there are plenty of people who don't want to know more about the list than they have to. Also access is tightly controlled through the CTC in any event. The good news is, the relative lack of oversight means that the list is one of the few intelligence items out there that isn't distorted by politics and corruption. The bad news is, the lack of the usual watered-down consensus means the product might offend some people."

I took a sip of coffee and considered. "If Crawley found out about Belghazi being on the list and was upset about it, why not just have him removed from it?"

This time he didn't even react to the mention of the name. "I don't know for sure, but probably because he doesn't want to draw too much attention to himself or his motives, whatever they are. Belghazi is practically the poster boy for terrorist infrastructure. It's easy to use a wink and nod and a slick line of bullshit about 'counterpart relations' and 'national security' to imply that someone's name shouldn't be added to something like the list, that there might be repercussions if it is. It's a lot harder to explain why you outright want the name off. You'd have a lot of explaining to do at the time. And people would remember afterward."

"So you think the Hong Kong team came from Belghazi."

There was a pause, then he said, "I see two possibilities. One is that the woman spotted you for what you are and didn't want you to interfere with whatever she's doing, so she's behind it. Two is that Belghazi is on to you, and the team in Hong Kong came from him. But

Belghazi seems the more likely of the two. I don't think all those phone calls, or the Belghazi/Mahfouz connection, are a coincidence."

His assessment tracked pretty closely with my own. I wondered whether he knew more than he was saying. Regardless, I didn't see him being behind the Hong Kong/Macau team. Since I had contacted him from Rio, he'd had numerous and better opportunities to set me up, if that's what he'd had in mind.

"Are you still tracking Belghazi?" I asked.

"Of course."

"Where is he now?"

"Still on Macau."

I looked at him. "How do you know that?"

He shrugged. "Let's just say there's a certain satellite phone that Belghazi thinks is clean, that isn't. Why are you asking?"

"Because it doesn't make sense that he'd still be in Macau. Why is he still there, do you think?"

He shrugged. "We've already talked about this. He has business in the area, and he's a gambler. We expected him to spend time at the casinos. He always does."

I nodded. "So you're telling me he's still there—to gamble? This is a guy who learns that he's been tracked to Macau, that one or maybe two contractors have been sent after him there, he's sufficiently concerned about this chain of events to call in a favor in the form of a six-man Saudi team to eliminate the threat, the team gets wiped out and the threat is still at large, and you're telling me he's still there because he doesn't want to interrupt his vacation?"

He looked at me, his cheeks flushing. After a long moment, he said, "You're right. That was stupid of me, not changing my interpretation of his behavior in light of subsequent facts. You're right. Let me think for a minute."

"You can think on your own time. If you want me to continue this op, you need to share information with me, not spend more time meditating on things in solitude."

His flush deepened, and I felt an odd twinge of sympathy. The kid was trying so hard. Managing characters like Dox and me would be tough on anyone, let alone someone as young as Kanezaki. He was actually doing well, too, and getting better all the time. He just wasn't as good yet as he wanted to be, and that was frustrating him. But he'd get there.

"All right," he said, "what do you want to know that I haven't already told you?"

"First, I want to know about Crawley. I want to know his interest in this, so I can understand whether, why, and how he's connected to Belghazi."

"I don't know," he said, again not bothering to argue with me about the name. "I'm going to try to find out."

So am I, I thought, thinking of the digital photos Dox had showed me. *And I bet I can get more information than you can.*

"Do that," I said. "Now, let's talk about Belghazi. You told me originally that he was in Southeast Asia to build up his distribution network, that Macau was just gambling, incidental to the real purpose of his trip."

He nodded. "That seems to have been incorrect."

"It does. So the question is, why Macau?"

He rubbed his chin. "Well, it's got good port facilities. Likewise for Hong Kong, of course. So a possible transshipment point for the arms he's selling to Jemaah Islamiah and Abu Sayyaf and other fundamentalist groups in the region."

"But you've got other ports in the area, too. Macau itself, Singapore, Manila—"

"True, but Hong Kong is the busiest. Busiest in the world, in fact."

"So?"

"So, if you're trying to hide something, obscure its appearance, you might want to send it through a port that handles, say, sixteen million containers a year. A needle in a haystack. Also, these guys have learned not to rely too much on any particular facility. They ship small and distributed. Then, even if any given shipment gets interdicted, the balance gets through. And overall, the distributed approach makes it much harder to shut down the pipeline, or even to get an accurate understanding of its true size. And Belghazi has been moving around, you know. We intercepted calls from Kuala Lumpur and Bangkok."

"Yeah, I know he was off Macau at one point," I said, remembering Delilah telling me that he had meetings in the region. I thought for a moment, wondering if there was an opportunity there. "How closely can you track him in those other cities?" I asked.

"As closely as we can in Macau. Which is to say, not very. We can only pinpoint his location for as long as he stays on the phone, and he tends to keep his calls short. Once he's off, we only know where the call came from."

I nodded, realizing that none of this would be enough for me to use if Belghazi's visits in the region were short-term. My best chance was still Macau, where something special seemed to be going on, and where I'd already familiarized myself with the local terrain.

Kanezaki said, "Maybe he's in Macau for the same infrastructure reasons that have taken him elsewhere."

"Maybe. But the thing is, if Macau were just one of

many distribution points for him, he wouldn't be there now. The benefit wouldn't be worth the risk, because he knows he's been tracked there. So why? More meetings there, like the ones he's doing elsewhere?"

He shook his head. "Maybe, but I don't think so. Southeast Asia is big for him now because of groups like Jemaah Islamiah. You don't have anything like that on Macau. The players, and likewise the meetings, would be elsewhere."

"Well, something is going on there. If you can find out what that is, why he's really there, what he's really doing, who he's really meeting with, I'll have a much better chance of getting close to him again."

"I understand."

I nodded slowly, then looked at him. Or rather I looked through him, as though he was somehow immaterial, a thing that mattered to me only slightly, something I could leave on or turn off as easily as I might flip a light switch. I said, "Kanezaki, I hope none of what you've told me today is untrue."

He looked at me, keeping his cool. "The facts are true," he said. "The speculation is only that. Keep in mind the difference before you decide to go precipitous on me, okay?"

I nodded again, still looking through him. "Oh, don't worry about that," I said.

I LEFT KANEZAKI and made my way to the Fiorentina trattoria, a restaurant in the new Grand Hyatt hotel, where I had told Tatsu to meet me. I arrived early, as I always do, and sipped iced coffee from a tall glass while I waited. I decided that I liked the restaurant, although not without some ambivalence. It was sleek without feeling artificial, with décor of leather and wood and other natural materials; good lighting; and lots of clean, vertical lines. Still, there was something vaguely disconcerting about how suddenly it, and the surrounding hotel and shopping complex, had sprung up. None of it had been here when I was living in Tokyo, and yet here was a virtual city within the city, which the planners had christened Roppongi Hills. You could almost imagine the Titan gods of the metropolis whipping a white sheet from over their newest creation and proclaiming with a flourish and a falsely modest bow that It Was Good.

And maybe it was good. Certainly the people around me seemed to be enjoying it. Still, the place had no history, and, somehow, no context. It was attractive, yes, but it all felt fearlessly forward-looking, miraculously unmindful of the past. And therefore, I thought, oddly American.

I smiled. No wonder I felt ambivalent. It was a transplant, like me.

An hour later, I saw Tatsu walk in through the lobby entrance, pause, and scope the room. A waitress approached and said something to him, probably an inquiry about seating him, and he responded by tilting his head in her direction but without taking his eyes off the room. Then he saw me. He nodded his head in recognition and muttered something to the waitress, then shuffled over.

I smiled as he approached and rose from my seat. There was something eternally endearing about that trademark shuffle, and about the interchangeably rumpled dark suits that always accompanied it. I realized how glad I was that Tatsu and I had found a way to live under a flag of truce. Partly because he could be such a formidable adversary, of course, but much more because he had proven himself a fine friend, albeit not one above requesting a "favor" when practicality demanded.

We bowed and shook hands, then looked each other over. "You look good," I told him in Japanese. And it was true. He'd lost a little weight, and seemed younger as a result.

He grunted, a suitably modest form of thanks, then said, "My wife has entered into a conspiracy with my doctor. She cooks differently now. No oil, no frying. I have to sneak into places like this one to satisfy my appetite."

I smiled. "She's on your side."

He grunted again and looked me up and down. "You're staying fit, I see?"

I shrugged. "I do what I can. It doesn't get easier."

We sat down. I said, "You know, Tatsu, that's the most small talk I've ever gotten out of you."

He nodded. "Don't tell my colleagues. It would ruin my reputation."

I smiled. "How's your family?"

He beamed. "Everyone is very fine. I will be a grandfather next month. A boy, the doctor says."

My smile broadened. "Good for you, my friend. Congratulations."

He nodded his thanks and looked at me. "And you?"

"Me . . ."

"Your family."

I looked at him. "You know there's no family, Tatsu."

He shrugged. "People get families by starting families."

Tatsu had set me up with a few women not long after I'd first returned to Japan, following the Late Unpleasantness. It hadn't worked out all that well.

"I think I'm pretty well committed to my exciting bachelor's existence," I told him. "You know, meet new people. See the world."

It came out less flip than I had intended, and maybe with a slightly bitter edge.

"'It doesn't get easier,'" he said. "As you noted."

I sighed. "Still trying to connect me to something larger than myself?"

"You need it," he said, his expression serious.

Christ, just what I always wanted—a maternal Tatsu. "Information is what I need," I said.

He nodded. "Does this mean our small talk is over?"

I laughed, surprised. "I didn't want to exhaust you. I know you're not accustomed to it."

"I was just warming up."

I laughed again, thinking, *Why not.*

We wound up discussing all sorts of little things: his joy at his daughter's pregnancy, and his fear that he and his wife might look at the child as some sort of replacement for the infant son they had lost; his frustration with bureaucratic inertia, with his inability to do more to fight the corruption that he believed was poisoning Japan; the way Tokyo, the way the country, was changing in front of his eyes. And I told him some things, too: how the Agency had tracked me down; how eventually I would have to move, and painstakingly reinvent myself again; how I tried not to despair at the thought that it would all once more prove futile, partly because in the end someone would always come looking for me, partly because some restless thing inside me seemed to insist that I move on regardless. We reminisced over some of the experiences we had shared in Vietnam, when Tatsu had been seconded to the war by the Keisatsucho's predecessor and I, because of my Japanese, was tasked with liaising with him; the people we had known there, the friends we had lost.

Once we got going, it was hard to stop. I realized how

much I missed this form of companionship, how virtu-
ally nonexistent it had become in my life. And Tatsu was
one of the few people, maybe the only remaining one, in
fact, who knew me all the way back to the time before
Vietnam and war and killing and everything else that
eventually came to define me, a time that, on those infrequent occasions when I care to consider the matter,
seems as disconnected and remote as a memory from
early childhood.

I realized, too, that this was part of what made me so
miss Midori. She made me feel like that previous incar-
nation, made me believe, foolishly, that I might even
shed my current skin and be baptized anew in the in-
carnation's unsullied body.

Not a bad dream, that one, as dreams go.

When we were done with the meal, and lingering over
tea for Tatsu and a second coffee for me, he said, "I
thought you might want to know that a gentleman
named Charles Crawley, who has U.S. State Department
accreditation, was in Tokyo recently. He contacted the
Keisatsucho and made inquiries about you. Do you
know this man?"

First Dox, then Kanezaki, now Tatsu. Mr. Crawley
was now firmly established on my radar screen.

"I know the name," I said. "What did you tell him?"

He shrugged. "That we had a whole file on you."

"And then?"

Another shrug. "We gave him the file."

I looked at him, incredulous. "You just gave him the
Keisatsucho file on me?"

He looked at me and said, "Of course," in his trademark *Why do I always have to spell everything out for
these people* tone, then paused before saying, "The official file."

I smiled a little at the wily bastard, relief and even some gratitude ameliorating the irritation I might otherwise have felt at him for playing with me. The "official" file would be bereft of the most meaningful information, the items Tatsu wouldn't entrust to anyone, and especially not to his superiors, the nuggets that might reveal too much about his occasional resort to extralegal methods in his battle with Japanese corruption.

"What does the official file conclude about my whereabouts?"

"That you are most likely still in Japan. Apparently there have been several sightings in major cities—Tokyo, Osaka, Fukuoka, Sapporo."

"Really," I said.

He shrugged. "Of course, I have my own notions about where you might have gone instead. But why would I want to clutter up an official file with speculation?"

He was telling me that he had doctored the file. That he had done me a favor. I knew there would be a favor in return. If not today, then another time, soon.

I nodded, thinking. *All right, then.* "Now, what about that fucking camera network of yours?" I asked.

Tatsu had access to the world's most advanced network of security cameras, all tied into an advanced facial recognition software system. He had used the network to find me after I had first left Tokyo and relocated to Osaka.

"No one is using it to track you. If that changes, I will let you know."

"Thank you. Now, tell me about the man I briefed you on through the bulletin board."

"Belghazi."

"Yes."

"I assume you already have plenty of background."

"I do. Give me the recent data first."

He nodded. "Belghazi supplies certain *yakuza* factions with small arms, working mostly through the Russian mob in Vladivostok. Lately he has been inquiring with these factions about you. I gather you did something to irritate him."

"That's possible."

"He doesn't seem like the kind of man one should irritate lightly."

"I'm beginning to figure that out."

"Would you care to tell me what you might have done to cause such grave offense?"

"I think you can guess."

He nodded, then said, "He is not a good man. He seems to be without loyalties."

"My detractors say the same thing about me."

He smiled. "They are mistaken. Your problem is that you are unable to acknowledge where your loyalties lie."

"Well, I appreciate your ongoing efforts to help me with that."

He smiled almost demurely. "We're friends, are we not?"

I thought for a minute. Maybe Belghazi, through his Saudi intelligence contact Mahfouz, sends the six Arabs after me in Macau and Hong Kong, as Kanezaki claimed to suspect. The team gets wiped out. Belghazi realizes the men were handicapped because of the way they stuck out there. Something big is happening on Macau or nearby, and Belghazi can't leave just yet. Now he feels vulnerable. Vulnerable to me. He decides he needs someone with greater local expertise, someone who can blend and get the job done right. He reaches out to the *yakuza*.

Yeah, I could see that sequence. See it clearly.

Damn, this guy was real trouble. I was beginning to wake up to the magnitude of the problem I faced.

"Belghazi's connection to the *yakuza,*" I said. "Is it close enough for them to help him with a problem elsewhere in Asia, if he asks?"

Tatsu nodded. "I would say so."

Shit.

I realized I was going to have to take Belghazi out. Not just for the money, but simply to survive. And then I realized, *He knows that. He's putting himself in your shoes, too. Which sharpens his imperative: to eliminate* you.

A vicious cycle, then. And winner take all.

All right. I needed to end this, and end it fast. I wanted this guy planted in the ground and no longer giving orders. "Natural causes," if possible; unnatural, if not.

"How can I help?" Tatsu asked.

I thought for a moment, then said, "You can get me the particulars for my new friend."

"Your new friend?"

I nodded. "Charles Crawley."

9

DELILAH HAD SAID Belghazi was off Macau for a day or two, and there wasn't much I could do for the moment with her in the way, anyway. I decided that my own brief departure would be a small enough risk to justify certain possible out-of-town gains.

I took the bullet train from Tokyo Station to Osaka, a less likely international departure point than Tokyo's Narita. I checked the bulletin board from an Internet kiosk. The information I had asked Tatsu for was waiting for me: Charles Crawley III. Home, work, and cell phone numbers; work address, supposedly the State Department but in fact CIA headquarters in Langley and therefore unlikely to be operationally useful; and home address: 2251 Pimmit Drive, West Falls Church. Unit #811. Suburban Virginia. Most likely an apartment complex, one with at least eight floors.

I booked a nonstop ANA flight to Washington Dulles for the next morning. Then I checked into a cheap hotel in Umeda for the night. I lay in bed, but sleep wouldn't come. Too much coffee. Too much to think about.

I got up, slipped into the *yukata* robe that even the lowest budget Japanese hotels can be counted on to provide, and sat in the cramped room's single chair. I left the lights off and waited to get tired enough to fall asleep. I could tell it would be a while.

The cheap rooms are always the hardest. A little luxury can numb like anesthetic. Take the anesthetic away, and pain rushes into its absence like frigid water through a punctured hull. I felt memories beginning to crowd forward, agitated, insistent, like ghosts newly emboldened by the dark around me.

I was eight the first time I saw my mother cry. She was a strong woman—she had to be, to give up her life and career in America to become my father's wife—and, until the moment I learned otherwise, I had assumed that she was incapable of tears.

One day, Mrs. Suzuki, our neighbor, came and picked me up in the middle of the afternoon at school, telling me only that I was needed at home. It was June and the air on the train ride back was close and hot and sticky. I looked out the window during the trip, wondering vaguely what was going on but confident that all was well and everything would be explained to me shortly.

My mother was waiting at the door of our tiny Tokyo apartment. She thanked Mrs. Suzuki, who held an extra low bow for a long moment before silently departing. Then my mother closed the door and walked me to the upholstered couch in the living room. Her manner was possessed of a ceremony, a gravity that I found odd and somehow ominous. She took my small hands in her larger ones and looked into my eyes. Hers seemed strange—weak and somehow frightened—and I glanced around, uncomfortable, afraid to look back.

"Jun," she said, her voice unnaturally low, "I have bad news and I need you to be very brave, as brave as you can." I nodded quickly to show her that of course she could always count on my bravery, but I sensed as children do that something was terribly wrong and my fear began to unfold, to spread out inside me.

"There's been an accident," she said, "and Papa ... Papa has died. *Nakunatta no.*" He's gone.

I wasn't completely unfamiliar with the concept of death. My paternal grandparents had a dog that had died when I was four, and my mother had explained to me at the time that *Hanzu,* Hans, had been very old and had gone to Heaven. But the concept that my father could be gone, *gone,* was too enormous for me to grasp. I shook my head, not really understanding, and it was then that my mother's composure buckled and her tears came flooding through.

And so that afternoon I made my first real acquaintance with death, as the thing that could make my strong mother cry.

I cried with her then, terrible tears of hurt and fear and confusion. And over the weeks and months that followed, as the lack of my father, previously such a commanding figure in my life, began to take root, my acquaintance with death deepened. I came to conceive of it as the wild card in a previously ordered universe, the sudden disrupter, the leering, lurking thief.

It took about five more years for me to complete my understanding that there was no more Papa, that he was represented now only by increasingly remote memories, like a series of crude cave paintings left behind by some long-vanished people. Now death was a place, a place to which people disappeared forever when they died, a place that gradually sucked away the clarity of memory afterward for a similar one-way journey.

At nineteen, I received the military telegram informing me that my mother had gone to that place, as well. Losing her was easier. I was older, for one thing. And at that point I had seen, indeed I had delivered, a great deal of death, as a soldier in Vietnam. Most important, perhaps, I was familiar with the process, the outcome of loss. Grief held no more mystery for me than did the bleeding, stanching, and eventual healing that accompany the infliction of a survivable bodily wound.

But familiarity diminishes only fear. It does considerably less for pain.

Midori isn't dead. Only gone. Maybe that's why I find myself thinking of her, more often than I should. I picture her face, and remember the sound of her voice, the touch of her hands, the feel of her body. I have no such power of recall for scent, but know I would recognize hers in an instant and wish that I could breathe it in even once more before I die. I miss her conversation. We talked about things I've never talked about with anyone. I miss the way she would kiss me, gently, on the forehead, the lids of my eyes, again and again after we had made love.

I still say her name, my sad little mantra. I find in those incanted syllables all that I can tangibly conjure of her, and that sometimes the conjuring contents me, however briefly. Even if I can't talk with her, I can at least talk to her. Something like that. Some consolation like that.

No, Midori isn't dead, but I deal with her memory by approaching my feelings as those of grief. My world is paler and poorer by her absence, but isn't this the case whenever we lose a loved one? I knew even as a teenager that my life would have been richer had my father survived my boyhood. I learned to accept this fact as immutable and, in the end, as perhaps not all that relevant. Midori wasn't dead, but she was an impossibility, and, for the imperatives of my grief, what was the real difference?

I rubbed my hands over my eyes, wishing for sleep,

for sleep's temporary oblivion. It wouldn't come. I would have to wait some more.

I sit in the dark of these empty rooms, and sometimes I think I can feel the presence of all the others who have done the same before me. Certainly the marks are there. The depression in the mattress, the line worn in the carpet between the bathroom and the door. Or the stains of sweat or saliva on the pillow, if you look beneath the case; or maybe of semen, of tears; sometimes of something darker, something like blood. I sit, the dark around me close but also boundless, and as my imagination slips into the vastness of that featureless bourn, I realize these marks are signs, artifacts of lives and moments that were but are no longer, like ashes in an empty hearth, or bones cast aside from some long ago supper, or a tattered shape that might have been a scarecrow in a field grown over with weeds. All just physical graffiti, unintentionally scrawled by other solitary travelers, detritus deposited by random men on their way to that common destination, and not just the marks of someone else's passage, but portents of my own.

The hours passed. A growing weariness finally suppressed my restless ruminations. I got back in bed, and, eventually, I slept.

I took the train to the airport the next morning. I called Crawley at home shortly before boarding the 12:10 flight. It was 9:45 the previous night in D.C.

Three rings. Then a nasal voice: "Yeah." It sounded as though I might have woken him.

"Oh, I'm sorry," I said in a fake falsetto. "I think I've dialed the wrong number."

"Christ," I heard him say. He hung up.

I smiled. I would have hated to fly all the way to Washington, only to learn that he was out of town.

The nonstop was a luxury. Ordinarily I prefer a more circuitous route, but this time I judged the imperative of catching Crawley while I knew where he was to be worth the risks inherent in a predictable route. Likewise, although business class was the usual compromise between comfort and anonymity, the constant travel was beginning to wear me down, and this time I flew first class. The east coast of the United States was over twelve hours away, and I wanted to be fresh when I got there.

I had already conceived the broad outlines of my plan, and now I needed to visualize the details. Once the plane had reached its cruising altitude and the annoying safety and entertainment announcements had ended, I closed my eyes and began a mental dress rehearsal of the entire operation: approach, reconnaissance, entry, waiting, action, egress, escape. Each stage of this mental walk-through revealed certain tools that would prove useful or necessary for the task at hand, and each tool became part of a growing mental checklist. Of course, additional items would be revealed during actual investigation of the target site, but those additional items would only properly present themselves in the context of an existing, organized plan.

Twenty minutes later I emerged from a deeply reflective state, knowing as well as I could, in the absence of further intelligence, what I would need and how it would work. I put the seat all the way back, covered myself with the first-class down quilt, and slept for the rest of the flight.

The plane touched down at a little before ten in the morning local time. I found a pay phone at the airport and called Crawley's office line. There was no answer. No problem, he was probably in a meeting.

I could have called his cell phone, but that wouldn't

have told me what I needed to know—where he was. I tried him at his apartment, and was unsurprised to get his answering machine. It was a weekday and I hadn't expected to find him at home, but one of the things you learn in war and in this business is never to assume. The day you think a house is going to be empty is the one day the owner stays home sick, or is there to let the washing machine repairman in, or has relatives visiting from out of town. You learn not to leave things like that to chance.

I rented a car with a GPS satellite navigation system and drove into D.C. for a little shopping expedition. At a hardware store, I bought twenty-five feet of clothesline, sheet plastic, Scotch tape, a roll of duct tape, and a disposable box cutter. Then a drugstore for a large tube of K-Y jelly, rubber surgical gloves, and a felt-tip pen. An optician for a pair of heavy black plastic, nonprescription eyeglasses. A wig shop for some new hair. At the Japan Information and Culture Center, I made off with a handful of flyers on upcoming JICC activities. And last stop, the Counter Spy shop on Connecticut Avenue, where I picked up a five-hundred-thousand-volt Panther stun gun, about the size of a cell phone, for $34.95 and tax.

I used the GPS nav system to pilot back to Virginia, where I did a preliminary drive-through of Crawley's apartment complex. There was a set of metal gates at the parking lot entrance. Although they were apparently left open during the day, their presence told me that I was dealing with a place that probably had decent security. I expected access to the building would require a key, and there might be a doorman, too. I saw no security cameras in the parking lot or under the large carport in front of the entrance to the building, but I thought I might encounter a few inside. I wasn't going to have a chance to confirm these issues beforehand, though; I would have to assume their existence and prepare accordingly. If things turned out to be easier than I had planned for, I would be pleasantly surprised.

The building was surrounded by thin suburban woods, through which there were some railroad tie stairs and trails leading to the street beyond. The West Falls Church Metro station was within walking distance from the building; presumably, the trails were used by commuters. They would do equally well for an unwelcome visitor bugging out after a failed op. There was a custodial entrance in back, a single, heavy metal door at the top of a short riser of concrete stairs. And, positioned over the door, as a deterrent to anyone who might want to break into the building through its less trafficked rear, a security camera.

I found a Nordstrom in a nearby shopping mall and bought a pair of galoshes, a gray windbreaker, a nice pair of deerskin gloves—thin enough to offer good tactile feedback; thick enough to avoid leaving fingerprints—a black wool overcoat, and a large leather briefcase. Then I stopped at a gas station near the mall, where, while engaged in a nonexistent conversation on the public phone, I tore out the listings for Chinese, Japanese, and Korean restaurants from the kiosk's Yellow Pages. I drove around until I found a place, Kim's Korean barbecue, that sold tee-shirts and baseball caps with the store's logo, a bright red box around red Korean lettering. I bought a shirt and a cap, along with a large lunch to go.

I drove back to Crawley's apartment. There was a Whole Foods organic supermarket in the strip mall across the street. I went in and fueled up with a couple of vegan sandwiches and a fruit smoothie. I washed it all down with a large coffee. It was good to eat so healthy on the job—usually the available operational menu consists of McDonald's and, if you're lucky, some other fast food possibilities, typically consumed cold and congealing. I enjoyed the repast, knowing it might be a while before I had a chance for another meal.

At two-thirty, I went to a pay phone and tried Crawley again at his office, ostensibly a State Department number but one I knew would in fact ring through to a CIA extension. He answered on the first ring.

"Crawley," I heard him say.

"Hello, I'm trying to reach the public affairs press liaison office?" I said, my voice a little uncertain. The title was sufficiently bureaucratic to make me confident that there would be dozens of similarly named working groups, at the Agency and elsewhere.

"Wrong extension," he said, and hung up.

I smiled and shook my head. People can be so rude.

I got back into the car and drove to a nearby residential street. I pulled over behind a few other parked cars and took a moment to slip on the galoshes and transfer my shopping items into the briefcase. I changed into the Kim's tee-shirt and pulled my windbreaker on over it, leaving it unzipped so the shirt's logo would show. The windbreaker, which I had deliberately purchased two sizes too large, would make me look smaller by comparison, awkward inside its volume, diminished. I donned the wig, the glasses, and the Kim's cap. I checked in the rearview, and liked the unfamiliar appearance I saw there.

I drove back toward Crawley's complex, parking in another strip mall parking lot that I would be able to reach on foot through the woods if things went sour and I had to leave in an unexpected hurry. I purged the contents of the car's GPS nav system and shut off the ignition. Then I spent a few minutes with my eyes closed, visualizing the next steps, getting into character. When I was ready, I got out and walked to Crawley's complex, carrying the Kim's bag with me.

I approached through the large carport, opened one of the two sets of double glass doors with the backs of two fingers, and stepped into a vestibule defined by another set of glass doors opposite the ones I had just come through. As I extended my hand to try one of the inner doors, a buzzer sounded. I looked through the glass and saw a young Caucasian girl, shoulder-length brown hair and freckles, who looked like a college student working a part-time doorman's gig so she could keep hitting the books while she worked. Part-time would be good. She wouldn't know the residents, the delivery people, the feel of the place, the way a full-timer would, and would be easier to deal with as a result.

I opened the door and moved into a lobby decorated in some sort of nouveau colonial style, lots of reproduction period furniture and wood paneling and shiny brass lamps. The girl sat behind an imposing built-in desk, behind which I imagined would be electronic access controls and video feeds from security cameras.

"Delivery?" she asked, with a friendly smile.

I nodded. I had multiple contingency stories prepared for the questions and events that might follow: *What apartment? Funny, they didn't mention a delivery. Wait a moment while I buzz them. Hmm, no answer. Are you sure about that number . . . ?*

But instead she asked, "Are you new?"

I nodded my head again, not liking the question, wondering where it was going.

She looked through the glass doors at the carport beyond. "Because you can park under the carport for deliveries. Sometimes it's tough to find a nearby space in the parking lot."

"Oh. Thank you," I said, in an indeterminate but thick Asian accent.

She looked at the logo on my shirt, then said something in a language that I couldn't understand, but that I recognized as Korean.

Oh fuck, I thought. *You can't be serious.*

"Uh, I not Korean," I said, keeping my expression and posture uncertain, vaguely subservient, not wanting to cause offense, just a recent immigrant, and not necessarily a legal one, working a minimum wage job and trying not to fall through the cracks.

"Oh!" she said, flushing. "My boyfriend is Korean, and I thought, because of the restaurant . . . never mind. Sorry."

Her embarrassment about the mistake, and my apparently embarrassed reaction to it, seemed to combine to cut off further questioning. Thank God.

"I just . . ." I said, gesturing vaguely to the area behind the desk, where the elevators would be.

"Yes, of course, go right ahead." She smiled again, and I nodded shyly in return.

I snuck a peek as I passed the desk. One open textbook, front center; one video monitor, off to the side. An easy bet as to which one got her hourly-pay attention.

I knew from the position of the custodial entrance in back that the access point would be to the left of the elevators, and I headed in that direction, passing an internal stairwell on the way. There it was, a swinging wooden door. Beyond it, a short corridor, lined in linoleum, at the end of which, the exterior door.

I looked the door over quickly. I couldn't tell if it was

alarmed. Its heft, and the presence of three large locks, indicated that the building's management might not have bothered. And even if it were alarmed, the alarm would likely be deactivated during business hours, when the door might be in use. There was a wooden doorstop on the floor, which supported the notion that there was no alarm or that it was currently disengaged. The custodians wouldn't be able to use the doorstop otherwise.

I used the cuff of the windbreaker to open the locks and turn the knob. I opened the door and examined the jamb. No alarms. I looked outside. There were several mops propped against the exterior wall, apparently to dry there, and a number of industrial-sized, gray plastic garbage containers on wheels, too.

I thought for a moment. The girl in front was obviously more interested in her books than she was in that monitor, and I had a feeling she would be habituated to seeing maintenance men moving in and out the back door during the course of the day. It looked doable.

I propped the door open a crack with the wooden doorstop and moved back inside. When I reached the elevators, an elderly black woman hobbling along with a four-way walker was emerging from one of them. She paused and squinted down at my galoshes, then looked at me. "Raining today?" she asked.

Christ, I thought. *They ought to hire* you *as the doorman.*

I shook my head. "New shoes," I said, still with the ersatz accent. *And if you speak Korean, too,* I thought, *I'll surrender here and now.* "I try decide if I keep, and like this no dirty soles." I leaned forward and lowered my voice. "Don't tell, okay?"

She laughed, exposing a bright row of dentures. "It'll be our secret, sonny," she said. She waved and moved slowly off.

I smiled, glad I'd had a lesser crime to which I was able to confess.

I couldn't very well leave with the Kim's bag after having supposedly entered the building for the express purpose of delivering its contents, so I deposited it at the bottom of a trashcan half full of junk mail in the mailroom to the right of the elevators. Then I counted off four minutes on my watch. I didn't want to pass the old woman again right away—she was a sharp one, and might wonder what had happened to the Kim's bag I'd been carrying just seconds before. If I overtook her in the lobby now, the four minutes could account for a quick delivery to a low floor, if the elevators had come right away. As for the longish time it had now been since I first passed the girl at the front desk, I deemed this acceptable. The main thing was that she should see me leave. She didn't strike me as the type who would pay attention to small discrepancies, like a deliveryman taking a little longer inside the building than might ordinarily be expected.

At four minutes, I walked out through the lobby. The old woman was gone. Maybe someone had picked her up in front. The girl at the desk looked up from her book and said, "Bye-bye." I waved and headed out to the carport, then left into the parking lot, beyond her field of vision.

Back at the car, I put the wig, glasses, and baseball cap in the glove box, zipped up the windbreaker, and pulled on the deerskin gloves. I grabbed the briefcase and headed back to the building, this time to the back. I hugged the exterior wall as I walked, wanting to get in and out of the camera's ambit as quickly as possible, and grabbed one of the mops and garbage cans on the way. As I reached the door, I leaned forward, as though there was something heavy in the garbage can and I was laboring to push it, and let the mop head obscure my face, which was in any event facing down as I pushed.

I pulled open the door and went straight in, pausing inside, waiting. If the girl at the front desk noticed something and came to investigate, she'd be here soon, and I wanted the door open if that happened for a maximally quick disappearing act.

I counted off thirty tense seconds, then slowly let my breath out. Good to go. She probably never even noticed the movement on the monitor. Maybe I was being overcautious.

As though such a thing were possible.

I closed and locked the door, parked the mop and garbage can next to it, and headed into the stairwell next to the elevators. A minute later I emerged on the eighth floor.

I took the JICC flyers out of the briefcase, walked down to 811, and knocked on the door. If someone answered, I would ask in Japanese-accented broken English if he or she would be interested in some of the exciting cultural activities planned by the JICC for the winter and leave one of the flyers to backstop the story. Then I would bow and depart and figure out some other way to get to Crawley.

But there was no answer. I tried the bell. Again, no answer.

I turned and taped one of the flyers to the door across the hallway from Crawley's, placing it so that it covered the peephole. It was the middle of the day and the complex had a quiet feel to it, most of its residents, doubtless, out at work. Still, best to take no chances on someone watching through the peephole for the minute or so it might take me to get inside.

The door had two locks—the knob unit and the dead

bolt above it. The knob unit would be a joke. The dead bolt was a Schlage. It looked like an ordinary five-pin, nothing particularly high security.

I put the flyers back in the briefcase and took out my key chain. On it, as always, were several slender home-made lengths of metal that I knew from experience worked nicely as picks for most household and other low-security locks. Next I took out the plastic felt-tip pen that I had picked up at the drugstore. I broke the metal pocket clip off the pen and inserted it into the knob unit, twisting it slightly to take up the slack. Then I worked one of the picks in. I had the lock open in less than ten seconds.

The dead bolt took longer, but not by much. Practice is the key. You can buy all the books and videos on lock picking that you want—and there are plenty out there—but if you want to get good, you buy the hardware, too: warded, disk tumbler, lever tumbler, pin tumbler, wafer tumbler, mushroom and spool pin tumbler, tubular cylinder, everything. You machine your own tools because the purpose-built stuff is illegal to buy if you're not a bonded locksmith. You approximate field conditions: gloves; darkness; time limitations; calisthenics to get your heart rate up and your hands slightly shaky. It's a lot of work. But it's worth it when the time comes.

When I had the lock open, I dropped the picks back in my pocket and opened the door. "Hello?" I called out.

No answer.

I pulled the flyer off the door opposite and entered Crawley's apartment, locking the door behind me.

I walked inside. Quick visual. Beige walls, beige carpet. Linoleum floor in the kitchen to my right. Large picture window and partially lowered white venetian blinds. Matching Ikea-style furniture: futon couch, lounge chairs, a glass coffee table with copies of *Forbes* and *Foreign Affairs* on it. Bookshelves jammed with serious-looking stuff on history and political science. A desk and a black leather chair. Large television set and speakers. A couple of potted plants.

There was a set of folding doors to my left. I opened them and saw a washing machine and dryer.

To my right was the kitchen. I walked in and looked around. The refrigerator held a quart-sized skim milk, some yogurt, a Tupperware container of pasta, a jar of spaghetti sauce. Everything was clean, neat, efficient. A functional place, used for making and ingesting simple meals and for nothing more than that. It seemed that Crawley lived alone. Single, or divorced with no children. Children, with visitation rights, would have meant a bigger place.

The bedroom and bathroom offered more of the same. A queen-sized bed on a platform, but only one night table next to it, with a reading lamp and digital alarm clock. In the bathroom, men's toiletries laid out neatly around the sink. A white bath towel hung on the glass shower door, the edges lined up. I removed a glove for a moment and touched it. It was slightly damp, no doubt from this morning's shower.

I imagined Crawley coming home this evening. How he might navigate the room would determine where I should wait. Where would he stop first? Let's see, come inside, drop the mail on the coffee table. It was cold out; probably he would have a coat. Next stop, coat closet?

There was a large closet off the living room. I checked it. Boxes for stereo equipment. A vacuum cleaner. A set of weights under a thin coating of dust. And a thick wooden dowel for hanging clothes, running the length of the space, with a handful of unused plastic hangers dangling along it. The dowel was supported at its center by an angle brace joined to the wall. I pressed down on it and was satisfied with its strength. Perfect.

But no coats. This closet seemed to be used for longer-term storage needs. I went back to the bedroom. On the wall adjacent to the bathroom was a closet behind a pair of folding doors. I slid the doors open. Yes, this was the clothes closet. Four suits, with an empty hanger for a fifth. Five dress shirts, five more empty hangers. One shirt on his back, I assumed, four at the dry cleaners. A dozen ties. One overcoat, one waist-length leather jacket. One more empty hanger.

I could see that he was a neat man, a man who liked things to be in their proper places. All right then, drop the mail off, then straight to the bedroom, hang the coat in the closet. Likewise for the suit, maybe use the bathroom, then back to the living room for the mail, turn on CNN or C-SPAN, maybe then the kitchen for something to eat. Fine.

I went back to the storage closet and took out the stun gun. I had already tested it on the drive from D.C. and it had worked as advertised, sending out a satisfying blue arc of electricity between its electrodes at the push of a discreet side trigger. I laid out some of the plastic along the closet floor, removed the other items from the briefcase, took off the windbreaker, folded it, and placed it and the briefcase items on the plastic. I didn't want any carpet particles on my clothes. The galoshes, which I was already wearing over my shoes, would protect my feet. Then I sat on one of the leather chairs and waited.

The room lit up briefly as the sun set outside the picture window, then gradually darkened as night came. I turned the closet light on. Night vision mode wouldn't be useful for this; Crawley would turn the lights on when he came in and I didn't want to have to adjust.

Every half hour I stood up and moved around to stay limber. The coffee was making its presence known, and three times I had to urinate. I used the bathroom sink for this purpose, letting the water run as I did so, avoiding the possibility that the toilet might still be running when Crawley came in and alert him to the presence of an intruder. Failing to flush would be unacceptable for similar reasons.

At eight o'clock, just after one of these quick trips to the bathroom, I heard the sound of a key in the lock. I got up noiselessly and moved to the closet. I held the door open a crack and turned off the light, the stun gun ready in my right hand.

A moment later I heard the apartment door open. The lights went on. Soft footfalls on the carpet. There he was, moving past me. Noting the curly, wheat-blond hair, the thin features I had seen in the photos Dox had taken, I watched him walk into the living room. He tossed the mail on the coffee table. I smiled. Call me psychic.

He shrugged out of an olive trench coat, grabbed a magazine, and made his way past me again, toward the bedroom. A minute passed, then another. And another.

He was taking longer to return to my position than I had expected. Then I realized: he was on the can, probably reading the magazine. I had planned to wait until he was back in the living room, but this was too good an opportunity to pass up. I picked up the spare sheet plastic and the duct tape and moved out of the closet.

I eased inside the bedroom and stood just outside the open door of the bathroom. I saw the trench coat, a suit, a dress shirt, and a tie on the bed. I set the plastic and duct tape down on the carpeting.

Another minute went by. I heard him stand up. The toilet flushed. I held the stun gun in my right hand at waist level, my thumb on the trigger. I breathed shallowly through my mouth.

I heard footsteps on the tile, then saw his profile as he emerged from the bathroom, wearing only a white tee-shirt and matching boxer shorts. I stepped in. His head started to swivel toward me and his body flinched back in surprise and alarm. I jammed the unit against his midsection and depressed the trigger. His teeth clacked shut and he jerked back into the doorjamb.

After four or five seconds, enough time to ensure that his central nervous system was adequately scrambled, I released the trigger and eased him down to the floor. He was grunting the way someone does when he's taken a solid shot to the solar plexus. His eyes were blinking rapidly.

I laid the plastic out on the floor and rolled him onto it. I placed his arms at his sides, then I wrapped the plastic around his body and secured it with duct tape, first at wrist level, then the ankles. He started to recover, so I zapped him again with the stun gun. By the time the effects were wearing off for the second time, I had him pretty well mummified in plastic and duct tape. Other than his head and toes, he was immobilized.

I grabbed a pillow off the bed and propped it under the base of his skull so he could see me better. Also so that, if he started thrashing, he wouldn't bruise the back of his head. My concern had less to do with consideration for him than it did with what might show up in a forensic examination.

I squatted down next to him and watched his eyes. First, they blinked and rolled. Second, they steadied and regained focus. Finally, they bulged in terrified recognition. He tried to move, and, when he found he couldn't, he began to hyperventilate.

"Calm down," I said to him, my voice low and reassuring. "I'm not going to hurt you." Which I supposed was the literal truth, after a fashion.

The hyperventilating went on. "Then . . . then why have you tied me up?" he panted.

Not an unfair question. I decided to level with him, at least partly. "You're right," I told him. "Let me amend what I said. I'm not going to hurt you, if you tell me what I want to know."

He swallowed hard and nodded. His eyes were still wide with terror, but I could see he was making an effort to pull himself together. "Okay," he said. "All right."

I paused to give him a moment to more fully appreciate his new reality. This guy was obviously no hard case. Sure, he was Agency, but the college-boy type, not one of the paramilitaries. The last violence he'd seen firsthand had probably been on the grade-school playground. And now, suddenly, he was tied up and helpless, with a known killer squatting next to him, looking at him like he was a frog about to be dissected. Of course he was terrified. And that was good. If I managed his terror correctly, there was a reasonable chance that he would tell me what I wanted to know.

"Well, Mr. Crawley," I said, "I guess what we need to talk about is why a nice guy like you would want to have me killed."

He pursed his lips and swallowed again, his breath whistling in and out of his nose. I could see that he was trying to decide how to handle this. Deny everything?

Blame someone else? Confess and beg for mercy? Something in between?

Watching him trying frantically to make up his mind, weighing the pros and cons of the feeble set of options before him, I sensed he understood that I knew what he was thinking, that I had seen it all before and would know just how to handle him regardless of which route he decided to use. So he would probably know enough not to outright deny everything. No, he looked savvy to me, even shrewd. At some level, he was probably thinking, *Don't deny it, he wouldn't be here if his information weren't good. And if you don't deny it, if you confess up to a point, he'll be more inclined to believe what follows.* It would be a variation of the galoshes game I had just played with the old lady with the walker. And he'd probably do a good job, too. A lot of these government guys are pretty adroit when it comes to lying.

Let's see, I thought, making a mental bet with myself, *probably it'll be something like, "I was only following orders."*

"It's not me," he said, unintentionally winning me the bet. "It's someone else."

"Who's that, then?"

"It's . . . look, Jesus Christ, I can't tell you these things!"

"But it's not you."

Hope flared in his eyes. "Yes, that's right."

I sighed. "Is there another Charles Crawley running around who looks and smells just like you?" I asked.

"What?"

"A twin. You don't have a twin?"

"What? No, no I don't."

"I didn't think so. But see, that's strange. Because a guy who looks exactly like you, and also named Crawley, although he called himself Johnson, went to a special operator recently and offered him a hundred thousand dollars to take me out. Went to him personally."

He glanced to his right, a neurolinguistic sign of imagination, not of recall. He was trying to make something up, to find a way out of the corner he had just painted himself into.

"Maybe, I don't know," he said. "Maybe there is someone using my name. Trying to set me up."

I sighed again. "The operator in question was carrying a cell phone with an integrated digital camera," I said. "He took about a half dozen pictures of you."

His pupils dilated. He licked his lips.

"I'm afraid this isn't going to end the way we were hoping," I said.

"All right, all right, I'm sorry, I was just afraid. That part was me. But look, I didn't want to do what I did, I just . . . I didn't have a choice."

"I'm listening."

He took a deep breath. "You were hired to . . . to go after someone recently. The problem you have, it's with that person."

I shook my head in mild disgust. It's been my experience that bureaucrats are to killing what the Victorians were to sex: they just can't bring themselves to call it by name.

I waited, letting the pressure of silence bear down on him. But he stayed cool, resisting the urge to talk. Okay, plan B.

I picked up the stun gun and held it an inch from his eyes, then depressed the trigger. Sharp tendrils of blue electric current crackled between the electrodes, and the acrid smell of ozone cut through the air. He tried to jerk his head away, but there was nowhere for him to go.

I released the trigger. "Remember, Mr. Crawley, my

assurance that I wouldn't hurt you had a condition attached. Let's not breach the condition, okay?"

The truth was, I didn't want to hurt him. Fear is a better motivator than pain. Fear is all about anticipation, imagination. Pain is real and quantifiable. Once the pain starts, the person is no longer in fear of it—it's right there, actually happening. The person might think, okay, this is bad, but I can take it. And he might even be right. So when you're interrogating someone, once you have to start actually hurting him, you've already lost a lot of your leverage. I wanted to avoid all that if I could.

I set the stun gun down. "It's important that we not hide behind euphemisms and vague references and undefined pronouns, okay?" I said, as though he was a child and I was just explaining the rules of the classroom to him. "It's important that you tell me exactly who's coming after me and why. If it turns out that you're just a bit player in all this, you'll survive the conversation."

Now I'd opened a little door of hope for him. All he had to do to march right through it was to betray a few people around him.

Fear of pain, the hope of release. Four out of five interrogators surveyed recommended this combination for . . .

"Okay," he said, nodding against the pillow, "okay. If I tell you everything I know about this, will you promise to let me go?"

Denial. A pathetic thing, really. But there are people who need it to get through the tough times. Crawley, it seemed, was one of them.

"Yes," I said. "But remember, there's a lot I know already. Otherwise I wouldn't be here. So I'll know if you're leaving something out."

"I understand," he said, nodding, seeing that door opening wider. "I won't leave anything out."

I said nothing. After a moment, he took another deep breath and said, "The man you were hired to . . . go after. He found out about you. That's how this started."

"Say his name."

"His name?"

"What did I just tell you about being vague? Are you trying to see how far you can push me? Say his fucking name."

There was a pause, during which he looked like he might be sick. He said, "Belghazi."

"Good. How did Belghazi 'find out' about me?"

"Someone was sent to Macau to kill him. At least, he thinks someone was. A Frenchman, guy named Nuchi, an independent contractor with a lot of Middle Eastern connections. Turned up dead in Macau less than a week ago with a broken neck, at the same time that the man . . . that Belghazi happened to be out there. Belghazi wanted to know what had happened. Did we know who had sent the guy, that kind of thing."

"What did you tell him?"

"That we didn't know anything about it. Which turned out to be true. Except that, when I started looking into it, I found out that we had sent someone, just not Nuchi. We sent you."

"But you didn't send the other guy."

"Who can say for sure? This shit is obviously being set up through outside channels, or you never would have been sent in the first place. But I don't think that even the idiots behind sending you would have been so stupid as to send two operators on the same op without informing them first."

He was getting more talkative, which was good. I wanted to keep him going, to continue to foster his new-found loquaciousness. This way, he would be used to the dynamic by the time we got to the heart of the matter, at which point the act of betraying secrets would seem to be not much more than what he had already said and done. Contrary to popular imagination, a good interrogation is much more like a seduction than it is like torture.

"Who do you think sent Nuchi, then?" I asked.

He shook his head. "Nobody knows. Nuchi does contract work for various Arab governments and terrorist groups, so the most likely explanation is that he was working for one of his usual clients. Maybe someone who Belghazi cheated, maybe someone trying to muscle in on Belghazi's sources or on his networks. It's actually good that the guy is dead. If you did it, you ought to get a medal."

"But instead of a medal, you warned Belghazi that I was coming after him."

There was a pause, during which he grappled silently with the realization that I knew this, too. Where possible, you want to give the subject the impression that you already know everything he's going to tell you. This makes him afraid to hold anything back, and helps him rationalize full disclosure: after all, he's not divulging anything you don't already know.

"Yes," he said, after a moment. "We warned him."

We, I thought. *Come back to that.*

"I'd like to hear more about why," I said.

He closed his eyes, again looking as though he might be sick. "There's a . . . relationship there," he said, after a moment.

Another vague reference, I thought. But I waited to see whether he would find a way past the mental logjam caused by his desire to protect his information, on the one hand, and his desire to still be alive when I left his apartment, on the other.

"He gives us information," he said finally. "So we . . . protect him."

"So Belghazi is a CIA asset," I said. My tone indicated that this was no great revelation to me, but in fact I was surprised.

He blanched at hearing it out loud. "In a way. He's not on the books as an asset, he hasn't been vetted that way, as a source he's too sensitive and we can't take a chance on the relationship being known outside the division. But he gives us information."

"NE Division?" I asked, showing him again that I knew a great deal.

"Jesus," he said. "How do you . . . yes, NE."

"And the information he gives you concerns . . . ?"

He sighed, perhaps now rationalizing at some level, *Well, I've come this far, what can it hurt, and he probably knows most of it anyway. . . .*

"Concerning the flow of arms, particularly WMD precursors, to groups that might use them against the United States."

"Precursors?"

"Precursors to weapons of mass destruction. Enriched uranium. Nuclear centrifuge designs. Anthrax culture. EMPTA, a chemical used in the production of VX gas. Etcetera."

"I'm confused," I said. "I thought Belghazi is heavily involved in all of this."

He shook his head. "Belghazi deals in the old-fashioned stuff. Guns and C-4 and RPGs. Stuff we're used to, that we can live with."

"I didn't realize the CIA could be so accommodating."

"Look, where do you think we get information on WMDs? From choirboys? Nobel Peace Prize winners?

Sure, Belghazi is bad, but he's an angel compared to some of the characters we're trying to stop."

"So he gives you information on some of the really bad guys out there . . ."

"And in exchange we protect him, let him continue with his trade." He paused and looked at me. "Look, I'm cooperating. Can you untie me? I think I'm losing circulation."

Nice try, I thought. I'd wrapped him up in such a way that the pressure of the bindings would be maximally distributed and no marks would be left. Accordingly, I knew his circulation was unimpaired.

"You're doing well," I said. "If you keep it up, I'll untie you enough so that you'll be able to get out of the rest of it by yourself, and I'll leave."

"All right," he said, no doubt comforted by our rational exchange, the civilized back-and-forth of bargaining. Denial again. A guy breaks into your apartment, lies in wait, knocks you out, ties you up, but—no problem!— you're willing to trust him to keep his word after that. At least you are if you desperately want to believe that you can trust him, glittering hope triumphing, as it often does, over the paler hues of common sense and gut instinct.

"So Belghazi gives you information, and you give him protection," I said, hoping to jar loose additional information by reflecting back what he'd already said.

"Yes. It's not an uncommon system. Police departments do it all the time. They couldn't fight crime without it."

"Belghazi is a snitch," I said.

"Exactly."

I noticed that he had moved us away from the specifics of the CIA's relationship with Belghazi to a more general discussion of these sorts of relationships in law enforcement. It was nicely done. Albeit futile.

"You say you 'protect' Belghazi," I said. "Tell me more about that."

His pupils dilated and his eyes shifted right again. He didn't want to tell me the truth, and was trying to come up with a substitute.

"I can see you don't want to talk about this, Mr. Crawley," I said, "and that you're about to try to fabricate. So, before you say anything, you should know that, if I sense that you're lying, or even being incomplete, I'm going to pull that pillow out from under your head and smother you with it. Imagine what that'll be like." I smiled as though I had just wished him a nice day.

He blanched, then nodded quickly. "All right. Sometimes we share information with him—say, about a rival broker, another deal that's getting put together. Belghazi can use that kind of intelligence to scuttle the other deal, or undercut it. Twice he's even used the information we provided to have a rival eliminated, which we generally view as a not undesirable outcome. Or if we learn that he's being watched by a rival intelligence service, or by law enforcement, we warn him."

I nodded. "But that's not what you were hoping not to tell me a moment ago," I said, my tone regretful, as though in anticipation of what I was going to have to do next.

"No, no it's not," he said quickly. "We also, sometimes, sometimes we put people on the ground. Oversee a transfer."

All right, here we go. The moment of truth.

"You keep saying 'we,'" I said. "Tell me who else is involved."

He closed his eyes and nodded his head for a long moment, as though trying to comfort himself. Then he said, "There's a former Near East Division officer. He's a NOC, nonofficial cover, based in Hong Kong, attached to the Counter Terrorism Center. He has a lot of autonomy, and a lot of authority. The other officers stationed there give him a lot of leeway and a lot of discretion."

"Why?"

He sighed. "The CTC guys are spooky. Area division personnel don't really know what the CTC types are up to. Hell, I don't generally know what they're up to—look how CTC in Langley decided to have Belghazi eliminated, I was totally in the dark about that. Anyway, the attitude is, those CTC guys are into the black arts, maybe I don't really even want to know. You know, they don't talk much about what they're up to, but they're doing God's work, don't ask, don't tell, just leave 'em alone and go out for drinks with the usual diplomatic suspects, write up an after-action report, call it a night."

"And this guy in Hong Kong . . ."

"He knows about Belghazi from his days with NE."

Finally, the link I'd been looking for: Belghazi to Mr. NOC to Crawley.

But Hong Kong . . . something about the Hong Kong connection was troubling me. I wasn't sure what it was.

"Is this guy, the NOC, how you learned about me?" I asked.

He nodded.

"Tell me," I said.

He swallowed. "Belghazi called the NOC about the dead Frenchman. The NOC checked with Headquarters CTC. He found out that Belghazi was on a list of terrorist infrastructure targets. And that we had sent someone after him in Macau."

"He found out who?"

He nodded. "Only your name. But the Agency has a whole file on you. Once I had your name, it was easy for me to get the file from Central Records."

"What was in the file?"

"You know, your history. A bio, suspected location, and activities."

"What else?"

"Just an old photo. That was all."

I thought about the photo, and about the way Belghazi had noticed me at the Lisboa. If the photo was military era, and I assumed it was, it would have been three decades out of date and wouldn't have accounted for the plastic surgery I'd had in the interim. Still, it might have been enough for Belghazi to confirm my identity. Or they could have digitized it, worked on it to bring it up to date. *Yeah, that was him,* I could imagine him saying. *The bastard sat right next to me in the VIP room of the Lisboa. Same night I got sick. Damn, he probably poisoned me.*

Then they would have distributed copies to the Saudi team in Hong Kong and Macau. I had been right about the way that spotter was scrutinizing me.

"Who else did you check with?" I asked, hiding the irritation that was building at the thought of these idiots relentlessly, robotically, ruining the little peace I might otherwise have known.

He looked at me, wondering, I sensed, just how much I knew, how much he could try to hold back.

"People in Japan," he said. "One of the Tokyo Station officers. Because the file said you were based there."

"Kanezaki?"

His eyes widened. "God all-fucking mighty," he said.

"What did Kanezaki tell you?"

"Not much," he said, recovering a little composure. "He's an asshole."

I almost smiled. From my perspective, that was the best character reference Kanezaki could ever have received.

"Who else?"

"Japanese liaison—the kay, kay something."

"Keisatsucho." Tatsu's outfit.

"Yeah. They had a file on you, too."

"What do you know about a woman named Delilah?" I asked, trying to catch him off guard, see if I got a reaction.

"Delilah?"

"Blond woman, cosmopolitan, probably Israeli, maybe European. Spending time with Belghazi."

He shook his head. "I've never heard of her. She's Israeli, spending time with Belghazi?"

I looked at him, ignoring the question. I didn't see any dissembling in his eyes.

I looked at my watch. We'd been chatting for five minutes.

"What's Belghazi doing in Macau, anyway?" I asked.

"What he always does. Meeting with customers, making sure the shipping infrastructure is in place, overseeing a delivery, that kind of thing. Business in Hong Kong, gambling in Macau. He likes to gamble."

I nodded, thinking. All right, Dox's story, Kanezaki's story, Tatsu's story, things were checking out.

Wait a minute. Dox. That was the Hong Kong connection, the thing that had nagged at me a second earlier. Dox had been using a photo to find me there. And apparently he had some local connections, connections that were sufficient to get the hotel staff's full attention over a "police matter."

"Who's the NOC?" I asked.

"I told you, a former NE Division officer, now attached to the CTC."

"His name."

His breathing shortened and quickened. "Please, please, don't make me tell you that. Why would you need to know, anyway? Please, I can't tell you something like that. I've told you everything else, I really have!"

I had thought that, by this point, we'd have enough momentum to get over this kind of bump. Apparently I'd been mistaken.

"Do you think, if he were in your shoes, he'd die before giving up your name?" I asked. "Because that's what you're choosing to do."

"I don't know what he'd do. I can't . . . I just can't tell you another officer's name. I'm sorry, I can't."

"Two things," I said. "First, I'm eighty percent certain I know who he is, and just want the confirmation." This was a lie, of course, but I wanted to make it easier for Crawley to rationalize if rationalizing was what it was going to take. "Second, I'm only interested in him because he can get me close to Belghazi. So, in not telling me the name, you're choosing to die to protect Belghazi, not to protect Agency personnel."

He closed his eyes, and tears began leaking out. "I'm sorry," he said, shaking his head. "I'm sorry."

Shit, his hope, real or false, was fading. My leverage would be fading with it.

"The operator you went to," I asked, fishing now. "To have me removed. He goes by the name of Dox. Is he the NOC?"

He didn't answer. He just continued to shake his head and silently weep. His reaction told me nothing.

"I'll give you one more chance," I said. "The NOC's name. Live or die, it's up to you."

He didn't answer, and I realized that at some level he might not even have heard me. He had made his decision and had already accepted the consequences. I could have tried some sort of crude torture, but was reluctant to do so. The benefits of information extracted by torture are usually minimal. The costs to the psyche tend to be significant.

Still, the next part wasn't going to be pleasant. I'd talked with him now, interacted with him, witnessed his tears and his fear and his misguided loyalty. All guaranteed to slice through decades of suddenly soft emotional callus and remind me that it was another human being whose life I was about to take.

But I didn't have much choice. I couldn't very well leave him alive after this encounter. He would warn Belghazi, warn the NOC in Hong Kong. And I'd mentioned Delilah, too. If he told Belghazi about her, she'd be dead that very night.

I wondered briefly if I'd mentioned her name to him to force my own hand, to clarify that, by sparing his life, I'd be ending hers.

I reminded myself that he had tried to have me killed. That, given the opportunity, he would certainly do so again.

Don't think. Just do it.

I felt a valve closing over my empathy like a watertight bulkhead. The bulkhead would open later, I knew, as the pressure built behind it, but it would hold long enough for me to finish the matter at hand.

I picked up the stun gun and jolted him again. He jerked violently from the shock, but the pillow kept him from marking his head. After about ten seconds I released the trigger and set the unit aside.

I sat him up and got behind him. I hooked my legs over his, wrapped my arms around his neck in a *hadaka-jime* strangle, and dropped back to the plastic-covered floor so that my body was under his. I put the strangle in carefully, using just enough pressure to close off the carotids, but not enough to damage his trachea or to cause any bruising. He didn't make a sound and he was unconscious within seconds. I held him that way for several minutes, until unconsciousness had deepened into death.

I got up and dragged him to the living room closet. The plastic was practically frictionless on the carpet and made the job easier.

I laid him down under the dowel in the storage closet and went back to the living room. I like to clean up as I go along—one step, one cleanup. Repeat. Makes it easier not to forget anything. I picked up the duct tape, then noticed something: a swath in the carpet where the fibers had all been pulled in the same direction by his plastic-assisted passage. I walked back and forth along the swath until it had been eradicated.

I went back to the closet, dropped the duct tape, and cut the plastic off him with the box cutter. I noticed that his boxers were damp—he'd pissed himself as he'd lost consciousness and died. Not uncommon. It was lucky he had just used the toilet or I might have had a more considerable mess to deal with.

I opened the folding doors near the entrance and turned on the washing machine. I added some detergent, then walked back to the closet, where I retrieved Crawley's shorts and tee-shirt. I threw them into the machine. Then I grabbed a couple of washcloths from the bathroom, which I used to clean him up. These, too, went into the wash, along with the contents of a plastic laundry basket that was sitting on top of the dryer. A small detail, but you don't want to leave loose ends, such as, *Why did the dead guy wash just his boxers, a tee-shirt, and two washcloths? Why didn't he throw in the rest of the dirty laundry, too?* I also took a moment to hang his coat, suit, shirt, and tie in the clothes closet.

I pulled off the deerskin gloves I'd been wearing, went to the storage closet, and pulled on the surgical pair. I grabbed the K-Y jelly and headed to the bathroom, where I squeezed out half the tube's contents into the sink, washing it all down with hot water. Then back to the closet, where I put Crawley's hands on the tube to ensure that it would be personalized with his fingerprints.

I set the tube on the ground and fashioned the clothesline into a slipknot. I pulled the knot over his head and ran the other end of the line over the hanging dowel, close to the angle brace where it would be strongest. Then I used the rope to haul him up onto his knees. He listed forward a few degrees, but the rope restrained him. I tied off the end on the dowel, cut off all but about three feet of the excess, and stepped back.

Diminished oxygen supply to the brain, called cerebral anoxia, can intensify sensations, making it, for some people, a good accompaniment to masturbation. The practice is known as autoerotic asphyxiation and usually remains a secret until the enthusiast dies accidentally in the midst of the proceedings. The statistics make extreme sports look safe by comparison: somewhere from five hundred to a thousand fatalities every year in the United States alone.

I looked at Crawley for a moment. *Make that a thousand and one.*

I applied a measure of K-Y jelly to his right hand and his genitals, then stepped back and observed. Yeah, that looked about right. The private life of a "State Department" bureaucrat. The quintessence of buttoned-down Washington Beltway seriousness by day; periodic bouts of autoerotic asphyxiation games by night. Really, you just never know what goes on behind closed doors. Especially closed closet doors.

A sudden thought nagged me: *Was he right-handed? Or left?*

Hmm, should have thought to find a way to check on that earlier. Sloppy. But the hell with it, no harm done. Maybe he enjoyed himself in private ambidextrously. Who could say one way or the other? The main thing was, the CIA wouldn't want this getting out. They'd want it dealt with quickly, quietly, and cleanly. They'd call it an embolism, a weak heart wall, something like that, and, wanting to believe this was the case, they'd repeat it until they did. Even if they had some suspicions, they would be reluctant to do anything that might cause this to leak. All of which would mean less pressure for me.

I pulled off the surgical gloves, dropped them inside out into the briefcase, and slipped once again into the deerskin pair. I eased into the overcoat. I rolled up the plastic, picked up the rest of the items, and put them in the briefcase, too, which I carried back into the living room. I looked around.

Take it backward, starting with the bathroom. I double-checked everything, then triple-checked. Nothing was out of place. No telltale signs. The washing machine was cycling through rinse. Crawley's things would be clean soon.

One last check of the closet. Everything was in order, Crawley included. He was canted forward, the rope preventing him from tipping onto his face, his knuckles resting alongside him against the carpeting. *Well, there are worse ways to go,* I thought. And I've seen plenty of them.

Ordinarily, I work under substantial time constraints, and don't have the opportunity for triple-checks, and certainly not for reflection, when the job is done. But this time, it seemed, I did.

I watched Crawley's lifeless form, thinking of all the death I had seen, of the deaths I had caused, starting with that unlucky Viet Cong near the Xe Kong river so many years before. I wondered what that poor bastard would be doing today if our paths had never crossed.

Probably he'd be dead anyway, I thought. *An accident or a disease or someone else would have killed him.*

Yeah, maybe. Or maybe he would have lived, and today he would be married, to a pretty Vietnamese girl, a fighter, as he had been, and they would have three or four children, who would revere their parents for the sacrifices they had made during the war. Maybe his first grandchild would have been born recently. Maybe he would have wept with terrible joy as he hugged his child's child to his own thin chest, thinking how strange life was, how precious.

Maybe.

I sighed, watching Crawley's oddly canted form. He looked relaxed, somehow, untroubled, as cadavers often do.

In developed countries most people live their lives without ever even seeing a body, or, if they do, it's an open-casket affair, where you have context and witness only the peaceful, ruddy-cheeked façade of the mortician's artifice. When Mom and Dad die, they're taken care of by strangers in a nursing home two towns over. The kids don't have to see them go. They don't even have to see them after. They just get a "we're sorry to inform you" call late that night from the institution's management, for whom such calls are as routine as putting out the weekly garbage is for a suburban homeowner. The funeral home picks up the body. The cemetery buries it. Unless you're a professional, you might live your whole life without seeing someone in the moment of leaving his own.

People don't know. They don't know the way the jaw goes slack, how the skin turns instantly waxy and yellow, how readily the eyelids close when you ease them shut. They don't know the awful smell of blood and entrails, or how, even if you can wash the stench from your skin, nothing can ever cleanse it from your memory. They don't know a hundred other things. You might as well ask them about the mechanics of butchering the animals that become the meat on their supper tables. They don't want to see any of that, either. And things are set up so they don't have to.

Sometimes I can forget the divide this knowledge produces, the way it separates me from those unburdened by its weight. Mostly, though, I can't. Midori sensed it even from the beginning, I think, although it wasn't until later that she fully grasped its essence.

Yeah, sometimes I can forget, but never for very long. Mostly I look at the innocents around me with disdain. Or resentment. Or envy, when I'm being honest with myself. Always with alienation. Always from a distance that has nothing to do with geography.

I walked over to the door and looked through the peephole. There was nothing out there.

I let myself out, checking to ensure that the door had locked behind me. I left through the front entrance, just another resident, heading out for the evening. Someone new was at the front desk. Even if the college girl had still been there, she wouldn't have recognized me. The light disguise I had been wearing earlier was gone, of course; but more than that, I was a different person now. Then, I had been a timid immigrant in a cheap, ill-fitting windbreaker, a visitor to the building. Now I walked as though I owned the place, a resident in a professional-looking overcoat, on his way out to a foreign car and thence to an important job at the office, a responsible position that no doubt occasionally required evening hours.

I left the building and crossed the street. I took off the galoshes, put them in the briefcase, and got in the car. I drove a few miles to another strip mall, where I changed into some of the clothes I was traveling with: gray worsted pants and an olive, lightweight merino wool crewneck sweater. I slipped the overcoat back on and was glad for its warmth.

For the next hour or so I drove around suburban Virginia, stopping at gas stations and convenience stores and fast food places, depositing a relic or two from the Crawley job at each of them until the briefcase was empty and it, too, had been discarded, in a Dumpster at a Roy Rogers. I pitched it in with the other refuse and watched a small avalanche of fast food wrappers cascade down and bury it.

I walked back to the car. The leafless trees along the road looked skeletal against the night sky beyond. I paused and stared for a long moment at that sky, at whatever might lie beyond it.

Oh, did I offend you? I thought. *Go ahead, then. Take your best shot. I'm right here.*

Nothing happened.

A minute passed. I started to shiver.

Suddenly I was exhausted. And hungry. I needed to get something to eat, and find a hotel.

I got in the car and pulled out onto the road again. I felt alone, and very far from home.

Wherever that might be.

PART THREE

She gives when our attention is distracted
And what she gives, gives with such supple
  confusions
That the giving famishes the craving . . .

T. S. ELIOT, *Gerontion*

PART THREE

10

THE TICKET I had bought to get from Osaka to Washington was a round-trip. One-ways attract unnecessary attention, especially post–September 11. When I'd left I wasn't sure that I'd be using the return, but I certainly had a reason now, and the morning after my chat with Crawley I caught a return flight from Dulles.

I slept well over the Pacific, all the way to the prelanding announcements, the flight attendants having kindly respected my wish not to be wakened, even for champagne and caviar service. Ah, first class.

I took the *rapito*, the Rapid Transport train, from Kansai International Airport to Namba's Nankai station in south Osaka. My ticket was for a window seat, and during the thirty-minute journey from airport to terminal station I sat and stared past my reflection in the glass. A sliver of sun had broken through the clouds at the edge of the horizon, shining like a sepia spotlight through an otherwise gray and undifferentiated firmament, and in the fading moments of the day I looked on at the scenes without, scenes that passed before me as disconnected and mute as images in a silent film. A rice paddy in the distance, tended by a lone woman who seemed lost in its sodden expanse. A man tiredly pedaling a bicycle, his dark suit seeming almost to sag from his frame as though wanting nothing more than to cease this purposeless forward momentum and succumb to gravity's heavy embrace. A child with a yellow knapsack paused before the lowered gate of the *rapito* railroad crossing, perhaps on his way to a *juku,* or cram school, which would stuff his head with facts for the next dozen years until it was time for them to be disgorged for college entrance exams, watching the passing train with an odd stoicism, as though aware of what the future held for him and already resigned to its weight.

I called Kanezaki from a pay phone in Namba. I told him to meet me that night, that he could find details on the bulletin board. I uploaded the necessary information from an Internet café. The Nozomi bullet train would take him about two and a half hours, and I expected he would leave quickly after getting my message.

I checked the bulletin board I had set up for Delilah, and was mildly surprised to find a message from her: *Call me.* There was a phone number.

I used it. The call might be traced back to Osaka, but I wasn't going to be in town long enough for it to matter.

"Allo," I heard her say.

"Hey," I answered.

"Hey. Thanks for calling."

"Sure."

"I wanted to tell you that it's almost done. To ask you to be patient for just a little while longer."

That was smart. She must have been concerned that, if I didn't hear from her, I might get frustrated. That I might decide she was playing me and go after Belghazi unilaterally again. And better to hear my voice, and let me hear hers, rather than a dry text message left floating in cyberspace.

"How much longer?"

"A day. Maybe two. It'll be worth it, you'll see."

I wondered for a moment, again, about the elevator at the Macau Mandarin Oriental. After what had happened subsequently, and after what I'd learned, my gut said that she hadn't been part of that attempt on me, that in fact she had tried to warn me, as she had claimed. What I couldn't understand was why. From her perspective, operationally, a warning would have been counterproductive.

I hated a loose end like that. But I couldn't make sense of it. I'd chew it over another time.

"Okay," I said.

"Thank you."

"Can I reach you at this number?"

"No. Not after this."

I paused, then said, "All right, then. Good luck."

"And you." She clicked off.

A LITTLE UNDER four hours later Kanezaki and I were sitting in Ashoka, a chain Indian restaurant in the Umeda underground mall that I had come to like during my time in Osaka. I had employed the usual security procedures beforehand and there had been no problems.

"You were right," I told him over Tandoor Murgh and Keema Naan and Panjabi Lassis. "There was a leak on your side. Crawley."

"How do you know?"

The question was straightforward and I detected no sign of suspicion behind it. Apparently he hadn't yet learned of Crawley's recent demise. When he did, he would come to his own conclusions. I saw no advantage in having him hear it from me.

"Your NE Division has a relationship with Belghazi," I said. "Belghazi gives them information about other people's deals, particularly in the WMD trade, and in return they protect him in a variety of ways, including overseeing transshipments through Hong Kong."

"Holy shit, how the hell did you learn this?"

I shrugged. "You're telling me you didn't know?"

"I've discovered a few things since we last spoke," he said, looking at me. "But I've got insider access, and you don't. Which is why I'm asking."

I smiled. "Forget about how. Call it 'sources and methods.' What matters is what—and who."

"Who—"

"There's a CIA NOC, based in Hong Kong, attached to the CTC, formerly with NE Division. He's the connection between Belghazi and Crawley."

I watched him closely, looking for a reaction. I didn't see anything.

"You know about the NOC?" I asked.

He nodded. "Of course."

"All right. My guess is, he's part of the reason that Belghazi seems to enjoy Macau so much. Belghazi likes to handle transfers in Hong Kong, where the CIA can help with the heavy lifting. Macau is right next door."

"You're saying it's not the gambling?"

I shrugged. "I'm sure he loves gambling. But he also knows that analysts focus on things like gambling when they're creating profiles. He knows that, if his movements are tracked to Macau, his profilers will just say, 'Ah, it's the gambling,' without probing deeper. He's using your expectations about his known habits to obscure whatever his real purpose is. Feeding you exactly what he wants you to eat, knowing you've already got a taste for it."

We were silent for a long moment, during which Kanezaki drummed his fingers on the table and ignored his food. Then he said, "You're right."

"I know."

He shook his head. "What I mean is, last time we met, when you suggested that Macau might not be a side trip for Belghazi, but maybe the main point, it got me thinking. I did some checking. Now, I told you that we've got a fix on Belghazi's sat phone. The units he uses are part of a low-earth-orbit network. People like the LEO networks because reception is clear and because the satellites' proximity to earth means reduced signal latency, but the networks are less secure."

"Because multiple satellites are picking up the signal?"

"Exactly. So you can always triangulate. It's not supposed to be possible because the signals are digitized and encrypted—it's like, okay, you know there's a needle in the haystack, but that's a far cry from actually being able to find the needle. But, trust me, if you use one of those phones, we can find you."

I thought for a moment. "You said 'units.' Has Belghazi switched phones recently?"

"Yeah, he has."

"I thought he might. He must have decided that the satellite phone was how he got tracked to Macau. What would the NOC have told him?"

"Probably to get a new phone."

"But you're able to track him anyway?"

He smiled. "Yeah."

"How?"

He shook his head. "I'm afraid that would come under the heading of 'sources and methods.'"

"What, have you got the NSA listening in for a digital voice imprint?"

He shook his head again. All right, I wasn't going to get the specifics. "Still think I'm paranoid for not using a cell phone?" I asked.

He smiled. "Maybe not. Anyway, I plotted out the co-ordinates of every Asian location to which we've tracked Belghazi's phone calls during the last two years. What you get looks like a semirandom collection of dots. Except for one place."

"Yes?"

"Three times in the last year, Belghazi has shown up at Kwai Chung in Hong Kong."

"The container port?"

"Yeah. Always at Container Terminal Nine, the new one on Tsing Li island. He makes a call from inside. Always between two and four in the morning."

"How's he getting in there?" I asking, thinking out loud. "It's got to be a secure facility."

"I wondered the same thing. I thought, maybe he's got an accomplice in there, a bribed Customs guy, night watchman, something like that. That's why always the same terminal. I did a little research. And I found out something interesting."

"Yes?"

"There's an access agent. Hong Kong Chinese, lives in the New Territories, works at Kwai Chung. Transferred to Terminal Nine when it came online in July 2003. Belghazi's first visit there was in August of the same year."

"Who was the recruiting officer?"

He looked at me. "The NOC."

I thought for a moment. I didn't see Dox in that role. He was a shooter, not a recruiter. But I couldn't be sure.

"So the NOC has the relationship with the port employee," I said. "He tells Belghazi, 'Hey, you can ship through Hong Kong, I've got the local connections to make sure it all goes smoothly.' A little service from your friendly neighborhood CIA officer in exchange for information on WMD precursors or whatever."

He nodded. "That sounds about right."

"What does the port guy do, do you think?"

"I'm not sure. I've been doing a ton of research on container shipping, though, and my guess is that this guy provides the physical access, shows Belghazi and the buyer or seller the merchandise in one of the containers, then takes care of the necessary EDI information to conceal the true origins and nature of the container cargo in question."

"'EDI?'"

"Electronic Data Interchange. Kwai Chung is the most heavily computerized container shipping terminal in the world. If the port guy has access to the EDI system and the physical containers, presumably he could change the necessary identification codes, country/size/type codes, etcetera, and ensure that the cargo in the container gets sent to wherever Belghazi wants it to go."

I thought for a moment. "Where is Belghazi now?"

"Still in Macau." He looked at me. "You learn anything new about the woman? The blonde?"

Delilah. Well, there had been that message, advising me that the wait was almost over. But of course it wouldn't do to mention any of that to Kanezaki.

"Nothing," I said. "You?"

He shook his head.

"What about Belghazi?" I asked. "Any calls from Terminal Nine?"

"Not yet."

"All right, then, we might still have a shot at him." Without pausing, making the request sound as smooth and obvious as possible, I said, "I'll need the names and particulars of the NOC and the access agent."

He shook his head. "No. No way."

Well, that didn't work. I looked at him. "Are you having second thoughts about this op?"

He shook his head again.

"Because you know now that there are people in your organization who find Belghazi useful, who want him to stay healthy."

He shrugged. "I don't know what game they're playing. I have my mandate, and my mandate is to have him removed. And knowing who he is, that mandate makes sense to me. If someone wants to disabuse me, they'll damn well have to be explicit about it."

"Good. I thought you were wavering there for a second."

"It's not wavering. It's just—"

"Look, I can't get to Belghazi directly anymore, okay? He's seen my face, he knows he's being hunted, he'll be taking extra precautions. My only realistic hope of getting close is through a third party. Like one of the ones you just mentioned."

"I understand what you're saying. But I can't give you the name of a CIA officer—especially a NOC—or the name of an asset. I've crossed a lot of lines with you, it's true, but I'm not crossing that one."

I could tell by his voice and his expression—and by recent experience with Crawley, who had refused to talk even in extremis—that he wasn't going to tell me what I wanted to know. It would be useless to ask about Dox. Even if I asked, I wouldn't be able to trust his answer.

I thought for a moment, and it occurred to me that there might still be a way to do Belghazi, even without the information Kanezaki was determined to hold back. It might involve calling off the wait that Delilah was counting on, but business is business.

"All right, let's go back to the beginning," I said. "What's the purpose of the 'natural causes' requirement with regard to Belghazi, anyway?"

He shrugged. "Well, originally, I was told that it had to look natural because Belghazi has protectors in other intelligence services. But now—"

"Now it seems that the more important objective was to avoid offending protectors in *your* intelligence service."

"Yeah, I know. Life at the CIA is funny that way."

"I told you the right hand and the left aren't exactly working in perfect harmony with you guys."

"I didn't disagree."

"And now, it seems, the right hand has learned that the left has taken a contract out on Belghazi."

He nodded. "So it seems."

"But they haven't complained to you. They haven't gone through channels. You've suggested they're afraid to do that."

"What are you getting at?"

I shrugged. "Maybe you were being overly strict in your interpretation of just how 'natural' Belghazi's demise needed to be. Because, if for whatever reason your people aren't in a position to complain about the existence of a contract on Belghazi, maybe they're not in a position to complain if the contract gets carried out."

He looked away and nodded, rubbing his chin.

I said, "I mean, the point of the 'natural' requirement is to avoid blame, right? Plausible deniability, that kind of thing?"

"What you and I agreed on involved a bit more than just plausible deniability," he said, shaking his head. "More like, Belghazi's death would happen in such a way that uncomfortable questions would never even get asked. There would be nothing to have to deny."

"Sure. But we've learned a few things since we had that conversation, haven't we? For example, we've learned that Belghazi seems to be in Hong Kong to oversee one of his arms transfers. You've got multiple parties involved—buyer, seller, middleman, bought-off port official, CIA overseer—and a lot of money changing hands."

He looked at me, and his mouth started to turn up into a smile. "Yes, that's true. A lot of players, a lot of money."

"Lots of potential for . . . complications."

His smile broadened. "And people to get greedy."

"Right," I said. "What does a bodyguard make a year? Not much, I'll tell you that. And he's spending all that time with Belghazi, securing Belghazi's hotel suites and then returning to his own tiny room, it's like watching *Lifestyles of the Rich and Famous* from the inside of a slum. He gets resentful, he gets jealous. He gets—"

"He gets greedy. And meanwhile he's learning Belghazi's plans—who he's meeting with, where and when."

"Maybe even . . . how much?" I said, raising my eyebrows slightly.

He nodded. "Yeah, he might learn that, too."

"He's the bodyguard, he accompanies Belghazi everywhere, including on those trips to Kwai Chung Container Terminal Nine. As the money is changing hands—"

"He shoots Belghazi, maybe a few other people, grabs the cash, hightails it."

"See? You can't trust anyone these days, not even your own bodyguards. And the way it goes down, both the bodyguard and the money are missing. It's obvious what happened and who did it. No uncomfortable questions for anyone else."

"What happens to the bodyguard?"

I shrugged. "I doubt he would be found afterward. I would expect him to just . . . disappear."

"And the money?"

I smiled. "I doubt that would get found, either."

He shook his head. "You're a devious bastard."

"Thank you."

"I don't think I meant it as a compliment."

"So? It goes down the way I just described, that's natural enough for our purposes?"

There was a pause, then he said, "It's not what we agreed on."

I closed my eyes for a moment, finding myself a little tired of his "this is a difficult concession" reflex.

"We didn't agree on my getting ratted out by your own people, either," I said, feeling like a rug merchant. "Under the circumstances, I ought to charge you double the original price. In fact, I think I will."

"Okay, I see your point."

"All right, then? What I've proposed, it's natural enough?"

He paused for a moment, then nodded. "It's natural enough."

I STILL HAD my doubts about Dox, about his role in this. About who the NOC was. But I knew I couldn't do Belghazi alone anymore. Delilah had been right about that. To make this work, I needed help, and I didn't have anyone else to turn to. And I couldn't just walk away, either. Belghazi had too much incentive to stay after me until he was sure I was gone for good.

And keeping Dox close would give me an opportunity to test him, maybe answer my questions indirectly. If I saw something I didn't like, I could always abort, reevaluate, come up with a new plan.

I called him on his cell phone. "Hello," he said, and it felt strangely good to hear his booming voice. *He's all right,* I told myself, and maybe he was.

"Are you still around?" I asked.

There was a pause, during which I imagined him grinning. I heard him say, "Depends on what you mean by 'around.' I'm in the area again, if that's what you mean."

"How soon can you be back in the same place we met last time?"

Another pause. "I can be there tomorrow, if you need me."

"I do. Same time as last time?"

"I'll see you then."

I hung up and, out of habit, wiped down the phone. Then I went to an Internet café for a bit of research on Hong Kong container shipping.

THE NEXT MORNING I caught a plane to Hong Kong. I sat in a coffee shop overlooking the restaurant where Dox and I had last eaten. He showed up an hour later, alone. I waited ten minutes, then went to join him.

"I didn't expect to see you again so soon," he told me, as I sat down.

"I missed you," I said.

He laughed. "You take care of our friend Mr. Crawley?"

I looked at him. "I don't know what you're talking about."

He laughed again. "All right, all right, I was just asking. May he rest in peace."

A waitress came over. "You know what you want?" I asked him.

"Can you get me some more of that caterpillar soup?"

"Glad you've developed a taste for it."

"Well, the taste is all right, sure. But it's the effects I really admire. Last time we ate here, that night, I showed two Thai ladies what love with Dox is all about. By the time the sun came up they were practically begging for mercy."

"I'm sure they were."

I ordered the food and looked at him. "How are your sniping skills?" I asked.

He scowled as though offended. "Shoot, partner, now you've gone and hurt my feelings, asking a question like that. You know marine snipers are the best in the world."

"What I mean is, you've been staying in shape?"

He smiled. "Well, let's just say that our friends at Christians In Action didn't hire me exclusively for my charm, considerable though it is."

"Do you have access to a rifle?"

"'Access'? Last job I did, I wanted to try out the new M-40A3. I had one waiting for me the next day, with a matching ANPVS-10 night scope, no questions asked."

"How'd you like it?"

"Liked it a lot. It's a little heavier than the M-40A1, but I like the adjustable cheek piece and the recoil pad on the butt stock."

"You used it in field conditions?"

He smiled. "With an M118LR round, chambered in 7.62mm. Drilled a certain malefactor through the eye in the middle of the night at four hundred yards. Nothing like seeing the pink mist to make a sniper feel alive, I'll tell you. Although in the night scope, it was more green than pink."

I nodded, satisfied. I'd seen some of Dox's exploits in Afghanistan. I knew he might enjoy exaggerating his prowess with women, but when it came to sniping, he was as good as he said.

"I've been on a job that's gotten more difficult as it's progressed," I said. "To finish it, I'm going to need help. If you're interested, I'll split the fee with you—two hundred thousand U.S., one hundred thousand each."

"Two hundred thousand? They're paying you that much? Shit, I've been getting shortchanged. I need to have a talk with that damn Kanezaki."

"Plus there might be some additional cash involved, although I don't think we'll know how much until the time comes."

"Well, I'm interested, all right. Tell me more."

I told him what he needed to know about Belghazi, the NOC, and the Hong Kong container port connection. He didn't react in any way that would have indicated prior knowledge or involvement, but you can't prove a negative, as they say.

"Well, first thing is, I need to see the terrain," he told me. "You say there's only one entrance to the terminal, that's where we're going to hit them, that's good. But can I get in and out of position without being seen? Will I have concealment? Can I shoot undetected? Will there be a clear line of sight to the target?"

I nodded and pulled out a sheaf of papers from inside my jacket. "These are printouts from the company that runs Container Terminal Nine," I told him. "They ought to be a good start."

I handed the papers to him and he started shuffling through them. "My gracious," he said, pausing at one of the pages, "is this a map of the terminal?"

I smiled. "It's amazing what you can get on the Web."

He nodded. "Well this is a nice head start, that's for sure. But I still need to do a walk-through."

"I've already rented a van. We'll drive over as soon as you've fortified yourself with the caterpillars."

"It might be less conspicuous if I do the reconnoitering by myself."

"Yeah, you're right, they get a lot of enormous, goateed white guys sniffing around Kwai Chung. I'm sure you'll blend right in."

He grinned. "Well, that's a persuasive point you make there, partner."

KWAI CHUNG and its massive container port are located in the New Territories, a name conferred by the British when they "leased" the area in 1898 and unchanged even after the transfer back to China almost a century later. Although its rolling hills are now obscured by ferroconcrete forests of residential skyscrapers, there's a timelessness about the place, a slower pace than is to be found on Hong Kong Island a few kilometers to the south, as though the area is gradually emerging from a long agrarian sleep and still suffused with the dreams of what it saw there.

We took Highway 3 north to the container port. Because we couldn't afford multiple passes of the port facility lest someone notice and get suspicious, we stopped along the way and bought a video camera.

I drove; Dox videotaped. When I took us along Cheung Fi road, the thoroughfare that leads to the Terminal Nine gate, Dox looked to the area opposite and said, "Well, this does look like fine sniping terrain. Fine, fine, fine."

I glanced over to see what had elicited his reaction, and saw a series of terraced hills, rising to what I estimated to be about one hundred and fifty meters above the road and overlooking the terminal entrance. Some of the hills were wooded, some were grass, some were cleared and home to what looked like partially constructed apartment buildings. Dox would have his pick of ingress and egress routes, cover, concealment, and an unobstructed field of fire. He was right. It was perfect.

We went to a tea shop in Tsim Sha Tsui to talk things over. Dox was pleased about the terrain, but I was uneasy.

"The problem is that our information is limited," I said. "Kanezaki says he'll know from Belghazi's sat phone when Belghazi is on his way to Hong Kong, so we'll have some warning about that. And the time window is manageable, too—apparently, Belghazi conducts his business at Kwai Chung between oh two hundred and oh four hundred. But we don't know what he'll be driving. We don't know whether he'll get out outside the gate, or stay in the car and drive in."

"What do you think he's been waiting for? He's been in Macau for you said, what, a week now?"

I shrugged. "Part of it probably really is the gambling. Part of it is the appearance he wants to cultivate for anyone who's trying to figure out what he's up to in the region—'Oh, he's just there to gamble.' And maybe part of it has to do with whatever shipment is being handled at Kwai Chung. There might have been some logistical problem along the way, the ship could have been delayed. A lot of things that could have kept him in place longer than he'd originally planned."

He was quiet for a moment, then said, "There's another thing. You said he's a careful man, and that he knows you're after him so he's extra nervous. What if he rents an armored vehicle for his little trip to the dockyards? A place like Hong Kong, with all the property magnates and such, would have armored Mercedeses and Bimmers available, I'm sure."

That was a good point. I thought for a moment. "What about armor piercing ammunition?"

"Well, I could use some, it's true. A 7.62 AP round will penetrate fifteen millimeters of armor at three hundred meters and take out a hundred and twenty millimeters of Plexiglas, too. But if I start capping these guys with that kind of ordnance, it won't exactly look like some bodyguard who decided to open up with a pistol from close range. And you said that if it didn't look like an inside job we might not get paid."

"We've got some flexibility on just how much of an inside job it needs to look like. The main thing is that it should look less like an assassination, and more like an arms deal gone to shit. We're going to have to play some of the details by ear."

"Okay, I'm just thinking out loud here."

"No, that's good, and you're right about the armor." I thought for a minute, then said, "What about two magazines, one with armor piercing, one with standard? You'd only need a few seconds' warning to switch as circumstances required, right?"

"That's right, yeah. We could do that."

I nodded. "All right, let's break it down. We know that, one morning soon, Belghazi is going to be visiting Container Terminal Nine. It's not reachable by train or realistically by foot, and the harbor approach is patrolled, so a boat isn't likely. Meaning we can assume he'll be coming in a car. The only approach is south along Cheung Fi road. Using that information, what do we need to do to make sure this is Belghazi's last road trip?"

"Well, the first thing is, we need to stop the car. Once it's inside the terminal or off Cheung Fi, we lose access to it."

"Right. Can we count on it stopping in front of the gate?"

He nodded for a moment as though considering. "I can't imagine the gate would already be open, not in the middle of the night. The car would have to at least pause outside it."

"Probably, but not definitely. Belghazi could call en route. His contact could be waiting for him with the gate open. In which case he drives right through. Plus, once the car turns in, you're looking at the vehicle's rear. If you start shooting but don't hit the driver, he'll floor it, blow through the gate, and we'll lose them."

"Yeah, that's true. Well, there's the approach along Cheung Fi. That's a quarter mile, so I'd have, say, fifteen seconds to take out the driver there. The problem is—"

"How are you going to know you've got the right car."

"Yeah, I'd hate to take out the pizza delivery man, I really would."

"So what we need to do is, I'm the spotter, positioned on the slope above Cheung Fi, but close to the road. I've got binoculars, I see the car coming. There won't be much traffic at that hour, and I guarantee you Belghazi will be arriving in something stylish, whether or not it's armored. It shouldn't be hard for me to confirm that it's him."

"What if the glass is smoked?"

"It might be, I know. But if I see a car like that heading toward Terminal Nine at oh two hundred on the same day Kanezaki tells us Belghazi is on his way, I'll be confident enough to take out the tires, and maybe the windows, and see what happens next. Also, it's possible they'll stop outside the gate, maybe roll down a window. In which case, even if I can't see what I need to, I might get to hear it. I'm going to ask Kanezaki to send a parabolic mike, compatible with the rest of the communications gear I want—earpieces and lapel mikes."

"I never used one of those parabolics," he said. "They really work?"

I nodded. "A good one will bring in conversation from three hundred yards out. The new ones fold up small, too. I'll be able to talk to you on one channel, then switch over and listen in on whoever arrives, then switch back."

"All right, so either visual or auditory or both, now you've got positive ID."

"Now I let you know, from my lapel mike straight to your earpiece."

"At which point—"

"At which point, you take your first clear shot. Any place between where I confirm that the target has arrived and the entry gate. In fact, earlier would be better. If this goes down right in front of the entry gate, we might have terminal security personnel to deal with, too. I don't want to take out bystanders, and the fewer witnesses, the better, anyway."

"Makes sense. I start with the driver, then just work my way through."

"Right. Count on a total of at least three—Belghazi, one bodyguard driving, one bodyguard passenger—but maybe more. And while you're shooting from up high, I'll be assaulting on foot with a sidearm. Anyone you've missed, I take out at close range."

He grinned. "Partner, marine snipers don't miss. By the time you reach the vehicle, all that'll be left is for you to reach through the shattered glass and retrieve a bag stuffed with cash, all right?"

And all that'll be left for you to do is take one last shot, I thought. *Then the cash will be all yours and you can walk away clean.*

I needed to find that opportunity to test him before the main event. I hadn't managed it yet.

I nodded and said, "Sounds like a plan."

OUR GEAR ARRIVED the next day. We had contacted Kanezaki independently with our requests for matériel, some of which was for commo gear and all of which was bound for Hong Kong, and he must have suspected that we were working together. But if he had any questions, he didn't ask. The Agency had moved it all through the diplomatic pouch and had left it in a golf bag at a pre-arranged dead drop. I had to admit, they could move fast when they wanted to.

Dox had asked for a Heckler & Koch PSG/1, semiautomatic, with a twenty-round magazine, tripod, 6x42mm illuminated mil-dot reticle scope, and integral suppressor. In the same package was a 7.62mm Tokarev for me. Unless Dox had to switch to armor-piercing ammunition, we would both be using frangible rounds, with relatively low penetration power but devastating results at the range from which we would be working.

Dox had been as excited as a kid with a new toy. He took the rifle over to the deserted south side of Hong Kong to take it through its paces. I joined him with the Tokarev and the commo gear. Everything was working fine. I was careful not to give him the opportunity to get downrange of me with the rifle. I still didn't trust him.

I was checking the bulletin board every hour, but no word from Kanezaki. Not the first day. Not the second.

On the evening of the second day, there was a message waiting for me: "He's on the way. Call me!"

I wondered if he'd thought to try Dox's cell phone first. Maybe I'd been wrong, and he hadn't figured out that this had become a joint operation.

I called him. He picked up immediately. *"Moshi moshi,"* he said,

"It's me."

"You got the message."

"Of course."

"'Of course.' How was I supposed to know, if you didn't call to confirm? I wish you would just use a damn cell phone. I really do."

"Do we have to have this conversation again?"

There was a pause, and I wondered whether he was smiling. "No, we don't," he said.

"I'll call you when it's done."

There was another pause, then he said, *"Ki o nuku na yo."* Be careful.

I smiled. *"Arigatou."* I hung up.

I picked up Dox and we drove to Kwai Chung. We parked the van in the parking lot of a nearby residential high-rise, reachable on foot from the hills overlooking the terminal entry gate. Each of us had a key to the van. If something went awry and only one of us made it back to the van, he'd still be able to drive away. We reviewed our plans one last time and separated to take up our positions. Dox was about thirty meters south of the gate, about a hundred and fifty meters distant and at maybe seventy meters elevation. I was thirty meters north, and much closer to the road. Dox would be doing the distance work; I would do the spotting, then follow up at close range. I was lying in a concrete-lined drainage culvert, which would provide cover from Dox's position in case I'd been wrong about him. But this was still dangerous. He was a sniper, more than capable of stealthily achieving a new position.

At a little after two o'clock, I saw a dark sedan coming down Cheung Fi road. I raised the binoculars—a gorgeous, mechanically stabilized Zeiss 20x60 unit with antireflective lenses—and looked through them. The approaching car was a Lexus LS 430. Two Caucasians in front. The back looked empty, but the car's interior was too dark to be sure.

I had been half-expecting to see Delilah in the car, although I knew the possibility was remote. She might not even know this meeting was going down tonight. And her role, as I understood it, was such that Belghazi would want to keep her separate from his business transactions. Most of all, I knew she was too specialized and valuable an operator to risk in an operation like a straightforward terrorist takedown.

"That him?" I heard Dox's voice clearly through the earpiece.

"I'm not sure yet," I said. "Too much glare on the windows from the streetlights, not enough light in the car. Hold on."

The car continued past my position. The driver-side backseat was empty. I couldn't be sure about the passenger side.

"Still no ID," I said. "Hold on."

The car pulled into the turnaround in front of the entrance, swung around so that it was facing the street, then backed up to within a couple of meters of the gate. The engine cut out. I watched through the binoculars, trying to imagine what this was, to understand why they weren't going inside.

The front doors opened and two men got out. They looked Slavic to me: broad cheekbones, wheat-colored hair crew cut, white skin shining unhealthily in the light cast by the shipping facility behind them. They seemed uncomfortable in their dark suits, neither of which fit particularly well, and each was wearing a bright red tie. Ex-military, maybe, men unaccustomed to any uniform that wasn't battle dress and choosing their ties in overreaction to a previous lifetime of nothing but olive drab. I decided to think of them as Russians. They looked around after exiting the car, and I thought their looks had the feel of an attempt at orientation. They certainly weren't locals.

"Looks like a drug deal in the making," I heard Dox say, and he was right, it did have that sort of illicit feel to it. I had expected them to drive into the container port, but it looked like the party was going to happen outside it. Which wasn't necessarily a bad thing.

"I think they're going to do the exchange right here," I said. "Let's see if our friend shows, too. As long as the gate stays closed, I'm going to let him pass my position. If he gets out of the car like these guys have done, you'll have a stationary target and a clearer shot. You're loaded up with the frangible ammo?"

"Unless you tell me to switch to the AP."

"Good. Hang tight."

"Roger that."

Five minutes later, two more vehicles pulled onto the access road: a white van, followed by a black Mercedes S-class. I glanced over at the previous arrival. The Russians, talking to each other, were smoking cigarettes. The gate was still closed.

"Two more vehicles approaching," I said.

"Roger that."

I saw two Arabs in the front seat of the van, neither of whom was the target.

Three men were in the Mercedes. The driver was Arab, and I recognized him as one of Belghazi's body-guards from Macau. It looked like there were two men in back, but I couldn't see well enough to know. Given the circumstances, though, I was reasonably sure about who the passengers were. Adrenaline kicked into my bloodstream.

"I think this is him," I said. "In the Mercedes. Let's let him go to the gate, like we said."

"Roger that."

The Mercedes stopped in front of the gate and backed in parallel to the Lexus. The van performed the identical procedure, parking so that the Mercedes was in the middle.

"They sure have fine taste in their automobiles," I heard Dox say.

The van doors opened and two Arabs got out. Three men exited from the Mercedes. One Arab. One white guy. And one half-French, half-Algerian. Belghazi. Bingo.

"He's here," I said. "The one who just got out from the passenger-side rear of the Mercedes."

Belghazi was walking over to the Russians. I watched as they shook hands.

"The one who's shaking hands now?"

"That one, yeah."

"Say the word and I'll drop him."

"Let's give them just a few more seconds. I don't see any money, and I don't want to have to dig it out of a locked trunk or something."

"Roger that."

"Hang on for a second, I'm going to see if I can listen in. Keep him in your sights now."

"He's not going anywhere."

I changed channels so the earpiece would receive from the parabolic mike. The reception was good. The men were exchanging pleasantries, in English. Good to see you, thanks for coming all this way. The two I'd been thinking of as the Russians had heavy accents that might have been Russian. I wasn't sure.

Belghazi shook the other Russian's hand. He motioned for the white guy to come over. Even before Belghazi had introduced him, I was pretty sure I knew who he was.

The NOC. Belghazi's protector. I let out a long breath as I eliminated this angle as a cause of potential untrustworthiness for Dox. This angle only, though. There was still the cash that we expected to be in play, the opportunity that, as he had put it in Rio, "only knocked once."

"Let me introduce you to our American friend," Belghazi told the men. "This is Mr. Hilger. He's here to make sure that we don't have to worry about problems with the authorities."

Hilger shook the Russians' hands. "And how do you do that, Mr. Hilger?" one of the Russians asked.

I looked around. The Russians were on their third or fourth cigarettes. Belghazi's Arab driver had just lit up. So had the two Arabs from the van. Everyone was obviously a little on edge. Everyone except Belghazi and Hilger.

"I'm fortunate enough to have some useful connections in both the U.S. and Hong Kong SAR governments," Hilger said, his voice low and reassuring. It didn't sound like a boast, just a calm response to a reasonable question. "On occasion, I ask those connections if they would be good enough to look the other way while I conduct some business. Tonight is one of those occasions."

The Russian might have pressed, but Hilger's self-possession seemed to settle the matter. The Russian nodded. "Cigarette?" he offered, extending a pack.

Hilger shook his head and said, "No, thank you."

I wanted to hear more. What was being exchanged tonight? Was this the moment Delilah had been waiting for, after which, she had assured me, she would give me the green light and help me get close?

And who were these "Russians"? Were any of these people connected to Nuchi, the Frenchman I had taken out in Macau, of whom Kanezaki claimed to have no knowledge?

Most of all, where was the money?

But at some point, the quest for perfect intelligence becomes an excuse for a failure to act. The situation seemed manageable for the moment, but it could easily change. I didn't want to delay any longer.

I took two deep breaths and switched back to Dox's channel.

"You ready?" I asked.

"Sure I am. Been waiting on you, that's all."

"Start with Belghazi. Then the white guy who came with him. Then the two white guys from the Lexus. I think they might be Russian. They look military to me, harder targets than Belghazi's usual retinue."

"Roger that."

"Take out as many as you can. The ones you don't drop are going to figure out the general direction the shots are coming from. Their only cover is the vehicles. When they move around the vehicles to get away from you, their backs will be to me. I'll close the pincer."

"Sounds like a plan, buddy. Here we go."

At that moment, Belghazi, Hilger, and the Russians moved around to the back of the van. I heard Dox say, "Damn, lost my shot."

"Hold on, I can still see him. They're just talking. Belghazi is gesturing to the inside of the van. I think they're talking about transport arrangements, something like that. Give me a second, I'm going to switch over again."

"Roger that."

The Russian was nodding his head as though satisfied with whatever Belghazi had explained to him. I watched Belghazi take out his satellite phone. I switched channels in time to hear him say, "We're ready for the cargo, please. Thank you."

He must have been talking to his contact inside. This wasn't what I had been expecting. I had thought the meeting would be just to inspect whatever the cargo was, confirm its contents, and exchange money. The port guy would take care of bills of lading and country of origin certifications and the other minutiae of Kwai Chung's EDI, then send the cargo off to its ultimate buyer. But it seemed that the goods were going to change hands right here.

And Belghazi had arrived with the van. I had assumed that he would be selling the cargo. Now I wondered if tonight he wasn't the buyer. I was fine either way. But I did want to know where that damn money was.

The Russians, it seemed, shared my concern. "You have the cash?" one of them asked Belghazi.

Belghazi nodded. He said something in Arabic to his driver, who walked over to the back of the Mercedes, where he retrieved a large black duffel bag from the trunk. He carried it back behind the van, set it on the ground, and unzipped it. It was stuffed with greenbacks.

"Would you like to count it?" Belghazi asked.

The Russian smiled. "It would take a long time to count five million dollars."

Holy shit, I thought, *what are these guys selling?*

"I doubt you would find it boring, though," Belghazi said, and they all laughed.

Come on, fuckers, move out from behind that van, I thought. But they all stayed put.

Five minutes went by. They all watched the gate. No one spoke. I switched back to Dox.

"They're still behind the van," I said.

"I figured. I'd have seen them if they'd gone anywhere else."

"Did you see that duffel bag?" I asked.

"Sure did. What's in it?"

"I'm reluctant to tell you. It might affect your shooting."

"Partner, nothing affects my shooting. When I'm looking through this scope, I could be getting a blow job and perineum massage from midget twins and I wouldn't even know it."

"Excuse me for a second. I need to drive a hot poker through my mind's eye."

He chuckled. "Well, what's in the bag?"

"Five million U.S., it sounds like."

"Well, that's good," he said. His tone was soft and even, and I realized he was telling the truth: when he was in sniping mode, he wasn't going to be distracted by anything not directly related to the task at hand.

A Chinese man on a powered hand truck was pulling up to the gate. Four large metal crates were stacked across the vehicle's tines.

"They're going to open the gate," I told Dox. "But I don't think anyone is going inside. They're going to load those crates into the van. Then the Russians are going to pick up the duffel bag and everyone will go back to his car. That's our moment."

"Roger that."

The gate opened and the hand truck came through. The driver lowered the crates into the van, backed out, then stepped off the vehicle. Belghazi and one of the Russians climbed into the van.

"I think they're inspecting whatever's in the crates," I said. "I can't see inside the van. Shouldn't be much longer."

"Roger that."

A minute later, Belghazi and the Russian came out of the van. They were smiling. Belghazi reached inside his jacket and handed a large envelope to the hand truck driver. The man nodded, got on the hand truck, and went back through the gate, which closed behind him.

One of the Russians picked up the duffel bag and zipped it shut. He shouldered it, then extended his hand to Belghazi. They smiled and shook. Everyone seemed to relax: the deal was done, money exchanged for merchandise, no unpleasant surprises.

Everyone, that is, but Belghazi's driver, the bodyguard who had carried the duffel bag over from the Mercedes. He was fidgeting, looking from one face to the next. Despite the coolness of the night I could see beads of perspiration on his forehead through the Zeiss binoculars.

No one else seemed to notice. They'd all been worried about so many things—betrayal, the law, problems with the merchandise, problems with payment—none of which had happened. It was natural that their guards were down now, if only for a moment.

Belghazi noticed first. He glanced over at the bodyguard, and his brow furrowed. He said something. With the earpiece switched to Dox I couldn't hear what. For a second, maybe less, an electric tension seemed to build.

I could see Belghazi getting ready to do something, his center of gravity dropping, his legs coiling beneath him. His instincts were excellent, perhaps dulled just slightly this one time because the source of the problem was a bodyguard, a direction from which he hadn't expected trouble to come.

Hilger looked over at the bodyguard, too. And, possessing a set of sharp instincts of his own but without the personal relationship that had perhaps fractionally slowed Belghazi's own reaction, he shot his hand toward the inside of his jacket.

But too late. The bodyguard had started his own move a second earlier. By the time Hilger's hand had disappeared under his jacket, the bodyguard had reached into his rear waistband and withdrawn a pistol. He pointed it at Hilger and said something.

Everyone froze. Hilger slowly removed his hand from inside his jacket. It was empty.

Belghazi was looking at the bodyguard, his expression incredulous. He shouted something.

"Holy shit," I said to Dox. "The bodyguard just pulled a gun on Belghazi."

"Say what?"

"I think the inside job we were going to simulate is happening for real."

"I'll be damned."

"I want to hear what they're saying. But if Belghazi shows his head, make sure you drop him. No more chances."

"Roger that."

I switched over. Belghazi was yelling at the bodyguard in Arabic, cursing him, from the tone. The bodyguard was yelling back, gesturing with the gun, pointing it from man to man. Everyone else seemed frozen.

"Achille, can you tell me what he's saying, please," Hilger said to Belghazi, the words slow and calm. "I don't speak Arabic."

"Yes, what in fuck is going on here!" one of the Russians added loudly.

"Take out your guns!" the bodyguard shouted. "Slowly! Put them on the ground! Slowly, slowly, or I will shoot you!"

Belghazi never took his eyes from his man. His lips had pulled back from his teeth, and his body was coiled like a panther about to pounce. It seemed that only the gun prevented him.

"He says that he is stealing the shipment," he said. Then he let out another hot stream of Arabic.

"Guns on ground!" the bodyguard yelled. "This is the last time I ask!"

The men did as he said. Each of them removed a pistol from a waistband or shoulder holster and slowly placed it on the ground.

"Now hands in the air! Hands in the air!" the bodyguard yelled. Everyone complied.

"Now kick the guns forward. Kick them!" Again, everyone complied.

The bodyguard turned his head to the Russians, but didn't take his eyes from Belghazi. "I am very sorry about this," he said in heavily accented English. "Very sorry. We tried to buy the missiles from you. But you wouldn't sell them."

"Who in fuck is 'we'?" the Russian spat.

"It doesn't matter," the bodyguard said. "What matters is, we offered you money, and you told us you already had a buyer—Belghazi. We offered to pay you more! But you wouldn't listen."

"Because we know this man, we have business with

this man," the Russian said. "With motherfucker we don't know, bullshit like this! You see?"

Belghazi let out another stream of Arabic abuse. Hilger said, "Achille, please, I need to know what's going on. Did he say 'missiles'?"

Belghazi flexed his hands open and closed, as though trying to burn off some surfeit of energy that would otherwise consume him. "Did you send that French piece of shit to Macau?" he said to the bodyguard. "It was you, wasn't it."

The man nodded. "I'm sorry, Mr. Belghazi, very sorry. But you were the only reason these men wouldn't sell us the Alazans."

Alazans? I thought.

"'Us.' Who is us?"

The man shook his head.

Belghazi threw up his hands and laughed. The laugh sounded dangerous, almost mad. "You're right, it doesn't matter! Because I would have sold you the Alazans! All you had to do was ask!"

The man shook his head again. "These are special, you know that, you know you would have quadrupled the price. Also you would have sold them off in small numbers to many buyers. But we need them all. We had to buy direct, and you were in the way. I'm sorry."

Belghazi said, "How are you going to move this merchandise off Hong Kong without my help, hmm?"

The bodyguard nodded almost sympathetically, as though he regretted putting his putative employer in such an embarrassing position. "We have made our own arrangements for the Alazans. Everything is taken care of."

Hilger said, "Achille, what are 'Alazans,' please? Are there missiles in that crate?"

Belghazi shrugged. He said, "Jim, don't ask me questions you don't want answered, all right?"

"You told me this was another small arms shipment," Hilger said, more to himself than to Belghazi. I could imagine the workings of his mind: *Five million sounded like way too much. I should have known right there something was rotten in Denmark. Damn it, these guys are trying to move some very bad shit. I've been had.*

The bodyguard turned his head to the Russians and, keeping his eyes on Belghazi, said, "We don't want the money. You can keep it, it's yours. It's the same amount we would have paid you, if you had trusted us. Maybe you will be able to trust us next time, because now we have 'done business,' as you say."

"We keep money?" one of the Russians said.

The man nodded. "All we want is the Alazans. And, for next time, your goodwill."

I wondered if the man was telling the truth. He might have been bluffing, holding out hope for the Russians as a way of persuading them to acquiesce in what was happening. Even if he was sincere at the moment, though, the Russians would have been fools to trust him. The psychology of a criminal who suddenly realizes his total dominion over another human life is rarely stable. His ambitions grow, his original aims change. A nervous armed robber, seeing his victims cowering before him, realizes that not only can he rob these people, he can do *anything* to them, and what started as a simple armed robbery escalates to sadism, often to rape. So if this went on for another minute or so, I could imagine the bodyguard thinking, *Why shouldn't I take that five million? It's for a worthy cause . . .* at which point he might also decide that it would be best not to leave witnesses, or anyone who might bear a grudge.

Hilger was watching the bodyguard carefully, his expression somehow dubious, and I thought he might be as acquainted with these less savory aspects of human psychology as I. In which case, I doubted he would remain passive for too much longer.

Also, he had seemed distinctly unhappy to learn that this shipment contained something other than small arms. I wondered if he had decided to try to do something about that.

The Russians started talking to each other, and I realized I had been right: they were using Russian. But again I wasn't sure of the accent. Were they Ukrainians? Belorussians? Or of some other group in the region?

I watched through the binoculars, amazed. With just a little luck, this really could go perfectly. The bodyguard executes the six men. Dox drops him as he goes to get in the van. Or they all start shooting at each other, and Dox and I take out the "survivors." I grab the duffel bag and we drive off.

But even as I imagined it, I knew it was too good to be true. Because I saw a new complication: a silver Toyota Camry, approaching from the south end of the access road. *Now what?* I thought.

The bodyguard glanced over at the approaching car, then back to the men in front of him. He didn't seem surprised; in fact, I thought I saw a little relief in his expression. I had a feeling the occupants of the car were his compatriots, perhaps having been signaled by the bodyguard through some electronic means that it was time for them to make their appearance.

Hilger was watching closely. I imagined him thinking: *He can't start shooting now because it's six against one. He couldn't drop us all before someone rushed him. But if the men in that car are with him, when they get here we're all dead.*

He was going to make his move before then. I could feel it.

"Well, gentlemen," one of the Russians said, "we brought Alazans, no? They are yours now. So this . . . not our problem."

Smart. He wasn't going to wait for that car, either. He picked up the duffel bag and nodded to his companion. They started walking to their car.

The bodyguard stepped back a few paces to maintain his ability to watch all the players, but he made no move to interfere with the Russians' departure. The one with the bag started to smile. Then his head exploded.

Maybe the bodyguard was willing to see that five million go. But Dox wasn't.

The bodyguard's mouth dropped open. And in that instant of his surprise and distraction, Hilger dropped down to one knee, drew a pistol free from an ankle holster, and shot him in the stomach. The man staggered backward and twisted around. Hilger shot again, and again. The bodyguard dove to the side of the car and I couldn't tell if Hilger's subsequent shots had hit home.

Apparently not. I saw muzzle fire come from under the car, from the bodyguard's position.

The second Russian grabbed the bag and started to dash for the Lexus. He took exactly two steps before Dox quietly blew his head off.

Belghazi jumped into the back of the van. I heard the doors slam behind him.

Hilger moved to the front of the van and pointed his pistol at the driver-side window. I thought, *Shit, he's going to drop Belghazi, his own asset. Remind me not to cross this guy unless I really need to.*

The Toyota screeched into the turnaround. I heard shots and saw muzzle flashes from the passenger-side window, explosions of dust in the dirt around Hilger and Belghazi's other men. The two Arabs dove behind the van. Hilger, still on one knee, turned from the van, took his gun hand in his free hand and coolly fired a half dozen shots, all of which hit the car. Either he hit the driver or the man panicked under the hail of gunfire, because a second later the car swerved and smashed into the concrete abutment on its right. It spun a hundred and eighty degrees and screeched backward along the abutment, its side throwing sparks into the air. A second after it had come to a stop, the driver-side door opened and a man jumped out. Another Arab. He knelt behind the door and started firing a pistol in Hilger's direction.

Hilger dove to the side of the van, seeking cover there. But there was none to be had. The van's engine roared to life, and it lurched forward. Belghazi must have scuttled forward, into the driver's seat. Hilger shot at its side, but apparently without effect.

I switched back to Dox's channel. "Take the shot!" I hissed.

"He's keeping down, I don't have a shot," I heard Dox say. Amid the gunfire and confusion, his voice was almost supernaturally calm. He was in his sniping zone.

"Then take out the tires!" I said.

A second passed. The van was pulling even with my position. I was going to have to try to take out the tires myself. From this distance and with only a pistol, I wasn't optimistic about my chances. And my fire would alert everyone to my position.

But there was no need. The front passenger tire exploded and the van lurched to the left. The rear followed a second later, and the van swerved hard to the right. It crashed through the container port's chain-link fence and slammed into a stack of containers about ten meters beyond. The containers, stacked five high, tumbled down on the roof, coming to rest behind the van and to the sides.

"Lost the shot," I heard Dox say. "Can't see past those containers."

"Cover me," I said. I doubted that anyone caught up in the firefight would notice me stealing across the road thirty meters north of their position, but I wanted backup just in case. I eased to my feet and scrambled down the embankment, my pistol out. I crossed the street in a crouch and ducked through the hole the van had punched in the fence.

Once inside, I slowed down and moved more cautiously. I held the gun in my right hand, the barrel angled down slightly, my wrist pressed tight against my solar plexus. My left hand was at chin level and further out from my body, where it could deflect an attack and keep Belghazi away from the gun if he sprang in suddenly.

The street was well lit, and the container area was dark by comparison. My eyes weren't fully adjusted. The van was obscured by the containers that had fallen around it. I couldn't see the driver-side door.

I moved up slowly, inching forward, my eyes scanning left and right, the gun tracking my searching vision. *Scan and breathe. Front foot down. Slide forward. Pause. Check position. Again.*

Belghazi's eyes wouldn't be any better adjusted than mine, but I knew the streetlights were backlighting me, exposing my position. I needed to move into the dark. I started to circle to my left.

Something hit me in the left ribs like a battering ram, finding its mark between my chin-level free hand and the stomach-level gun. There was an explosion of pain and I went flying backward. As I hit the ground I could hear Delilah's voice: *With his kicks he can break individual ribs.*

Or maybe three or four at a time.

My body did a judo *ukemi* breakfall of its own accord, a quarter century of muscle memory taking over without any input from my conscious mind. The breakfall distributed the impact and saved me from further damage. Lying on my back now, I tried to bring the gun up to where I thought he would be, but he had already moved in. His foot blurred off his chambered hip in some sort of *fouette* or spiral kick and the gun blew out of my hand. I felt the shock up to my shoulder.

He reached inside his jacket. What he pulled out flashed in the lights reflected from the street and I realized *razor,* just as Delilah had warned me.

I brought my legs up to try to kick him away, and was surprised to see him take a step back. I thought, *He knows your background, he's being careful about closing, even with the razor,* but then I saw him wiping blood from his eyes and realized the pause was driven more by necessity than by tactics. He must have gotten smacked around when the van hit the containers.

He swayed for a second, and in that second I rolled backward and sprang to my feet. I felt a hot stab in the ribs where he had nailed me and thought, *If I get out of this, I* will *carry a blade, I don't give a shit about all the good reasons not to.*

I took two more steps back to buy a little distance, then glanced down at the ground. I didn't see the gun. There were too many shadows, and too much junk lying around: cracked wooden pallets, container doors, sections of chain-link fence. To my right was a pile of what looked like oversized metal hubcaps. I swept one up, liking its heft. If there had been a handle on it, I might have used it as a shield. Instead, I slung it like a Frisbee. It hissed through the air straight for Belghazi's midsection. He jumped left and it sailed past him. Damn, even with the head injury, he was light on his feet, more like a dancer than a typical kickboxer. He started to move toward me and I snatched up another of the metal disks, seeing as I did so that after two more I would be out of ammo. I sent it flying. He dodged again. I grabbed the third and fourth and flung them rapid-fire. The first went high and he managed to duck under it. But the duck cost him his mobility, and he couldn't get out of the way of the next one, which was heading straight for his head. He raised his razor hand to protect himself and the disk slammed into it, knocking it back into his head. I saw the razor tumble out of his grip and felt a rush of satisfaction.

He stood up and glanced down, and I immediately took two long steps toward him. He looked up at me, knowing that he wasn't going to have time to grope for and recover the weapon, and we stood facing each other for a moment, each of us breathing hard. He hitched his pants up slightly, creating a little more freedom of movement for his legs. *That's it,* I thought. *Give me one of those fucking legs. I promise to give it back when I'm done with it.*

I had to be careful, though. His physical skills and toughness were obvious, but more than that I expected his tactics to be sound, too. Old-style *savateurs* practice what they call *malice,* or dirty fighting, using improvised weapons, deception, anything to get the job done. It becomes a mind-set, a mind-set with which I am firsthand familiar. I expected that Belghazi would be equally so.

I circled left, my hands up in a boxer's stance. He did the same, his hands held lower, his posture looser, again moving fluidly, light on his feet. Of course I had no intention of boxing with him or otherwise trying to engage him at a distance. That was his game, not mine. But if I offered him a familiar appearance, say, the appearance of the kind of opponent he was accustomed to facing in the gym and in the ring, his body might automatically respond to the recognizable stimuli, much as mine had done a moment earlier when I had landed with a judo *ukemi.* In which case he would begin to approach me as though I was another *savateur,* thereby, I hoped, creating an opportunity for me to close with him. He wouldn't be unacquainted with grappling—*savateurs* call their grappling style *lutte,* a derivative of Greco-Roman wrestling designed more to maim than to restrain—but I had little doubt that, if I could take him to the ground, the advantage would be mine.

He chambered his right leg, feinted, then returned the foot to the ground. He repeated the maneuver. And again. The upraised leg started to return to the ground and I saw my opening. I shot forward. But the third time had been no feint, or in fact it had been the real feint, and the leg reversed course and whipped in from my left. I covered up with my left elbow and the toe of his shoe caught me between the biceps and triceps. It felt like I'd been hit with a hammer. He retracted the kick, then shot it in again, this time toward my forward knee. I lifted the leg just as his heel landed, and, although it hurt, the impact was dissipated enough to prevent meaningful damage.

He replanted his right foot and I shot my own kick in, a basic front kick off the back leg aimed at his knee. He twisted clockwise off the line of attack and parried inward with his left hand. I reached out and managed to snag his left sleeve with my right hand. I rotated counterclockwise, dragging his sleeve down and around, ruining his balance and forcing his body to follow. As he spiraled in toward the ground, I changed direction and brought my left hand up under his hand. I swept my right leg around clockwise along the ground and levered his arm backward, trying to break it. Even with his balance destroyed, though, his reflexes were quick. Rather than resisting the wristlock, he launched his body into it, getting ahead of the lock's momentum and saving his arm.

He landed on his back and I immediately dropped onto his solar plexus, my left knee leading the way. He grunted and I heard the wind being driven out of him. I kept his arm and dragged it upward, simultaneously sliding my left foot under his ribs, preparing to fall back in a *jujigatame* armlock and take out his elbow. But again he showed both quick reflexes and sound training: as I whipped my right leg across his face and dropped back into the lock, he spun his body in my direction and retracted his arm like a man trying to yank out of a straitjacket sleeve. His reaction cost me some of my leverage, but I still held enough arm to damage him. He reached around with his left hand and grabbed his right wrist to prevent me from straightening his arm. I brought my left leg up and hacked at his wrist with my heel. His grip broke. I popped backward and levered his arm against the natural movement of the elbow joint. I felt an instant of resistance from the surrounding ligaments, then felt the joint break with a resounding crack. He screamed and writhed under me.

And in that instant I realized I had lost track of his other arm. It had disappeared from my view. My stomach lurched with the knowledge. Then, as that lurch rolled sickeningly through me, his right arm flashed into view, light glinting off the surgical steel he was holding in it. A second razor, deployed after the attacker had been lulled by disarming him of the first. *Malice.*

I clamped his head tighter with my right leg and squeezed my knees together, increasing the pressure on his ruined elbow. He screamed again, but he was fighting for his life now and wasn't going to be stopped by pain alone. He slashed at my thigh with the razor. I tried to grab his wrist but missed, and the blade cut deep into my quadriceps. He pulled back, then immediately cut me again. There was no pain, really, adrenaline taking care of that for the moment, but a gout of blood spouted out of the wounds. He slashed again. Again I missed the grab, and this time he cut my wrist. The next time I caught him. Immediately I shifted my leg off his head and blasted a hammer fist into his face, snapping my body forward to generate momentum and getting my weight into the blow. Once. Twice. Again.

I felt his body go limp and the razor dropped from his hand. I transferred his wrist to my left hand and groped for the razor with my right. There it was, on the ground, next to his thigh. I grabbed it carefully and slid off him. His face was a bloody mess and he was groaning, seemingly semiconscious.

I knelt beside him and hooked the fingers of my free hand under his jawline. I hauled his head back and raised the razor.

A voice cried out sharply in Japanese from behind me. *"Yamero!"* Stop!

I froze, thinking, *What the fuck?*

I looked back over my shoulder. Two serious-looking Japanese stared back at me, each with a pistol pointing at my face. *"Yamero!"* one of them said again. *"Kamisori otose!"* Drop the razor!

I did as he asked and started to stand. My right leg wobbled, then went out under me. I looked down and saw why. My thigh was gashed wide open and spurting blood. My wrist was doing the same.

I sank down to my knees and looked at them. "You must be Belghazi's new *yakuza* friends, is that right?" I asked them in Japanese.

They ignored me. Beside me, Belghazi stirred.

He must have had them positioned up the road as backup, and they'd moved in when the shooting started. Maybe they'd been accompanying him since Macau. Sure, he knew I would be looking for Arabs again, and he'd even supplied a few—distractions at the periphery, diverting me from the real players. Tatsu had been right.

Belghazi groaned and sat up, then got unsteadily to his feet. I watched him, my face impassive. I was already kneeling, and now I placed my hands calmly across my bloody thighs, the fingers pressed lightly together and pointed in at forty-five degrees. I drew my head and shoulders up into *seiza,* or natural posture, the formal attitude of traditional Japanese culture, an integral element of martial arts, of the tea ceremony, and, perhaps most of all, of the dignified moments before *seppuku,* or ritual suicide.

Belghazi rocked on his feet, cradling his broken arm, blood running down his face from a gash in his forehead. It looked like one of the hammer fists had broken his nose. His body convulsed, then he leaned forward and vomited. His men watched and said nothing.

He spat a few times and wiped his face with his good hand. For a few moments he stood leaning that way, catching his breath. Finally he straightened and said to me in English, his voice ragged, "How have you been tracking me?"

I ignored him. It seemed that my luck had finally run out. I expected no help from Dox. There was a bag with five million dollars in it being contested in front of his position. I couldn't reasonably expect him to abandon it. I was alone now, fittingly enough, and I had no good options.

"Tell me how you have been tracking me, and I promise to kill you quickly. If you don't, I will make you suffer."

My mind began to drift. I barely heard his questions. The urgency of his tone seemed strange to me, irrelevant. I wondered at some level whether I was suffering from the effects of blood loss.

"I will ask you a final time," he was saying. I noticed that he had picked up the razor. "Then I will slice your face apart."

I looked out at the harbor and had the oddest sense that I was connected with it somehow, that my spirit was leaving my body and expanding outward. I was vaguely surprised at how unafraid I was. Death catches everyone eventually, and I had never harbored any illusions about its ability to catch me. That it had hesitated so long to do so seemed born more of a desire to mock me than of any real inclination to wait. Death had tired of that game, and had finally moved in to collect what we all owe.

Well, come and get it, I thought. *Go ahead, take what's yours. Choke on it.*

There was a strange sound, softer than the pop of a champagne cork, louder than the fizzing of a seltzer bottle. I looked over and was surprised to see a fine mist erupting out of one of the *yakuza*'s heads. Probably I should have done something about that. But the event seemed to have little to do with me.

The other *yakuza* had turned to look at his partner, whose body was sliding straight to the ground like a suddenly liquefying pole. The *yakuza*'s mouth was hanging open, as though in shock or incomprehension. But only for a second. Because then his head was erupting, too.

Even in his battered condition, Belghazi recognized what had happened. He was able to process it, and somehow to react. He turned and began to run. But something unseen knocked him down. He landed on his face, and immediately pulled himself to his feet. He staggered for a second, then got an unsteady foot in front of him. Something knocked him down again. This time he didn't get up.

I looked out at the harbor again. Wherever I was going, I was already halfway there. All the commotion around me seemed trivial, even silly. I wished it would stop and leave me alone.

I heard soft footfalls to my right. I sighed and looked over. It was Dox. He had approached through the hole in the fence and was moving smoothly toward us, the rifle shouldered and pointed downrange.

Maybe he'd recovered the five million. If so, it would be time to tie up loose ends. Belghazi. Then, I supposed, me. Game over.

I looked out at the harbor again, feeling myself slipping toward it, into it. The water was warm. The feeling was not at all unpleasant.

"You all right?" I heard Dox ask. I looked over. I saw his eyes move to Belghazi's prone form, then scan left and right, then back again.

I didn't answer. The question might have been cruel, given what he was about to do to me, yet somehow it struck me as almost funny. I looked at him and smiled.

"That mean yes?" he asked, pulling abreast of me now. He raised the rifle to eye level. There was a soft *crack* and a flash from the end of the suppressor.

I looked over at Belghazi. He was totally still. Dox had put a last round into his head.

I felt tired, so tired. The ground underneath me was soaking wet and warm, and for a moment I thought I was back near the Xe Kong river, where I had killed that young Viet Cong. He, too, had been lying on earth saturated with his own blood, and in that instant it was as though I was seeing the world through his eyes. As though he was calling to me from across time, from across the grave.

Dox was looking at me now. I saw concern in his expression. He lowered the rifle.

Suddenly I was confused.

"I thought I was dead," I said, trying to explain. My voice sounded odd to me, slow and unnaturally low.

"Well, you don't look so hot, but I'm pretty sure you ain't dead. I would say, though, that we ought to get out of here."

"Mmmmmm," I said, looking past him at a dark and suddenly retreating shape that flickered at the edge of my vision. *Only teasing,* Death seemed to be saying over his shoulder with a rictus smile, with good humor and an oddly paternal affection. *Take care of yourself, okay? We'll play again.*

Dox stooped and got his head under my arm, then straightened. We started walking toward the fence.

"What about . . . what about the money?" I asked, not understanding what was happening.

"Well, it was a heartbreaker, I won't deny it, but I had to abandon the big payday and come to your rescue. I meant to get here sooner, but there was a lot going on back at the ranch and I had a fair amount of ground to cover. Plus these PSG/1's are heavy, even for muscle-men like me."

"You just . . . you just let it go?" I asked, trying to take it in.

I felt him shrug. "I don't give a damn about money if my buddy's in trouble, partner, and I know you feel the same."

I didn't respond. "What about . . . what happened in front of the gate? That other car?"

I lost my footing for a second, but Dox's arm, tight around my waist, kept me going. "Now there's one no-body would believe if I were to tell 'em," he said. "I don't know who Belghazi's pal is, the white fella, I mean, but he's quite a shooter. He dropped one of the men in that Toyota, and then, when the two Arabs who came in the van got up from humping the ground, he capped them both point-blank. They seemed a bit surprised at the time. He and the other fella from the Toyota had each other pinned down after that. They both had good cover, and I couldn't wait for a shot 'cause I thought you might need my help. Too bad, too. If I'd been able to take them both down, that bag would be waiting for us right now. Well, it might be, still. We'll see in a minute."

"Hilger . . . he was shooting them all?"

"Hilger? Ah, the white one. Yeah, he sure was. I don't think that boy wanted anyone around to contradict the story he was making up about how all this carnage oc-curred and his role in it. He's a resourceful one, and cold-blooded, too. Hell, Kanezaki ought to hire him for the shit we do."

We got to the street and paused. I heard gunshots from in front of the gate, then return fire from inside the Toyota.

"Damn, those boys haven't killed each other yet," Dox said. "Looks like we're shit out of luck. Here we go."

He pulled me across the street fast. If Hilger or the Arab noticed, they gave no sign of it. They had each other to worry about.

A few seconds later we were on the other side, heading upward, enveloped by darkness. I lost my footing again and this time couldn't find it. For a moment I felt I was floating on water, that some sea creature had risen up beneath me and lifted me onto its snout. My head cleared, and I realized Dox had picked me up over an enormous shoulder and was carrying me.

"Wait," I said. "Put me down. The money's right there, if you can drop those two."

"Partner, you are bleeding out," I heard him say from under me. He didn't even break stride. "Don't worry about the money. We'll get another chance."

I drifted away again. When I came to, we were back at the van we had rented. Dox laid me out in the rear and slammed the door. The engine gunned and we drove off. A moment later, I heard him on the cell phone. His tone was urgent but I was fading in and out again and couldn't make out what he was saying. Something about a doctor, maybe.

"Come on, man," I heard him bellowing from somewhere in front of me. It seemed that his voice was coming from a great distance. "Stay with me now. Kanezaki's scrambling a doctor and I need to know your blood type."

"AB," I said, my lips moving thickly. "AB negative."

"Well, thank God for small miracles! A universal recipient! Come on down!"

I WAS GONE a long time after that. When I woke up, I was in a bed in a dingy room. I looked around. Taupe drapes from another millennium. An old television on a cheap dresser. A metal door with a peephole. It was a hotel room.

Dox was in a chair next to the bed, facing the door, his head slumped forward, the rifle set across his lap.

I pulled back the blanket and looked down at my thigh. It was heavily bandaged. Likewise for my wrist. The thigh and wrist hurt, and the ribs were worse, but none of it was terrible. My head felt fuzzy, though, and I realized someone had given me something for pain.

"Hey," I said.

Dox's eyes popped open and his head snapped up. "Well, all right," he said, flashing me the grin. "It's damn good to see you, man. You had me worried there for a while."

"Where the fuck are we?"

"A little Motel 6 kind of place on Lantau Island. I didn't want anyone bothering us while you were recuperating."

"Who bandaged me?"

"Your uncle Kanezaki made a few phone calls and took care of everything. Got a local doctor out here pronto. He sewed you up, but you'd lost a lot of blood. Luckily I was on hand to lend you a quart or so. So don't be surprised if your dick's grown to about twice as big as you remember."

I laughed weakly. "Am I going to start looking at sheep differently, too?"

He grinned again. "You should only be so lucky. But

one way or the other, take comfort from the fact that you've got a quart of Dox sloshing around inside you. There's people who'd pay good money for the privilege, and here it's yours for free."

I nodded, taking it all in. "Thank you," I said, looking at him.

He shook his head. "Forget about it. Like I told you, you were good to me in 'Stan. I don't forget."

"Well, I reckon we're even, then," I said.

His eyebrows shot north. "Did he say 'reckon'? My God, son, it's working already!"

WE CALLED KANEZAKI the next day, after we had changed hotels. We put him on the speakerphone on Dox's cell phone.

"I was always afraid the two of you were going to join forces," he said.

Dox grinned. "Well, someone's gotta save western civilization from the forces of darkness," he said.

"You're closer to the truth there than you know," Kanezaki replied.

"What are you talking about?" I asked.

"I can't go into it now. But it'll all be in the news tomorrow. We'll talk after that."

"The two hundred thousand?" I asked.

"The balance has already been transferred. Congratulations."

That was good. In our haste to depart, Dox and I had left behind the binoculars and parabolic microphone, and I had been mildly concerned that Kanezaki might argue that this evidence made things look too well planned to be attributable to the kind of straightforward inside job we'd discussed. Apparently there wasn't a problem. I was looking forward to finding out why.

"Speaking of the two hundred thousand," Dox said, "you've been shortchanging me, son. My price just went up."

"See, this is what I was afraid of," Kanezaki said. "A damn union."

We all laughed. Kanezaki asked, "How'd that doctor work out?" Reminding me of how he'd come through when I needed him.

"Well, he gave me a quart of Dox's blood," I said. "That ought to be grounds for malpractice."

"Crimson Viagra!" Dox crowed, and we all laughed again.

"Check the papers," Kanezaki said. "You'll see what you've done. You should be damn proud, no shit."

It was on CNN that night. A joint Hong Kong police/CIA operation had stopped a transfer of radiologically tipped missiles at Kwai Chung port container facility. Several Arab terrorists involved had been killed in a shootout. A CIA officer, whose identity could not be revealed, was wounded in the operation. All missiles were recovered. No one mentioned anything about a duffel bag with five million U.S. in it.

So Hilger must have survived. Maybe he'd finally managed to put a round in the last Arab. No wonder Kanezaki hadn't been uptight about the abandoned binoculars and parabolic microphone. Apparently their presence hadn't been inconsistent with the new cover story.

The next morning I checked the appropriate offshore account. The two hundred thousand was in there, as Kanezaki had promised—fifty thousand that had been paid up front, one hundred fifty moved in the day before.

Dox had given me the number of his own account. I

transferred him all two hundred. My way of saying thank you.

I called Kanezaki from a pay phone.

"I saw the news," I said. "Another heroic success for the defenders of the free world."

He chuckled. "Be happy. The cleanup suits everyone—you, especially. No one here is disputing the official story. They're all scrambling to try to make themselves part of it, in fact. So no one's arguing about the definition of 'natural.'"

"What are those missiles?" I asked.

"They're called Alazans. They're surface-to-surface rockets with a ten-mile range. They were originally designed by Soviet scientists for weather experiments, but seemed to work better as a terror weapon. Conventional versions were employed by Azerbaijan forces in the war with Armenia over the disputed enclave of Nagorno-Karabakh, and by separatists in South Ossetia in clashes with Georgian troops."

"The news said the ones recovered were radiologically tipped."

"Yeah, two years ago, we uncovered documents showing that at one time one of the Alazan batteries had been fitted with radiological warheads—turning the rockets into 'dirty bombs.' The radiological battery was stored in Transdniester, a separatist enclave that broke away from Moldova twelve years ago. Transdniester is currently recognized by no government but its own, and, with its huge stockpiles of Soviet-era arms, it's become a clearinghouse for black arms weapons."

"Those two guys," I said, thinking aloud. "The Russians. They were from Transdniester?"

"Yeah, the military junta that's running Transdniester now is pro-Russian. The rest of the enclave speaks

Moldovan, which is really just Romanian. It's complicated."

"Sounds it."

"Anyway, what you've got now is a small clique that runs the 'country' of Transdniester by its own rules. Much of the enclave's trade is controlled by a single company, Sheriff, which is owned by the son of Transdniester's president. The son also heads the Transdniester Customs Service, which oversees all the goods flowing in and out of the country. The shipments move through the Tiraspol airport; overland by truck to Ukraine or Moldova; and on a rail-to-ship line that connects the capital to Odessa."

"Or through Hong Kong."

"Not a likely route, if you look at a map, but brilliant if you had the local connections that Belghazi was using. He was snowing his handlers in NE Division. They thought he was a 'good' arms dealer who was informing on the 'bad' arms dealers. In fact, he was informing on his competitors, and meanwhile dealing in whatever would make him the most money. The Alazans were probably just one example. Who knows what he was moving right under the Agency's nose."

"Not anymore."

"That's right. I meant it when I said you should be proud. The people who he would have sold those missiles to would have used them anywhere they could. If they had been smuggled into the U.S., it would have been catastrophic."

"The two who died at Kwai Chung," I said. "What was their connection to Transdniester's president? And his son?"

"Why?"

"I just like to keep tabs on people who might want to take me off their Christmas card list."

There was a pause. "Nephews of the president. Cousins of the son."

I thought about that for a moment. "The family is probably unhappy about losing them," I said. "Just guessing."

"They have no way of connecting you with what happened at Kwai Chung."

"What about Hilger?"

"Hilger?"

Kanezaki might have been playing dumb. Or the "Hilger" moniker might have been a pseudo, used operationally, that Kanezaki didn't know. It didn't really matter.

"The NOC," I said.

There was a pause, during which he digested the fact that I had learned the NOC's identity, or at least an operational pseudo. "Without confirming any names," he said, "I can say that everyone involved has an incentive to stick to the official story. This was a joint CIA/Hong Kong law enforcement operation."

"It sounds like Dox and I ought to get a bonus," I said. "You got a lot more than you bargained for."

"I can't do that," he said, "but you can charge me more for the next job. I don't think anyone would argue."

"Where'd the money go?"

"The money for the missiles?"

"Yeah."

"It was recovered at the scene."

"How much was recovered?"

"About three million."

I laughed. "'About three million'? Anyone wonder why such an odd amount?"

"What do you mean?"

"I mean your man Hilger scooped out about two mil-

lion after executing the remaining people at the scene.
It was dark and he was in a hurry, though, so he couldn't
very well count it all out bill by hundred-dollar bill."

"No. Why wouldn't he have taken all of it?"

"This was a sale. It would have looked suspicious if
there had been no funds at the point of purchase. Hilger
is smarter than he is greedy."

There was a long pause. "Let me ask you something,"
he said. "Do you think he knew what was in those shipping crates?"

I considered for a moment. "I don't think he knew beforehand, no. He seemed surprised when he heard the
word 'missiles,' and Belghazi said something to him
about not asking questions he didn't want answered."

"Yeah, but still, to just stand by for something like
this . . ."

"For what it's worth, I think he might have decided to
try to prevent the deal from going down, once he figured out what it was all about. But should he have
known beforehand? Could he have, if he'd cared? Hell,
yes. Until circumstances made rationalization and denial impossible, he was probably happy to look the
other way because he was getting such good 'intel' from
Belghazi."

There was another long pause while he took it in.
"That's what I thought. Anyway, there's not much I can
do about the money he took. Not this time."

That's all right, I thought. *I know who he is now. I've
seen his face, up close through those Zeiss binoculars.
And I know he uses the name Hilger, at least operationally. Dox and I might want to have a chat with him,
tell him it isn't nice not to share.*

"You ought to think about the arrangement NE had
with Belghazi," I said. "I doubt that it's unique."

"It isn't."

"Then you're getting jerked around by other 'good' guys?"

"Look, the people who have the dirt are dirty. Belghazi was poor execution, but that doesn't mean the concept itself is flawed."

"You spend all this time with people who are dirty, what does that make you?"

"You don't want to get dirty, better stay out of the sandbox."

I laughed. "He was playing you."

"Of course he was. Opposing sides always play each other. It doesn't mean a deal doesn't get done. As long as there's something in it for everyone, it all gets worked out."

"Incredible."

"Not really. It's just the way of the world. Look at America. All the interest groups donate to both political parties, knowing that, whoever wins, the winner will be in their debt."

I paused, thinking, then said, "There's something I want you to do."

"Name it."

"You've got a file about me. The file mentions Rio de Janeiro. It mentions Naomi Nascimento."

"Yes."

"I want those references deleted."

"I can do that."

"Good," I said. "I'm going to tell you something now. And the information comes with responsibility. Heavy responsibility."

There was a pause, then, "All right."

"I care about that woman. It's over between us, but I care about her. I owe her something. If someone from your organization, or through your organization, hurts her or even just tries to follow her to get to me, and I learn about it, I will make you pay."

"I understand."

"Good," I said again.

There was another pause. "I hope you'll let me know when you're ready for the next job," he said. "There's a lot of work to do."

"There always is," I said, and hung up.

BEFORE I LEFT Hong Kong, Dox told me he couldn't take the money I'd wired him. Told me a deal's a deal, and we had said 50/50. I told him I couldn't give him less than a hundred percent after what he'd done for me, after what he'd walked away from to do it. I couldn't convince him.

"We'll have another opportunity," he told me, patting me on the shoulder, suddenly avuncular. "Just you wait and see."

"I thought you said it only knocks once."

"It does. This one wasn't our time, that's all."

I nodded. "All right. You win. Send it back to me."

"I will. Just give me the account number."

I scratched my head. "Damn, I can't remember it."

"C'mon now, that's not fair."

"If it comes to me, I'll write you."

"Damn, you are a stubborn one, I'll say that for you."

I smiled. "Thanks, Dox. You're a good man."

He smiled back. "You're just saying that 'cause it's true."

I held out my hand. He took it, then pulled me in for a hug.

Jesus Christ, I thought. But damn if I didn't hug him back.

*   *   *

I WENT BACK to Rio.

The city was warm. It was summer there, south of the equator, and it felt good to be back, to walk the beaches and wade in the ocean and listen to *choro* and drink *caipirinha*s and live, for a while, as Yamada again.

I knew there were people now who might think to look for me in Rio. But I'm not that easy to get to, even if you know the right city. And, strangely enough, when I thought about the people who knew, I didn't feel threatened.

Of course, a secret isn't a secret once other people know about it. I thought I could trust Kanezaki to doctor the file as I had instructed, but you never really know. And, even if he did what I had asked, there might be other copies. I'd made a few new enemies with my latest escapades. If they looked hard enough, who knows what they might find.

But I felt all right for the moment. I'd just keep my nose to the wind, see what I could learn from Tatsu, from Kanezaki. Think about what I wanted to do next.

My wrist and leg took their time healing. My ribs took longer. The protein shakes and other supplements didn't seem to be helping the way they should. I wanted to get back to my workouts, to jujitsu in Barra. But for a long time all I could reasonably manage was slow walks in the tropical evening air.

The long healing process was probably good for me, though. It reinforced something I needed to come to grips with: I was getting older. Time was, I would have ripped through a guy like Belghazi before he could have damaged me in return. But now, although my skills, my tactics, were better than those of my younger self, my quickness, and my resiliency, were declining. If I had been working alone that night at Kwai Chung, as I ordinarily do, I would have died there.

I tried to tell myself that it would have been all right, that it wouldn't have been a bad death and you have to die of something. But that was bullshit. Almost dying had been a powerful reminder that I wanted to still be alive. I couldn't articulate why, exactly. But it wasn't just the sight of sunsets or sound of jazz or taste of whiskey.

What had Delilah said, both dismissively and sympathetically, when I had ticked off those items? *All things.*

And: *If you live only for yourself, dying is an especially scary proposition.*

The walks got longer. I began to supplement them with bike rides. My wounds lessened, but their presence continued to serve as a paradoxical reminder both of certain mortality and of continued life.

My city by the sea was still beautiful. But over time, I noticed that Rio no longer relaxed me the way it once had. In fact, in the oddest way, I found myself longing for Tokyo, for something I once had there, although at the time I hadn't properly appreciated it for what it was.

Tokyo's suddenly renewed presence in my thoughts was strange, because I had never thought of the city as home while I lived there. Strange, too, because, despite a childhood spent partly in the city and twenty-five subsequent years there as an adult, the associations that had welled up when I had returned were all about Midori.

Well, maybe that's what home would always be to me—the place I'd miss when I had to move on. Love seemed like that, too. Because the woman I loved was the one I couldn't have.

What had most defined Tokyo for me, I realized after Kwai Chung, was that it had always made me feel like there was something there, something I might find that would fulfill me, some answer to a question I couldn't quite pose. Whatever that thing was, though, if it existed at all, it had always eluded me, frustrated me. It took without giving back.

But I realized now that the thing's elusiveness didn't mean I should stop seeking it. Life after Kwai Chung felt like a reprieve, a second chance. What a waste, not to make something of that.

I wasn't sure how much longer I would stay in Rio. But I was equally unsure of where else I would go. I was like a kite suddenly cut loose from its line: for the moment exhilaratingly free, yet certain now to lose the wind that had borne it aloft and plummet back to earth.

I needed to find that line again. But I didn't know where to reach for it.

There was Naomi, of course. Sometimes I thought about going to see her. But I never did. Maybe she was getting over the way things had ended between us. Maybe she was moving on. I didn't want to interfere with any of that. Most of all, I didn't want an association with me to be the thing that got her hurt, or worse than hurt.

Still, there were nights when I would lie in bed, listening to *"De Mais Ninguém,"* the song that had been playing in Scenarium the night I had gone to see her, or listening to some of the other music she had played in her apartment while we made love there, and the thought of how near she was would be almost unbearable.

I thought of Delilah, too. I wondered how things had turned out for her. I wondered how much of what she had told me had been true. I asked myself inane "what if" questions. I found myself wanting to believe her, wanting to believe that something was there, or could have been there, and I found this reaction weak and somewhat foolish.

Yeah. But look at Dox. He surprised you.

Yeah, he did. But not enough to reverse my whole view of human nature.

I'd been back for about two months when I found a message on one of my bulletin boards. The message said, "I'm vacationing in a wonderful city. Every morning I swim at the most famous beach there. The older beach, the one further north. I wish you could join me."

It was the bulletin board I had been using with Delilah, password Peninsula. No one else knew of it.

I stared at that message for a long time. Then, without even being conscious of a decision having been made, I started packing a bag.

That night I checked into the Copacabana Palace Hotel, Rio's grandest, positioned on its eponymous beach. I took an ocean-view room on the fifth floor. I had brought along a pair of binoculars—not quite the quality of the Zeiss model that I had employed at Kwai Chung, but good enough for gazing at the ocean. Or the beach.

I slept poorly. At sunup I started watching. At ten o'clock, she showed.

She was wearing a dark thong bikini, navy, almost midnight blue. I decided it would have been a crime for her to wear anything else.

She swam for twenty minutes, then lay down on a towel in the sun. She seemed to be alone, but the beach was filling up. I had no way of really knowing.

I told myself that she had no reason to try to set me up. And that was true. But the funny thing was, I just didn't care. For the moment, I didn't even care how she knew where, or almost where, to find me.

I pulled on a bathing suit and a hotel robe and walked out to the beach. The sun was beating down hot from overhead, and I squinted against the glare coming off the ocean and the sand. I put the robe down next to her and sat on it.

"Is this spot taken?" I asked.

She opened her eyes. They were bluer than I had ever seen them, taking on some of the hues of the sea and sky.

She smiled and sat up and looked at me for a long moment. Then she said, "You got my message."

I nodded. "It was a surprise. Pleasant surprise."

"You want to know how I found you."

She was beautiful. She was just . . . beautiful. I said, "I want to know how you've been."

She didn't say a word. She just looked into my eyes, leaned in, and kissed me. The taste of her, the feel of her mouth, the fact of her presence, it was all like a waking dream.

I pulled back and looked around us.

"It's all right," she said. "I would, too, if our positions were reversed."

I looked at her for a moment. It was good to be with someone who understood my habits. Who shared them.

She glanced at my arm and my thigh. The dressings were gone now, and the slowly healing results of Belghazi's handiwork were clearly visible. Whoever had patched me up must have been more concerned about closing the wounds than with their subsequent cosmetic appearance. It looked as though I'd been attacked by a pissed-off lawn mower.

"I know what you did at Kwai Chung in Hong Kong," she said.

I shrugged. "What, that thing? I read that was the CIA and Hong Kong police."

She chuckled. "You know where those missiles were going?"

I shook my head.

"To Saudi-funded groups that would have used them against Jerusalem and Haifa and Tel Aviv. The missiles have a ten-mile range. Israel is nine miles across at her waist. They could have reached anywhere."

"So it was the missiles you were after?"

She nodded. "We didn't have a fix on the seller. But we were tracking Belghazi, tracking him closely, as you know. Once he took possession, the shipping information would have been in his computer. He kept everything in it. Encrypted, of course, but we have people who could have cracked it."

"What then?"

"We would have tracked the ship that we learned was moving the missiles. Almost certainly it would have been destined for a Saudi port or to Dubai. So in the South China Sea, the ship would have been boarded by naval commandos, the cargo confirmed and appropriated."

"Lots of pirates in that part of the world," I noted.

"And not all 'pirate' activity is publicized, either. Some shipping companies would prefer to keep a theft quiet. Depending on the cargo involved, of course."

"So it was the handoff, and the shipping information, you were waiting for."

"Yes. If something happened to Belghazi before then, we would have lost track of the missiles. There would have been another buyer."

I nodded, thinking. "I don't think Belghazi was planning on moving those missiles through ordinary container port shipping. From what I understand, one of his last acts was to have them loaded into a van."

"The information we've been able to piece together suggests as much. The Alazans were an unusual shipment for all parties concerned. They were using unusual means of movement."

"I got that feeling."

"What I mean is, if we had proceeded with our original plan, we might have lost track of the shipment. That would have been disastrous. You have a lot of admirers right now among the people I work with."

I smiled, but the smile felt sad. "I have a feeling there's a job offer in all of this."

"There is."

I laughed and looked away. I'd really been hoping there, for a minute. One glimpse of a thong bikini and my brain had gone to mush. It was ridiculous.

"At least you're not pissed that I didn't wait for your signal," I said.

I heard her say, "I'm not. But none of that is why I'm here."

I wasn't going to buy it. "Yeah?" I said.

"I'm taking a long vacation, a long decompression, standard practice after living undercover and in danger of discovery for so long. My organization is generous this way, and sensible. They understand the stresses."

It sounded depressingly like a sales pitch. "I'm sure they do."

"Usually I go a little crazy for a while when an assignment is finished. I travel, hook up with some handsome young thing, try to blot out recent memories with a lot of wine, a lot of passion. No one knows where I go, and no one asks. I come back when I'm ready."

"This time?"

"This time I thought I'd spend some time with a man I met. If he's interested."

I looked out at the water. A breeze was kicking up whitecaps. They flashed under the sun.

"Tell me how you found me," I said, having waited long enough.

"After Kwai Chung, priority was given to tracking you. We put together a lot of information quickly. The more we learned about you, the more we were able to find out. And we were able to access Hong Kong Customs records, going back over a year. Smart people made assumptions, technicians fed data into supercomputers. They tracked you to South America. After that, you were gone."

"Not gone enough, it seems."

"You forget, I know you. We spent time together. At the Oparium Café, in Macau, you ordered *caipirinhas.*"

I shrugged. "They're popular all over the world."

"You said *'por favor'* when you ordered."

"No."

She nodded. "The waitress was ethnic Portuguese, so at the time I thought you were just using some trivial knowledge of the language. But, when the technicians said they had tracked you to South America, I started thinking about what you had ordered, the way you had ordered it, your accent, the Japanese community in Brazil—"

"That's the problem with being multilingual," I said. "You forget what the hell language you're speaking."

She laughed. "Tell me about it. Can you imagine what Belghazi would have said if I had greeted him, *'Shalom'*?"

We both laughed. She said, "Anyway, Rio felt right to me. Partly because of what you said about retiring to a sunny place, a place with beaches. But partly because . . . it just felt right. I decided to give it a try. São Paulo would have been my second choice. But a *caipirinha* wouldn't taste nearly as good there, would it?"

"You want to get one now?"

She smiled. "It's ten in the morning."

I shrugged. "I've got a room at the Copacabana Palace, right behind us. We could kill some time first."

Her smile broadened. "That sounds nice," she said.

Maybe it was all part of some larger plan, wheels within wheels. Maybe this *was* the job offer, and she was my signing bonus.

I supposed I would never know. Her motives, I understood, would remain a mystery, the time I might share with her a mirage, a kaleidoscope animated by the engine of my own foolish hopes, an attractive illusion, a projection.

On the other hand, she had warned me about that guy who'd been waiting for me in my room in Macau. That was the one thing that refused to fit, the one telling detail. Because, based on everything I'd learned since, I still couldn't see any operational benefit that she would have derived from that warning. And if operational imperatives couldn't explain it, it had to be something else.

Watching her there on the sand, I realized I'd been evaluating her too one-dimensionally, perhaps in unconscious and unflattering reflection of the way I view myself. She had refused to answer at the time when I'd asked her why she'd warned me. She might not even have known herself. But now I thought I might know. It was the desire, in the midst of a horrible business full of deceit and killing and regret, not to be responsible for an additional death. To expiate the sins of righteous butchery by saving a single life.

I could understand that. I could even hope for it. It was a pretty slim reed on which to try to build trust, but it was something.

It was a start.

I looked at her and asked, "How long are you going to be in town?"

She smiled. "A while, I hope."

I held out my hand. She took it and we stood. Then we walked back to the hotel.

AUTHOR'S NOTE

The Hong Kong, Macau, Rio, Tokyo, and Virginia locales that appear in this book are described, as always, as I have found them. The backstory of Transdniester and the Alazan missiles is real.

ACKNOWLEDGMENTS

Deepest thanks:

To my agents, Nat Sobel and Judith Weber of Sobel Weber Associates, for the conception; to my editor, David Highfill of Putnam, for the execution; and to Michael Barson and the Barsonians of Putnam, for the dissemination. What a team!

To Lori Andreini, for her continued insights into what sophisticated, sexy women like Delilah wear and how they think, and for helpful comments on the manuscript.

To my once and future *sensei* Koichiro Fukasawa of Wasabi Communications, for years of insight, humor, and friendship, and, as always, for helpful comments on the manuscript.

To Doug Patteson, for consistently pointing me in the right direction, for refining numerous ideas for the book's backstory, and for his enthusiasm for John Rain generally.

To Evan Rosen, M.D., Ph.D., and Peter Zimetbaum, M.D., for once again offering (reluctant) expert advice on some of the killing techniques in this book, and for helpful comments on the manuscript.

To Ernie Tibaldi, a thirty-one-year veteran agent of the FBI, for continuing to generously share his encyclopedic knowledge of law enforcement and personal safety issues, and for helpful comments on the manuscript; to Michael Stapleton, a thirty-three-year veteran Special Agent of the FBI, for sharing his expertise on fingerprinting and DNA forensic science; and to a certain active-duty FBI agent, who must remain nameless, for sharing his expertise on defending against improvised explosive devices.

To Amelia Chan, Monica Chan, Norman Chan, Daniel Fok, and Kai Cheong Fok, for being such wonderful hosts and guides during my research visits to Macau; for training Rain in how to look like a local and blend thereby; and for sharing their many insights about the territory and the region.

To Alika Yamamura, *carioca* and *edokko,* for imparting her firsthand insights on what it means to share Japanese ethnicity and Brazilian nationality, and for furthering my understanding of Brazil and Brazilians.

To Bob Baer, for his excellent *Sleeping with the Devil: How Washington Sold Our Soul for Saudi Crude,* to which Kanezaki owes some of his thinking regarding the U.S.–Saudi relationship, including his comments about a conspiracy of silence and "incest."

To Gavin De Becker for *The Gift of Fear,* which has helped Rain (and countless others) spot subtle signs of danger and effectively deal with potential violence.

To Lt. Colonel Dave Grossman and Loren W. Christensen for *On Combat,* which has helped Rain—and, more importantly, is helping countless military and law enforcement personal—successfully manage deadly force encounters. Thanks too to Dave for helpful comments on the manuscript.

To Maj. John L. Plaster USAR (Ret.), for *The Ultimate Sniper: An Advanced Training Manual for Military*

& *Police Snipers,* and for his other excellent books and videos on sniping, all of which provided invaluable background on and tactics for Dox; and for *SOG: The Secret Wars of America's Commandos in Vietnam,* which continues to provide critical insight into the combat crucible that shaped Rain's character.

To Paulo Rocco and Ana Martins of Rocco, my Brazilian publisher, for showing me around Rio, for patiently answering all my questions, and for introducing me to the joys of *caipirinha* (while, it must be said, failing to mention that more than two over lunch can be dangerous). In particular, my thanks to Ana for introducing me to the marvelous bar/restaurant Scenarium in Lapa and to the music of *choro,* both of which appear in this book.

To Ralph Gracie, Sandro "Batata" Santiago, Dave Camarillo, Cameron Earle, Misho Ceko, Tom Cicero, Alan "Gumby" Marques, and my other instructors, formal and informal, and training partners at the Ralph Gracie Jiu-Jitsu Academy, for teaching me some of the moves that help Rain keep his edge. Special thanks to Misho for helping me choreograph the Sambo grappling techniques that appear in Dox's confrontation with Rain, and for being such a patient teacher and all-round *ii hito.*

To Carlinhos Gracie and everyone at Gracie Barra in Rio, for so warmly welcoming me to train with them while I was visiting Brazil for research, for teaching me some great moves while I was there, and for tapping me out with such graciousness and good humor, and to Scottie Nelson of OnTheMat.com for showing me around town.

To Randy Adams, for teaching Rain baccarat, and to Allan Murphy, for introducing Rain to Ben's Café in Takadanobaba, Tokyo.

To Dr. Wolfgang Gilliar, Doctor of Osteopathic, for overcoming his queasiness about my questions just enough to explain exactly what would happen to a knee that has been victimized by a sambo foot lock.

To Tom Hayse, for helping me understand how satellite phones work and how their signals are intercepted, and for helpful comments on the manuscript.

To Seb Belisarius, ex-SEAL and shootfighting and combatives instructor; Craig Douglas, former Army Ranger, narcotics agent, and combatives instructor; and Dennis Martin, VIP Protection and close quarters combatives instructor, for sharing their incredible knowledge about surveillance, close quarters combat, and tactical awareness, and in particular for making sure that Rain includes in his EDC (Every Day Carry) an E1e SureFire flashlight, a Traser wristwatch, duct tape, a pen that can be used as a tension wrench, and some other handy and devious items.

To Tony Blauer, for sharing his decades of research and experience on effectively managing violence, and in particular for his feedback on Rain's mind-set and tactics in the final confrontation in the book.

To Matt Furey, for devising the Combat Conditioning system that Rain uses to maintain his edge, and for sharing some of his incomparable grappling expertise to make Rain's neck cranks the deadly weapons they are.

To Marc MacYoung, Dianna Gordon, and the rest of the Animal List denizens who hang out at *www.nonon-senseselfdefense.com,* the most eclectic, eccentric bunch of experts on everything anyone could ever imagine. In particular, thanks to Dave Bean, mad scientist and moral philosopher, for sharing his knowledge of firearms and the results of his experiments on what really works and how to do it; Alain Burrese, former army sniper, for helping me understand Dox and refine his tactics; Ed Fanning, for his thoughts on martial arts, self-defense, and the difference between the two; Jack "Spook" Finch, veteran of the Vietnam war's Easter offensive, Operation Just Cause, Operation Desert Storm, and Silver Star awardee, for sharing his knowledge of firearms and his thoughts on living with the experience of combat and killing; Frank "Pancho" Garza, for his frequent philosophizing on violence, street etiquette, and sheep; Montie Guthrie, Peter Huston, Michael "Mama Duck" Johnson, and Justin Kocher, for sharing their well-founded thoughts on how "heavy hitters" carry themselves; Marc, for his observation that snipers tend to be a soft-spoken breed and for his continued insights into personal safety, violence, and street etiquette; Kevin Menard, Savate Silver Glove, for helping me get up to speed on how Savateurs fight and outfitting Belghazi thereby; Slugg, for sharing his knowledge of firearms, his thoughts on invisibility in crowds, and his cough syrup recipe; Tristan Sutrisno, former army Special Forces, Vietnam veteran, and keeper of the dreaded Nessie, for sharing his thoughts on living with the experience of combat and killing.

To Naomi Andrews and Dan Levin, Eve Bridberg, Alan Eisler, Judy Eisler, Shari Gersten and David Rosenblatt, Joe Konrath, Matthew Powers, Owen Rennert, Ted Schlein, Hank Shiffman, Pete Wenzel, and Jonathan Zimmerman, for helpful comments on the manuscript and many valuable suggestions and insights along the way.

To my friends at Café Borrone in Menlo Park, California, for serving the best breakfasts—and especially coffee—that any writer could ask for.

Most of all, always and forever, to the best of everything, my wife, Laura.

KILLING ISN'T the hard part. Gangbangers and other fear biters do it every day. Anger pumps you up, panic cancels consideration, you grab the gun, close your eyes, pull the trigger, Christ, an ape could do it, you don't even need to be a man.

No, the truth is, killing is the easy part. Getting close to the target, though, that takes some talent. And making it look "natural," which is my specialty, well, I've only known of one other operator who could consistently get that right, and I'm not sure he should count because I'm the one who killed him. And leaving no trail back to yourself, that's no cakewalk, either.

But the hardest part? The part that you can't plan for, that you can only really understand when it's already too late? Living with it after. Bearing up under the weight of what you've done. That's the hardest. Even with limitations like mine—no women, no children, no acts against nonprincipals—you're not the same person after. You never draw the same breath again, or dream the same dreams. Trust me, I know.

As much as you can, you try to dehumanize the target. Accepting the target as human, a man just like you, creates empathy. Empathy makes killing more difficult and produces caustic regret.

So you employ euphemisms: in Vietnam we never killed people; we only "wasted gooks" or "engaged the enemy," the same as in all wars. When possible, you prefer distance: air strikes are nice; bayonet range is horrible. You diffuse responsibility: crew-served weapons, long chains of command, systematic replacement of the soldier's sense of self with an identification with the platoon or regiment or other group. You obscure features: the hood is used not to comfort the condemned, but to enable each member of the firing squad to pull the trigger without an anguished face to remember afterward.

But it's been a long time since any of these emotional stratagems has been available to me. I typically operate alone, so there's no group with whom to share responsibility. I don't discuss my work, so euphemisms would be pointless. And what I do, I need to do from a very personal distance. By the time I'm that close, it's too late to try to cover the target's face or otherwise conceal his humanity.

All bad enough, even under the usual circumstances. But this time I was watching the target enjoy a Sunday outing in Manila with his obviously adoring Filipino family just before I killed him, and it was making things worse.

The target. See? Everyone does it. If I'm different than most, it's only in that I try to be more honest. "More" honest. A matter of degree.

Manheim Lavi was his name, "Manny" to his business associates. Manny was an Israeli national, resident of South Africa, and citizen of the world, which he traveled much of the year sharing bomb-making expertise with a network of people who put the knowledge to increasingly grisly use. Vocations like Manny's once offered a reasonable risk-to-reward ratio, but post-9/11, if you sold your expertise to the wrong people, you could lose your rewards pretty fast. That was Manny's story, as I was given to understand it, a tragic fall from a certain government's grace.

Manny had arrived in Manila from Johannesburg that evening. A black Mercedes from the small Peninsula fleet had picked him up at Ninoy Aquino Airport and whisked him straight to the hotel. Dox and I were already staying there, outfitted with first-rate ersatz identities and the latest communication and other gear, all courtesy of Israeli intelligence, my client of the moment. Dox, an ex-marine sniper and former comrade-in-arms of mine, had recently walked away from a five-million-dollar payday to save my life in Hong Kong. Bringing him in on this job was in part my way of trying to repay him for that.

Dox was waiting in the lobby when Manny arrived. I was in my room on the sixth floor, a tiny, flesh-colored, Danish-designed wireless earpiece nestled in my ear canal, a wireless mike secured to the underside of the left lapel of the navy blazer I was wearing. Dox was similarly equipped.

"Okay, partner," I heard him say softly in his Southern twang, "our friend just got here, him and the world's biggest, butt-ugliest bodyguard. They're checking in right now."

I nodded. It had been a while since I'd worked with a partner, and not so long ago Dox had proven himself a damn good one.

"Good. Let's see if you can get the name he's using and a room number."

"Roger that."

Having to get this information on our own wasn't ideal, but the Philippines wasn't exactly the Israelis' backyard, and they hadn't been able to offer all that much. Manny traveled to Manila frequently from his nominal home in Johannesburg, taking as many as ten trips in a year. He never stayed for less than a week; the longest of these visits had lasted two months. He'd been doing this for a decade: presumably because customs control in Manila isn't as tight as it is in, say, Singapore, making the Philippines a good place for meetings with the MNLF, Abu Sayef, Jemaah Islamiah, and other violent groups in the region; possibly because he liked the price and variety of Manila's well-known nightlife, as well. He always stayed at the Peninsula. There were a few surveillance photos. That was all.

With less than the usual dossier to go on, I knew we would have to improvise. Where to hit Manny, for one thing. The hotel was our only current nexus and so presented a logical choice. But if Manny died in the hotel, it would absolutely have to look natural; otherwise, there would be too much investigative attention on the other guests, including Dox and me. Staying elsewhere wouldn't have helped; it would have kept us too far from the action.

The level of "naturalness" a hotel hit itself would require isn't easy, but there were other problems, as well. Most of the ruses I typically use to get into someone's room depend on the target's anonymity, yet Manny was well known to the hotel. And even if I did get into the room while Manny was out and then waited for him to return, what if the bodyguard swept the room immediately before his arrival? What if Manny came back with a bar girl? In the current terrain, I couldn't control for these variables, and I didn't like that.

Still, I wanted the room number. Partly in case a better opportunity didn't present itself and we had to use the Hotel Room Expiration as Plan B; more important, so we would know on which floor to place the video camera that we would use to track his movements. We could have tried placing a camera in the lobby, which would have been easier because it would have saved us the trouble of finding out what floor he was on. But there were downsides to the lobby, too. With all the people coming and going through the hotel entrance, we'd have to scrutinize the grainy feed constantly to pick Manny out of the crowd. And if the lobby was always our first chance to see him on the move, we'd have to scramble to follow him out of the hotel—behavior that any decent bodyguard would key on in a heartbeat. So I decided we would use the lobby only if we had to.

Even low-end hotels don't give out their guests' room numbers, though, and the regal Peninsula Manila, with its expansive, marble-lined lobby and white-uniformed bellhops, was anything but low-end. And even if we found an indiscreet employee, we wouldn't have known whom to ask for because we didn't know what name Manny would be staying under. So, while leaning forward to ask some typical questions about Manila and environs, Dox had taken the liberty of placing a few adhesive-backed transmitters under the long front edge of the marble reception desk. When Manny checked in, Dox would be able to listen in on his conversation with the clerk.

I waited two minutes, then heard the twang again. "Well, it's good news and bad news. Our friend is here under the name Mr. Hartman. But all the clerk said to him is 'Mr. Hartman, your room number is written here.' "

I'd received the same treatment when I checked in and wasn't surprised. The hotel staff was well trained.

"Anything else?" I asked.

"Sure, there's something else," I heard him say, and I could imagine his trademark grin. "He took the elevator on the Ayala Tower side."

The hotel had two separate wings—the Ayala and the Makati. Now we knew which set of elevators to focus on. We were beginning to triangulate.

"You get on with him?" I asked.

"I tried to. But the bodyguard was awfully polite and insisted that I just head on up by my lonesome."

All right, his bodyguard had some tactical sense. Not a surprise. "Did he get a good look at you?"

"Good enough. I think we can expect him to recognize the best-looking fella in Manila next time he sees me."

I nodded. Letting Dox run ahead was a calculated risk. Soon enough we would be double-teaming Manny, and it would be hard for his bodyguard to avoid getting distracted by sightings of Caucasian Dox, with his linebacker's physique and good ol' boy's grin. Distracted enough to completely overlook the smaller, unassuming Asian guy Dox was working with.

There were about two hundred sixty rooms on the Ayala side, and I thought about calling each of them from the house phone, offering, "May we have someone draw you a bath, Mr. Hartman?" until I hit the right room. But if Manny was reasonably paranoid, a call like that could make him suspicious. He might phone the front desk to confirm. Or he might just accept the offer, which would create its own set of problems. Enormous, goateed Dox showing up to draw you a bath isn't everyone's idea of proper hygiene.

So I'd hold off on Plan Bath, and use it only if our more subtle attempts came to nothing. "Think you can get anything else?" I asked.

"You know I'm working on it. Give me five minutes."

The next part of the plan was for Dox to make his way to the gift shop, where he would buy a book or something and charge it to his room. The clerk would check Dox's name and room number against a list to ensure that the transaction was legitimate. Dox would be holding a high-resolution camera cell phone. Using whatever social engineering was necessary, Dox would position himself so that he could use the camera to capture what was on the list, including, presumably, the name Hartman and an accompanying room number. We'd tested the system earlier, and it had worked perfectly. Now that we had the right name, it was time to see whether it would work when it counted.

Five minutes later there was a knock on my door. I padded quietly over and flipped up a small piece of cardboard I had taped over the peephole—no sense blocking the light from behind with my approach and alerting a visitor to my presence—and looked through. It was Dox.

Personal Safety Tips
from Assassin John Rain

PART OF THE APPEAL of my series about the half-American, half-Japanese assassin John Rain seems to be Rain's realistic tactics. It's true that Rain, like his author, has a black belt in judo and is a veteran of certain government firearms and other defensive tactics courses, but these have relatively little to do with Rain's continued longevity. Rather, Rain's ultimate expertise, and the key to his survival, lies in his ability to think like the opposition.

Okay, get out your highlighter, because:

All effective personal protection, all effective security, all true self-defense, is based on the ability and willingness to think like the opposition.

I'm writing this article on my laptop in a crowded coffee shop that I like. There are a number of other people around me similarly engaged. I think to myself, *If I wanted to steal a laptop, this would be a pretty good place to do it. You come in, order coffee and a muffin, sit, and wait. Eventually, one of these computer users is going to get up and make a quick trip to the bathroom. He'll be thinking, "Hey, I'll only be gone for a minute." He doesn't know that a minute is all I need to get up and walk out with his three thousand dollar PowerBook.* (Note how criminals are adept at thinking like their victims. You need to treat them with the same respect.)

Okay. I've determined where the opposition is planning on carrying out his crime (this coffee shop), and I know how he's going to do it (snatch and dash). I now have options for security:

1) avoid the coffee shop entirely (avoid *where* the crime will occur)

2) hope to catch the thief in the act, chase him down, engage him with violence

3) secure my laptop to a chair with a twenty-dollar Kensington security cable (avoid *how* the crime will occur—it's hard to unobtrusively employ bolt cutters in a coffee shop, or to carry out a laptop that's got a chair hanging off it)

Of these three options, #3 makes the most sense for me. The first is too costly—I like this coffee shop and get a lot of work done here. The second is also too costly, and too uncertain. Why fight when you could have avoided the fight in the first place? This is self-*defense* we're talking about, remember, self-*protection*. Not fighting, not melodrama. As for the third, yes, it's true that these measures won't render the crime impossible. But what measures ever do? The point is to make the crime difficult enough to carry out that the criminal chooses to pursue his aims elsewhere. Yes, if twenty-seven ninjas have dedicated their lives to stealing your laptop and have managed to track you to the coffee shop, they'll probably manage to get your laptop while you're in the bathroom even if you've secured it to a chair. But more likely, your opposition will be someone who is as happy stealing your laptop as someone else's. By making yours the marginally more difficult target, you will encourage him to steal someone else's.

Which brings us to an unpleasant, but vitally true, point:

If you and your friend are jogging in the woods, and you get chased by a bear, you don't have to outrun the bear. You just have to outrun your friend.

Except at the level of very high-value executive protection (presidents, high-profile businessmen, ambassadors and other dignitaries), you are not trying to outrun the bear. You are trying only to outrun your friend.

Let's combine these two concepts—thinking like the opposition, outrunning your friend—with an example from the realm of home security. And let's add an additional critical element: that all good security is *layered*.

If you wanted to burglarize a house, what would you look for? And what would you avoid?

Generally speaking, your high-level objectives are to get cash and property, and to get away (home invasion is a separate subject, but is addressed, like all self-protection, by reference to the same principles). You'd start by looking at lots of houses. Remember, you're not trying to rob a certain address; you just want to rob a house. Which ones are dark? Which are set back from the road and neighbors? Are there any cars in the driveway? Lights and noise in the house? Signs of an alarm system? A barking dog?

Thinking like a burglar, you are now ready to implement the outer layer of your home security. By some combination of installing motion sensor lights, keeping bushes trimmed so as to avoid concealment opportunities, putting up signs advertising an alarm system, buying a dog, keeping a car or cars in the driveway, and leaving on appropriate lights and the television and making sure there are no newspapers in the driveway or mail left on the porch when you're away, you help the burglar to immediately decide during his "casing" or "surveillance" phase that he should rob someone else's house.

If the burglar isn't immediately dissuaded by the outer layer, he receives further discouragement at the next layer in. He takes a closer look, and sees that you have dead bolt locks on all the doors, and that your advertisement was not a bluff—the windows are in fact alarmed. If he takes a crack at the doorjamb, he discovers that it's reinforced. If he tries breaking a window, he realizes that the glass is shatter resistant. Whoops—time to go somewhere else, somewhere easier.

Okay, the guy is stupid. He keeps trying anyway. Now the second layer of security described above, which failed to *deter* him, *delays* him. It's taking him a long time to get in. He's making noise. At some point, the time and noise might combine to convince him to abort (back to deterrence). But if he insists on plunging ahead, the noise has alerted you, and you have bought yourself time to implement further inner layers of security: accessing a firearm; calling the police; retreating to a safe room; most of all, preparing yourself mentally and emotionally for danger and possible violence.

Another example: personal protection from an overseas kidnapping attempt. As with everything else, this form of protection starts with you thinking like the bad guy. Your objective is to kidnap a foreigner. Not a certain Jim Smith, for example; high-value targets are a separate problem (although, again, subject to the same principles). Just any old foreigner, perhaps in particular an American. Now what do you need to do to carry out your plan?

First, you need to pick a target. This part is easy—any foreigner will do. Next, you need to assess the foreigner's vulnerability. Where will you be able to grab him, and when? To answer these questions, you need to follow the target around. If he's punctual, a creature of habit, if he likes to travel the same route to work at the same times of day, you are going to start to feel encouraged.

But what if instead, during the assessment stage, you watch the target go out to his car and carefully check it for improvised explosive devices. Your immediate thought will be: *hard target. Security conscious. Too difficult—kidnap someone else.* As the potential target, your display of security consciousness becomes the outermost layer of your security.

But suppose the would-be kidnapper wants to assess a bit further. Now he learns that you never travel the same route to work. You never come and go at the same times. He can't get a fix on your *where* and *when*. How is he going to plan a kidnapping now?

Note that, by putting yourself in the opposition's shoes, you have identified a behavior pattern in which he must engage before carrying out his crime: surveillance. Before you are kidnapped, you will be assessed. Assessment entails surveillance. Now you know what preincident behavior to look for. If you were trying to follow you, how would you go about it? That's what to look for.

Perhaps the would-be kidnapper will discover choke points— a certain bridge, for example—that you have to cross every day on your way to the office. This would be a good place for him to try to lay an ambush. But, because you know this, too, you will be unusually alert as you approach potential choke points. As he watches your "choke point" behavior, he realizes again that you are security conscious, and thus a poor target. Again, deterrence. If he is rash and acts at this point anyway, the possible inner layers of your security—locked and armored vehicles; defensive driving tactics; presence of a bodyguard; access to a firearm; again, most of all, preparing yourself mentally and emotionally for danger and possible violence—all have time to come into play.

Other examples: If you needed fast cash, where would you look to rob someone? Maybe on the victim's way from an

ATM? If so, what kind of ATM would you pick? Where would you wait? What about if you wanted to steal a car? Assuming you're not a pro who can pick locks and hotwire ignitions, where would you go? Maybe outside a video store, or a dry cleaner, somewhere people leave the keys in the ignition because they'll "only be gone for a minute"? Now, armed with a better understanding of the criminal's goals and tactics, how should you behave to better protect yourself?

One common element you might see in all of this is the vital need for alertness, for situational awareness. Understanding where threats are likely to come from and how they are likely to materialize will help you properly tune your alertness. If you are not properly alert to a threat, you almost certainly will be unable to defend yourself against it when it materializes.

Notice that so far the discussion has been devoid of any mention of martial arts. This is because martial arts, self-defense, fighting, and combat, while related subjects, are not identical. The relationship and differences between these areas is outside the scope of this article; for more, check the suggestions for further reading below, especially http://www.nononsenseselfdefense.com. For now, suffice to say that martial arts can be thought of as an inner layer of self-defense. If you are called upon to use your martial arts moves, then almost certainly some outer layer of your security has been breached and you are in a worse position than you would have been had the outer layers held fast.

To put it another way:

Thinking like the opposition; taking threats seriously and not being in denial about their existence; and maintaining proper situational awareness, is infinitely more cost effective for self-defense than is training in martial arts.

Note that I have been doing martial arts of one kind or another since I was a teenager. I love the martial arts for many reasons. I do not dispute and am not discussing their *value*, but rather am emphasizing their *cost effectiveness* in achieving a given objective—here, effective personal protection. No matter what his martial arts skills, the person who recognizes in advance and can therefore steer clear of an ambush has a much better chance of surviving it than does the person who wanders into the ambush and then has to fight his way out.

John Rain and his author are particularly indebted for

much of what appears in this article to the wisdom and experience of Marc MacYoung and http://www.nononsenseselfdefense.com. There is much, much more to this subject; this article is only a start. To learn more, I suggest: Gavin DeBecker, *The Gift of Fear*, http://www.gdbinc.com/home.cfm; Marc MacYoung, *Cheap Shots, Ambushes, and Other Lessons*, http://www.nononsenseselfdefense.com; Peyton Quinn, *A Bouncer's Guide to Barroom Brawling*.

If you're interested in going deeper on the mechanics and psychology of violence, then: Tony Blauer's tapes and courses, http://www.tonyblauer.com; Alain Burrese, Hard Won Wisdom from the School of Hard Knocks, available through http://www.burrese.com; Loren Christensen's books and videos, available through http://www.lwcbooks.com; Marc MacYoung's books and videos, available through http://www.nononsenseselfdefense.com; Peyton Quinn, *Real Fighting* http://www.rmcat.com.

If you want to go beyond self-defense and into the realm of combat and killing, then: Dave Grossman, *On Killing* and *On Combat* http://www.killology.com.

Barry Eisler's thrillers, featuring the half-Japanese, half-American freelance assassin John Rain, have been included in numerous "Best Of" lists, including *Publishers Weeklys* Best Books of 2002 and Amazon.com's Editors Picks of 2003; have been translated into over a dozen languages; and have been optioned for film by Barrie Osborne, Oscar-winning producer of the *Lord of the Rings* trilogy. The fourth book in the series, *Killing Rain*, will be published in July 2005. http: www.barryeisler.com.

[Originally published in issue 4 of *Crimespree Magazine*, http://www.crimespreemag.com.]

Penguin Group (USA)
is proud to present
GREAT READS—GUARANTEED!

**We are so confident that you will love
this book that we are offering a
100% money-back guarantee!**

If you are not 100% satisfied with
this publication, Penguin Group (USA)
will refund your money!
Simply return the book before
September 1, 2005 for a full refund.

**With a guarantee like this one,
you have nothing to lose!**